The File

Gary Born

The File

Addison & Highsmith

Addison & Highsmith Publishers

Las Vegas ◊ Chicago ◊ Palm Beach

Published in the United States of America by
Histria Books
7181 N. Hualapai Way, Ste. 130-86
Las Vegas, NV 89166 USA
HistriaBooks.com

Addison & Highsmith is an imprint of Histria Books. Titles published under the imprints of Histria Books are distributed worldwide.

Library of Congress Control Number: 2023932037

ISBN 978-1-59211-205-0 (hardcover)
ISBN 978-1-59211-270-8 (eBook)

Chapter 1
Sara West

She looked across the lake as the sun began to set. Her eyes were grey, like the waves washing against the shore.

She stood at the window of the hotel room. The windowpanes were dirty, cracked in a few places and never repaired. Thick, rusted bars were anchored into wooden beams at the top and bottom of the window frame. She looked between the bars, up and down the dusty road, for signs of the men who were hunting her. An old woman returning home from the market, wrapped in a length of faded cloth, balanced a basket on her head as she picked her way past the potholes. But otherwise, the road was empty.

She opened the window and reached through the bars to close the shutters. They were weathered, with slats missing in a handful of places, and creaked as she pulled them shut. She closed the window and drew the curtain, shutting out the evening light.

She turned away from the window and walked across the room. The concrete floor was rough, and she could feel the grit beneath her feet. The room was nearly empty, the white-washed walls and ceiling barely visible in the half-light. A single cot with threadbare sheets stood against the wall. Mosquito netting hung from the ceiling above the bed, mended in a dozen places and streaked where guests had killed the insects that came in from the lake.

She had found the hotel earlier that day. It was all she needed — it took cash, no questions asked, and had a room with a sink and a mirror. The sink was chipped and missing one of the faucets. The mirror was older, with faded glass. A single bulb was mounted over the mirror and cast feeble yellow light into the darkness of the room.

She turned on the one faucet that still worked and washed her hands, using what was left of the bar of coarse soap to scrub away the mud from weeks in the jungle. When she finished, she dried her hands and opened the backpack that lay on the cot next to the sink. She took out the thick stack of papers that had almost cost her life and laid it aside. She searched inside the pack and found the candle and matches. She lit the candle and let wax drip onto the bedside table, before fixing the candle stick upright. Deeper in her pack, she found the medical kit, bright red with yellow Cyrillic lettering, and took out the iodine, bandages, and package with the sterilized needle, then arranged them on the table.

She looked into the mirror above the sink. She had thick blonde hair, tangled and dirty from the jungle, pulled back from high cheekbones still lightly streaked with mud. Her eyes were almond-shaped, half-blue, half-grey, wide-set and large. Their gaze was cold and wary, as if they were watching something in the distance. She looked away from the mirror, barely recognizing the reflection.

She wore jeans, torn in a half-dozen places and caked with dirt, rubbed deep into the creases. Her t-shirt was once white, but now was grey and brown, mottled with white where her sweat had dried. On her left side, the cloth was dark brown and stiff.

She took a breath and then lifted the t-shirt up, gently, over her left breast. The gash was twenty centimeters long, starting at the end of her collar bone and running diagonally down to the place where the swell of her breast began. It had been made by a machete, wielded by one of the men who was hunting her in the jungle. The man had barely missed her throat, as she wheeled, cat-like, away from his blade, gleaming silver in the moonlight, pivoting so that he almost missed her entirely. But he hadn't, and instead the tip of his blade had caught her, tracing a glistening slash across her left breast.

She looked back into the mirror, eyes locked in the faded glass, and let her fear rise. She let it wash over her, the way she had practiced, and then steadied herself, leaning against the sink. She put aside the fear, and the sadness, that had stalked her through the jungle for the last three weeks. She picked up the iodine and drenched the wound above her breast, before swabbing it clean, trying to ignore the surge of pain that followed. There were no more painkillers. She had taken the last of the tablets the day before.

She opened the package that contained the needle, already threaded with a length of surgical thread. She held the tip in the candle's flame, then wiped it clean. She leaned forward further, hips pressed tightly against the sink, and held the top of the wound closed, then drew another breath. She poised the needle against her skin, on one side of the wound, before pushing it in, forcing the metal through her skin, watching the droplets of blood well up out of the puncture. Then she drew the needle slowly through that side of the wound, followed by the surgical thread, before pushing the point of the needle into the other side of the gash and forcing it back into her flesh. She could feel the thread slide through her skin as she pulled it tight, the knot tugging against the wound.

She stopped and leaned against the sink, bracing herself against the pain. Then she rested the tip of the needle against the side of the wound again, less than half a centimeter from the first stitch, and did it once more. She pulled the thread through her skin to finish the second stitch, feeling the pain bore its way through her breast. She stopped again for a moment, to wipe the sweat from her face and the blood from her fingers, then forced herself to take up the needle, and sew another stitch into her skin, and then another. And another.

Twice, she almost cried out, the pain overwhelming her resolve. But each time she caught herself and leaned in against the edge of the sink, forcing herself to stop, to breathe, and, after a moment, to turn back to her task, eyes fixed on her wound in the mirror. She stopped after every few stitches to dry her fingers on the towel. They were slippery with her blood, making it hard to push the needle through the sides of the wound. Halfway through her task, she had to re-thread the needle with a fresh length of surgical thread, gleaming white against the blood on her fingers.

In all, it took nearly an hour. Forty minutes of gut-wrenching pain that clawed through her stomach, leaving her panting with exhaustion. Thirty stitches in all, spaced along the gash, closing it tightly, just the way she had learned in medical school. It wouldn't ever be pretty, but it would save her life, letting the wound heal, even in the jungle damp.

When she was finished, she washed her hands again. She used the towel to wipe the blood and the sweat off her breast and stomach, and then to dry her hands. She dripped what was left of the iodine along the gash again, drenching the wound so that it wouldn't fester. Then she used the bandages from the medical kit, taping them loosely over the wound, leaving it room to dry. Next, she looked into the backpack once more and found her other t-shirt, this one also filthy, but not as badly blood-stained as the one she had been wearing, and pulled it on.

Before she left, she reached into the pack one more time and found the gun. It was an Uzi machine pistol. She had taken it from the man who tried to kill her with his machete in the jungle. He hadn't protested, or even noticed, as she had taken the gun and medical kit from his pack. He had been focused on trying to pull the bamboo stake out of his chest, where she had planted it with all her weight, standing astride him, one boot on either side of his body. He hadn't been able to, and she had left him there, pinned into the mud on the floor of the clearing, as she slipped into the bushes, three nights ago.

She pushed the gun into the waistband of her jeans, where nobody would be able to see it. She pulled her t-shirt out over the weapon, and then picked up her backpack. It was badly worn but large, with enough room for her poncho and fleece, the medical kit, and the large package of papers. She slung the pack over her shoulder in a single, fluid motion that she had repeated hundreds of times over the past three weeks.

She scanned the room again, to make sure she was leaving nothing behind, then opened the door, and went out into the hallway. It was brightly lit by a bare fluorescent tube attached to the ceiling, and she paused to let her eyes adjust after the dark of the room. Then she closed the door behind her and headed silently down the hall towards the stairs, to find the men who were hunting her.

Chapter 2
SS Oberkommandant Heinrich von Wolff

They say that the darkest hour is always just before dawn. SS Oberkommandant Heinrich von Wolff prayed that was true.

Berlin's streets in the early morning of April 24th, 1945 were nearly dark. The city's streetlights had failed days before, the last power stations crippled by the U.S. and British bombers. The city was shrouded in dust and smoke, from weeks of Allied bombs and Soviet artillery. Fires burned out of control across the city, ignited by the night's bombing raids. The glow of the flames was caught by the clouds, their undersides painted orange-red. Artillery thundered in the distance.

The streets on the way to Tempelhof, the only Nazi airport in the city that remained in operation, were littered with rubble and wrecked vehicles. Von Wolff's car led a convoy of four trucks and an armored personnel carrier. The trucks were the latest Wehrmacht models, freshly painted and in mint condition. Their doors bore the SS Leib-Standarte's insignia — the Führer's elite guard. Even now, with Soviet and Allied tanks only miles away and the Führer silent in his bunker, the authority of the SS was unquestioned. The convoy rolled past three checkpoints on the way from the bunker to Tempelhof, with the Wehrmacht troops hardly glancing at von Wolff's papers. When they did, the Führer's signature, and his orders, dated only hours before, sent the convoy speeding on its way.

Even at 4 a.m., Berlin's streets were crowded. Returning from the front, those Nazi soldiers who could walk trudged silently around the bomb craters and piles of debris, while fresh troops headed the opposite direction, towards the battle lines. Von Wolff watched the new recruits impassively: men who looked like teenagers or grandfathers, marching into battle in street shoes with hunting rifles against Soviet T-34 tanks. He had no illusions that these reinforcements would be able to hold back the Soviet armor for more than a few days. Berlin would fall within the week, and with it, what remained of the Third Reich.

Security at the Tempelhof airfield was non-existent. The massive entrance had been bombed repeatedly, but still loomed over the road, smooth whitish-brown stone walls pale against the night sky. Stylized imperial eagles stood on the building's roof, the crowning touch to a masterpiece of Fascist architecture. But the airfield's main gates were unmanned, and the fence around the runway had been breached in multiple places. The terminal was darkened, and the runways deserted. The Luftwaffe, unchallenged in the early years of the war, lay in wreckage. The last Nazi fighters had been shot down or destroyed where they sat on the ground weeks before. Their wrecks had littered the airstrip, until von Wolff ordered them cleared away the day before.

The convoy drove to the far end of the terminal. Two guards in SS uniforms stood at attention before a massive, blast-proof door. Von Wolff's Mercedes pulled to a halt, and he stepped out of the car. He was tall, blonde and blue-eyed, with a hawk-like nose. His uniform was jet-black, crisply pressed, with gleaming silver insignia. His custom-made boots were polished to a high gloss.

Von Wolff was accompanied by his two closest aides, Kasimir Merkels and Siegfrid von Hauptmann. Both SS officers had fought with him since the beginning of the war, first rolling east, nearly to the suburbs of Moscow, and then on the endless retreat back to the Fatherland, before he had been reassigned last year to the Führer's staff in Berlin. The two men were like brothers to him. They would give their lives for him, if ever he should ask.

The guards in front of the hangar snapped to attention and barked "*Heil Hitler.*" Von Wolff returned the salute and signaled for the convoy to halt alongside the terminal. The remaining SS vehicles followed, sleek grey shapes in the dawn's half-darkness. He remembered the first time he saw trucks like these in action, on the outskirts of Warsaw, when the Wehrmacht was still the world's most fearsome army. He had commanded a division then, elite SS troops that had fought their way through Poland, the Baltics, and then Russia. Those had been the days — the intoxicating days of the Third Reich's rise to power.

His convoy was manned by twenty SS Waffen troops. Their uniforms were worn from combat in scores of battles all across Central Europe, but clean and carefully mended. Their weapons were painstakingly maintained and, like their uniforms, battle-worn. The troops disembarked in front of the blast-proof door at the end of the terminal, securing a perimeter. Four guards remained inside the last truck and two more waited in front of it, all six men scanning the airfield for signs of intruders.

At his command, the massive door to the hangar wheeled open, creaking noisily over the sound of the convoy's engines. The interior of the hangar was enormous, and, despite Berlin's power outages, brightly illuminated. A diesel generator growled in the background. The room was tidy, with tools ordered neatly on rows of benches and workstations. It was also, he noted with satisfaction, empty. No technicians or soldiers were to be seen.

In the center of the hangar stood a Junkers Ju-290, the largest Nazi bomber in service. Even the Americans and British had nothing that could match it. The plane's fuselage bore no Nazi insignia, a precaution that he had ordered days before. Next to the bomber stood two smaller Messerschmitt Me-262 jet fighters. These were the fastest, most agile fighters in service, superior to even the best of the U.S. Air Force planes. These proudly bore Nazi markings, a white and black battle cross, on their wings and fuselage. All three planes were in perfect condition, showing no signs of the hurried repairs and cannibalization of parts that other Nazi equipment had suffered since the long, bitter retreat from Moscow and Stalingrad began.

We were so close then, he thought. If only fate had granted us another month, we would have won. None of this would have happened, this last desperate mission wouldn't have become necessary.

Von Wolff dismissed his reverie and surveyed the Tempelhof runway. His orders had been followed perfectly. The wrecks of the Luftwaffe's last fighters had been towed to one side of the concrete, and the largest craters on the airstrip had been filled. Everything had been done overnight, in the dark, so the Allies wouldn't see. He turned back to the hangar and issued the next command.

"Deploy the planes. *Sofort.*"

The SS guards towed the bomber and two fighters onto the runway. They needed to hurry. A single Allied bomber, or even a fighter, might catch the planes on the ground at this point, destroying his entire project just as it began. At the same time, four pilots climbed hastily out of the last truck, two boarding the bomber and one climbing into each of the fighters. Moments later, their engines roared to life, the first time in more than a week that a Nazi warplane had used the field.

"Unload the cargo," von Wolff directed.

Merkels and von Hauptmann hurried to the last truck in the convoy and returned, followed by two SS soldiers carrying a long grey box — a metal file cabinet. The box was handcuffed to the wrist of one of the guards. Two more guards accompanied the men, still surveying the runway for signs of intruders. The guards carried the file cabinet across the runway and carefully maneuvered it up the ramp to the cargo hold of the bomber and disappeared inside. Von Wolff followed, his boot steps just audible above the roar of the planes' engines. Merkels and von Hauptmann waited outside the aircraft, while the remaining SS troops maintained their security cordon.

It took a moment for his eyes to adjust to the dark in the cargo hold. The SS guards carried the file cabinet to the front of the hold, away from the cargo door, and secured it on the floor. Von Wolff dismissed one of the guards and produced the key for the remaining guard to unlock the handcuffs that secured the file cabinet to his wrist. As the soldier fumbled with the lock, von Wolff drew his SS dagger and stepped silently behind the guard, watching him for a moment. Then, with a single slash, he cut the man's throat, holding his mouth with a gloved hand. The soldier collapsed against the file cabinet, dying without a sound.

Von Wolff wiped the blade against the man's tunic, and then sheathed the knife. He knew he didn't need to have taken this chance, and that he shouldn't have done this himself, with a knife. But he hadn't been able to resist. The day's excitement, and the prospect of success, of the fruition of his plan, laid carefully, painstakingly over the last year, left him reckless and hungry for a kill. He smiled to himself. The risk had been worth taking.

He walked out of the cargo hold, adjusting his officer's cap as he left the plane. The pilots on all three planes signaled that they were ready for take-off. Von Wolff summoned his two aides, who called the SS soldiers to attention. Twenty-one SS troopers, standing in two neat grey rows, as dawn started to break over Tempelhof. The combat-hardened veterans of dozens of battles, facing the runway, waiting for him to issue their next orders. He watched them silently for a moment.

On his signal, Merkels and von Hauptmann turned their machine pistols onto the backs of the SS troops, laying down a withering crossfire that left no one standing. A few of the men struggled, to raise their weapons, or attempt to flee, but most fell into silent heaps on the concrete. Merkels and von Hauptmann then went man to man among the corpses, dispatching the wounded with further shots. In only minutes, the runway was silent again, save for the three planes' engines. It was a tragic waste. Von Wolff regretted that. They had been good, brave men. His men. But nothing would stop the Allied advance now, and it was imperative that his operation remain secret. There was no other option.

He boarded the bomber, followed by Merkels and von Hauptmann, and all three men seated themselves on the canvas seats that ran along the fuselage. The metal file cabinet lay at the front of the hold, still handcuffed to the SS soldier's body. Minutes later, the jet fighters taxied down the airstrip and climbed into the sky over Berlin. A moment later, the bomber was powering down the runway, bumping over the recent repairs, engines roaring angrily as the plane gathered speed. The three men gripped the sides of the canvas seats, as the aircraft careened from side to side, swerving to avoid the remaining obstacles on the runway. And then they were airborne. Staying low, according to the plan, and banking sharply to the south, over the remains of Berlin, before heading out over the Havel and the Wannsee, into Allied territory.

This was the riskiest part of the mission. The skies around Berlin were thick with Allied aircraft. But hardly any German planes had taken off for weeks, and no one would have imagined that three Nazi warplanes would appear that morning. The two Nazi fighters led the way, clearing the sky and protecting the bomber from Allied planes, as all three aircraft flew south. One of the Messerschmitts caught a U.S. P-51 Mustang from behind and above, raking its cockpit with machine gun fire; the other Messerschmitt took a British Thunderbolt from the side, turning more quickly than its prey and tearing off one wing with long bursts of bullets. The Nazi fighter pilots were the best of what remained of the Luftwaffe, highly trained and even more experienced. Together, the two German fighters dispatched nearly a dozen Allied planes, as they fought their way out of Berlin.

After twenty minutes or so, he began to believe they had reached safety. The three men sat in the darkness of the cargo hold, lit only by a dim bluish light mounted near the cockpit. There were no windows in the fuselage, and they could not see what progress the planes were making. But as the minutes crept by, the sounds of battle became progressively fainter, the bomber's flight smoother.

Just when von Wolff was convinced that they had escaped, he heard the whine of another flight of Allied fighters. The Mustangs finally caught one of the Messerschmitts from behind, their bullets finding its fuel line. The Nazi fighter exploded in a ball of flames that engulfed one of its attackers, then spiraled down into the darkness that surrounded Berlin. He clung to his seat in the darkness of the cargo hold as the bomber dove wildly to escape the American fighters. The shriek of their engines and the rattle of machine gun fire were deafening.

All three men stared rigidly into the dark, at the sides of the fuselage, praying that their luck would hold and that the pilots' maneuvers would shake off their pursuers. It seemed like an eternity, but the sound of the Americans' engines and guns gradually receded again. At last, the bomber's flight leveled off and, in another thirty minutes, the two Nazi aircraft were free of the Allied blockade. As the morning sun edged over the horizon, the planes and their cargo flew south, the skies now empty.

Three hours later, the pilots reported that they had cleared the Greek coastline. The experimental long-range fuel tanks functioned flawlessly and were still nearly

70% full. The engines were running smoothly, and the pilots estimated another twelve hours to their destination.

Von Wolff allowed himself to relax, for the first time in weeks. Merkels and von Hauptmann were both asleep now, heads leaned back against the fuselage, their faces barely visible in the dim blue light. He checked again to make sure that the file cabinet was still securely stowed, and then let his thoughts drift. He might have succeeded. Against all conceivable odds, he had persuaded the half-comatose Führer to sign his orders and hand over the files, and then they had escaped from the wreckage of Berlin, encircled by Allied tanks and planes. Just as unlikely, and just as important, the contents of the file cabinet were intact. All of it. In hours, they would land and he could start anew, beginning the long slow task of rebuilding, just the way he had planned. As the plane passed over the Egyptian coastline, von Wolff finally closed his eyes and drifted off to sleep.

Chapter 3
Professor Michael West

The camp was small and neat. Twenty-five tents, pitched in three rows, were arranged alongside a streamed on the floor of the valley. The valley lay between two jungle-covered ridges, rising up sharply from the plain, less than a kilometer apart. The valley was at the edge of the Rwenzori Mountains, on the border between western Uganda and the Congo in Central Africa. The nearest town was Goma, some 260 kilometers to the southwest, in the eastern Congo.

The camp was in some of the world's most forbidding terrain. The Rwenzoris sat on the Equator, with rich volcanic soil, tropical temperatures and exceptionally heavy rainfall — nearly 300 centimeters per year. That combination produced lush, almost impenetrable, rainforest — a dense jungle that carpeted the sheer cliffs and ridges of a range of uninhabited mountains. It was one of the most remote regions on the African continent, also home to some of the most unusual plants in the world. Underfoot, the Rwenzori's soil was dark and fertile, perpetually moist because of the heavy rainfall. During the rainy seasons, the soil turned into mud — a thick, viscous mud that reeked of decaying vegetation and clung stubbornly to anything it touched.

It was early afternoon. The monsoon rains had not yet come that day, and the sky was clear. At one end of the camp, in the center of the valley, was a fire pit, surrounded on one side by camp tables and chairs. A dozen foreigners — mostly European and American — were seated around the fire, nursing mugs of tea or coffee. Most were dressed in t-shirts and loose trousers or shorts. They all wore hiking boots.

The conversation was led by Michael West, the expedition leader. West was one of the world's most distinguished botanists. He had discovered hundreds of plant species over the past thirty years and held tenured chairs at Harvard and Oxford. He was wrapping up the group's weekly briefing, which was the last briefing that he would give on this expedition. They had accomplished all of their goals over the past twelve weeks and planned to finish their work in the next few days, before the monsoon season hit with full force.

He congratulated the group on their achievements, and then outlined preparations for breaking camp and heading back to Kampala, and civilization, at the end of the week. When West finished, the group's conversation wandered, before turning to him, the closest thing that botanists had to a rock star. This kind of talk made him uncomfortable, but he'd given up protesting years before.

One of his colleagues remarked, "Michael, you look sad to leave. Don't you want a proper bed and meal? Like the rest of us?"

He laughed. "I love it out here. It's clean and quiet. And beautiful. So much better than some crowded city. I wouldn't trade it for anything."

"This must be your tenth trip here, no? Just how many times have you done field research here in Uganda?" asked one of the graduate students.

He smiled again. "Yeah. It seems like home. Nearly fifteen summers, counting the Congo. Almost every other year since Sara was born," he said, nodding at his daughter, who was seated across the fire from him.

"I guess that's why she's better in the jungle than our so-called local guides then," commented one of the graduate students seated near the fire.

It was Robert Lamb, a botany lecturer at Oxford. Lamb was the envy of every male on the expedition. His girlfriend, Sara West, was not just West's daughter, but also stunningly beautiful. Large, liquid grey eyes, set above high cheek bones, and even, smooth skin, framed by a thick mane of blonde hair. She was tall, with long, slender legs, a blend of the best that an American father and an Afghan mother could offer.

Lamb's compliment irritated her. "That's silly. The guides grew up in the forest. This is their home. None of us know it the way they do," she retorted.

She rose effortlessly from the ground near the fire where she had been sitting, then walked gracefully to a nearby camp table and began to fill a battered kettle with water.

West laughed. "She hates compliments. You must know that by now, Robert."

"It's my fault, I guess," West continued, trying to shift the subject. "She's spent more time out here on expeditions than in civilization. That's probably why she ended up being a botanist."

Professor Pierre Richoux, a prominent botanist at the Sorbonne, was impatient with the small talk. He interjected, peering over his reading glasses.

"Seriously, your father/daughter discovery of a new epiphytic species is remarkable. Who would have imagined a family of giant orchids growing here with those characteristics. It will be one of the most important botanical discoveries of the decade. Of this, I have no doubt."

"Well, let's hope so," West said. "It took a huge effort, by all of you. It never would have happened without that."

As the conversation paused, the camp foreman, Isaac Godfrey, caught their attention. Godfrey was a tribesman who lived in one of the villages at the edge of the mountains. He had never interrupted the "Professors" discussions before. He held his woolen cap nervously in both hands, in front of him, as if he were making an offering.

"I am so sorry, Professor... Sirs... I am sorry, but my son, Jackson, he found something. Something in the jungle... He want you to look. He say it is important. Very important." Godfrey nodded vigorously as he spoke.

One of the graduate students stepped in. "Where's Jackson? What does he say he found?"

"Just coming, Professor," Godfrey replied with relief. "Jackson just come down from the mountain."

Isaac's son, Jackson Godfrey, approached the fire. Jackson was 28 years old, a serious-looking young man, who was also the best guide in the group. He always knew, unerringly, exactly where he needed to go in the jungle. Jackson was just as reliable. They had trusted him, the month before, to take Sara on a three-week trek, only the two of them, through the jungle, to the far side of the Rwenzoris, across the Congolese border. Jackson had guided them through the rainforest, using only game tracks and occasional hunter's trails, almost never losing his way during the twenty-five days.

But what Jackson had to say that afternoon sounded anything but reliable and serious to him. Instead, it sounded like a bad joke.

Jackson's voice was stubborn, as if he expected to be challenged: "I found a machine. Very big machine. Old one. Old machine. Up on the ridge."

"What? What do you mean, a machine in the jungle?" demanded Professor Richoux.

"Yes. Yes." Jackson was more nervous now. "I saw it. Very old machine. Hidden under the trees."

Lamb interrupted. "We are 120 kilometers from the nearest road. There can't be any machinery here. What are you saying?"

"I saw it. I swear. Big one. Big machine. Bigger than five tents. Up there," Jackson said, pointing at the western ridge, that rose steeply along one side of the valley.

Professor Richoux laughed loudly. "*Non.* That cannot be so. There is no machine anywhere near here. Except, maybe, in your imagination." He laughed again.

Sara's voice was soft, but it cut through the laughter. "Show me where, Jackson."

She had rejoined the group and handed Jackson a pair of binoculars. He scanned the ridge, pausing several times before pinpointing a location.

"Just there. By the tall mahogany tree," he said, returning the binoculars.

She trained the glasses onto the forest and looked intently where Jackson pointed.

"I can't see anything," she said after a moment. "It's too dense."

"It is there. A big machine. I swear it," Jackson insisted.

Richoux chuckled again, joined now by Lamb and a couple of the other graduate students around the fire pit, who began to turn back to their conversations.

Sara thought for a moment, and then said, "Take me up there, Jackson. We go look now, while you still remember the way."

Jackson beamed. "Yes. We go now. Take boots. Trail very muddy today."

West thought for a moment, then interjected. He doubted he could change his daughter's mind, but he wanted to try.

"Sweetie. It's almost 3:00. Are you sure you want to climb the ridge now? It's at least 700 meters up. Whatever's up there will still be there in the morning."

"Don't worry Daddy. I think it's more like 950 meters. But we'll be fine." She was already lacing up her boots.

West thought for a moment about joining her, but then Lamb rose to his feet.

"I'll go too then," Lamb said, putting his hand in hers. "Get your pack, too. We need to be back by sundown."

Professor Richoux laughed again, shaking his head. "Good luck, Robert, looking for that machine. The big one."

Sara ignored the comment and slipped into her pack, then came over and gave her father a hug.

"We'll be fine. And back by sunset. I promise," she said.

"OK, honey. Just be careful." He hadn't expected anything else. Once she decided on something, it wasn't easy to change her mind.

Then she turned and headed out of the camp, leading Jackson and Lamb along the path headed towards the ridge. West followed for one hundred meters or so, watching the threesome walking along the valley floor towards the ridge. He stopped after a few minutes and stood for a moment, remembering when she had barely been a teenager, struggling along the trail under a pack that was almost her size. It seemed like yesterday.

Then he turned away, to look back at the encampment. He savored the moment, the tidiness of the camp and the quiet of the valley, watching the tents against the backdrop of the mountains. He wondered how many more of these trips he could do. He wasn't getting any younger; someday he would have to stop. Then he shook the thought away and headed back to the camp, to start work on the list of tasks that needed to be finished before they returned to Kampala.

Chapter 4
Sara West

They made their way towards the ridge in single file, with Jackson leading. In twenty minutes, they had reached the far side of the plain, where the mountains rose up steeply from the valley floor. The path up the mountainside was almost non-existent for the first kilometer, a barely visible trail that climbed abruptly out of the valley along the flank of the ridge. For the first few hundred meters, the way was fairly easy, with only a little mud and water on the path. Afterwards, however, the track disappeared almost entirely, and the threesome bushwhacked through thickly jungled forest, only occasionally along sodden, muddy game trails.

Jackson continued to lead the way, over and along fallen tree trunks and through dense, thorny vegetation. The bushes and trees were a wall of green on either side of the trail. There was every imaginable shade of green, from the light, fresh green of recent shoots, to the silvery green of lichens, to the dark, almost black, green of older leaves. Vines hung from the centuries-old trees, which towered more than one hundred meters above them, twisted and gnarled, dangling in the shade of the jungle canopy.

The incline was steep, and the trail was slippery, particularly when it crossed a stream. But Jackson led them steadily higher, always picking the best routes, instinctively avoiding thickets and other obstacles. Still, all three of them were breathing hard and drenched in sweat when they stopped for a break after an hour or so.

"I know it's there. I'm sure I find it again," Jackson said, uneasily now.

"I know. I believe you," she said, her voice reassuring. Lamb remained silent, moving his hand up to her shoulder.

Half an hour later, they reached the top of the ridge. The final push, through thickets of rhododendron and bushes, had been even steeper and muddier than the first hour. Jackson paused and surveyed the ridge. He headed to the north, down the slope of the ridge, then halted, and started in the opposite direction.

"I thought he never got lost," Lamb commented.

She ignored him. Fifteen minutes later, all three of them were winded again, having made their way laboriously through dense forest along the edge of the ridge top. With no signs of any machine, Lamb looked at his watch, then up at the sun.

"We have to be back by sunset. It wouldn't do to get caught up here at night." His voice was serious. She knew he was right.

"Going down always faster," Jackson said. "It is here."

"Then find it," she said, her voice still soft, but firm enough to make Jackson swallow nervously.

He led them further through the foliage, now impenetrable in most places. Ten minutes later, his brow dripping with sweat, Lamb looked at his watch again, clearing his throat loudly.

And then, suddenly, Jackson shouted: "There. The machine." His face beamed with relief.

Perched at the edge of the ridge lay a long grey metal cylinder, with a massive motor almost buried in the bushes nearby. The cylinder was covered in vines and moss, nearly invisible among the trees and undergrowth. Even knowing where to look, from twenty-five meters away, she could barely see the object.

She worked her way through the undergrowth surrounding the cylinder. Five meters from the engine, she stopped, waiting for Lamb and Jackson to join her.

"A machine. I said it was here," Jackson declared proudly.

"Yes. You were right." She smiled at him, resting her hand on his daypack.

"It's a plane," Lamb finally said, a little grudgingly.

The aircraft lay on its belly, almost looking over the edge of the ridge. Where they could still be seen, underneath the vegetation, the plane's original colors had long since faded. At the front of the plane, the cockpit was still intact, its interior blackened by smoke. The rear of the aircraft was also intact, the fuselage lodged solidly on the jungle floor. A cargo door was marked in faded red paint and appeared untouched.

"It must be fifty or sixty years old. It's been here for ages," Lamb said.

"Yes, at least. Where did it come from?" she wondered aloud.

"Kenya? Or Egypt? I can't imagine what the Royal Air Force was doing here," he replied.

"Are you sure it's RAF? Not someone else?"

"Who else? It must have been British, no?" Lamb asked.

Instead of answering him, she forced her way through the bushes surrounding the plane and made her way to the cargo door. There was an emergency mechanism for opening the cargo hatch from the outside, and she followed the pictorial instructions, calling for Lamb's help as she worked.

Together, they released the door's safety latches and disengaged the locking mechanism. The door refused to budge, until Jackson used his machete to trim away the vines along its edges. Although it had been closed for decades, the cargo door finally swung open, with barely a sound. Whoever had engineered the plane had done so with painstaking precision, that had survived decades in the jungle.

The interior was dark and cool, the air musty and slightly metallic. She searched in her pack and found a flashlight, then shined its beam around the cargo hold. It was small — seven meters by three and a half meters or so, squeezed into the fuselage, just behind the pilots' cabin. There was hardly anything in the hold. Spartan canvas seats, bolted to the sides of the hull, ran along the fuselage. Oxygen masks dangled from the ceiling in the darkness.

And there were four bodies, all in uniforms — in what looked like German military uniforms. Three of the bodies were strapped into their safety harnesses along the sides of the fuselage. The fourth corpse lay on the floor, curled up in a half-fetal position. One of the seated figures, the tallest one, still wore his military cap. There were silver marks of rank on his shoulders and a chest-full of medals.

All four had been dead for decades, and what was left of their flesh was mummi-fied, dried like leather, worked into gruesome masks, staring up at them from their seats.

The scene was too much for Jackson. "Bad place, Miss Sara, very bad place. We go now," he insisted.

"Easy, Jackson. They're dead. They won't be hurting anyone now," she said reassuringly.

"No, Miss Sara," Jackson retorted. "Evil spirits here. Bad things in this place. They will curse us."

"You go outside, Jackson. I'll come in just a minute."

Jackson would ordinarily never have left her side. They had spent three weeks alone together in the jungle and Jackson would no sooner have left her in danger than he would have cut off his own arm. But the four ghoulish faces, staring va-cantly into the dark, were more than he could bear. Fighting back panic, he made his way to the cargo door and waited, just outside the fuselage, for her to finish her inspection.

The hold was almost empty, apart from the corpses. She nearly missed the file cabinet. It lay under one row of seats, running lengthwise next to the fuselage, near the pilots' cabin. It was a long, grey metal box. A meter and a half long, half a meter deep and wide.

She shined her flashlight on the box. It was a dull grey, with no markings on its side. She pulled the box out from under the seats, into the aisle of the hold. There was a small coat of arms, worked into the metal of the top of the box. The only thing she could make out was the swastika, gleaming in black and white enamel, as if it had been painted yesterday.

On the side of the box was a keyhole, but nothing else. She tried the lid, but it wouldn't move, not even a hint of give. She hesitated, and then gingerly reached into the pockets of the uniform on the body lying on the floor, next to the box. No keys. There were none on the corpse's belt either.

She eyed the other bodies seated along the fuselage warily, then chose the tallest one. Avoiding the figure's eyeless gaze, she unbuckled the corpse's seat belt and lifted aside the fabric of the uniform. She forced herself to reach inside, and checked the man's pockets, first the trousers, then the jacket, until she found it, in a buttoned pocket on the inside of the jacket. It was a single key, on a finely worked silver key chain, with another Nazi insignia — the SS coat of arms — worked into the key.

"Just another minute, Jackson," she called out.

"Yes, Miss Sara. No worries." His voice sounded very worried.

She fit the key snugly into the hole on the side of the metal box. Even after sixty years, it turned smoothly, almost like clockwork, and the locking mechanism released with a delicate click. She carefully lifted the lid of the box and let it rest on its hinges, shining her light into the long, rectangular space.

She was disappointed. It was full of papers. She checked underneath the papers and at the sides of the box. Nothing else. Just a file cabinet filled with old papers — stacks of files, full of old documents.

She flipped through some of the papers. Some were faded or molded, but many seemed to be in good condition. They were in German, typewritten on various kinds of paper. Almost all of the documents were on some sort of letterhead, mostly embossed with Nazi swastikas and stylized eagles. She could tell, even from skimming a few of the papers, that they were official documents, probably Nazi government records.

She paused for a moment. It would take hours to examine the contents of the file, and they had to start back down the ridge very soon. In fact, they should already have left for the camp.

But the plane and its cargo had captured her imagination. Where had it been going? What was its cargo? Who were its passengers? She carefully extracted the contents of the first few folders in the file cabinet and slid them into her pack, wrapped in the rain jacket that she always carried in her pack. Then she closed the lid of the metal box, locked it, and walked back to the cargo door. Before she exited, she took half a dozen photos of the cargo hold and the passengers' remains with her phone.

Once outside, she repeated the process, photographing the cargo door, the plane's fuselage and the cockpit.

Jackson's face broke into a broad smile when she finished.

"We go now?" he asked hopefully.

"Yes. We go. Back to the camp."

They worked their way down the ridge in the fading light. It was much easier descending, and they remembered parts of the trail. By the time the sun had reached the horizon, they were on the valley floor, and familiar terrain. Still, they did not reach camp until the sky was nearly dark.

Her father waited anxiously for them at the edge of the camp. Even in the twilight his worry was unmistakable.

She greeted him. "Hi, Daddy. Sorry we're late."

"Honey, you frightened us. Me most of all," he said.

"I'm sorry. But you won't believe what Jackson found. And you should know by now, I'm safer out there than most other places," she answered, softening her response with a hug and a kiss on his cheek. "And I had Jackson there to protect me. Jackson and Robert."

Jackson beamed again. "All good, Professor. All very good."

They walked into the camp, where dinner was being served around the fire pit. Large pots of pasta rested on rocks around the fire, and the expedition members ate family style, helping themselves to large portions. Kerosene lanterns glowed on the tables, and guitar music played from a sound system.

Professor Richoux rose and greeted them, with an effusive welcome and playful smile. "My friends, finally back. And the machine. The huge machine in the jungle. You must tell us all about it."

She let Lamb answer. "I'm not quite sure what we found. But whatever it is, Pierre, you won't believe it," he said.

Then he described the plane site, the wreckage, the four bodies and the files. When he was finished, they passed around her phone, inspecting the photos and speculating about what they meant.

"Well, you're right. I can't believe it," her father finally said. "It doesn't make any sense."

"*Oui, oui,*" nodded Richoux.

"It looks like a Nazi bomber, from WWII," said Lamb. "Look at the uniforms and the swastika on the box. But how did a Nazi bomber end up here?"

There were a variety of theories. Flights gone astray from Rommel's Egypt or Mussolini's Ethiopia. Diplomatic missions to God-only-knows-where. Spy flights. But none of the possibilities provoked more than skeptical frowns.

"What's in the file, then?" asked another of the graduate students.

"I haven't looked closely yet," Sara said. "Do any of you read German?"

"Dieter and Michael do. But they've just gone back to Kampala. I spoke a bit in my teens, but doubt I can help much," said Lamb.

"That's fine. My German's rusty but will do. I should be able to get a quick review done tomorrow afternoon, after we pack," she replied.

They finished dinner, with talk returning to the expedition's work and the trip back to Kampala. The plane and its cargo were put aside as the expedition's participants turned to the tasks ahead of them in the next few days.

Later that night, she walked her father back to his tent. He turned on the lantern in the living space, which doubled as the expedition's office, and logged onto the camp's one computer with internet access. Together, they composed a brief email report on the last few days' work for the four universities that were sponsoring the expedition. At the end of the email, they described the unusual discovery that Jackson had made. Then she handed him her phone, which he connected to the computer, before letting her attach her photos to the email. When they were finished, he clicked send, confirmed that the email had been sent, and turned the computer off for the night.

He walked her to the door of the tent and opened the flap for her. They stood there for a moment, watching the glow of the fire pit against the mountains. Then she hugged him again, holding him tight against her windbreaker, before saying good night and walking back to her tent.

The camp was still, peaceful and quiet in the night. As she snuggled into her sleeping bag, her thoughts drifted back to the plane, up in the jungle on the ridge. After a moment, she put the images away, a mysterious puzzle, but nothing to distract her from the list of chores she needed to finish in the next few days.

Chapter 5
Ivan Petronov

Ivan Petronov left the black London cab three streets away from the Mayfair address. He always did that. Then he took a circuitous route home, checking twice for tails. He knew there would be none, but training was training. He had learned the tools of espionage during almost twenty years at the KGB, and its successor, the Federal Security Service. The bureaucracies had never suited him, but the two spy agencies had taught him well. Their training had been invaluable over the past decade, ever since he had left the FSS and gone into business for himself.

After ten minutes, he reached No. 34, a quietly elegant house, standing between two large mansions. It was brick, Victorian, and at this point, one of his many excellent investments, having almost doubled its £10 million purchase price over the past four years. He rang the bell twice, to let her know that it was him, and then deactivated the three security systems.

He was fifty-four years old, on the short side and heavily built. His face was pale and pudgy, with small dark eyes set closely together beneath thick, bushy eyebrows and oily brown hair. His hands were slender, with long, tapered fingers and manicured nails. They looked out of place at the end of thick, fatty arms, as if they belonged to someone else. He was dressed for travel, in custom-made grey slacks from Saville Row and a white cotton shirt, tailored in Hong Kong. He perspired slightly in the late spring afternoon.

He shut the door behind him, locking it and re-activating the security systems, before he went inside. The ground floor reception room was grand — although they never used it for receptions, or any other entertaining. The house was their retreat, where visitors were never invited. The floors in the reception room were mahogany, a rich brown that set off the gold-colored silk wallpaper and Persian carpets. Antique furniture and early twentieth-century Soviet constructivist paintings completed the picture. Classical music, Tchaikovsky, played softly in the background. She had to be home.

He climbed the stairs up from the ground floor, pausing for a moment on the landing to catch his breath. She was in her bedroom on the second floor, looking over the garden. Her room was cool, with ivory wallpaper, light cream curtains, and a large bed with white lace pillows. A single scroll, with the Chinese character for "courage" drawn in elegant black brushstrokes, hung across from the bed.

She sat, cross-legged, on the floor — eyes closed, hands folded in her lap. Her hair, dark and shining, fell loosely down her back, nearly to her waist. Her face was a perfect oval, with soft, delicate features. Her lips were full and red, moistened slightly and partly open. Tiny wisps of fine hair, almost like feathers, ran along her hairline. She wore nothing. Her breasts were small and firm, uplifted with dark, pointed nipples. Her waist was slim, legs long and lithe. Her skin was light brown, smooth and perfectly even.

He felt the stirring in his loins, as he did whenever he saw her this way. So soft and vulnerable. He knew that she wanted to be left alone until she finished her exercises, but he couldn't resist. He had been gone for three days and was hungry for her. He kicked aside his shoes, noting how she tensed ever so slightly. He smiled at her anticipation. She didn't mind the interruption all that much, he told himself.

He lifted her roughly from the floor, without saying a word. She was slightly built, almost childlike. He dropped her on the bed, turned her over, face down, legs just at the edge of her bed, her tawny skin warm against the crisply pressed linen. He touched her from behind, between her buttocks, then spat into his hand, since she wasn't wet yet, using the saliva to moisten her, forcing his fingers inside her, feeling her clench in response.

He unbuckled his belt, dropping his trousers. Then he held her firm, one hand on the back of her neck, pinning her down, while he pushed into her. She was tight as he thrust, one time after another. His hairy thighs and belly, pale and sweaty, at least a dozen kilograms overweight, contrasted with her smooth, even skin, no hint of wrinkles or marks, and perfect figure.

He shifted his grip, both hands now on her hips, holding her tightly as he fucked her hard. His breath came ragged now, as he pumped deeper, hammering into her soft warmth. He heard her moan, softly, as if she wanted to conceal it, and the sound drove him over the edge. He came hard, his last spurts jetting onto her back as he slipped out of her, sperm splashing across her butt and his hand. He lay there, panting, bent over her for a moment, regaining his breath.

Then he wiped his hand across the back of her leg, leaving a glistening streak of sperm against the soft brown of her skin, before he rolled her over and looked down into her eyes. They were dark, almost black, and calm, even and steady. It was as if she were watching a landscape, far away in the distance. There was a thin sheen of sweat above her lips and her breath was faster. He could tell that she had liked it.

"Did you miss me?" he asked.

"I so wanted that. Can you do it again?" she said with a mischievous smile.

He laughed. She must know how good that made him feel, even if he couldn't. "Soon, baby. Don't worry."

He rested against her again, still half-panting, his sweat matting the hairs on his pale chest. The sun was going down and the sounds of London's evening traffic came in through the window.

"How was your trip?" she asked, after a moment of silence.

"Fine. They can get me access to the Stasi archives in Berlin. That much is pretty clear. But it won't be cheap."

"What do they want?"

"They said 1.5 million Euro. But maybe half that," he replied.

"That's not cheap. Can they deliver?"

"I think so. They showed me samples of a few of the files we asked about. They must have some sort of high-level access."

He was silent for a moment, and then stood, his shirt open over his ample belly. He ought to use that gym again, he thought in passing. But his attention was elsewhere.

"Give me a minute," he said, and kicked off his pants, before walking out of her room and across the hallway to his own bedroom.

His computer was on the desk, an antique writing table, and he turned it on. He completed the log-in procedures. They took longer than most, but the security was worth it. After the system booted up, he logged in. He checked his main email account first, replying noncommittally in an encrypted email to the couple he had just visited in Berlin. Then he logged into his special account, the one that only his friends in Moscow, at the FSS, used. Unusually, there was an email waiting. It had just arrived, also encrypted. He felt his throat tighten. Dealing with his old friends always made him nervous. Hopefully, not bad news.

The email was short. It said only "FYI," and attached another email — an intercept by Russian intelligence services. The attachment was in English, with four photos attached to it in turn. The email was a report, by a botanist, about his expedition's work in Western Uganda. At first, he thought that the attachment was a mistake — that the wrong item had been forwarded to him.

But then he skipped down to the final paragraph of the email. It was short:

"By the way, we also stumbled on a very unusual thing today – it looks like a Nazi aircraft that crashed here in the jungle and seems to have been untouched since 1945 or so. Attached are photographs. There were remains of two pilots and four passengers, which might need to be reported to the authorities. Can you have someone in Kampala advise on formalities when you have a moment? Many thanks."

The attached photos showed a WWII Nazi warplane, overgrown by jungle vegetation, as well as an interior shot of the cargo hold. The latter photograph was dark, but he could make out four bodies in military uniforms, as well as a long grey metal box, lying on the floor of the plane.

He sat stock still, heart pounding. He wasn't sure that he could believe his eyes. His thoughts whirled. Elation, that his hunches and his stubborn instincts over all these years had been right, and that the Nazi files were within his reach. Astonishment, that his search might be so close to its goal. Anxiety, that others might be on the same trail that he was. Or that they would be soon. He re-read the email, and then called her.

"Yan. Come here," he barked.

She padded into his room. She had slipped on white silk pajamas and pulled her hair up. She looked over his shoulder at his computer. She was silent too for a moment.

Then she asked, "Is it real?"

"I can't believe it's not," he said.

"You found it then," she said quietly. "That's exactly what your sources said. A perfect match."

She rested her hand gently on his shoulder. She watched him, through cool, even eyes, while he sat there, long, slender fingers fidgeting with his keychain, as he thought about the things they needed to do.

"And it looks undamaged. I waited so long for this. It's finally in my reach." He spoke rapidly, excitedly. "We have to move now, though. Immediately. There may be many others listening in. And once the files are reviewed, others will definitely be interested."

"Where is it? The plane wreck?" she asked.

"In Africa. The Ugandan-Congolese border. In the middle of nowhere," he said.

"So we need to get there. Now," she said.

"Yes. And not alone. We'll need help."

"Your Russian friends? No one else?"

"Nobody else. No one. This is perfect for my old friends."

"They won't be cheap."

"This is worth it. Worth many times what they will charge. And we can afford it. Dozens of times over. Now let me do this."

He turned to his computer, dismissing her. He needed to think carefully now, about how to approach his contacts at the FSS. They would take what he had found in a heartbeat, if they ever figured out what it was worth. He needed to make sure they wouldn't ever know enough to do that. He hunched over his computer, lost in thought as he constructed what he would tell his friends.

She watched him for a moment, then walked silently back to her bedroom and closed the door behind her. She sat down on the floor and resumed her exercises, sitting alone in the middle of the darkened room, facing the scroll on the wall.

Chapter 6
Franklin Kerrington III

The newspapers lay on the dining table, next to his breakfast setting. Samuel had poured the coffee, freshly brewed and still steaming, as Franklin Kerrington III came down the staircase. The coffee cup was nineteenth-century porcelain, a special edition by Meissen, with an intricate blue and cream pattern. The set had been in the Kerrington family for generations. He eased into the chair at the head of the table — both elegantly proportioned Chippendale antiques that gleamed in the morning light.

The room was long — twelve by five meters — with high ceilings and floor-to-ceiling French doors along one side. The shutters were open, and sunlight streamed in from the internal courtyard. He could hear the fountain through the doors, which Samuel had opened to let the morning air come in. There was no traffic — it was 6 a.m. on a Saturday morning, and Georgetown had not yet started the day.

The courtyard was spacious, with four grassy squares, finely cut, surrounding the fountain. His grandfather had brought the fountain home with him after a summer in Rome nearly eighty years ago. It was by Bernini, with two heroic figures, Honor and Duty, gazing into the basin. The fountain's marble, still crystalline white after four centuries, was tinged green with moss at its base. The paths that quartered the lawn were laid with white pebbles, glistening in the morning dew, framed by rounded arches of walkways that ran along three sides of the courtyard.

He walked to the window, sipping his coffee. This view always grounded him. It reminded him of a cloister, the courtyard of some monastic order, devoted to a higher calling, detached from the troubles of the day.

The rest of the mansion was more imposing — he knew that. The reception rooms were grand, stretching nearly the entire Georgetown block, with rich teak floors, soaring ceilings and six identical Venetian chandeliers. The double staircase, with ornate marble balustrades and carpeted stairs, was equally splendid. The residence projected wealth and power — he knew that as well and valued it. But it was here, looking onto the quiet, ordered silence of the cloistered courtyard, that he was most at home. He treasured the mansion's history — the authority it projected, its elegance and refinement — but it was the secluded garden, curtained off from the guests, where he spent his time when he could choose.

He turned back to the table and refilled his coffee. Samuel appeared again, this time with orange juice, freshly squeezed, in a thickly cut crystal glass, and a single porcelain plate with fruit — two plump figs and three dates. He placed the glass and the plate silently on the table and withdrew; he never spoke unless Kerrington directed a question to him.

He savored his second cup of coffee and nibbled at the fruit. The dates were delicious — golden brown with crinkled, translucent skin — imported from Beirut, courtesy of a Lebanese merchant he had known for decades. The first fig was delicious as well, juicy and bursting with flavor. But the second was spoiled — a half-rotted mass of rancid flesh, that he put aside in disgust, thankful that he hadn't bitten fully into what had looked so healthy from the outside. He consoled himself with the last date and another cup of Samuel's coffee.

He skimmed the headlines in the newspapers, digesting Congress' antics and the ineffectual young President's newest round of missteps. He spent longer with the business pages, pausing for a moment on rumors of one defense contractor's courtship of another. He made a note to follow up on the last item, and then moved on to an article about corruption in Russia, losing interest when he realized that the authors had nothing remotely new to report, at least not to him. But then, few reporters did.

He was the Deputy Director of the CIA. At 62, he had occupied the office for more than a decade. He had seen three directors of the Agency come and go, as well as two presidents. There were few secrets, few secrets that really mattered, either in Washington or anywhere else, that he didn't know.

But he was the soul of discretion — respected by both political parties for his judgment and wisdom. In 21st-century American politics, that was no small achievement. Republicans and Democrats, whatever their stripe, also credited him with a healthy proportion of the last decade's foreign policy successes — and none of its failures. His reputation for competence and foresight was unparalleled. And, the pundits wrote, his humility was just as unique. In a city dominated by egos and self-aggrandizement, Franklin Kerrington III was different — a man content to do the nation's business, and to leave glory and power to the politicians. That was his reputation.

Honor and duty, the figures on the fountain and the motto of his family, were his watchwords as well. Like his father and grandfather before him, who had served in the Senate, he was celebrated for his patriotism, his devotion to honor and duty. He valued that, the reputation which his family had built over generations, as much as the mansion and the immense family fortune, which he had also inherited from them.

When he was finished with the newspapers, he crossed the hallway to his private study, using the key in the pocket of his dressing gown to let himself into the room. The key hung alone on a finely worked silver key chain. It fit snugly into the keyhole, turned smoothly with a delicate click, and the door swung soundlessly inwards — a wood-paneled slab of steel, on precisely engineered hinges, that could stop all but the best-equipped intruders. And no intruder would have the time needed to get beyond the door, given the round-the-clock CIA security detail on call nearby.

He sat down behind the desk. It was an English antique, finely carved and gleaming. It was tidy, almost bare. Silver-framed photographs, black and white, of his father and grandfather, were arranged on one side of the desktop. They were dressed formally, as they always had been, and gazed directly at the camera, still imperious long after their deaths. They looked every bit like men who had directed the U.S. Senate, as they had. Kerrington had the same gaze — large dark brown eyes beneath imposing grey eyebrows, set in patrician features that could have belonged to an English viceroy or Venetian doge. An aquiline nose, thin lips and silver hair, combed back from a high forehead, without a strand out of place, completed the portrait.

The final photograph on the desk was of his wife, years ago, on their horse farm, smiling regally. For the last decade or so, she had spent most of her time at the farm, in the Virginian countryside, bored by Washington life and a Georgetown mansion that was usually empty. That suited him perfectly, giving him time to continue building the Kerrington family's fortune and reputation.

Also on the desk was a sleek black computer. It was a custom-built device, constructed at jaw-dropping expense by three former Agency IT engineers who had struck out as freelancers when the budget cuts of the previous decades had reduced the attractions of CIA work. This product of their efforts was exceptionally powerful — and protected by equally exceptional security. It took him the better part of three minutes, working his way through passwords, fingerprints and retina scans, before he was online. Despite the time it took, he logged onto this computer once each day.

Once online, he checked three separate email accounts, each with different usernames. Most days, all three accounts were empty. Even when he received a message, it was usually irrelevant. That was the case again today — with two of the accounts. The third account was different though. The third account contained a single email, with a single attachment.

The attachment was another email, along with four photos. It had been intercepted and forwarded to him by one of the three firms he had hired, through an impenetrable series of front companies, to provide him with information on various matters. Matters that he didn't want the CIA, or anyone else, to know that he was interested in.

He read slowly, putting down his coffee when he reached the final paragraph. He paused, read the paragraph again and then opened the attached photographs. The email was a report by a botanist, a well-known one from Harvard, his alma mater, about a research expedition in Uganda. The final paragraph reported, in a matter-of-fact tone, on the discovery of a WWII bomber, with six corpses.

His breath came shallowly, and his stomach clenched tight around a thick ball of dread that he had felt only a few times in his life. It was not as if he hadn't endured dangerous times, on assignments in Aleppo, Caracas, Kinshasa and elsewhere. He had risked his life — really risked it, with bombs exploding and bullets flying past him — more times than he could count, more than most Agency field operatives. But he had hardly ever felt the dark knot of fear, deep in his gut, the way that he did now.

He forced himself to breathe, to think. He sat motionless, first for a moment, then for nearly a quarter hour, calming himself, and then working through the possibilities. When he was finished, he exhaled. He had to assume the worst — that the bomber in the jungle was the same one that he had heard reports of, and that the plane contained the Nazi records, the ones that his father had warned him about. He could hardly bring himself to recall those reports, and their stories of Nazi conspiracies and the tainted roots of the Kerrington dynasty. But he had to, because they threatened his reputation, fortune, and power, all that he and the Kerrington family had built.

Eventually, he picked up the secure phone that sat on the edge of the desk. It looked like a normal mobile phone, but it was another product of his IT contractors — heavily encrypted and untraceable. That meant untraceable by anyone, including the technicians at the CIA. He dialed a number, which answered after a moment — and after multiple re-routings. The voice on the other end was flat, shielded by its own encryption.

"This is a nice surprise," the voice answered.

"I'm glad you think so." Kerrington was curt.

"You must need some help."

"I do. Fast."

"It will cost," the man said.

"We'll see about that. Don't forget how you got to where you are."

"How could I? But business is business."

He knew the man well, despite their tone. They had worked together on more operations than either could remember — Nicaragua, Iran, Yemen, Serbia, and countless other hotspots around the world. He had helped the man leave the Agency, a decade ago, to start his own security firm, handling projects that the U.S. government couldn't do itself. Truth be told, Kerrington had encouraged the man to set up shop on his own, exactly so that he would have someone to do the things that Congress and the press kept the Agency out of. When the man had wavered, Kerrington had secretly blocked the man's career at the CIA, making the choice a lot simpler for him. Of course, the man never found out what he had done. And he was instead deeply loyal to Kerrington, who was also the main source of business for his private operation.

The two men turned to business. Kerrington outlined the mission: locate the wreckage of an aircraft in the remotest regions of Western Uganda, retrieve the plane's cargo and return it to Washington. Kill anyone who interfered. Spare no expense. The man on the phone hesitated, which was uncharacteristic. He hardly ever hesitated.

He finally said: "We can do it, but it's complicated. It won't be cheap or easy. Not at all. But we can do it."

"Of course. It needs to happen right away. The targets may move."

"Understood."

Kerrington continued. "One more thing. There may be competition. And I will be sending one of my own men."

"That's two things. Doable, but it's going to be expensive."

"What are you thinking?" he asked.

"Ten million, U.S., plus expenses."

"You might retire on that. We wouldn't want that."

"I can retire already. The price reflects the risk."

"Done then."

"Half now. Half on completion."

"10% now; the rest on completion. Successful completion."

"Of course. 25% upfront and we have a deal," the man countered.

"Done. But don't fail me. Not on this one."

"Of course not. We won't."

"My guy will be in touch this afternoon. An ex-Agency man. He'll be branching out on his own today."

"That sounds familiar. I am sure I'll be fine with him."

Kerrington hung up. The knot in his stomach was slightly more manageable. There were multiple scenarios that posed no risks at all for him. The plane might have nothing to do with his family; its cargo might have disappeared or better, been destroyed; the cargo might not incriminate his father or grandfather, might not suggest the origins of the family's wealth. All of these possibilities were more likely, much more likely, than a disaster scenario. The possibility that a collection of secret Nazi files, which somehow incriminated his grandparents and parents, would turn up after seventy years in a Ugandan rainforest was preposterous. He was worrying about goblins beneath the bed. But, then again, that was why he had survived for so long.

He had work to do then. He needed to organize funding — that would be fairly straightforward. His fortune was massive and largely secret, supposedly in blind trusts; but he could arrange these payments without anyone raising an eyebrow.

The man he wanted to send on the mission was more complicated. He had to be the best. And loyal — completely loyal — to him. No cowboy, but a reliable man whom he could trust. The mission would be dangerous. And there would be no Agency backup; this operation would be completely off the books. Just as important, the man would need to bring him the cargo from the plane, if there was any, as well as deal with the botanists and the competition — Russians and Israelis were the obvious risks.

He had been grooming two men at the Agency for a day like this one, but he wasn't sure either one was ready yet, especially on short notice. He would have a final look at their files, talk to them, and make up his mind. And then theirs.

He dressed for work, the way he did every day. Samuel had laid out his suit, hand-tailored in Italy, and shirt, white Egyptian cotton with French cuffs. By 7:30 a.m., he was in his car — a Lincoln Continental, armored, courtesy of the CIA and U.S. taxpayer. He made telephone calls on his way to work, tying off loose ends on a variety of problems at the Agency and on Capitol Hill. By 8 a.m., he was at Langley's front gate, ready to start the day. The knot in his stomach had eased further, but it still made his throat tighten when he thought about what secrets might be hidden in the Nazi plane out there in the jungle.

Chapter 7
Peter Abramov

The Crimea was anchored one hundred kilometers off the Kenyan coastline, near the Somali border, in the Indian Ocean. The captains of most vessels in that part of the world would have been worried about pirates. Peter Abramov was not.

Abramov's freighter was at least fifty years old — a Russian-flagged survivor from the Soviet Union. It had plied the coast of Africa for decades, first servicing the African regimes that shared fraternal Socialist bonds with the USSR and, more recently, doing business with anyone who was willing to pay rock-bottom prices for no-frills service and no questions. It made a bad target, for pirates or anyone else.

The vessel was rusty and in disrepair, too small for modern containers and too dilapidated for most self-respecting shippers. The windows on the main deck were greasy, cracked or repaired in countless places, and boarded over in another two or three. The deck was weather-beaten, with decades-old wooden timbers that received the bare minimum of care. The ship stank of diesel, burned badly in an engine that wasn't properly maintained, and the scents of its native crew — bodies that went unwashed for weeks on end, cheap cigarettes, spicy African food, and overcrowded toilets. Clouds of oily black smoke spewed out of the vessel's smoke-stack, adding to the layers of dirt and smells.

Despite endless challenges, he had managed to keep the vessel running for the past several decades. He survived the dark times after the Soviet Union disinte-grated, privatizing and then rebuilding what was now his own business, step by painful step. The years had taken their toll. His hair was nearly white, and his face was furrowed and leathery, from countless days in the African sun and even more nights of too much alcohol and fitful sleep. But Abramov felt now that his fortunes had at last turned, with this latest contract. It was risky, and no doubt broke the laws of a dozen countries. But much of what he did was no different, so who really cared?

The assignment had come suddenly, from an old FSS contact whom he hadn't heard from in years. It was simple: allow two helicopters to land, resupply, and take off from the Crimea, together with their crews and cargo. And the contract price was more than the entire amount that he would earn in some years. He had no regrets, even when the two helicopters that had arrived during the afternoon had been military aircraft, loaded with men who looked like ex-Spetsnaz Russian special forces troops. That wasn't his business; his bank account, which had a larger balance than ever before, was all he cared about.

The two helicopters that now sat aft of the bridge were the latest model Russian attack crafts, Mi-28s, sparkling in the evening sunlight. They were painted with desert camouflage colors, dark and light browns, and carried the newest generation of Russian air-to-surface missiles. Their armaments were fully loaded, S-8 missiles slung low on either side of the helicopters' fuselages, machine guns mounted above the missiles. The cockpits were fitted with thick, bulletproof glass and the doors were armored. He couldn't help but notice that, despite their obvious Russian origins, the two aircrafts bore no identification markings.

Swarming over both helicopters were technicians, checking the weapon loads, fueling the two aircrafts and double-checking their equipment. The technicians wore uniforms with the logos of Rostec, the helicopter manufacturer. Despite the sweltering heat, nearly 40° in the shade, the technicians went about their work with military efficiency.

Lounging in the shade beneath the bridge were twenty or so heavily muscled men. They had short hair, military fatigues, and were idly chatting in Russian or checking their weapons. Several of the soldiers were cleaning AK-103s, standard issue assault rifles for Spetsnaz commando forces. Another was stripping down a grenade launcher, while the largest, a tall blonde man, tinkered with the scope on a wickedly long sniper rifle. The men were almost all in their late twenties, in peak physical condition, muscles rippling beneath their t-shirts and tattoos. A few of the soldiers exercised or practiced martial arts on the deck.

He had swallowed hard when the soldiers had clambered out the helicopters that afternoon. He was well-accustomed to tough customers, but these men were more menacing than Somali pirates or Kenyan thugs. They were serious professionals, not ordinary soldiers, brutal and hardened, and armed to the teeth. They made no secret of their contempt for his vessel and its native crew. They spoke loudly, mockingly, in Russian, knowing perfectly well that he could understand, ridiculing him, his ship, and his crew.

He looked forward to dusk, when the helicopters and their cargo would leave. Even the technicians who serviced the aircraft were uncomfortable around the soldiers. They were as eager as he was for the helicopters to depart. They gave the soldiers a wide berth and directed all their questions to Igor Vilchoy, the FSS contact who had sent Abramov this assignment, and the $500,000 in his bank account.

Vilchoy was civilized, a gentleman, who had bargained hard, but fair, and who kept his word, paying the price that they agreed, on time and fully. Vilchoy's woman, the Chinese girl, was civilized too and just as beautiful. She had thanked Abramov with a shy smile when he directed her to the toilet beneath the deck. She insisted on bringing her bags with her, refusing his offers of help with the luggage, then softening her refusal with another smile. After she disappeared into the toilet with her bags, locking the door behind her, one of Vilchoy's men demanded Abramov's presence on the deck and he reluctantly went to the bridge.

When he reached the deck, one of the Spetsnaz soldiers beckoned him over. Although it was his ship, and he was the captain, he obeyed. The young blonde man directed him to bring his supply of vodka and whiskey — just the unopened bottles, the man specified with a sneer — up to the deck. Abramov started to protest and the blonde man was on him like a panther, sweeping his legs out from under him with a vicious kick and then pinning him down against the deck, a long knife suddenly out and pressed into his throat. The blonde man spoke slowly, telling him that he would not repeat the order again, before allowing him to stand.

Abramov was fit, hardened by three decades of life on the open sea. But he felt like a child in the blonde soldier's grip, well aware that the man could have slit his throat in a heartbeat.

He stumbled away and headed beneath the deck, back to the galley. He was relieved, then, that Vilchoy appeared in the doorway. He was dressed casually, in linen trousers and a fine white shirt that looked out of place amidst the grime of the Crimea. Vilchoy reassured him.

"Don't worry, my friend. They are only boys. Give them a few bottles of liquor. Your fee will cover it, and if it doesn't, this will." He handed over two crisp €500 notes, smiling easily, like an old comrade.

Abramov was still resentful, but the bottles he surrendered wouldn't have cost a fraction of the notes that Vilchoy handed him. He collected part of what was left of the ship's liquor supplies and returned to the deck. The blonde Spetsnaz soldier took the bottles silently, with a mocking smile, then returned to adjusting the sight on his sniper rifle.

By 6:00 p.m., the sun was touching the top of the Kenyan coast. The helicopters were pronounced ready and the ex-Spetsnaz troops loaded their gear onto the aircraft. Vilchoy came over and repeated what he had said before.

"Remember. This never happened. No matter who asks, we were never here."

"Of course."

He half-wished that were true but comforted himself with thoughts of his bank account.

Vilchoy and the woman boarded one of the helicopters. As they climbed onto the aircraft, Abramov noticed for the first time that both of them carried Uzi machine pistols, in well-used shoulder holsters. Then Vilchoy shut the cockpit door behind them, and the two helicopters took off, one following the other over the railings of the ship and out above the ocean.

The downdraft of the rotors, and screaming of their engines, forced Abramov and his crew into the main cabin of the Crimea. They watched the two helicopters bank to the left and then head towards the African coast, into the setting sun. The two silhouettes were suspended for a moment, like giant insects, against the blood red sun, the roar of their motors still loud over the waves.

Abramov breathed a sigh of relief. He had promised himself another vodka when they were gone, and he made his way down the stairway from the main deck to his cabin. He opened the door to the dark, damp room, hardly the size of a closet, that had been his home for the last 30 years and opened the bookcase. Tolstoy, Chekhov, Dostoyevsky, and Stolichnaya.

He chose Stoli, pouring a healthy shot. The water glass was chipped and dirty, as always, but the liquor was clean and sharp, biting his throat as he swallowed. He sat upright on his cot, back against the hull. He took another breath and thought of the $500,000 payment as his stomach warmed. The dingy cabin seemed brighter and more spacious than it had for ages. He smiled again.

The explosion shattered the quiet. It came from the main deck and rocked the entire ship, slamming it down into the ocean, and then shaking the vessel violently, side to side. The screams of his crew and the Russian technicians pierced the dusk. The ship lost its power a moment later and the passageway was dark as he groped his way up to the deck. Another blast, this one deep below the decks, near the toilets, rocked the vessel again. It was followed by more screams.

He stared at the wreckage of the deck. The steering wheel and navigation equipment were gone, replaced by twisted metal — smoke and flames starting to pour from the sides of the cabin. The ship began to list heavily; the explosion below the deck, down by the toilets, must have holed the hull. The water rushing into the Crimea's hold would sink her in a matter of minutes, he knew with cold certainty.

He made his way to the main cabin, hoping that the radio might somehow have survived the explosion. It hadn't. In fact, nothing in the cabin had survived. Then, over the crackling of the fires on the deck and the screams of injured sailors, he heard the whine of approaching helicopter engines. He turned towards the sounds and shouted wildly, with joy, waving his arms over his head. Vilchoy was a decent man; he would rescue them, would rescue Abramov. He could start over, with the money that was in his bank account.

Then he saw the flashes from the muzzles along the sides of each helicopter. He watched the tracers streaming through the darkening sky, raking across the deck and the blackened cabin of the ship. He felt the slugs slam into his legs, feeling the impact that hurled him against the deck, but barely registered the pain. As the first helicopter roared past, only meters from his sinking ship he glimpsed the Chinese woman through the window for an instant. She was smiling peacefully, and her eyes watched him coolly. Then he saw the missiles detach from the second copter and streak across the night sky towards what was left of the Crimea. That was the last thing he ever saw.

Chapter 8
Sara West

She woke early, with the rising sun and African songbirds. She lay there a moment, letting the morning peace embrace her, before the camp began to stir. Robert lay next to her, snoring, his head tilted back and mouth open. His arms were folded protectively across his chest as he slept, his brow wrinkled with a frown. She watched him for a moment, wondering what might be worrying him. While she slept like a baby in the wild, Robert complained about the jungle noises and the dreams he said they produced.

She pulled aside the mosquito netting that hung over the cot and slipped into her clothes. They were the same things she wore every day — worn blue jeans, a t-shirt, and hiking boots. She checked the boots for insects before she put them on, a habit she had learned early from her father, on one of their expeditions into the wilderness.

The early morning air had a chill, and she pulled on a fleece as well. She walked across the tent to the camp-table and collected her backpack, with the stack of papers she had brought down from the plane wreck three days ago. The intervening days had been a whirl of preparations for their return to Kampala. She had barely thought about, much less looked at, the file of documents, the way she had planned to do. But now she had at least an hour of quiet time before the others were awake.

She found a stool by the fire, still smoldering from last night's dinner. The cook brought her a mug of coffee. While she waited for the coffee to cool, she watched the mist that wreathed the higher peaks, up at the far end of the valley. The clouds curled heavily into the treetops on the ridge, and then, higher up around the peaks, were light and wispy — not like the dark thunder clouds that would follow when the monsoons arrived in full force.

She studied the ridge again, trying to locate the plane's wreckage. But even though she knew exactly where to look, there was no sign of what lay below, buried in the rain forest. The foliage of the canopy was a solid green wall, carpeting the entire ridge. There wasn't a hint that anything might be hidden beneath the jungle. She could see why the Rwenzoris were nicknamed the Mountains of the Moon. They were the roughest terrain she had ever seen.

She opened her pack and took out one of the files from the plane. It was a cardboard folder, with a Nazi swastika and eagle embossed on the cover. Large red type warned "Streng vertraulich" — strictly confidential. A faded red velvet tie secured the flap.

Inside the folder were a hundred pages or so, type-written for the most part, in chunky font with archaic German spellings. Virtually everything in the file was in German, with a few pages in English or French, and one in Russian. Most of the documents were thin and brittle, almost like tracing paper, with faded print, making it almost impossible to read in some places. A few of the pages broke apart, along the creases where they had been folded, when she opened them up. They smelled musty, like old clothes in a suitcase at the back of an attic.

She sipped her coffee and started with the first pages of the file. Her German was almost fluent, thanks to her mother — born in Afghanistan, but educated at a German university in Heidelberg — who had made sure that her daughter learned her adopted language. Despite that, the German of the file was slow going. Even where the faded text was fully legible, antiquated spelling, an obtuse, bureaucratic style and impossibly long sentences made it difficult to read. With concentration, though, she could follow.

The first document in the folder was a memorandum, six pages secured by an old-fashioned paper clip. The memorandum had no addressees and was dated September 17th, 1944. It began with a summary of Germany's military position in the

Summer of 1944. It made an effort to present an optimistic scenario, citing Wehrmacht battlefield successes and, even more hopefully, advances in Nazi weapons development.

Nonetheless, the memorandum described a recent decision to prepare for a less-than-optimal result in the war. The focus was on a negotiated peace that left Germany weakened, as World War I had, with a puppet regime installed by the Allies. Her eyes widened slightly when she read the reference, in passing, to the decision having been approved by the Führer. The decision was to be treated with the highest security classification, to avoid affecting German morale or compromising the post-war efforts that the memorandum contemplated.

The memorandum was only a summary. It didn't explain what actions the Führer had decided to take, or the steps that had already been taken. But the things that the memorandum did describe let her see the outlines of what was envisioned. Steps would be taken to collect a vast war-chest, which would provide a post-war survival fund for the Third Reich. Assets would be assembled from across the Reich — the valuables looted from the Jews and others, assets taken from the occupied territories, profits from state-owned firms, and spoils of war. All of this was to be collected under a central control, and then secreted, hidden outside Germany behind a web of front companies, banks, and trusts.

The memorandum recommended that the entire fund be controlled by only two people — the Führer and his chief adviser on economic security. No mention was made of the Third Reich's other leaders — Himmler, Göhring, Göbbels — who were apparently not to be either informed or involved. The memorandum underscored the critical importance of absolute secrecy. It also recorded the Führer's decision that the funds and their documentation be centralized in secret accounts with a Swiss bank, which was unnamed, but with which the Nazi regime had done business for many years.

The second half of the memorandum outlined the purposes of the fund. If the war went badly, and ended with Germany accepting another intolerable peace, then the fund, properly deployed, would ensure that the Reich could rise again. Money would be used to protect ex-Nazi leaders, educate a new generation of leaders, eliminate opposition, and fund street fighters and make friends abroad. The memorandum also referred to an existing network of Nazi supporters, in the highest positions in countries around the world, including in each of the Allied powers. These men, a small circle of influential politicians and opinion-makers, had supported the Nazi regime in the past, and had pledged to do so in the future. They would be cultivated and drawn together into a network of powerful supporters, whose assistance a new Reich, a Fourth Reich, could count on in the future.

The memorandum was signed in faded, barely legible ink by the Führer's chief adviser on economic security — Heinrich von Wolff. She had been wrong that there was no addressee of the memorandum. There was one, identified at the end of the memorandum. Her eyes widened again. It was the Führer. Nobody else was shown receiving copies. The memorandum was initialed on the final page, also in faded ink, by "A. Hitler."

The other documents in the folder seemed less remarkable. Again, many of the pages were faded and hard to read. They seemed to be a random assortment of banking and corporate documents — lists of bank accounts, bank statements and account details, certificates of incorporation, minutes of shareholder's meetings, some signed and completed, others not.

The last document in the folder was a cover memorandum with a number of attachments. The memorandum contained little more than a list of names, some with titles, some with contact details, and others without. The list was short — only thirty or so names. It was titled "Freundeskreis" — Circle of Friends. Many of the names were familiar now, even seventy years later. A leading British politician, outwardly an outspoken detractor of Hitler; a prominent French politician and sometime poet; a well-connected American industrialist and politician; and a member of the Soviet Politbüro. Attached to the memorandum were several dozen tabs. There was a separate tab for each name in the circle of friends, with each tab followed by an assortment of reports and letters.

She closed the folder and took a deep breath. It was hard to believe. If it wasn't some elaborate hoax, it was a new piece of Nazi history. It was also political dynamite. Some of the names on the list were leading statesmen in their countries and others had gone on to higher public office — one was instrumental in founding the European Communities, another was a leading UK politician. It was a collection of the international great and good. Except they had all been Nazi spies.

And what had become of the Nazi treasure, the hidden bank accounts? Had the war chest ever been funded? Was the treasure still there, waiting to be deployed — if it had not already been? Where was it, if it still existed?

"Guten Morgen, Fräulein."

She whirled around with a start, nearly spilling what was left of her coffee. Robert's smile turned into an apologetic grin when he saw her reaction.

"I'm so sorry, darling. I didn't mean to startle you."

"Of course you didn't, honey. I was just lost in these papers," she said, then started to tell him what she had read.

Robert cut her off and turned to the day's routine. "Tell me later, baby. We need to finish today's samples or the whole project will be delayed. Your dad and the team are waiting for me."

"OK. But I really need to talk to you. I need to talk to both you and Dad. This file is unbelievable."

She started again to summarize what she had read, but he stopped her in mid-sentence.

"You're right. It really does sound bizarre. But tell us this afternoon," he said hastily. "We'll be back to camp around 3:00, and I'm dying to hear. But tell me then. Big kisses, honey."

He gave her a hurried hug. Then he released her, glancing at the morning sun and his watch, eager to get on with his lab work.

"O.K. Talk tonight," she said, as he turned to leave.

Robert disappeared through the tents, heading up towards the trail. She turned back to the stack of documents and continued to read. After a moment though, she realized that she needed to go back to the wreck. She had taken what looked like the most important documents from the file, but only based on a few minutes' review. She needed to properly examine what remained — or at least examine as much as she could manage in the time they had.

She also realized that they shouldn't leave the files up there in the jungle. They were historical archives, maybe very important historical records, that ought to be preserved. That gave her one more thing to do today, before they closed down the camp. She would take Jackson up to the wreck, and together they should be able to bring down the contents of the file cabinet.

She spent the morning racing through the tasks that she had planned for herself and packing their gear for the porters to carry back to the road to Kampala. She left her fleece and raingear out of the crates, in case she needed them in the morning, as well as her sleeping bag. She put the clothes and the sleeping bag in her largest backpack, instead of her daypack — she would need the larger pack to bring the files down from the wreck.

Then she went around to the villagers who tended the camp, thanking each of them with smiles and hugs. They were friends at this point, after three months in the bush with no visitors. The goodbyes took the better part of two hours. She and Jackson weren't ready to start for the ridge until nearly 1 p.m.

The sun was beating down as they shouldered their packs. The air was heavy with moisture, and she suspected that the monsoon rains might come that afternoon. She felt mildly ridiculous, lugging a half-full pack up a thousand-meter cliff in the heat, laden with rain gear and a sleeping bag. But her father had always taught her that you never knew when the weather might change, or whether you would pick that day to lose the trail and have to spend the night in the wild. So she sweat under the weight of the pack as Jackson led them across the valley and up the trail on the side of the ridge.

There was really no trail to lose, she thought, as they slogged their way through the dense undergrowth. Only the faintest signs of use, often missing for dozens of meters or more, hinted at the direction that they should head. When they reached the edge of the rain forest, the shade stole the breeze, but also shielded them from the sun, while they worked their way along the muddy paths and through the fallen tree trunks and undergrowth. It took them nearly two hours to reach the edge of the ridge. They were both drenched in sweat and breathing hard when the wreck finally came into sight.

It sat there, silent and forbidding, in the undergrowth at the edge of the ridge. Nothing had moved in the last three days. She made her way to the back of the plane and let herself into the cargo hold again. In the meantime, Jackson headed off further up the ridge, taking his hunting rifle and hopes of a deer, one of the small duiker that lived in the rainforest on the cooler hills, above the valley floor.

The cargo hold was still dark and cool. She walked to the front of the hold and opened the metal box that lay on the floor and began sorting through its contents. She worked by the light of her flashlight — she had brought extra batteries and used the light freely.

The papers in the file were a hodgepodge. Some of them looked like they had been dumped into the cabinet without any care, almost as if they had been scooped up at the last minute. There were stacks of account statements and corporate certificates, files of shareholder minutes, telegrams, and a collection of other papers. She had no clue what most of these meant, if anything, and had no idea how to figure it out. She placed these papers into a large bag they had brought, that Jackson would carry down from the site.

There were a few more detailed files on the secret circle of Nazi supporters — these she collected and put into her pack. There was also a file folder of correspondence with a Swiss bank, together with some official-looking legal documents. She put those papers into her pack as well. And that was almost it.

There was one other thick cardboard folder, like the first one she had taken, that contained an interim report on the collection of assets for the post-war survival fund. The report was dated December 1944, only three months after the first memorandum, and it listed an impressive collection of corporate shares, real estate, artwork, and bank accounts, the proceeds of which had already been deposited into the Nazi fund. It was clear as well that this was just the start, the tip of the iceberg. There was a rough estimate at the end of the memorandum of the total value of the fund — 15 billion Nazi Reichsmarks or $3 billion, in 1944 dollars.

The memorandum concluded with the observation that this was a reasonable start, but not even 5% of the overall target. She drew another breath, then closed the file. She hadn't focused on the amounts of money that the project involved. The figures were staggering. She wondered what the Nazi fund would be worth today, if it still existed. She wondered where the money had gone.

There was one more place she needed to look before leaving. She steeled her nerves and walked over to the three corpses, strapped into their seats along the fuselage. She inspected their uniforms, trying hard to ignore the gaping eye sockets and toothy smiles. The name plates were tarnished, but still legible. Two names meant nothing to her. Two faceless Nazi officers. The third name — the tallest one, whose decorations were the most elaborate — rang a bell. "Von Wolff." Then she remembered the author of the memorandum, the Führer's adviser on economic security. She smiled to herself, pleased that she had figured out this little bit of the plane's mystery.

"And what do you, Herr von Wolff, have here in your uniform?" she asked.

It took her a moment, and then she found a silver locket, with the faded photograph of a beautiful woman, and a heavy gold fountain pen. In another pocket she found a leather wallet, with two carefully folded sheets of paper — but nothing else. The same was true of the other bodies. A few personal belongings, but nothing more.

She went outside with her pack and von Wolff's wallet and found a log to sit on, away from the corpses. She opened the wallet and scanned the two letters. More surprises, although she might have guessed.

The first letter was addressed to a Rhodesian banker, recording the Führer's friendship, thanking him for having supported the Nazi cause so faithfully, and commending von Wolff to his care. The other letter, more peremptory and businesslike, was addressed to the head of the management board of a leading Swiss private bank — an old bank, that even she had heard of. The letter directed the bank to comply with von Wolff's directions and referred to the protocol of a meeting in Berlin in late 1944. Both letters were signed "A. Hitler."

She folded up the letters and tucked them into her pack, alongside the other papers from the file. By this point, her collection was bulky — twenty centimeters of papers, two thousand pages or so — and took up one compartment of her backpack.

While she waited for Jackson to return, she made her way to the front of the plane wreck, at the edge of the ridge. The jungle there was thick, with dense stands of saplings and almost impenetrable thorn bushes. But her jeans and windbreaker protected her, as she forced her way through the vegetation to the front of the fuselage. She noticed then that there was a break in the foliage at the side of the ridge, and that she could look down the valley to where the camp lay, two or three kilometers away. If she sat on a dead log near the edge of the ridge, she could even make out figures in the camp. She watched for a moment, then opened up her pack, took out the file, and continued to read.

Chapter 9
Jeb Fisher

The room was long, with windows along one side, looking out onto the dirt runway. A single ancient air conditioner struggled noisily against the midday heat, dripping water onto the bare concrete floor. The walls of the room were plain, painted white years ago, with a well-used blackboard at the front of the room, facing thirty or so wooden chairs, arranged in haphazard rows. The faded photograph of a handsome black man, dressed in a general's uniform, hung above the blackboard. Most of the windows were open and the smell of dust, smoke from cooking fires, animal dung, and gasoline came in with the breeze.

Fifteen men sat in the chairs. Most had flown overnight, connecting through various airports around the world, to arrive in Addis Ababa, Ethiopia, earlier that morning. They had been escorted, without passing through immigration or customs, to a hangar at the end of the Addis Ababa airfield, where they had boarded a privately chartered plane. Hours later, they had landed at a military airstrip somewhere in South Sudan.

Nobody had told the men where they were, or the name of the nearby native village — a dusty collection of mud huts. Before they disembarked from the plane, they had been told what to do: take your bags and go into the main building, next to the airstrip. Then wait for instructions. The orders had come over the plane's loudspeaker system, delivered in clipped military commands by one of the two older men who sat at the front of the aircraft.

As they disembarked at the South Sudanese airfield, a single African soldier appeared for a moment. He was a Dinka — tall, lanky, and black as asphalt — wearing a uniform with no insignia or badges. His only interest in the group was to collect a small package from the grey-haired man who had given them their orders on the plane. The soldier's bearing was erect and poised as he opened the package and thumbed through the banknotes it contained. When he was finished, the soldier nodded with satisfaction and walked back towards the buildings on the opposite side of the airstrip. The only other signs of life came from a handful of local troops who patrolled the perimeter of the airfield in the distance, keeping whoever might be curious away — and keeping the visitors inside.

Jeb Fisher sat in one of the chairs, near the back of the room. His hair was dark brown, just touching the tops of his ears. At thirty-seven, the first hints of gray were starting to show at his temples, framing deep blue eyes and clean-shaven cheeks. He was smaller than most of the men in the room, standing 1.85 meters and weighing eighty kilos. His arms were sinewy, like his torso, tapering to a slim waist and powerfully muscled legs. He sat alone, apart from the other clusters of men, who were laughing and telling tales of supposed exploits in battlefields and brothels around the world.

Until two days before, he had been one of the CIA's star field agents. He had grown up in Allentown, Pennsylvania, the fourth of seven children of a steel mill foreman. After Catholic high school, he attended Princeton, courtesy of a track scholarship. Four years of straight As, a Political Science major, and two Ivy League records in the long jump followed.

In his senior year, life after college had loomed. He had no idea what to do next. The Peace Corps and life as an Outward Bound instructor were the least unattractive choices that he could identify. Wall Street and consulting jobs had been easy to come by, and his father, then unemployed, and his girlfriend, lobbied hard for investment banking or business school. But sitting in a box as a junior analyst in a New York bank, gambling with other peoples' money, was pretty close to his idea of hell on earth, and he kept finding excuses not to accept any of the offers that filled his mailbox.

He was close to capitulating when a notice in the career office caught his eye — the CIA was looking for fluent Spanish speakers. An on-campus interview, which he attended as much for fun as anything else, further whetted his interest.

A week later, he spent a day at the CIA headquarters in Langley, Virginia, without telling either his father or his friends. After that day, though, he was sure about what he wanted to do. The idea of fighting for his country, in exotic places around the world, hooked him. He had been brought up in a world of right and wrong, good and evil, and the Agency promised to let him join the forces of good. And to have lots of fun along the way. Three months later, minus a girlfriend, he was in the middle of CIA orientation in rural Virginia with a couple dozen other recruits.

His performance in the Agency's training program was exceptional. His scores on all the tests — mental, physical, and emotional — were among the best in Agency history. After a month of training, he was dispatching martial arts instructors with a combination of feline agility and overpowering strength. He outwitted the drafters of logic games and puzzles, both in the classroom and in training exercises. And he endured the toughest marches, climbs, and obstacle courses that his trainers could devise. He graduated from training school with some of the highest expectations in CIA history.

His career as an operative fulfilled the promise of his training. He worked undercover throughout Latin America, infiltrating a Columbian drug-lord's inner circle for more than a year. The information he collected about the gang's operations would have been invaluable in rolling the organization up. But he conceived, and then ran, an operation that lured the members of both that gang and its main rival into a bloody showdown at the drug lord's estate, letting them wipe one another out in a way that no DEA prosecution would have begun to achieve. He walked away from the cartel's former headquarters without a scratch, leaving behind fifty corpses, including two of the DEA's ten most wanted fugitives.

He was just as resourceful, and ruthless, in a series of other operations, first in Nicaragua and then in Brazil, before moving on to Africa. He hunted Russian arms dealers in the Congo, Al Qaeda in Sudan, and slave traders in Hong Kong, again eliminating scores of serious evildoers with brutal efficiency — all without running afoul of CIA regulations. Along the way, he attracted the attention of Franklin Kerrington, the Agency's Deputy Director, who made sure that Fisher got the recognition, and the support, that he needed.

He hadn't planned to leave the Agency. But two days ago, Kerrington summoned him for a one-on-one meeting. They met for coffee at Kerrington's home, in an opulent room looking onto a sunlit courtyard. The Deputy Director outlined a proposal — one that Fisher really had little choice but to accept.

The proposal was that Fisher join a firm run by another former Agency star, who had left the CIA a decade ago to found a company specializing in assignments that nobody else could do, charging prices that nobody else dared quote. Kerrington assured him that the company wanted his services, and that it would offer a salary that added a zero to his Agency wages, plus performance bonuses. Kerrington said that he had already talked with the company's principal shareholder and CEO — Reginald Reid — and confirmed the offer. It was a chance to do the right thing, to do even more for his country than he could at the Agency. And, although Kerrington didn't threaten him, he worked in a reference to the pending proposal for a retirement policy at the CIA — which would be twenty years for field operatives. Who knew what might be on offer for Fisher in another three years?

Kerrington also mentioned the times that he had stepped in with help — in internal political squabbles of the sort that Fisher hated. Kerrington promised to be there, with the same help, if Fisher joined the private sector. Fisher was pretty sure that the promises were real ones, and that life would be better outside the Agency from here on, than inside it. Kerrington sealed the deal by confiding that he needed his own eyes and ears at Reid's company. Reid and his team were first-class and had been delivering tremendous results. But the outfit had grown, and Kerrington wanted to be able to keep a closer eye on things, if the need arose. He wanted someone who he could be sure had the Agency, and the country, fully in mind at all times. And he wanted Fisher to be that man.

That convinced him. Kerrington was his idea of a perfect boss. A man he admired and respected. He wasn't another Washington politician, but a man dedicated to the Agency and to doing the right thing. And Kerrington promised again to give him the freedom and the tools that he needed to do the right thing himself. They had shaken hands on his new job over glasses of 40-year-old Scotch, Kerrington's firm handshake and level gaze leaving him with no doubt that this was the right decision.

Later that day, Fisher spoke with Reid by telephone, and then met with two of his team, at what looked like corporate offices on M Street near Georgetown. He hadn't expected things to move slowly, but also hadn't expected them to move quite so quickly. Over dinner, he was listening to one of Reid's men outline a mission that had him leaving for Ethiopia the next day.

The operation was simple on one level: find a plane wreck, whose approximate GPS coordinates would be provided, and recover the plane's cargo. It was the details of the mission that were more complicated, a lot more complicated — but then, he loved challenges. It turned out that the wreckage of the plane was in a remote part of Uganda, or maybe the Congo, and that there was likely to be a Russian special forces team hunting for the same cargo.

Reid's lieutenant, a former Agency operative named Sam Wilson, was a slightly built man, with none of the muscle of many in their business. But when Wilson caught his eyes, there was nothing soft about him.

"The cargo isn't a nice to have. It's critical to this country's security. It doesn't matter what we have to do, or who gets in the way. That cargo comes back here with us. Period. Got it?"

Fisher nodded. He refrained from asking the obvious question — "What was the cargo?"

He knew the answer already. They would tell him when, and if, he needed to know.

"And if the Russians get in the way?" he asked. He was pretty sure he knew the answer to this question too.

"Then we deal with them. One way or another. If they are after this cargo, then they are very bad guys. We'll have all the equipment and back-up that we need if things get ugly."

One thing nagged at him: "Why such a rush?"

"I wish it wasn't so," Wilson replied. "But we just found this thing and it may be moving. Plus, we have to beat the competition. The Russians, and maybe others. We need to staff up right away."

That made sense. It all did. It was different, and a challenge. But it was fighting bad people, alongside other good people, and that was why he joined the Agency. And now, it was why he was leaving the Agency.

Wilson instructed him to show up the next day, early afternoon, at Dulles Airport's cargo terminal. The Agency used the facility for its operations. One of the benefits of Kerrington's support for Reid's team was that they could use it as well. Wilson passed over a folder of papers. It included an itinerary, a list of clothing and personal items, plus some maps, as if this were a package tour. He also handed over a sheet of paper with instructions for accessing a bank account. A numbered Swiss bank account.

"Check it tonight. There should be a $100K balance. Your signing bonus. But you can't withdraw it until we're back."

If we're back, Fisher thought to himself. But instead, he smiled. "Very generous. Thanks."

"You'll see. That's how things are done here. Good to have you on the team."

He overcame any hesitations the next day. The men he met at Dulles were tough. A mix of Agency, Green Beret, SEALs and others — all combat–hardened and serious. No cowboys or thugs. They seemed just like him; they wanted to fight evil and terror, just on a longer leash, with better pay. The equipment was also top-of-the-line. The latest U.S. special forces weaponry, best electronics and other gear, all carefully selected for the region. The details of the mission remained sketchy, but that made sense. "Need to know" was a sound operating principle. And the $100K wasn't irrelevant. His parents' home needed a new roof, and his mom needed a new hip. This would make all that easy.

Reid entered the room looking out on the dusty Sudanese airstrip at exactly 1 p.m., accompanied by Wilson and two other civilians. He stood at the front of the room and delivered a briefing, speaking for thirty minutes, without slides or notes, in short, precise sentences. Reid's voice was deep, with a slow, almost rhythmic, cadence. He was grudgingly impressed. The briefing was concise, but it hit everything the team needed to know, while projecting authority and absolute confidence.

The plan was simple, but well thought out. The men would board three helicopters at the South Sudanese air base that night. They would fly south-west over the border and across Uganda. The destination was a remote mountain ridge, in the Rwenzori Mountain range, where they would locate the wreckage of an aircraft, secure the plane's cargo and return with it to their South Sudanese base. The men were divided into three teams — to secure the site, to guard the perimeter and to extract the cargo. The skills of the men in the room were what he would have chosen himself, a mix of combat troops and tech guys.

When Reid was done, he called out assignments, detailing the men to the three teams. He was assigned to the extraction team, headed by Wilson. When the plane had been located, and any opposition neutralized, they would secure and extract the cargo, and then return it to the U.S. They spent the next two hours going over what they knew about the mission and working up a more detailed action plan. By the end of the session, his hesitations about the mission had receded even further. This was a new team, but it was just as good and just as focused on fighting bad guys as the old one.

They boarded the helicopters just before sunset. Painted light brown, with no markings, they waited at the edge of the runway. They looked suspiciously like U.S. Marine attack helicopters that had seen action in Iraq or Afghanistan. He smiled as he imagined how the three aircrafts had made their way here. It helped to have someone like Kerrington on your side.

The helicopters took off in rapid succession, each whipping up a storm of dust and pebbles. The airfield was still empty, and there was no one to watch them lift off, and then rise over the African scrubland and start their journey south. They flew low – three hundred meters or so — and without lights. There was no moon and, even if there had been anyone awake to watch, there would have been nothing to see. He sat in the back of one of the copters, working through the mission in his mind, well after the rest of the team had nodded off. Somewhere over northern Uganda, he finally surrendered to sleep.

Chapter 10
Sara West

She sat on the log at the edge of the ridge, working through the documents from the file, looking out over the valley from time to time. It was hot and humid, even in the late afternoon. She wiped the sweat off her face every few minutes, to make sure it didn't drip onto the papers.

Over the drone of the insects, and the squawking of jungle birds, she heard a harsher metallic sound, one she hadn't heard before. It was a sharp whine, like some giant hornet, that came from behind the ridge and then began to clatter rhythmically, its low thumps filling the valley as it came closer. The sound grew fainter for an instant, and she almost lost it, but after a moment it returned. Then, roaring only meters above the jungle canopy, the noise was on her before it rushed past, followed seconds later by another wave of deafening sound, just the same. Craning her neck, and looking out over the valley, she could see them — two helicopters, painted with camouflage colors, barely a hundred meters away, headed down into the valley.

How strange, she thought. The helicopters looked like military aircraft, with what seemed to be machine guns mounted along their sides. It must be the Ugandan Air Force. A strange place for training flights, she thought, but at least there were no villagers to frighten up here in the jungle. She watched the two gunships fly along the valley floor, noses tilted slightly downwards, like bloodhounds following a trail. She watched them reach the expedition's camp, peaceful in the distance, like a child's model, then tilt and circle it, descending lower.

Then, as if in a dream, she watched the gunships spout bright flashes of orange and yellow from their sides. She watched the puffs of white smoke emerge from missile pods on the sides of the helicopters, followed by wispy trails of vapor that streaked towards the camp. She watched the streams of fire light up the paths between the tents, and then the trails of vapor spawn silent eruptions of dirt and smoke around the camp's perimeter. She watched her friends, watched the native bearers, looking up with bewilderment, and then fright, before turning to flee, as streams of fire knocked them off their feet.

She found her binoculars in the backpack and watched the camp through them in disbelief. She saw the cook, saw her best friend from grad school, saw the porters, saw them all crumple, falling into miniature heaps on the valley floor. And now she could hear the rattle of gunfire and the muffled sounds of explosions as the missiles struck home around the outskirts of the camp. She watched one of the helicopters descend slowly and then land, while the other gunship hovered watchfully above the camp. The clatter of the machine guns had mostly stopped now, but she could hear the methodical cracks of rifle shots, as someone in the helicopter picked off first one and then another of those who survived the initial attack and tried to escape.

Men had poured out of one of the helicopters, men in khaki shorts with guns, who were going from tent to tent, rounding up the camp's remaining occupants. They killed the Ugandan workers straightaway, wherever they found them. The only exception was Isaac, the camp foreman, who was dragged by two of the soldiers into one of the tents. The others, the Westerners, were forced into a circle around the fire pit in the middle of the camp.

She watched through her binoculars. She searched, with rising panic, for her father and Robert. They were nowhere to be seen. A half dozen of her friends and colleagues huddled around the fire pit. She spotted Kim — her closest friend from grad school. Blood poured from a gash on his forehead and one eye was already swollen nearly shut. Another of her friends, Jason, was doubled over on the ground, writhing in pain. Four muscular men from the helicopter, with crew-cuts and automatic weapons, lazily stood guard, watchful, but apparently joking with each other. She should see their mouths moving, and their smiles and laughter through her binoculars, but couldn't hear a sound.

Two more of the attackers came into the camp. They were herding her father and Robert at gunpoint. They both looked unhurt. Other men, also armed with automatic weapons and sidearms, emerged from the tents they had been searching. They brought computers and papers with them, depositing them near the fire pit.

She watched as an older, heavy-set man, accompanied by a slim, dark-haired woman, began surveying the materials that had been collected. The man paid particular attention to the lab books and research folders, not reading them, but flipping through each in turn, as if to make sure everything was there. He seemed to be frustrated by the inspection, and when he was finished, he shouted at the guards, pointing at the tents. Several of the men returned to the tents, disappearing into first one and then the other, occasionally appearing with more papers or a backpack.

While this search continued, the heavy-set man strolled over to the circle of frightened prisoners around the fire pit. He seemed to be talking to them, then awaiting an answer. Again dissatisfied, he waved one arm, wielding a pistol, at the guards. She watched then, horrified, as the guards dragged Kim over to the fire pit. Two guards collared him, forcing him to the ground by the fire, then holding him by the hair and pressing his face down into the burning embers. She could hardly bear to look, blinking away tears of fear and panic, half-imagining that she could hear Kim's screams, even where she sat.

And then, suddenly, she realized why the men were there, understanding with absolute clarity why the attackers had come to their camp. Kim lay sprawled motionless on the ground now, his face still lying in the coals, his hair smoking. Another one of the prisoners, it looked like Jason, was pointing, mouth wide and face contorted, pointing at the ridge further up the valley. Pointing with his arm, hand gesticulating, and mouth flapping open and shut. The heavy-set man approached him and seemed to speak. Jason shook his head. She could see him struggle to swallow and wipe away his tears with the back of his hand. The heavy-set man seemed to speak again, and again, Jason shook his head.

Then, in a terrifying, dream-like sequence, as if from a slow-motion film, the heavy-set man lifted his pistol, leveled it against Jason's head and, shaking his own head, pulled the trigger. The retort came an instant later, after the gun kicked the man's arm up and after Jason's head jerked back, exploding in gouts of blood that she could see even from where she sat.

She watched in terror now, tears streaming down her face, misting the lenses of the binoculars, as the guards returned to the remaining hostages. After brief exchanges, the heavy-set man coolly shot first one, and then the next, of her friends. Sally died on her knees, hands clasped together, as if in prayer. William tried to rush the man but was halted in his tracks by simultaneous shots from three of the guards. They had been standing casually by the fire pit, almost disinterested, as the heavy-set man went about his work. But they reacted instantaneously, in unison, the second that Will crouched to charge the man.

With a sick knot of fear in her stomach, she watched the heavy-set man approach her father and Robert, who were seated near the camp table. She knew now what the man was looking for, why the men were here. They were looking for the Nazi plane, for the files from the long metal box. Somehow, they had learned of the discovery, and for some reason, they wanted it for themselves. They wanted the papers in the file very badly, badly enough to come here from half-way around the world, and badly enough to kill for them, to kill innocent strangers to get what they wanted.

That thought was driven away then, by another wave of terror. The heavy-set man appeared to order her father to his feet. She prayed that he would point up the valley, that he would point out the place where she and Jackson had entered the jungle at the base of the ridge. She showed him three days ago, through her binoculars, exactly where the wreck was and where the trail climbed the ridge. He knew. He could tell the man.

She prayed that he would answer the heavy-set man, whose mouth was issuing soundless demands. Her heart sank then. She knew that pose, the slight lifting of her father's chin, his gaze leveled at the man, his lips set in a grim, implacable line. She prayed that he would relent, that he would tell the man where she was. But, of course, he didn't.

The single shot followed, echoing dully up the valley. Her eyes went dark, her heart stopped beating. She sat, on the edge of shock, transfixed, not even noticing that Jackson had arrived, that he was shaking her.

"Lady, my lady. What happens there? This is bad."

His frantic queries and trembling hands reached through the clouds of shock and despair. She forced herself to look back and to try and think. Blinking away the tears, she watched the heavy-set man turn on Robert. Her world had ended once already that day. The crumbled, bloodstained bodies of her friends, that last terrifying image of her father's face, locked in grim defiance, had killed her father, and with him, a part of her, ending the life she had known.

She looked back into the valley through her binoculars. Robert was pointing now. Pointing up at her, at the ridge where she sat, then down the ridge at the place where the path disappeared into the jungle. Tears were streaming down his face, and she could see his lips quaver through the binoculars.

She realized, with slightly detached surprise, that she had never seen Robert cry. She had never seen him look anything like the way he did now. It was as if he were a different person, someone she had never seen before. She didn't know whether to be thankful — Robert was saving his life, or if she should be afraid — with his betrayal, the men would be coming for her soon, coming up the path through the jungle, up the ridge, to the wreck where she sat.

She watched dully as Robert led the men through the camp to the trail across the valley, then pointed out where the hunter's track, imperceptible if you didn't know where to look, split off from the main path and disappeared into the trees. A dozen or so of the men went with Robert, forcing him in a half-jog along the path. The men wore shorts, t-shirts, and military boots. They had guns, each one carrying at least two guns — a large grey one, like a hunting rifle, but bigger, with a curved clip for bullets, and a pistol. The last soldier, a tall, blonde man, carried a longer weapon, again like a rifle, but with a long scope mounted above the barrel.

When she looked back, Robert was kneeling. She could see his mouth moving. He was still crying, probably begging for his life. The lead soldier was laughing now. He lifted his weapon, and with an easy, almost nonchalant motion, fired a single shot at Robert's head, hurling him back, head over heels, to lie motionless beside the path. She watched, dull again, unable to cry and beyond fear. First, his betrayal, her fiancé telling the soldiers where they could find her, then the shooting, and now his body, like a bundle of rags by the side of the trail.

She looked back now at the other soldiers. She realized, with a start, that the last of the men, the tall, blonde man, had stopped by the side of the trail and was pointing his weapon up at the ridge, looking through the scope on the top of the barrel. He was slowly, methodically sweeping back and forth, systematically searching the jungle. Searching the jungle for her.

The blonde man stopped. His weapon was pointed right at her. The gun spat fire and jerked. A second later, she heard the shot, followed almost instantly by Jackson's cry. She dropped the binoculars, clambering down off the log where she was perched, rushing to his side. There was a gaping hole in his shoulder, blood streaming down one arm, as if someone had opened up a faucet. She touched his face, hoping this was some horrible dream, another terrible dream. But it wasn't.

Nor was the sharp crack that followed, from down in the valley, or the slug that gouged into the tree next to her. Nor the clattering metallic whine of the helicopters coming low up the valley towards the ridge. She pulled Jackson into the shade of the plane, away from the sight of the sniper. It took all her strength to drag him those few meters, even with his help. He was conscious but grimacing with pain, blood streaming out of the wound in his shoulder.

"Lady. You go. You go fast." Jackson's voice was ragged.

"Jackson. Don't talk. You'll be OK. We'll take care of you."

"Lady. Listen now to me. You go. You take path we took before. Last month, on the long hike. You go fast, down to Congo. You run. I stay here."

She knew he was right. He was dying. He couldn't walk, much less run. The soldiers would kill them both if they caught them. If she wanted to live, she had to go, to run the way he said, as fast and far as she could.

She looked into his eyes, dark and solemn. He had guided her for weeks through the jungle, taught her the trails and local plants. He helped her when she slipped, nursed her the time she was sick, because she had drunk bad water. And he told her stories at night about his baby girl, how much he missed her.

She choked back another wave of sobs and hugged him close, feeling the warm, sticky blood from his shoulder soak through her t-shirt. Then she helped him crawl behind one of the engines of the plane, and, on his instructions, brought him his hunting rifle and the spare box of ammunition in his pack. She took his canteen, again as he directed, and the pack of dried meat and cornbread that he always carried and put them in her own pack.

"Lady. You go fast. You get away. Tell my baby, tell my wife, tell them I love them.... Go fast now, lady. God bless you."

"God bless you, Jackson." Her voice was hardly a whisper.

And then she was gone, slipping silently into the jungle, wiping away her tears as she went.

The last vision that she had of Jackson was of him curled up behind the huge grey engine, blood dripping off his hand as he sighted his old hunting rifle through the jungle. His face was set like her father's had been, the last time she saw him. A hard, cold gaze, tinged with resignation, in contrast to her father's defiance. But the same grim determination as he waited for the soldiers to arrive.

She turned then and followed the trail, the way he had taken them before, knowing it would lead her up the ridge, then down to the next watercourse, and onto the trail they had hiked last month. She couldn't bring herself to think about the last half hour. She could only do what Jackson told her — run, run fast and far, as fast and far as she could.

Chapter 11
Reginald Reid

He looked out of the helicopter, over what was left of the camp, then swore again. The weather had turned against them early in the morning, two hours before the sun rose. As they flew south, the clouds thickened. When they landed to refuel at another nameless airstrip, this one in central Uganda, the rains had already begun. Nearly blinded at times, and buffeted by heavy winds, the helicopters slowed to half their usual speed. Twice, they were nearly forced to land. By the time they reached the target zone on the Congolese border, hours behind schedule, rain from the monsoon clouds had been cascading down for most of the final leg of the flight.

The next part of the plan was almost as bad. They set the helicopters down in the middle of the morning, five kilometers from the expedition's campsite. The plan called for two of Reid's team to dress as hikers and walk into the camp, to reconnoiter the area. They managed to land without incident, but the two "hikers" lost the trail in the driving rain and uncharted wilderness. The rain turned the ground into a swamp of oozing mud, which clung to the men's boots and reduced their progress to a crawl. Eventually, in the mid-afternoon, even further behind their timetable, the two men arrived at what was left of the expedition's camp.

Their report, over the walkie-talkies, turned things from bad to very bad. They described the carnage at the campsite, with piles of bodies scattered around the camp, now sodden with blood and water, and partially burned tents. Someone else had arrived before them. It was a fucking disaster.

He ordered all three helicopters to the expedition's camp as soon as he received the report. Barely restraining his fury, he directed a dozen men to scour the camp for survivors and evidence of what had happened. While that search progressed, he instructed Rogers and Wilson to comb through what remained of a pile of log-books, notes, and laptops that they found in the center of the camp.

He told the men to look for a file of documents, mostly in German. Kerring-ton hadn't told him much more — just that there was a file of old Nazi documents that had to be recovered.

Someone had tried to burn the files and computers that were piled next to the fire pit. They reeked of gasoline and most of the folders were partially burned. But the torrential monsoon rains had prevented further damage. On his instructions, Rogers and Wilson went through the materials that remained with a fine-tooth comb. They inspected each of the dozens of logbooks, paging through daily reports of field research and routine lists of samples, looking for out-of-place materials or files in German.

When they were finished, they turned to the laptops. Most of the computers couldn't be accessed and these were set carefully aside. Those that could still be operated were booted up and became the subject of intense scrutiny. Wilson, with the help of an IT specialist, methodically worked his way through the files and emails on all of the computers that still functioned.

Reid directed the men who had searched the camp to report to him. He lis-tened impassively, asking occasional questions. He was a tall, powerfully built man, in his late fifties with grey hair, clipped close, and a military bearing. He had served in the Green Berets during the 1980s but left after ten years for something with more action. As far as he was concerned, operations like Panama and Grenada were for beginners. He wanted real combat.

After drifting through a series of mercenary assignments in forgotten corners of Africa, he had ended up at the Agency, working for Kerrington. He hadn't al-ways gotten the battle-field combat that he sought, but he found something at least as good. Kerrington gave him broad freedom to go after terrorists, drug lords, and similar targets. It was clear that if something went wrong, the Agency would cut him off, denying that it had ever heard of him. But Kerrington made sure that he had all the resources, and protection from oversight, that he needed to get his job done.

He returned the trust with lethal results. First, it was ex-Soviet scientists gone rogue with weapons plans and nuclear material. Next came drug barons and their financiers, which took him from Medellin and Caracas to Geneva. Operations in Lebanon, Yemen, Iraq, and Syria ended badly for a variety of Al Qaeda terrorists and their supporters. More recently, it had been Iranian nuclear weapons designers and North Korean hackers.

He loved his work at the CIA. He couldn't imagine anything better than roaming the world with a semi-automatic and the best available high-tech support. He was the ultimate mercenary, doing the difficult work for Kerrington and the Agency that nobody else could handle. He rankled under the Agency's restrictions and occasional threats of congressional and press review, but on the whole, it was just what he had wanted to do. Everywhere, he was on the front line. He planned the operations and then led them himself, still hungry for action after more than twenty years of field work.

When Kerrington proposed a new structure, twelve years ago or so, where Reid would go into the private sector, but continue to work for Kerrington with even more action and better pay, he thought for a couple days, and then accepted. The new job was even better than his old one. There was a wider pool of enemies, now including corporate spies, freelance hackers and corrupt foreign politicians. And he began to be rewarded handsomely for his work — something he came to appreciate after years of government salaries.

Sitting in one of the team's helicopters, still parked on the valley floor, he digested the reports he had received. His mood progressively darkened throughout the afternoon, matching the dark monsoon clouds that hung low over the valley floor. The picture was at least partially clear, and completely unacceptable.

A team of professionals, almost certainly Russian Spetsnaz troops, had surprised the scientists the day before, probably in the late afternoon. From the boot prints and cartridges that littered the area, there were at least a dozen attackers. They came in two helicopters, very likely military crafts, and had used missiles and machine guns, as well as semi-automatic AK-103s, standard Spetsnaz weaponry.

The Russians had been ruthless — some forty-five locals and foreigners had been killed, many in execution-style shootings. They had also tortured one of the locals, whose ruined body Reid's men found inside a tent in the center of the camp, stripped to the waist and soaked in blood. The attackers had also searched the camp thoroughly for something, collecting every scrap of paper, computer, and phone they could find. And they had made hurried efforts to cover their tracks.

Fortunately, the Russians left clues to the location of the wreck site. The trail of boot-prints heading up the valley was thick — nearly the entire team must have headed that direction on foot. Three hundred meters from the expedition's camp, they found the body of one of the scientists. He had been shot in the head at close range — another execution-style killing. An effort had been made to conceal the body in the bushes by the trail, but it was half-hearted and hurried. Ten meters further up the trail, Reid's men found a path, now marked with the boot-prints of a dozen or so men, leading up towards the ridge on one side of the valley. He ordered four of his men to follow the path and sent two of the helicopters to scour the side and top of the ridge from the air.

It took a couple of hours, but they found the wreck. It lay on the edge of the ridge, up at the top, mostly blanketed by jungle foliage. It would have been completely covered by the jungle canopy, but there had been a fire. As nearly as his men could tell, the attackers had hit the plane with machine gun fire, or possibly a rocket grenade, igniting whatever was left in its fuel tank. The fire had been fairly small, but nonetheless destroyed much of the plane.

Next to the plane, behind one of the engines, was the body of a local hunter, holding an antiquated hunting rifle, with one hand still on a nearly empty box of cartridges. The hunter's shirt was soaked in blood, from a gaping wound in his chest. The bodies of three men were scattered in the jungle near the plane, each with a single rifle-shot wound in the head. The men were obviously military. They carried no identification, but their weapons, and one man's tattoo, left no doubt that they were Russian. Lenin's visage and an FSS insignia above one man's bicep made that clear.

He finally knew enough to report. Ordinarily, he would never call Kerrington, instead waiting to be contacted. But Kerrington had said that he wanted reports as soon as new information was available. Reid made the call on his encrypted phone and grimly summarized what they had found. He barely restrained his anger at having failed to secure the plane's cargo and at having been beaten by the Russians. He hated losing, and it hardly ever happened. Plus, he had a lot to lose on this one — the $10 million fee for the job, his very rewarding business with Kerrington and maybe more.

He saved the most important for last, hoping it would be a silver lining in the cloud. "We ID'd the bodies against the list of people on the expedition. One scientist, a student, is missing. An American woman, 28 years old. Name of Sara West. We think she's headed west, into the jungle, with ten to fifteen Spetsnaz special forces troops hot on her tail."

Kerrington was silent.

He continued his report. "We retrieved her laptop. The Russians missed it. She was the one who found the wreck, plus what she said was a stash of top-secret Nazi documents. She apparently took some of the files with her back to camp. At least that's what she was going to tell a friend in an email; she never sent it, but it looks real."

"Did she say what the papers contained?" Kerrington asked sharply.

"Nope. Just secret Nazi documents. Her email said that they were hard to believe, but nothing else."

There was a long pause. Kerrington didn't usually pause. Then he asked: "What about the plane? Were there any files there?"

"Nope. The Russians torched the plane by mistake during the fire fight. We found a metal file box in the wreck. It looked like it was mostly empty, apart from some charred bits of paper. There was also a garbage bag, a plastic one, that the girl seems to have filled with papers, probably from the file box. But it was almost completely burned as well. We secured the ashes for analysis, but they're in pretty bad shape. I doubt we'll get anything," Reid reported.

Kerrington was silent again. Then he asked, sharply again: "Are you sure about that? Did you see what was retrieved? What papers were recovered?"

"I'm sorry, but there was nothing to recover, sir. It all burned. There's nothing but a couple shoeboxes of ashes and melted plastic. No papers or anything else survived the fire. Not even fragments of papers. I checked the site myself while the team was going over it."

Kerrington's reaction to this was surprising. He didn't seem angry. Instead, he paused once more, and after a moment directed that the ashes be sent to Langley. Immediately. Kerrington would make sure that they got analyzed.

Kerrington continued: "What about the files the girl took from the plane? Where are they?"

"We aren't sure. Our best judgment is that the girl still has those files. Which might explain why the Russians are chasing her. If they had the files, you wouldn't think they'd bother with her."

There was another pause. Reid knew better than to try and fill the silence. He waited for Kerrington's reaction. It wasn't nearly as bad as he had feared.

"I'm not happy. This shouldn't have happened. You have to get the girl now and retrieve whatever files she took. And if the Russians get in the way, take care of them. Don't let them beat you again."

"Understood, sir. We won't."

Kerrington hung up without saying goodbye.

Reid exhaled. It could have been worse. Much worse. In fact, Kerrington didn't seem upset about the destruction of the files on the plane. But they still had to find the girl and whatever files she had taken. If he failed again, there would be no forgiveness. Kerrington had made very clear that failure was not an option on this mission. And he had seen what happened to others who had failed to deliver what Kerrington demanded.

When he finished his report to Kerrington, Reid held another briefing for the team down in the camp. One helicopter continued to stand guard, hovering further up the valley. His briefing was short and to the point. He was as up-beat as possible, but also made it clear that they had messed up badly and that they couldn't fail again.

One team — with a total of eleven men — would track the girl and the Russians. The team would keep a very low profile and avoid contact with the Spetsnaz troops unless they were sure that the Russians had retrieved the files from the girl. The other team, including Reid, would leapfrog both the girl and the Russians, and set up a screen further to the west, with the aim of trapping the girl when she emerged from the jungle. This would involve posting men along the possible exit points from the rainforest — in both Uganda and the Congo, across the border. Locals would be hired to provide manpower. Even if the girl somehow eluded the Russians, she would stand out like a sore thumb — a lone white Western woman — wherever she went. This part shouldn't be that hard.

The focus of the first team was on tracking the girl and the Russians in the jungle. He told himself that she couldn't escape them; it was only a matter of time before a single girl, without military training and alone in the jungle would be caught. The only real issue was the Russians. They had a head start and might well get to her first. In that event, though, the prey would be the Russians. They would have no idea Reid's men were shadowing them and would be easy prey if it came to that.

Reid's briefing concluded with a simple order. The girl was not to be allowed to escape again. He passed around photos of her, which they had pulled off the internet. He also provided the men with an explanation for why they were chasing her. Most of the team wouldn't care; orders were orders. But it was still good to have a rationale, if only to stop speculation.

Despite her innocent appearance, Reid explained that the girl was a cold-blooded traitor, who had betrayed the Agency, selling out to the Russians. Now she had betrayed the Russians as well, selling the same intelligence again to the Chinese, or someone else. The documents she had were a scientific masterstroke, which the Nazis had achieved in the dying days of the Third Reich. Nazi scientists had discovered, and the girl had stolen, the key to a whole new type of weapon, a virus that could be targeted based on genetic factors. The details were classified, but her theft was a critical national security threat. They could not fail again. The country's security, as well as their bonuses, depended on succeeding.

He also had Wilson put together a cover story for the local authorities and press. The expedition had been attacked by a renegade band of rebels from the Congo. Cross-border incursions were rare, but the expedition had been unlucky. The rebels had been ruthless, killing everyone, and destroying what they didn't loot. There was no hint that the Russians or anyone else had been there.

The sun was setting as his team headed up the ridge again. The men were fit and highly trained, but the jungle paths were steep and treacherous, slick with mud, shrouded in the half-light of the rain forest, beneath the jungle canopy. The monsoon rains returned intermittently throughout the evening, drenching the men, as well as their packs, which were already weighed down by the array of equipment that twenty-first-century soldiers require. By nightfall, they were still on the ridge, barely a kilometer from the wreck, cursing the mud, the leeches, and the mosquitos.

Reid sat in the cockpit of the third helicopter. It was crossing over the Rwenzoris, into the Congo, flying low above the densely forested ridges, so they couldn't be spotted. The high peaks were to the north, and a thousand or more kilometers of rain forest stretched as far as the eye could see to the west. A vast ocean of uncharted green, with no roads or towns to break the jungle canopy. No place for an amateur, he thought to himself.

He leaned back in the seat. He still had to struggle to restrain his anger. But, despite the setbacks, the mission was back on track. Notwithstanding the fiasco, he had retained Kerrington's confidence. And he was sure that there was no way that the girl could escape his men and their helicopters. It was just a matter of time before they caught her.

Chapter 12
Sara West

She ran. She ran up the ridge, along the same hunter's track that she and Jackson had returned over, coming back to the camp from the Congo only weeks before. But now she wasn't coming home — to her father and friends. Instead, she was running away, running in terror from the men who killed her father and destroyed her life. She forced those thoughts out of her mind. And ran, as fast and hard as she could.

The trail was wet — muddy and treacherous. The mud was thick, inches deep in some places, clinging to her boots, as if it wanted to hold on to her feet. Elsewhere, the trail was slippery, like an ice rink, with water-coating mossy logs and rocks. The path was especially bad on the slopes, when it climbed or descended to the streambeds that crisscrossed the ridge.

On one descent, she slipped on a moss-covered log, then slid head-first down a five-meter slope, before tumbling into the bushes that surrounded the trail, their thorny branches raking her arms. She stumbled to her feet, wiping the tears from her eyes with the backs of muddy hands, then found the trail, and ran again.

The monsoon rains began as evening came, making the trail even more treacherous. The rocks in the path that usually provided footholds turned slippery, like patches of ice. As she scrambled over three fallen logs, layered one on top of another across the trail, she slipped and slammed her forehead against a low-hanging branch. The pain stunned her, stars flashing before her eyes. She forced herself to get up and run, but then fell two more times in quick succession.

She stopped in the center of the trail in the fading light, head down and backpack resting on a log, panting until her sides ached. When she could finally catch her breath, she forced herself to think. She had to slow her pace. At least she was still on the trail. But the light was fading quickly. The path had been hard to follow even in daylight, and it would be impossible at night, after darkness fell. Even if she somehow stayed on the path, she would never be able to keep her footing. At some point, she would twist an ankle or a leg. Then the men would be on her and that would be the end.

She stood by herself in the darkness on the jungle path. Her face and clothes were drenched in rain and sweat, streaked with mud and Jackson's blood. She looked around her, at the trees and bushes. They were a solid green wall, nearly impenetrable, dark and alien, surrounding her in every direction, for as far as she could see. She was alone in a trackless jungle, being hunted by a dozen trained killers. She fought back the waves of terror that suddenly had her gasping for breath again. She forced herself to breathe, deeply, wrestling the panic down, with an effort that took every bit of her remaining willpower.

Thoughts raced wildly through her mind. She thought about surrendering, giving the file to the men who were chasing her. But they wouldn't let her go. That was clear. They would kill her too, like they killed everyone else, just to silence her. She thought about hiding, curling up under a log or in the bushes until they were gone. But they would find her. They would track her and they would find her. She had to run. There was no other choice. She swallowed and turned back to the trail, forcing herself to keep moving, more slowly now, but away from the men who were chasing her.

The jungle around her grew louder as night fell. First, the insects — crickets and cicadas and beetles — in an infinite variety of clicks, buzzes, and whines, from every corner of the jungle. And mosquitos, flies and moths, buzzing around her head, entangling themselves in her hair and batting blindly against her face. Then the frogs, birds, and monkeys, with their own croaks, hoots, and calls.

There was another sound now — at first, a metallic whine that she could hear faintly in the distance. But the whine grew steadily louder, until it threatened to drown out the jungle cacophony. Then she saw a light, sweeping back and forth through the rain forest, its pale glare lighting up the jungle floor and casting spiky shadows onto the tree trunks. She froze, petrified as the helicopter's searchlight swept past her, and then was gone.

Down the ridge, less than a kilometer away, she could see other lights, faint, momentary flashes, through the foliage and the rain. It must be the flashlights of her pursuers, as they came along the trail leading up from the wreck. They must have been dropped onto the ridge by the helicopters. There was no way they could have made it up the ridge on foot that quickly.

She turned and continued up the trail, despairing at the prints her boots left in the mud. Those prints would lead her pursuers right to her. She ran along a smoother section of the trail, then over a rocky ridge, down the other side, where she nearly lost her footing again. A streambed ran through the ravine, which she crossed, then headed up the other side of the ravine and over the top, onto a flat plateau.

She stopped at the top of the ravine, panting again, and forced herself to breathe, to think and to try and plan. The path divided here, one fork dropping down to the west, where Jackson had told her to go, and the other path curling east and north, back into Uganda, the direction she had come. She stood for a moment at the crossroads, then took the eastern fork and hurried along. She and Jackson had started down this path last month, by mistake. The trail had taken them to a marshland a few hundred meters ahead. She ran now, ignoring the mud and branches, heedless of the prints that she left on the trail. She heard noises behind her, further back along the ridge. She strained to make them out, but the rain and jungle noises drowned out most sounds that were more than a couple dozen meters away. She ran on, as fast as she dared.

She finally reached the marsh. It was right where she remembered. She headed into it, to the left, wading now through knee-deep water overgrown with reeds and rushes. She forced herself not to think about the snakes or leeches or other things that lived in the water and concentrated on keeping her balance. The bottom of the marsh was muddy, clogged with leaves and vines, slippery underfoot.

As she went, she made sure to leave a trail. She broke the stalk of a rush, smeared blood from the cut on her forehead onto the leaves of a bush further along, then dropped a leaf onto the surface of the water. The water deepened, nearly reaching her waist. Steadying herself on the muddy floor, she unfastened the pin that held her hair back. It was a carved wooden bird, brightly painted, that Robert had given her on their anniversary two years before. She threw it, as far as she could, deeper into the marshland. She heard the splash but couldn't see where it landed. She hoped it would float.

Then she turned around and headed back to the edge of the marsh. She retraced her steps, trying to return exactly the way she had come. She moved less quickly now, disturbing as little as possible. She lost her bearings once and used her flashlight, for just an instant, praying that the light wouldn't be spotted by the men who were chasing her. A wave of relief swept over her when she realized she hadn't gone astray and saw the broken rush that she had left only meters ahead.

When she reached the shore of the marshland, she carefully stepped up onto solid ground, and then retraced her steps for thirty meters or so, walking backwards with painstaking care, either stepping on rocks or placing her boots in the tracks she had made only minutes before.

She could hear them now, coming up the opposite slope. They were shouting to one another, in what sounded like Russian. They had to be less than one hundred meters away. She reached the streambed in the middle of the ravine, where she had paused only moments before. Forcing herself to move slowly, she eased into the water. It was only a few feet deep, but she made sure not to touch the bottom, floating with the current, helping it carry her along the ridge, inching away from the trail that she had taken the opposite direction into the marsh.

After two hundred meters or so, the stream widened into an enormous swamp, just where she recalled it. The current stopped here, and the water was stagnant and fetid. It stank of rotting leaves and mud. She eased herself deeper into the swamp, only inching along, taking care to leave no traces. She maneuvered, half-floating, around a tangle of roots, which supported a decaying kapok trunk, one of the larger species of trees in the rainforest.

At some point, years before, the tree stood eighty meters high, draped in vines and moss. A decade ago, the top half of the tree had broken off, toppling down against the tree's own trunk. New plants — vines, flowers, and ferns — took root on the dying branches of what was left of the tree, producing an enormous clump of dense, tangled vegetation which descended all the way down to the surface of the swamp water. She pulled herself under that canopy of leaves, ducking beneath the vines and branches, wiggling in between the roots that protruded out of the water. When she was entirely underneath the thicket of roots and branches, with the swamp water at her neck, she stopped. She was hidden here, wedged between the roots of the tree, impossible for the soldiers to see from the outside, even with their flashlights.

She waited, trying not to breathe. The noises came even closer, the men systematically scouring the trail for her tracks. She heard their voices, a few of them only meters away, then saw their flashlights, searching the bushes and undergrowth for her prints. The helicopter returned, clattering overhead, while its floodlights lit up the waters of the swamp around the tree.

She forced herself not to move, not to breathe, to crouch motionless, feet buried in the mud at the bottom of the swamp, face pressed against one massive root of the dead tree. The water of the swamp stank, a stench of sulfurous decay. After a few minutes, she felt things beneath the surface of the water, working their way up the legs of her jeans, along her calves and thighs. They felt like thick, clammy fingers, pulling blindly at her skin, hunting for places to feed. She wanted to brush them away, to get them off her legs, but she didn't dare make a sound or disturb the waters of the swamp. She forced herself to stand motionless, ignoring the things that were feeding on her, while the men kept searching for her trail along the swamp.

Over her head, in the tangle of roots and leaves, beetles and centipedes moved, slowly, making furtive sounds, their brittle shells rasping against dry leaves. Occasionally, something would drop down onto her hair or face, before crawling away. She stood motionless in the stinking water, holding her breath and trying not to imagine what made each of the sounds. Mosquitos hummed incessantly, all around her head. She could feel the itchy welts start to form around her neck and prayed that her anti-malaria prophylactics would work as advertised.

She tried not to think about her friends, about her father, about what the soldiers had done to them. The image of her father, his face set like stone, before that final moment, kept replaying before her eyes. She had never felt so empty, so desolate, in her entire life. She forced herself not to watch those images, or to remember what had happened, and instead to listen and watch, straining in the dark, while she tried to survive the night.

The sounds of the men gradually receded, as they moved back to the path, and then into the marshland that she had left only minutes before. She heard the splashes, first a few men and then more. Even through the rain, she could hear their shouts and the occasional metallic bark of their walkie-talkies. Gradually, almost imperceptibly, the sounds moved further into the marsh, as the men spread out to hunt for her, following the trail she had left. As they searched, she waited there in the dark, crouched in the swamp water underneath the dying tree, tears silently streaming down her cheeks. And she knew then, with absolute certainty, that it was only a matter of time before they would find her, and then, before they would kill her.

Chapter 13
Franklin Kerrington III

The late afternoon sun spilled through the venetian blinds, golden on the teakwood floor. Classical music played in the background. Kerrington stood at the window, gazing into the courtyard. He sipped the tea — a rare Darjeeling blend — and watched the water dancing in the fountain.

The last report from Reid was an improvement. His team had located the plane and confirmed that there were no papers at the site of the wreck. Most of the files that had been on the Nazi plane were destroyed in the fire and nothing legible remained. The camp was clean as well and the girl hadn't sent emails to anyone describing what, if anything, she had read. Nobody else had either. The problem was contained: just the girl with what was at most a few files, and the Russian Spetsnaz team, assuming that they ever caught her. These were problems, but they were manageable. His team was larger and tougher, with more resources; they could do this.

He thought about what would happen if Reid's team didn't succeed. He didn't know what exactly the Nazi files contained. But he did know from what he had pieced together over the years that the contents of the files could be disastrous. He knew that the files might describe his family's support for the Third Reich before and during WWII. Not just moral sympathy, but active support and concrete assistance. The Kerringtons had used their political, financial, and other resources to assist Hitler, in every way they could. They had traded secretly with the Nazis, helping them get access to hard currency and critical raw materials. And his grandfather had run a small, but very effective, spy ring, passing along information about U.S. military forces, weapons, and political intentions.

Just as bad, the files might also reveal the real source of the Kerrington fortune — the secret financial infusions from Germany during the 1930s that compensated for a decade of drunken mismanagement at the end of his grandfather's life. Those revelations would destroy his family's reputation and, in all likelihood, its fortune. The press alone would do that. The lawsuits and regulatory investigations would eat up whatever survived. Everything that the Kerrington dynasty had worked so hard to build over the past century would be gone. All because of the file that the girl had found in the jungle.

He couldn't let that happen. He took another sip of tea, watching the sunlight on the fountain. Then he walked across the room and picked up the secure CIA phone that had been installed at his house. He made three short calls, businesslike and carefully choreographed.

By the time he was finished, the NSA was executing orders to position one of its satellites over western Uganda and eavesdrop on all communications in the region. The ostensible purpose of the effort was to track down a Russian arms dealer, reportedly carrying plans for a new type of biological weapon. An Agency team was being dispatched to the region at the same time. The mission leader was handpicked by Kerrington. The man was a CIA veteran who had worked with Kerrington and Reid a dozen times before, who would help track the girl and the Russians, but do nothing to interfere with Reid's operation. It would tilt the odds even further in their favor. He would leave nothing to chance.

He turned to the cartographic atlas that had been delivered earlier that day from the CIA. It contained a selection of maps of the Rwenzoris, where the girl had disappeared. He had arranged for the Agency's cartographic department to prepare them for him the night before.

He studied the terrain, first on the larger-scale maps and then the small-scale ones. The area was remote, and almost entirely unpopulated. It was also impossibly rugged. He followed the contour lines of the small-scale maps, trying to picture the sheer cliffs and ravines. There were no roads, no towns, and no villages — basically nothing for nearly two hundred kilometers. Just empty mountains and jungle. The nearest town to the west was Goma, on the shores of Lake Kivu in the Congo. It was 250 kilometers away from the plane wreck, on the other side of a rugged mountain range and an uncharted jungle.

He smiled to himself. It was perfect. A perfect place to hunt the girl, with nobody there to see. There was no way she could survive for more than a few days in that wilderness, much less make it 250 kilometers to the nearest town. All Reid had to do was execute. The rest would be easy, just a matter of time.

He checked his watch, making sure that he wouldn't be late for dinner with the President's National Security Adviser. The watch had belonged to his grandfather. Its case was lustrous gold, smooth and solid. His grandfather's name was engraved on the back. His father had worn the watch when he served in the Senate and had given it to Kerrington on his twenty-first birthday. His father accompanied the gift with a story.

It was an ancient Roman story, about duty and honor. A story about a man's sacrifice for his family, about a man giving his youth, his freedom and then his life, so that his family and its honor could survive. Kerrington never forgot his father's story. He lived his life according to that story. He married a woman whom he never loved, in order to build the family's honor, and then sent his boys away to schools when they were not yet teenagers, so that they could better do the same. And he spent his life building the family's honor and fortune, leaving time for hardly anything else, hardly any of the things that he wanted. Surrounded by the wealth and dignity of his family's house, he swore that he wouldn't let that honor be lost now.

Chapter 14
Sara West

She woke inside a cathedral. She was lying on the floor, looking up into the interior of the church. The cathedral's pillars were greenish-gray stone, massive columns soaring up to a vaulted ceiling, which was worked in an intricate, leafy pattern. The stained-glass windows let the sunlight in, its rays slanting in the early morning. The windows were like lace, delicately detailed with patterns that shimmered like jewels in the light. The church was silent and peaceful, the way a place of worship was meant to be. She imagined how the choir would sound, filling the nave with music. She hardly ever prayed, much less went to church, but wondered now why she didn't.

The cathedral's peace was broken by the growl of engines and then the whine of helicopter rotors. She awoke from her dream in panic. She was lying under a clump of bushes, next to the swamp, where she had pulled herself in the early morning, after hours in the water. She hadn't even managed to crawl into her sleeping bag, instead collapsing onto the shore at the edge of the marsh, curled up around her backpack.

Somehow, they hadn't found her. Somehow, she had survived the night. She fought back a wave of terror as she remembered where she was. Images from the day before and her headlong flight through the jungle came back, replaying themselves before her eyes.

She started to cry again, wrenching sobs that she couldn't control. She cried, on the banks of the swamp, like a lost child. She cried for everything she had lost – her father, Robert and her trust in him, Jackson, her friends. And she cried in anger, in bitter fury at the men who had done all that. She lay there, tears streaming down her muddy face, sobs wracking her body, alone in the swamp.

It seemed to take forever, but she finally managed to calm herself, holding back the tears, and forcing herself to take deep, slow breaths. Long breaths, that she held inside until she regained her balance. Her mouth was parched, and she found her water bottle in the backpack. At least she hadn't lost that. She drank thirstily, draining the flask. She refilled it from the swamp, using the iodine and the filter in her pack to treat the brackish water. Then she forced herself to take stock.

Her face and neck had been bitten a dozen times by mosquitos and the things that crawled down out of the tree in the swamp during the night. She prayed that none of them were too poisonous. She recalled dimly that one had been a thick, brittle-shelled centipede that she had pulled off the back of her neck in the middle of the night. Her legs itched and she lifted up her trousers, then stifled a scream. Dozens of leeches had attached themselves up and down her legs. Many of them were fat now, bloated with her blood. She plucked them off, using her knife when they resisted, leaving the thick, black creatures to inch their way back into the swamp.

She couldn't hear the Russians, but she knew they were out there, methodically searching for her in the marshland, on the opposite side of the ridge. Their hunt would go more quickly in the daylight. When they had convinced themselves that she wasn't there, in the marsh, they would probably start over at its edges and then search outwards, looking for her trail. At some point though, they would backtrack and start looking at other possibilities. If she were unlucky, she had left a print or another clue, somewhere along the trail that she had taken. And then they would be after her again.

She cleaned up the place where she had slept beneath the bushes. She used water from the swamp to wash away any sign she had been there and checked that she hadn't broken any twigs or disturbed any leaves. Then she pulled on her backpack and slipped back into the swamp, its brown, brackish waters swallowing her once more. She half-floated through the water again, careful not to leave any traces. Slowly, she made her way deeper into the swampland. Most of the time, the swamp was silent, except for the rustle of the wind. Occasionally, in the distance, she heard the sound of a walkie-talkie, but these sounds faded, then disappeared, as the day wore on.

For hours, she inched, crab-like, through the water. Her pace was painfully slow — a few hundred meters every hour. She was chilled, frozen to the bone, by the water of the swamp, but she forced herself to continue. Twice, during the afternoon, the monsoon rains returned, pouring out of the swollen grey clouds in heavy sheets. At least that would make it even harder for the soldiers and their helicopters to follow her trail, she thought, as she wiped the water out of her eyes.

She continued to inch her way along, until the swamp gave way to an open grassy plain, dotted with hillocks and trees and crisscrossed with streambeds. She found what looked like one of the larger streams, flowing west across the plain. She eased herself into it, then half-floated and half-swam, moving against the gentle current. Once, she heard the rhythmic beat of helicopter blades in the distance and froze under the leafy ferns along one bank of the stream. It seemed like a lifetime later, when the sound had faded away, that she could continue her painstaking crawl along the stream and across the plain.

It was nightfall when she reached the far side of the plain, where another ridge reared up, abruptly, from the valley floor, its steep sides overgrown with tangled jungle. She waited in the water of the stream, even colder now as the sun went down, until darkness had fully descended. The sky turned grey, then darker, when the stars came out, half visible between the clouds. Wild birds and bats swooped low over her head as night fell. And with them, she crept out of the water, first over logs by the stream bed, and then, gingerly, onto the trail that Jackson had followed a month ago — the hunters' trail that snaked up the side of the next ridge, over it, then down through the jungle to the rainforest beyond.

She knew that she had to sleep, and searched, in the fading light, for a shelter. She found it, near the game trail, half an hour later. It was under a fallen tree, sheathed in vines and underbrush, where the jungle floor was clean, that she finally collapsed. She forced herself to eat a handful of Jackson's dried meat, and part of the cornbread. Then she crawled into her sleeping bag and cried herself to sleep again, curled up in a tight little ball around her pack, in the ravine at the bottom of the ridge.

The next day, and the ones after that, were a blur. A blur of trees, bushes, leaves, and vines, punctuated only by drenching rain storms and sleepless nights hidden in the undergrowth. A blur of mosquitos, beetles, centipedes, spiders, columns of ants, and endless jungle trails, which she crept along in terror, praying that she wouldn't leave a track, a broken branch or a displaced leaf. At first, her pace was heartbreakingly slow, only a handful of kilometers a day. And she lost her way a half dozen times or more each day, leaving her terrified, alone again in the trackless expanse of the jungle, with no idea where to turn.

Somehow, though, each time, she found her way back to the hunters' trails — the network of almost imperceptible tracks that led through the jungle. It helped that she had come this way only weeks before. And, as the shock of the attack on the camp began to recede, her wilderness experience took over. She made her way along the trails with long, graceful strides that began to eat up the distance. She instinctively avoided low-hanging branches, thorny bushes along the sides of the path and columns of ants that swarmed in shiny, foot-wide ropes across the trail. She had done this, hiked across rugged terrain, countless times before and she forced herself to concentrate on doing the same again, hour after hour, leaving the Russians further behind each day.

When darkness fell, she slept under logs or bushes, inside her sleeping bag and curled up around her pack. Each night, she lay there, alone, crying silent tears of sadness and fear, until the morning came, and she had to run again. Each night, she cursed the thick file of documents which was carefully tucked in her backpack, away from the rain and the wet. It was that file, those papers, that had killed her father, and that kept the Russians on her trail. None of this would have happened if she hadn't found those papers.

On the fifth day, she dared to imagine that she might have escaped. She hadn't heard or seen her pursuers for nearly three days. It had been a day and a half since she had seen one of the helicopters, although she could still occasionally hear them in the distance. She stepped up her pace, covering nearly fifteen kilometers that day, before the sun started to fade.

The terrain was broken and uneven here, but heavily forested, and she could make good time. She continued heading west, towards another large ridge, rising steeply five hundred meters off the floor of the valley, which she had to cross on the way to the Congo. She remembered that the trails leading up its sides were especially treacherous.

As the light began to fade, she watched for a shelter for the night. She spotted a fallen log, in a clearing dotted with palms, thirty meters or so from the trail. She debated for a moment whether it was worth risking a minute's exposure in the open for the sake of a dry, secure shelter.

She surveyed the horizon, then listened for the sound of the helicopters. The sky was empty. Taking a deep breath, she made her way out of the bushes at the edge of the clearing. She was halfway to the shelter when the sky erupted in angry metallic clattering. One of the Russian helicopters had come over the ridge ahead of her; the ridge must have blocked the sounds of the copter's rotors, until it had emerged almost above her, flying fast and low across the hilly plain.

She froze, trying desperately to make herself as small and still as she could. The helicopter continued past her, barreling along the valley, intent on other missions. She didn't move a muscle, didn't look up over her shoulder at the copter, and instead crouched motionless, willing the sound to move along, to grow fainter, finally to disappear.

It didn't. Instead, the sound paused for a moment in the distance, neither fading nor coming closer, like a coin standing on its side, about to fall. And then, first imperceptibly and after that like a freight train, the sound bore down on her. She forced herself to look up and the terror returned. They had seen her. The helicopter had turned around and was headed back up the valley, right at her. Somehow, someone in the helicopter had spotted her in the field, and now they were coming back for her.

She turned and ran again, ran in terror, back into the undergrowth, onto the hunters' trail, then through the forest towards the ridge rising up from the floor of the valley. Behind her, the helicopter roared angrily, hunting for a place to land.

The rough terrain of the valley saved her life, at least for another few hours. It took the pilot nearly fifteen minutes to find somewhere to set the aircraft down. And when he did, it was another few hundred meters away from the ridge. That gave her a precious thirty minutes lead on the two men who scrambled out of the helicopter and came rushing after her.

She used that lead as well as she could. She ran headlong along the trail, putting all the distance that she could between herself and the soldiers. When she reached the edge of the valley, she took the trail that ascended the ridge most directly and started up. The path was strewn with fallen logs and branches. In places, the trail was entirely on fallen trees, whose trunks were slick with moss and water. She had to slow her pace here, where a fall could send her tumbling down the slope, or a misstep would leave her ankle twisted or her boot trapped between the logs. But she pressed on, as fast as she dared, ascending through the darkened jungle up the side of the ridge.

Night fell before the men found her trail again. Even with the moon, it would be difficult now for them to follow. Another monsoon rainstorm of cold, drenching drops, made it even harder for them and their helicopters. She heard them, from time to time, and occasionally saw their lights far down the slope through the trees and rain. She was faster here, though, than they were, and she knew where she was going, steadily widening the gap as she made her way up the ridge. She heard the helicopters again, later in the night, when she finally reached the top of the ridge. The jungle was too thick for the copters to land, but they crisscrossed the ridgeline, searchlights probing the rainforest's canopy for openings, hunting for her among the trees and bushes.

She crossed the top of the ridge, then started down the opposite side. The trail was just as bad as the one she had just ascended — tangles of wet and mossy fallen logs, ankle-deep mud, and a path that disappeared at every turn into walls of bushes or undergrowth. She was tired, exhausted from five days of flight, no real sleep, and barely enough food. But she made her way, meter by painful meter, down the side of the ridge, losing and then finding the trail a handful of times along the way, the countless times that she had hiked similar paths in the past keeping her from going too far astray. By the time she had reached the bottom of the ridge, the night was half gone. The jungle was thicker here, the clouds and the canopy shutting out even the dim light of the moon. There was little point to continuing now. She was sure to lose the trail and, even if she didn't, she would cover hardly any ground.

She found a place to shelter. It was under a bush, only slightly larger than its neighbors, thirty meters or so off the trail. She curled up in her sleeping bag, bone-tired and shattered.

It was only then, lying in the bushes, drenched with sweat, straining to listen for the sounds of her pursuers above the jungle noises, that she realized how hopeless her chances were. She thought she had eluded them. They had lost her trail, she was sure of that. And each day had put her further away, another ten or fifteen kilometers further away.

But the Russians' helicopters, and their numbers, were an advantage she would never overcome. They would spread out, searching the area, until one of them spotted her — as they almost inevitably would. And then he would call the others and they would be there, on her trail again. It might take a week, or two weeks, but she would make another mistake at some point. She would slip and twist an ankle or knee. Or she would leave one track too many. Or she would drink bad water and become too sick to walk. And then the soldiers would have her. It was just a matter of time. She cried herself to sleep again, weeping tears of fear and frustration — fear of what the men would do to her and frustration at being helpless, being chased like an animal.

She awoke with a start, instantly wide awake, heart pounding again. She didn't know what time it was. But she must have slept only an hour or so — it was still pitch dark. She lay there in the dark, the jungle night alive with sound, the noises of frogs, birds, beetles, monkeys, and all the other things that came out in the dark. Most nights, she had loved these sounds. She had grown up with them, on two dozen different expeditions and three times as many treks into the wild. She could name what made the sounds, one by one, if she wanted to. But tonight, they were alien and hostile.

She lay there in the dark, curled around her pack, and cried again. Cried for her father, for her friends, and for Jackson. Cried in fear of the men that chased her and in frustration at the thick file of papers that had caused all this.

It wasn't an idea at first. It was instead a slow, imperceptible gathering of resolve, like clouds before a storm. It steadied her somehow and then stopped her tears. It turned her fear into anger, a dark fury, an angry bitterness, thirsty for vengeance. And then, after a while, her fury turned into thought, into an idea. The thought was that she would not lie there in the dark and cry anymore, like a lost child. She would not run, in panic, like an animal, through the jungle, until the soldiers finally caught her. She would not be hunted.

Instead, she would hunt. This was her home, the place where she had grown up, where her father raised her. They would not hunt her here. Instead, she would hunt them. She would not wait until she made a mistake. Instead, she would wait until they did. She wiped the tears away from her eyes with her mud-stained hands, pulled back her hair, away from her face, and sat up, cross-legged, in the dark in the middle of the jungle. And began to think of the ways that she could kill the men who were chasing her.

She sat motionless there under the tree for hours. She looked like a monk or a nun, lost in contemplation and prayer, eyes half-closed, hands peacefully folded in her lap. But her thoughts were not peaceful; they were grim and bloody. She catalogued her tools — Jackson's machete, her pocketknife, the nylon rope in her pack — as well as what the jungle would provide — bamboo, poisons from a dozen species of plants, heavy logs.

And then she enacted scenes, set there in the jungle, where she confronted her pursuers. Most of the scenes ended badly, with her body torn by bullets or machete blows, lying dead in the mud. But a few scenarios ended differently, with her facing the men who chased her, and surviving. She took these scenes and reenacted them, again and again, probing for weak points and opportunities, playing through different ways that something might go wrong, and leave her dead.

The sun was rising above the jungle canopy when she finally stirred. She drank from the canteen, the water brackish and foul-tasting. She allowed herself another piece of Jackson's cornbread and dried meat, her mouth watering at the taste of food. She eased to her feet and then started carefully along the trail, making sure again that she didn't leave a trace on the path. Barely noticing that she did so, she sidestepped the muddy places on the trail, used the fallen logs, roots, and rocks as stepping stones, and avoided the ferns and leaves that lined the sides of the path. After three hours or so, she found what she was looking for — a stand of bamboo, fifty meters or so from the game track, surrounded by undergrowth and barely visible from the trail. She had almost missed it herself, through the vines and bushes.

She crept through the undergrowth with even more care than usual. It took her half an hour, but eventually she made it. The bamboo stand was huge — hundreds of greenish shafts, clustered together, thrusting out of the undergrowth, up towards the treetops. The larger stalks were fifteen-twenty centimeters in diameter and towered ten or fifteen meters above her, thick green columns whose fronds cut off the sunlight that made it down from the jungle canopy. Around the edges of the bamboo stand, she found what she needed — smaller bamboo shafts, two or three centimeters across, five or six meters long.

She used the machete the way Jackson had taught her to cut down four of the smaller bamboo stalks. She grimaced at the sounds she made, chopping through the hard, resilient fibers. She prayed that no one was there to hear. She angled her blows diagonally, down at the base of the bamboo, so it would not look as if anything had been disturbed. And then she used the machete again, to chop off the top meter and a half of each stalk. She hid the remnants beneath a pile of leaves. And then she sharpened the thinner end of one of the bamboo stalks, first using her machete and then her knife, until the end of the stalk was razor sharp and pointed. She did this again, on another bamboo stalk, and then again, until she had four spears, light and easy for her to carry, but nearly as strong as metal poles, with a wicked, slightly jagged point at the end.

She crept further into the jungle, leaving the bamboo spears hidden next to the stand. After an hour of searching, she found a cluster of the plants that she needed — thick, greyish-green leaves and crimson flowers. They looked sinister, with a deathly pallor, and their poison was worse. Her father had showed her this plant when she was just a teenager, warning her about its poison, and describing how the native tribes harvested it for hunting larger game.

She used the machete again, to make incisions along the bottom of the leaves. She made sure that the creamy fluid that oozed out of the leaves didn't touch her hands. Instead, she let it drip into one of the plastic specimen vials that she always carried in her pack. When the vial was full, she replaced the cap and secured it, then repositioned the leaves of the plant, so that it was impossible to see her hand-iwork. When she was finished, she returned to the bamboo stand and her spears.

Night was falling now, and she found a fallen tree. She crept under the vines and roots, easing aside the bushes, until she found a bare patch of soil where she could lie down. She took off the backpack and curled into her sleeping bag, leaving the bamboo spears next to her in the dark. She lay there, hugging her pack, and for the first time in six nights, she didn't cry herself to sleep.

Chapter 15
Ivan Ivanchenko

He moved through the jungle like a machine. He wore leather mountain boots that protected his feet against the mud, the damp, and the snakes. He carried a heavy pack, laden with a tent, food, water, communications gear, a medical kit, and other supplies, together with ammunition for his three weapons. The pack weighed more than thirty kilos, but he was built like a slab of concrete, and carried the weight easily. As he walked, he methodically scanned the trail in front of him, searching for the slightest trace of the girl — anything that might put them back on her trail.

They lost the girl a week ago, on the other side of the valley, in a trackless marsh. They scoured the marshland for a day and a half but hadn't found a trace of where she might have gone. After that, they widened their search again, fanning out in all directions to pick up her trail. She was very good — they all now realized that. She might not have had military training, but she had managed to escape that night, when a dozen ex-Spetsnaz commandos were only minutes away from her, and then hide in the forest for the next week. She had covered seventy kilometers, over brutal terrain, leaving no tracks and avoiding all of her pursuers.

But she couldn't survive forever. They had spotted her again a couple days ago with one of the helicopters, and then transported their team to the valley where she had been seen. They would fan out and pick up her trail again. Or she would slip and hurt herself or run out of food. It was only a matter of time.

Ivanchenko whispered into his walkie-talkie. Peter was three hundred meters or so ahead of him, on the same game trail. Mikhail was off to the right, five hundred or so meters away, on another one of the jungle paths, while Igor was to the left working his way through the jungle. They checked in with each other every thirty minutes, just as their protocol provided. Earlier that morning, Mikhail said he had seen a partial boot print, which might have come from the girl. No one else had seen or heard a thing.

They hiked until well past nightfall, using their flashlights in the dark. At 8 p.m., they stopped for the night. They did not regroup, each one instead bivouacking alone, again, according to their protocol. They all had ample supplies of dehydrated food and used their butane stoves to produce the semblance of a meal. It didn't taste like much, but it was nutritious and filling. As he prepared his meal, he wondered idly what the girl would be eating — nothing, he assumed. If they didn't catch her first, then hunger would. And they would follow the vultures and crows to her body.

When he was finished with his dinner, he opened a new bottle of whiskey. It was Johnny Walker Blue — almost as good as vodka. Strictly speaking, they weren't permitted alcohol. But, of course, they ignored that. They would die of boredom, and never get to sleep, without their private stashes. He enjoyed a long swallow, letting the warmth fill his stomach, and listened to the jungle sounds. The noises were wild, like Jurassic Park. He had been on lots of hard-core missions, but this place was the roughest. None of them had ever seen mountains and jungle this difficult, not to mention the bugs and rain and mud. It made Chechnya look like the suburbs.

After a few moments, he crawled into the one-man tent, which he had pitched next to the trail. It protected him from the snakes and ants and other creeping things in the jungle, as well as from the monsoon showers. The tent could be seen from at least a hundred meters away; it was camouflage colored, but its sleek lines still stood out in the jungle. He didn't mind that, though. They were hunting the girl, not the other way around. If she saw them, and panicked, so much the better. He drifted off to sleep, helped along by few more swigs of Johnny Walker.

He awoke with a start and looked at his watch. It was 3:30 a.m. and the jungle was still dark. Someone had turned their walkie-talkie on to transmit and started to say something. The short metallic squawk had awakened him. Half-asleep, he considered checking in with the others, and then decided against it. Somebody must have imagined that they heard something, then thought better of it. No reason to wake everyone else up. He was back asleep in minutes.

The sun had nearly risen when he woke. He crawled out of his sleeping bag, unzipped the mosquito fly, and eased through the flaps. The jungle air was already thick and humid. He stretched lazily, his heavily muscled arms locked behind his head. When he was finished, he lit the stove and set the kettle on to boil. While the water heated, he took down his tent. By the time the water had boiled, the tent and his other supplies were stowed in his pack. He emptied two packets of instant coffee and sugar into the water and waited for the metal cup to cool.

While he waited, he used the walkie-talkie to check in with the rest of the team. Within seconds, Peter and Igor had answered. They joked easily, complaining about the heat and bugs. Mikhail was slow in responding, provoking another round of jokes, focused on speculation about pygmy women and masturbation. They signed off to finish their breakfasts and prepared to continue the search. He drained the cup, grimacing at the aftertaste of the instant coffee, then shouldered his pack and switched the walkie-talkie to transmit, trying again to reach Mikhail. Still no answer. He tried once more.

"Mikhail. Pick up, man. You know the protocol."

Still no response. He gave it another couple of minutes, and then tried again. There was still no reply, with nothing but static on the line. He waited, wondering why Mikhail wasn't answering.

"What do you think?"

He started. But the voice from the walkie-talkie was Peter's, not Mikhail's.

"I don't know. Maybe his walkie-talkie is broken," he replied.

"Maybe. Or maybe the idiot lost it or gave it to the pygmy girl." Peter always played the clown.

"That's it. What's her name then. Let's call her." Igor and Peter laughed at their little game.

"Fuck it. Let me get over to his trail and see," he replied in disgust.

He didn't relish working his way through four hundred meters of jungle to the game trail that Mikhail was following. The undergrowth was thick and tangled. Ants, spiders, and beetles crawled along the leaves and vines. Snakes too, if he was unlucky. Razor-sharp leaves and thorns added to the delight.

It took him forty-five minutes, and two long scratches on one leg, to reach the trail that Mikhail was following. The undergrowth was even thicker than he had expected. He used his machete repeatedly, chopping aside branches and leaves so that he could fit his two-meter frame through the dense bushes. Once, he disturbed a column of red ants that retaliated by swarming silently onto his boots, then up his bare legs. Dozens of the insects made their way up his shins before he noticed. He tried to brush them away, but their pincers had already locked into his skin. It took ten minutes to pick them off, one by one, leaving a collection of red welts behind. The bites itched even worse than they looked.

Thirty minutes later, he spotted Mikhail's tent, pitched in a clearing off to one side of the trail, fifty meters ahead or so. He started to shout Mikhail's name, then thought better of it. Flipping off the safety of his AK-103, he crept along the trail, edging up to the rear of the tent.

He was nearly there when he saw the poles — long bamboo poles, protruding up a meter out of the top of Mikhail's tent, through the mosquito vents in its roof. The air in the clearing was thick with flies, their buzzing drowning out the other jungle sounds as he moved closer to the tent. He padded forward, trying to ignore the flies.

"Igor. Peter," he spoke quietly into his walkie-talkie.

"Yes, boss." It was Igor. His voice was serious now as well.

"I'm at Mikhail's tent. Something's wrong here. Not sure what. I'm going to check," he said.

"Copy that boss."

He edged forward, even more cautiously now. He scanned the bushes and trees around the tent. They stood there silently — a curtain of greens and browns. When he reached the tent, it was as bad as he feared. The long bamboo poles were spears. The spears had been thrust down through the roof of the tent, into the interior space. One spear was buried in Mikhail's right eye, the other in his chest, pinning him to the ground. The bottom of the tent was a pool of dark red blood, trapped by the waterproof floor, congealing in the heat. Ants, flies, and fat white worms gorged on the crimson puddle, as well as on Mikhail's swollen face.

He looked silently, in disgust, at the column of ants that made its way up the side of the tent on the outside, then down the inside, then onto Mikhail's arm and up to his ruined eye. How stupid could the man be? Who could have done this shit? It must have been the girl. There was nobody else here. How could Mikhail let a girl do this to him? He sighed and lifted his walkie-talkie.

Her third spear caught him in the back of his head, just behind the ear. He hardly felt it. It had been thrust with cold fury and all the strength that she could summon. He didn't feel the next spear at all. She planted it in his chest, right in the center, just underneath his ribs. The spear was light and supple, but as hard as steel. She had sharpened it to a needle point, which drove through his muscled torso like driving a tent peg into the mud. Her thrust had all her weight behind it, as she stood over him, boots planted on either side of his body, driving the shaft through his chest and down, into the soft mud beneath him.

Ivanchenko lay there, pinned to the jungle soil just like Mikhail, for the next two hours. His body was covered with ants and beetles and worms when Igor and Peter finally arrived. His pack lay open on the ground, next to Mikhail's, as if someone had hurriedly rifled through it. His food and water were missing. They searched the campsite, and then the surrounding jungle. They didn't find a trace of her, not even a boot print. After they were done searching, Igor used his satellite phone to call Petronov. He leaned against a tree, looking at what was left of Ivanchenko and Mikhail, as he waited for Petronov to answer.

Chapter 16
Reginald Reid

Their camp was in a deserted village, which didn't seem to have a name, on the Congolese side of the border with Uganda, in the lowlands that stretched out at the foot of the Rwenzoris. The countryside around the village had once been fertile farmland but was now empty, devastated by two decades of civil war between shifting factions of Congolese, Ugandan, and Rwandan militias. The local military commander had been on the CIA payroll for years and was delighted for an excuse to demand an increase in his monthly retainer. The commander's rag-tag troops stood guard, a respectful distance from the village, leaving the Americans to their own devices.

Reid didn't just rely on the local troops to guard the village. He knew better than that. He had established his own perimeter inside what was left of the village. Six of his team manned positions in burnt-out huts, their night scopes and binoculars scanning the landscape around them.

The remainder of his team was seated under a giant baobab tree that stood in the center of the village, towering over the reddish-orange soil and the handful of thatched huts that were still standing. Next to the tree, the team's three helicopters were parked neatly alongside one another, their rotors casting circles of geometric shadows onto the hard-packed ground.

There wasn't much for the men to do, apart from wait. They had stripped down and oiled their weapons and checked their supplies more times in the past week than they could count. When it was dry, the men worked out, doing push-ups in front of their huts. But it rained twice a day, in torrential downpours that cascaded off the badly thatched roofs of the huts, turning parts of the village into miniature ponds. And it was brutally hot, a humid heat that made it hard just to sit up. They spent most of each day inside, reading cheap paperbacks, sleeping, or trading stories.

It was late in the afternoon when he walked out underneath the baobab tree and clapped his hands twice. His men knew by now that this was a call to order, and they climbed out of their hammocks and put away their weapons. They arranged themselves in a semi-circle around the tree's trunk where he stood. It was their sixth day in the village, but his khakis were still neatly pressed, his shirt spotless white. He wore mirrored aviator sunglasses. He stood motionless under the tree, his face impassive. He prided himself on his appearance, no matter what the circumstances. He was in control of his environment, not the other way around.

"There are new developments," Reid said. "Good ones. But you need to be ready to move and move fast. We need everyone able to depart in five minutes if I give the order. We need everything packed and ready to go. Got that?"

It wasn't really a question. The men nonetheless murmured assent.

"So. New intel. It seems that the girl is a little tougher than the Russkies thought. We're still piecing together the intercepts, but it looks like she took out two of the Russians last night. Killed them both with bamboo spears. Left them to bleed to death in their tents, pinned to the ground with stakes through their chests."

Reid continued. "Then she helped herself to their weapons and supplies. And now has at least half a day's lead on the rest of the Russians. She's one nasty bitch, that's for sure. Double-crossed these guys and then put spears through their hearts. We don't know who trained her, but she's evil. And good."

"And she's coming our way. We're pretty sure of that. Her trail has come across the mountains, heading west towards the Congo, ever since she left the crash site. There's no reason to think that she's going to change course now."

He went on. "We need to be ready for either of two possibilities. First, the Russians catch her, in which case we take the Russians, and then we take her and her files. Second, she escapes the Russkies and we just take her ourselves. I want teams to work on scenarios for each possibility. Ramirez, you lead the Russian scenario; Wilson, you handle the girl-only scenario. Get back with me as soon as you have something up and running. And remember. Total radio silence. Our Russian friends don't know we're here. We have to keep it that way."

"Remember too, we need to recover the data she's carrying. It's top priority. It doesn't matter whether she's dead or alive. Frankly, better dead, because then she won't double-cross us and won't talk. And the same thing for the Russians. This is 'take no prisoners' mode."

Reid dismissed them, before motioning Ramirez and Wilson over to his hut. He knew that he could count on both of them. They were ex-Agency and as tough as anyone in the business. He walked through the operations that he wanted each of them to plan. They listed the equipment that the men would need and arranged for some new supplies to be flown in from Ethiopia. He lectured them again on the mission's importance and the extent of the girl's treachery. They could not afford to mess up.

He sat on the one old chair that they had found in the village, looking out of the hut at the helicopters, wondering if he had missed anything. He hadn't expected anything like this from the girl. Nobody had.

He hadn't told the men what they knew about the girl. They all thought that she was a trained agent, working for herself now. But Reid knew that she was really just a 28-year-old grad student. She was alone. Untrained. With no weapons or food. A college student. It was a miracle that she had survived for more than a day or two. Much less that she had imagined fighting back.

But despite everything that had happened, she was still dead. The Russians had a dozen men on her trail. Plus their copters. It was still just a matter of time. And it was also just a matter of time before Reid's team took down the Russians. They didn't know he was here, watching and listening to their every move. And they didn't know what kind of armaments his helicopters carried. He just had to be patient. He just had to execute and things would fall into place.

He looked out at the half-burned huts and barren trees, the results of years of senseless war. He let his thoughts wander, an indulgence he almost never allowed himself. He thought about the girl again, out there alone, somewhere in the jungle. The truth was, she was just an unlucky civilian. If he had ever had a daughter, she would have been around the girl's age. The girl hadn't done anything to bring this on herself, he thought. She hadn't double-crossed anyone or stolen anything. She hadn't done anything at all, in fact, except been in the wrong place at the wrong time. Except get her hands on something that Kerrington and the Russians didn't want her to have. He wondered what it might be. What she had found. What would justify an operation like this.

He put the thoughts out of his mind. They didn't matter. This girl wasn't his daughter. And it didn't matter what she had taken. What mattered was Kerrington's instructions. And the $10 million fee. That was all that mattered. He went through their plans again, double-checking his orders, making sure that he hadn't overlooked anything. That was his job — just execute, efficiently and flawlessly. That was all he needed to do, and they would have her.

Chapter 17
Ivan Petronov

The villa was in the suburbs of Kampala, up in the hills looking over the city. It had once been a colonial bungalow. Now, it was augmented with modern additions, producing a tasteful mix of old and new — ancient ceiling fans and first-class air conditioning, tribal masks and modern art, dark teak floors and bright Scandinavian carpets, plus a luxurious pool in the back. All courtesy of a local businessman, who owed Petronov more favors than he wanted to recall.

They sat together next to the pool. The air was thick and humid, hanging from the low grey clouds like wet blankets on a clothesline. Petronov wore swim trunks and no shirt. He sat in the morning sun, which had already turned his pale chest and stomach pinkish-red. Sweat dripped off his back onto the tiles beneath his chair. He had slept badly and woken angry and frustrated. His eyes were red, set deep in dark sockets, sleep still crusted in the corner of one eye. He hadn't shaved in a couple of days, and his hair hadn't been washed in even longer.

A map of the region was spread out on a table next to his chair. He spent the morning trying to trace the girl's trail through the jungle and decide where to deploy his men. He hadn't made much progress. The map didn't show any roads or trails — just an empty expanse of jungle-covered ridges and valleys.

"I don't see how that could have happened," he said. "Those guys are the best there are. She couldn't have killed even one of them, much less two. I don't even see how she could have gotten away. Not for even a day. Goddamn cunt."

He paused and drank from the bottle of local beer. It was early, but he needed to relax, to take the edge off the tension. Two empty bottles stood on the table under the umbrella. He hated the endless waiting, for little fragments of information that were never what he wanted to hear. He hated the helplessness even more, depending on others whom he didn't trust.

"Who is this girl?" he demanded angrily. "How could she do this?"

Yan didn't answer. She was dressed simply, in loose white silk trousers, a cotton blouse, and a sun hat. She sat in the shade, beneath one of the umbrellas that stood around the pool. Her skin was smooth, without a trace of perspiration or worry; her eyes were clear and rested.

Flecks of frothy saliva sparkled on his lips in the sunlight as he spoke. He drank again. The bottle was cold, with drops of moisture beaded on the dark brown glass. The beer was good. German brewers had successfully transplanted their craft to Africa. He took another drink and savored the taste. It cut the darkness of his mood, lifting his spirits a bit. He belched into his hand, then studied the map again.

"I think the girl is a dangerous one, my love," Yan spoke softly.

He laughed. "She is just a girl. Alone in the middle of nowhere."

She was quiet for a moment, then spoke again, still softly. "The girl is a child of the jungle. She grew up there. She's spent more time there than any of our men. We know that now. And she hates.... They killed her father, and her lover. And now they hunt her. She has no choice but to fight back. They underestimate her."

She said "they," not "we." Not "you."

He was silent, mulling what she said. Then he answered. "So, what if this is right? What does it matter?"

He was about to continue, then paused. His anger rose again. It was fucking ridiculous to sit here, in Kampala of all places, while a bunch of overpaid Spetsnaz commandos chased a girl for weeks through the jungle. The waiting drove him crazy. The fucking bitch.

She waited again, not saying a word.

"We need to find her." His voice was thick with rage again.

He hurled the bottle he was drinking from against the wall. It exploded in a thousand shards, glittering in the morning sunlight.

"We fucking need to fucking catch the fucking bitch. She has the files. All of them. Unless we get her, unless we get the files, this is all a waste. Ten years wasted. And billions of dollars gone."

He swore again, spittle arching onto the tiled floor. He felt out of control, trapped in a stinking African jungle. The money didn't really matter. He had more money than he could ever spend. But the wasted time and opportunities drove him into a frenzy.

She stood and walked over to him. She walked lightly, like a dancer. Her breasts moved gently against the fabric of the white blouse. Her hair was soft, pulled back, with two or three strands escaping. She took off her sunglasses, then knelt between his knees, looking up at him, one arm on each of his legs.

"My love. We will catch her. You and I. We will take the files and then we will take the money. All of it. I trust you. I know you can." She leaned forward slightly.

He looked down at her, into her dark, still eyes. He could see the swell of her breasts, the dark points of her nipples against the thin blouse. She looked up again, just at that moment, eyes uplifted. His loins stirred. The darkness lifted again.

She watched him, then eased slowly back and sat a little straighter, smoothing her blouse. And said, softly, again, "Maybe we don't worry where she is now. The men are doing that. Offer a bonus. A big one. For whoever finds her. And what we do is think where she will go next. If she escapes us in the jungle, where will she run?"

Petronov paused, then looked back at the map for a moment and smiled. "There is only one place. She must go to Goma. There is no other way. She can't come back; we will get her. She can't go farther west; the rebels will get her. She can't go north; there's nothing there but rebels. If she goes to Goma, she can get transport. A flight. A car to Rwanda. It's on the border with Rwanda. The only place to run."

He continued. "So we go there. To Goma. And we wait. While the boys hunt her."

"Yes," she said. "That's so clever. That must be right." She rested one arm gently on his leg.

He was silent for a while, then spoke again. "But maybe we wait a day or two. It's nice here. We don't need to rush."

She didn't argue. After a moment, she said. "Maybe the boys watch the road to Goma. There's only one road. She will have to take it. And I don't think there are so many white women out there on that road these days."

She waited again. He started to relax, thinking about the things he needed to do. The men needed to be organized, directed to Goma, and the road leading south to it.

"I wonder if your FSS friends in Moscow could help," she continued after a few moments.

He looked up quickly. Then thought for a moment.

"How then?" he asked.

"Didn't the men say that she took Mikhail's phone?" she asked, her voice tentative.

"Yes, they did say that. You mean track her? Track the phone?"

"Can your friends do it? Can we trust them?" she asked again.

He thought again. It was a clever idea. Very clever. He liked it.

"Maybe. Maybe Alexei could. We could trust him," he said, still lost in thought.

She remained silent.

"Yes," he said, after a moment. His spirits lifted again. "That's it. I'll have Alexei track the phone, and then feed us her coordinates. The dumb bitch. She won't know what hit her."

He chuckled loudly and reached for another beer.

She got up and returned to her chair. She watched him from beneath her sun hat as he placed the call, then spoke to Alexei in Russian. Alexei was happy to help. The FSS could start tracking the phone right away. It would cost a little more, but not that much, especially given the value of the information. He smiled to himself while they talked. Things were under control again. He took another drink from the bottle, the beer cold and smooth as he swallowed.

She continued watching him from under the umbrella while he spoke with Alexei. She lowered her eyes and straightened her blouse again. A tiny shard of glass from his bottle had lodged itself in the fabric. She carefully pried it out, making sure not to cut herself, and dropped it onto the tiles, where it couldn't hurt her. It sparkled in the morning sunshine, like the other remnants of his bottle.

Chapter 18
Vladimir Grotzky

There were four of them in his squad. Grotzky was the leader. He was forty-five years old, seasoned by fighting in Ukraine and Syria, and stood more than two meters tall, 110 kilograms of solid muscle. He had the strength and endurance of a man ten years younger, and the experience of someone twenty years older. Scars crisscrossed his arms and legs — the tracks left by shrapnel, barbed wire, and one long session in the hands of Syrian rebels. He had survived, though, and he intended to survive this mission as well. Survive, and earn enough to retire from these jungle adventures. Especially with Petronov's new bonus, $250,000 for whoever got the girl.

Igor, Sergei, and Peter were ahead of him on the trail. Six other men were fanned out to the left and right. Each group was following a different game trail, searching for traces of their quarry. "The blonde bitch" — that was what they called her now. Vladimir hoped they would catch her alive. They had all liked Mikhail and Ivan. They were comrades, brothers in arms. It would be good to make the bitch suffer the way Mikhail and Ivan had suffered. They knew how to do that. They just had to catch her. They'd been trying without success for more than a week now.

But at last, they'd had a break. He looked at the GPS coordinates on his iPad. They were getting close now, very close. It was dark, more than two hours past sundown, and they needed to move slowly. They edged cautiously through the forest, without lights, not making a sound. There was a ravine ahead, four hundred meters away. That was where they had pin-pointed the signal from her phone. She had probably stopped there for the night.

He smiled to himself. She finally made a mistake. Taking Mikhail's phone. And then turning it on. Maybe she thought she could call someone for help. Stupid bitch. That mistake let Petronov's friends at the FSS track her and feed her coordinates back to them. They would wait and, when she was asleep, they would pounce on her. This time, they wouldn't take any chances.

An hour later, they found her camp. He had to admit that she knew what she was doing. Well off the game trail, buried in the underbrush, in the shelter of what looked like a fallen tree, she had pitched a tarp, a camouflaged Russian military tarp that she took from Mikhail's pack. It would have been hard to see in the daylight. At night, even with their night scopes, it was all but impossible. They would never have found her without the FSS's spy satellites.

They had already planned their next steps. He whispered into his walkie-talkie, alerting everyone that they had found her. Peter and Sergei would continue ahead, looping around behind the girl's camp, trapping her between the four of them. He and Igor would wait on this side of the camp, and once Peter and Sergei were in position, they would move in and take her. If, by some fluke, the girl escaped from the camp and fled, Peter and Sergei would be waiting for her.

It took another hour. Peter and Sergei were slow, inching forward as quietly as cats. He smiled, imagining two Siberian tigers stalking through the jungle, silently creeping up on unsuspecting prey. He settled onto the jungle floor, made himself as comfortable as he could, and waited. Igor was six meters to his right, also waiting patiently.

When Peter and Sergei were finally in position, Grotzky's walkie-talkie blinked red — the agreed signal. They were only fifteen meters away from the girl, their walkie-talkies in silent mode. He signaled Igor and the two of them crept forward, just as silently as Peter and Sergei had. Two more tigers on the prowl. He smiled in anticipation. This would be good. He hoped that he would get her first.

They stopped seven meters away from her, at the far end of the fallen tree where her tarp was pitched. Through their night scopes they could see her now. She was curled up inside Mikhail's taken sleeping bag. They could see her hair, long blonde hair, that had come undone and fallen out of the sleeping bag. Her head was buried in her arm, half-hidden under the edge of the bag. Her gun, the Uzi she had taken from Mikhail, wasn't in sight. She must be clutching it next to her body, thinking it would protect her. He smiled again, then signaled Igor to close in. They inched forward, soundlessly, across the jungle floor.

It happened in a heartbeat. Only an arms' length away, Igor suddenly stumbled forward. It looked as if he had sunk down into the ground, a meter and a half into the jungle floor. Then Igor's scream pierced the night, a shriek of animal anguish, like a cat caught in the jaws of a steel trap. He waved his arms desperately, like a man drowning, flailing wildly against the side of the tree trunk that was next to him, all the time shrieking. The jungle first went completely silent, and then burst alive again with sounds, even more loudly than before. Birds, monkeys, wild cats, and everything else that lived in the jungle, joining Igor's wild night cries.

An instant later, Peter and Sergei opened fire on the girl. He had been about to do so himself, but they were faster. Their bullets ripped through the tarp into the sleeping bag. One of them triggered another short burst, just to make sure. But they had got her. There was no way she could have survived the point-blank crossfire from two AK-103s.

Grotzky made his way over to Igor, whose screams had turned into moans, wet and bubbly. He had fallen into a hole. A deep one. He must have broken something. His breathing was labored, panting now, even wetter than before. Igor tried to speak, but he couldn't. It was as if his throat and lungs were filled with liquid. He clutched in panic at the sides of the hole that he had fallen into, trying to pull himself out, but he couldn't. Grotzky tried to lift him out, leaning over the hole with both arms and pulling, but he couldn't budge the man. He must be wedged in deep, with something broken.

Grotzky tried to calm him. "Igor. Brother. You'll be fine. I'll be right back. Let me get the bitch's head for you. You can talk to her while we get you out."

Igor didn't answer, just stared vacantly off into the distance. He stopped struggling. Christ, Grotzky thought. The man must be hurt bad.

He turned and opened up the walkie-talkie channel. "I am going in. Don't shoot."

"Got that," Peter replied.

He walked cautiously towards the tarp, where the girl's body lay hidden in the sleeping bag. He had nearly reached it when the ground fell out from under his feet. It suddenly gave way and he dropped, feet first, straight down into empty space. Just the way Igor had. An instant later, he felt the searing pain of spikes driving themselves up into his legs, deep into his calves and thighs. He almost screamed but held it back. He had been lucky. Igor must have been impaled, must have taken a spike up into his stomach or groin. He was luckier. It was only his legs. Once he got loose, he would be fine. The fucking bitch. She had got him too.

He shouted into his walkie-talkie. "Watch out. There are traps. Igor fell into one. He's hurt. And I am too. There are pits. Fucking holes in the ground. With spikes. Fucking sharp spikes. Come get us out. But be careful."

He waited there in the dark. He tried to free one leg, but he couldn't. His efforts produced only another wave of pain, which shot through both legs. The spikes must have stuck themselves pretty deep. He could feel the blood dripping down his calves, pooling into his boots. And he could hear the flies, attracted now by the scent of food. Just the way they had fed on Mikhail and Ivan.

"Igor," he spoke into the walkie-talkie. There was no answer.

"Igor, boy. Answer me." Still no answer.

Grotzky heard Peter and Sergei pushing through the undergrowth. They must be using machetes to cut a new path through the jungle. That was smart. It would take a while, but it was safer. They would avoid the bitch's pits.

He felt tired, sleepy. He realized that the wounds in his legs didn't hurt as much as before. He could barely feel them now. He looked into the bushes that surrounded him. They were beautiful. Green waves, geometric patterns, pulsing with energy. He smiled. He wanted to sing, sing to the bushes. He couldn't though. He couldn't speak. Couldn't form a word. He wondered why. But he didn't care. It didn't matter. He closed his eyes to rest for a moment. He wanted to rest. Then he would be able to sing. Sing to the bushes and the trees.

He didn't see Peter and Sergei reach the tarp. He didn't watch Sergei lift up the top of the sleeping bag, to reveal the girl's face. And he didn't hear Sergei's curse, followed by the thundering detonation of the grenade. If he had heard the sound, he would have recognized it in an instant. It was standard Russian special forces issue — a fragmentation grenade, deadly against infantry. It sprayed lethal shards of metal ten meters in every direction. It was what they carried in their packs, what Mikhail was carrying in his pack, before the girl killed him three days ago.

He also didn't see her enter the camp, from out of the jungle, ten minutes later. She moved silently. She checked Igor's body, then his, making sure that they were dead. She moved along and checked Peter and Sergei as well. Making sure they too were dead. He also didn't see the girl retrieve her pack and gun from underneath the tarp, then loot the packs of her pursuers.

There was no one there to watch as she took a medical kit and fresh rations. This time she left their phones. She also left another one of their grenades, tucked beneath Sergei's shoulder, armed and ready to detonate when his body was disturbed. As she turned to go, she surveyed the scene again with cold satisfaction, making sure she hadn't left anything behind. And then she slipped silently past his body and disappeared back into the jungle.

Chapter 19
Yan wu

They were having a late breakfast on the veranda of the villa in Kampala. It was a beautiful morning, with no signs yet of the monsoon clouds that would arrive later in the day. The air was scented, like jasmine, from the flowers that hung down over the patio.

The cook had made tea for them, rich and strong from a local blend, as well as an omelet, a dozen of slices of bacon and toast for him. He was eating noisily, while she sipped her tea and watched the wind in the flowers at the edge of the garden. She could tell that he was in good spirits. They were back on the girl's trail, very close now, with the FSS tracking her every move.

His mobile phone rang, the encrypted one. It would be Vladimir, with a report. They must have got the girl. There was no other reason for Vladimir to call. She watched him smile with anticipation. He answered, putting the call on his speaker phone, so she could hear the good news. But the call wasn't from Vladimir. It was from someone new. Maxim, Maxim somebody. His report was brief and to the point. It wasn't what they expected, and it wasn't good news.

There were five more dead that night, in a series of ambushes. Two men were dead in concealed holes, dug 1.5 meters deep into the jungle floor, with razor-sharp bamboo stakes planted in the bottom, pointing upwards. The pits had been dug with a Russian trenching tool, one that the girl took from Mikhail's pack. The stakes were poisoned. They weren't sure with what, but it was lethal.

Two more men were dead from a grenade booby-trap. The girl used one of their own grenades. It had been very simple, and a little lucky. She had taken the pin out of the grenade and wedged it under a branch in her sleeping bag. When they disturbed the sleeping bag, the grenade exploded, killing Peter and Sergei.

And the back-up team then blundered into yet another trap that she left for them — this one a live grenade tucked beneath Sergei's body. It almost killed another four men. Instead, Yuri took the full blast of the grenade in his face and chest. It killed him instantly, but the other men in the back-up team survived with only superficial wounds. They had been lucky. Luckier than the others.

He hung up. She had heard it all. She waited quietly, hands folded on her lap, stomach clenched with worry.

"Goddamn bitch. How can they be so fucking stupid?" He cursed, staring into the garden. His eyes were dark, his face a mask of rage.

She needed to be careful. She didn't argue. She rose from her seat across the table and walked over to stand next to him. She put her hand gently on his arm and leaned against his shoulder with her body, while he stared across the garden.

"Water, baby?" she said, after a moment.

He didn't answer, so she fetched him a glass, cool and sparkly. He took it, without a word, and drank deeply. He had drunk too much vodka the night before. Again.

"Damn. I don't believe it," he said after a moment. He seemed calmer. Worried, not angry.

"Who is that girl? Who is she?" he asked.

She was silent. She moved her hand up to his neck.

He stared into the garden. "At least we know where she is. Or was."

He continued: "Maybe you were right. She will need to go to a town. It has to be Goma."

"Yes, darling," she said again.

Her stomach began to unclench. He hadn't lost control. He was thinking, thinking what to do next. That was good.

He was silent. "Let's go there then," he said at last.

"I think so, baby," she said, feeling the tension slowly seep away. "And maybe we watch the roads. The one to Goma. Get local people on the payroll."

"Yes," he said. "We will do that now."

She put her arm around him while he thought. She shook her head, so that he would be sure to smell the scent on her hair. She leaned gently against him, watching him through half-open eyes.

"The phone was a trap. It was her trap," he said after a moment.

She tightened inside. She needed to be very careful. He was right, of course. And it had been her idea to use Mikhail's phone to track the girl. She had fallen for the girl's trap. The girl was clever. She must have taken Mikhail's phone, then turned it on just so that they could track her. She had used the phone, and herself, as bait. That was smart. And daring. The girl was a dangerous enemy.

"I should have thought of that," he said.

She felt a wave of relief wash through her again. "No, baby. The team was careless. It was right to track the phone. It got them closer. Got them right to her. The men were stupid though. They let her turn the tables, and then escape."

She had thought of this before. Blame the men. They were the stupid ones.

He was quiet again. "Yes," he said finally. "That's it. They fucked up. You fuck up in this business and you die," he said. He took another swallow of water.

She stroked his hair and whispered to him, "We won't do that. This is ours, baby. Billions of dollars. It's still ours." She watched him, seeing how he would turn.

"You can do it, baby. We can do it," she said softly.

She pressed her face against the back of his neck, already sweating as the heat of the day began to rise. His hair smelled stale, of oil and sweat. She hated the smell. It made her feel dirty, reminded her of the past. But she didn't pull away. Instead, she turned her face, letting her hair rub softly against his neck, and looked out into the garden, and the brightly colored bougainvillea bushes lining the courtyard.

The view of the garden calmed her, reminded her of another courtyard she had watched in moments like this, long ago, in what seemed like another life. She waited, kneeling there, watching the flowers, as he thought about what to do next.

Chapter 20
Jeb Fisher

The four men listened to the latest report from the NSA in the hut that served as Reid's command center. Fisher couldn't resist smiling. Five more Russian special forces troops dead. Three of them by their own grenades. Two more by poisoned bamboo spikes. And the girl escaped again. Best of all: she had ambushed them, luring her Spetsnaz pursuers into a trap and then taking them down with ruthless efficiency. She had at least a half day's lead on them now, maybe more. They hadn't reckoned with anything remotely like that. Nobody had.

The Russians now seemed to think that the girl would head to Goma, a ramshackle local town along the shore of Lake Kivu near the Congo-Uganda border. The Russians were also headed in that direction, still trying to track her in the jungle, but also planning to catch her on the roads along the way to Goma, and if not, when she reached the town. It was a decent plan. But it didn't take Reid and his men into account.

Reid spent the afternoon on the phone with Kerrington and a couple of Agency analysts. They gave him a full briefing on NSA intercepts from the Russians, plus reports from an Agency team that was already in position in Goma. And they'd emailed Reid maps and photos of Goma and the area surrounding it. As a result, they also had a plan, a better one than the Russians, that Reid had worked out with Kerrington.

Fisher waited, along with Ramirez and Wilson, all three men facing Reid and waiting for him to begin.

"OK. This needs careful handling, but it's very doable. The girl is heading into Goma, on this side of the border. She'll probably try and hitch a ride on a truck or a car, when she hits the main north-south road. I doubt that our Russian friends will find her before she gets to the town. They haven't managed so far, and I've got to say that my money is on the girl at this point."

Reid continued. "The Russians aren't stupid though. They'll put a watch on the places she may go — hotels, bus stations, whatever. And they'll get people into the police checkpoints along the road to Goma. And then they grab her when she shows up somewhere. They snatch her, take the data, and are gone."

"Here's our plan then. We shadow the Russkies' stakeouts. The minute we spot her, or they grab her, we take both the Russians and the girl. At the same time, we whack their copters. With the air-to-air missiles on our copters. Then we take the girl, the files, and head back home. And we're heroes — rich ones."

Reid went on. "For what it's worth, I'm betting she makes it into Goma. So, what we need is a mobile team in the town. Eight guys based in Goma, who can show up wherever we want, whenever we want, with full battle gear. They need transport, weapons, and a cover." Reid was looking to Wilson on this. Wilson was their logistics guy.

Reid continued. "Goma is full of UN personnel. They mostly drive nice, new Range Rovers. Big, white and blue, with tinted windows. Get us three or four of them. We stick our teams in those, and they'll have the run of the town, with all their gear. Wherever the girl goes, wherever the Russians grab her, we show up, ready to roll. But total radio silence until we hit them."

"Remember. If things get rough with the Russians, we leave nothing to chance. I don't care how much noise, how many casualties, or who they are. We take down all the bad guys and grab the files and the girl, dead or alive. You all got that?"

All three of them nodded. Reid's plan was simple and effective. They could make it happen.

"How do we exit?" Ramirez asked.

"Our copters will take out the Russians' transport, either in the air or on the ground. Courtesy of the NSA, we know exactly where they are. And we'll know if they move, in real-time. After we hit them, our copters set down by the lakeside.

The mobile team does a rendezvous with the copters and we fly across the border, into Uganda and then back home the way we came."

Ramirez interjected. "What exactly do we do with the girl? And what if she stashes the files somewhere? We don't want them floating around the Congo."

Reid answered curtly. "The girl is evil. A real menace. She's as good to us dead as alive. Maybe better dead. And there's also nothing to suggest that she left the files anywhere. But don't kill her until we confirm. We might have to ask her a few questions. The number one priority is securing the files, so figure out how we do that."

The three men nodded their assent to Reid's directive. But Fisher wasn't sure about this part of Reid's explanation anymore. Not sure at all. The expedition camp had been real. It was just a bunch of scientists looking for flowers in the jungle. There was doubt about that.

He had also googled the girl, out of curiosity as much as anything else. He wanted to see who she was, who they were chasing. And it turned out that she really was just a graduate student. A graduate student in biology with no conceivable connection to the spy business. No connection to the FSS, the Agency, arms dealers or anyone else in intelligence. According to numerous universities and other websites, she was a serious researcher, with a handful of publications about obscure plants — real articles in real scientific journals and blogs. There was no way all that was made up.

The truth was that she had been on a research expedition with her father, who was a real scientific superstar. That wasn't made up either. He'd read the countless stories, publications, and awards. He had also seen their father/daughter pictures on the web. The father in tweed jackets and horn-rimmed glasses. The daughter in scruffy sweaters and jeans, admiring plants and flowers in the Amazon, the Congo, the Volta, and elsewhere, year after year, over the last decade. There was no way it was all a cover.

Reid's story that the girl had been spying for the Russians and then double-crossed them, stealing plans along the way for some high-tech biological weapons that the Nazis had supposedly discovered made no sense. Fisher was pretty sure that it was all made up. Or at least that big pieces of the story were made up.

Fisher remained silent though. Reid must have reasons for his cover story. Even if it was a lie, those reasons might make sense. That was possible. Still, he was skeptical. Things didn't add up and he couldn't see why Reid, and Kerrington too, would lie to him. He wondered what the truth was, why they really wanted the girl and her files so badly.

He parked those thoughts for later. He turned his mind back to the more immediate problems of securing Range Rovers and suitable places for the team to stay in Goma. He used an encrypted phone to give instructions to one of the CIA's local contacts, working through the equipment that they would need and the layout of the town.

By the time he was finished, the sun was going down over the forest around the village and the night sounds had begun. As the sun set, he went outside and leaned against the side of one of the huts, nursing a lukewarm beer and watching the jungle foliage moving in the breeze.

His thoughts returned to the girl. He couldn't help but admire her, notwithstanding Reid's story. Twenty-eight years old, with no military experience or training at all. Not just surviving the attack on the camp and eluding fifteen or so Spetsnaz troops for a week, but then turning the tables and attacking them. He doubted that many of the men on Reid's team would have survived what the girl had. He wasn't sure he would have. He watched the jungle beyond their perimeter disappear into the darkness as the sun set, wondering what the girl would be doing out there in the jungle, wondering what she would be planning next, what she must be thinking.

Chapter 21
Sara West

It was dusk. She was moving fast, making the most of the fading light as she came down out of the Rwenzori's foothills. The paths here were wider and well-used. The jungle wasn't as dense here, and there were only occasional tree branches, reaching out across the trail. She avoided them unconsciously, brushing the leaves aside from time to time. She moved along the darkened trail with the same grace that she had admired in Jackson, feet automatically avoiding the roots and holes, eyes scanning the trail for obstacles.

She had heard the road for the first time that afternoon. First, faint metallic clanks, far away in the distance. Later, the sounds of engines and horns, made by trucks grinding along the north-south road to Goma. She had hurried at first. On the road, she could find help — a ride south into Goma, or north towards Beni, further away in the opposite direction. The road would take her out of the jungle and away from the men who were chasing her, back to civilization.

Later in the afternoon she had slowed her pace. She realized that the road meant new dangers, as well as civilization. In fact, the road meant worse dangers. The jungle hid her. It had hidden her from the soldiers and their helicopters for the last fourteen days. She was their match in the rainforest, more experienced, quicker and harder for them to find. On the road, she would be out in the open, exposed to their helicopters and cars and teams of men. They would be waiting for her, somewhere along the road. Their training, their weapons, and their helicopters would give them even more advantages out in the open.

She stopped in the middle of the afternoon, resting beside the trail, waiting for night to come. She used the time to think, and to plan how she could escape. She needed to get to Goma, one way or another. She couldn't spend the rest of her life in the jungle. And she needed food. The rations that she had taken from the Russians were running low. She made up her mind and put her doubts aside. A local truck would be the fastest way. She could hitch a ride, quietly, without attracting attention, on a truck headed south to Goma.

When the shadows turned to darkness, and the jungle's night sounds began, she slipped back onto the trail, hurrying along it until she reached the road. Once, before the Belgians had left the Congo in the 1950s, the road was paved, one lane running in each direction. Today, it was a single lane, mostly dirt, rutted and muddy.

She surveyed the road cautiously from the bushes. It was empty, dark, in both directions. The only sounds were the jungle noises. There were no trucks and no people that she could see in either direction. She waited for more than an hour, crouched at the edge of the forest. The road was about four meters wide here, almost entirely dirt, with occasional patches of pot-holed pavement. The jungle crowded along both sides of the track, slowly reclaiming what little was left of the concrete surface. Nothing moved, apart from occasional birds and bats, the entire time.

She heard the truck long before she could see it. Its engine was pounding, gears grinding on the hills. Then, it finally appeared, as if from out of the jungle, two hundred meters away - two unevenly mounted headlights, casting ghostly shadows along the road. She watched the truck approach. Even in the dark, she could see that it was an ancient European model, repaired by generations of local mechanics. The truck ground closer to her, laboring along the bumpy track. It was time now, the time for her to step out of the bushes, into the truck's headlights and wave. That would stop the truck. Her white face and blonde hair certainly would.

But something stopped her at the last moment. Something held her back in the bushes, and kept her watching. She saw the driver flash past, the interior light in the cab of the truck illuminating his black face and white eyes, fixed on the road ahead. She imagined the inside of the cab. It would be dirty, air thick with cigarette smoke and the driver's scent. But it would be civilization — music from a sound system, beer or bottled water. And the driver would have coffee, food that he had bought in the last village, fried pork or chicken, spicy with chilies and onions. Maybe rice or flat bread.

She had eaten nothing but Jackson's dried meat and cornbread, plus the packages of rations she had looted from the Russians, for nearly two weeks. Her mouth watered again, a sudden, uncontrollable flood of saliva. She could almost taste the driver's food. And she would be able to stop walking, and ride instead, watching the truck eat up the kilometers.

She shook her head and watched the taillights disappear into the night. When the truck was gone, she slipped out of the bushes, and walked across the rutted surface of the road. It was night now, but the moon had risen, and its light helped her find where the trail continued on the opposite side of the road — the western side of the road — and then where it disappeared into the trees. She walked back into the forest, then hurried again along the trail, now away from the road.

The Russians would be waiting for her all along the road, their people checking the trucks and cars. Their helicopters would patrol from above. There would probably be checkpoints, with police or soldiers — all looking for her, for a lone white woman. They might have her photograph at the checkpoints, waiting for her to arrive. Let them wait, she thought. Let them search the trucks and the cars. Let them patrol the road and search the jungle where she had been, east of the road. She walked due west now, away from the road, deeper into the Congolese jungle, away from civilization, back into the rainforest, where nobody would think to look.

After another three hours, she turned onto a smaller trail, this one heading south, finding her way by the light of the moon. The road was far away now. Too far away for her even to hear the trucks. It was almost the same here, in the jungle, as it had been east of the road. The rainforest was mostly empty, with nothing but endless stretches of jungle. There was a crisscrossing network of trails that a few local hunters and farmers used. The area was slightly more populated than east of the road, up in the mountains, but it was still mostly empty, trackless rainforest.

She walked south until she found a dense thicket away from the trails, where she wouldn't be seen. Then she left the trail and crept into the bushes, in between the branches and leaves. She found a flat, mostly dry, place on the floor of the jungle, and unrolled her sleeping bag. She took another one of the Russian combat rations from her backpack and forced herself to eat the cubes of processed cheese and meat. She couldn't avoid thoughts of fried pork, with chili and onions, as she chewed the rations. They were tasteless, as if she were eating plastic.

But she had done the right thing. She was safe here. She settled into her sleeping bag as she ate and let her thoughts wander. She still couldn't bear to think about what she had seen that afternoon two weeks ago, up on the ridge, when the Russian soldiers had attacked their camp. There was a part of her, inside, that felt dead and empty, as if she would never laugh or smile again. Even her anger, the fury that had built over the past weeks, didn't touch that part of her, that empty sadness and despair. But she forced those thoughts, and the sadness, away. She turned her thoughts back to the present, back to dealing with the jungle trails and the Russians, and back to surviving.

When she was finished eating, she curled up in her sleeping bag. Tomorrow, she would work her way south, along the jungle paths. She would go slowly, and mostly at night, to avoid the local farmers. It would take her days to reach the town, but it would be safe. She slept soundly that night, hidden in the bushes, amidst the noises of the forest.

Chapter 22
Gregori Karpov

He couldn't sit at the checkpoint for another minute. He had been there, in the sweltering, humid jungle for five days, by himself, except for two teenage soldiers, who spoke nothing but some incomprehensible African dialect. There had been nothing to do but watch the occasional local truck stop at the side of the road, and then question the driver and check the vehicle for the girl. They hadn't found her. And none of the truck drivers had seen her. Fucking Petronov. He hadn't signed up to play policeman in the middle of the jungle. He was a Spetsnaz commando, not a piss-ass constable.

He scratched at the sores on his arms. They were covered in bites, from the mosquitos and bed bugs that infested the squalid little room where he slept. He swatted the flies away and then got up and left the hut that they called a checkpoint. The two local soldiers were both asleep, heads buried in their arms on the wooden shelf beneath the window looking onto the road. They had been sleeping all afternoon.

He started to walk along the road, in the direction of the town, then thought better of it. There was nothing in that direction, nothing for at least a half-dozen kilometers. He had walked that way the day before. And he'd walked along the road in the opposite direction, to the north, a couple of days previously. There was nothing there either. He'd try the jungle today. At least it would be out of the sun. He'd walk a few kilometers, away from the heat and smell of the checkpoint.

The trails were wider than they were up in the hills that they had come through on the way down from Uganda. He was only twenty-five kilometers or so from Goma, and the trails were well-worn by local farmers, traveling to the markets in the town. He walked fast along the trail, his long steps eating up the distance. After a day sitting at the checkpoint, it felt good to get out in the open. An hour later, he paused where two paths met at a crossroad in the jungle. He needed to turn back soon. It would be dark in another hour, and he'd rather spend the night in the hut than out here. He decided to walk for another twenty minutes along the new path, that ran north-south, parallel to the road. Then he would turn back.

He almost missed it. It was half a boot print, freshly made, and deeply imprinted in the mud on the side of the trail. African farmers didn't wear hiking boots. Only Petronov's team wore boots. And the girl. She also wore hiking boots. The print had to be hers. None of Petronov's other men were out here.

He thought about the $250,000 bonus they'd been promised. He debated going back to the checkpoint. He hadn't brought his walkie-talkie, or his AK-103. He thought about hurrying back to the checkpoint. But it would take an hour to get back to the road, and then it would be dark. She might disappear again. And he had his machete. Which he wouldn't need. He could take the girl with his hands if he needed. He must be almost twice her size. All he needed to do was track her down, before it got too dark.

Spotting her print was a stroke of luck. He hurried along the trail, eyes scanning the mud for more boot prints. They were there. Every dozen meters or so, he found another track, all the same, all headed towards the town. It had to be her. And the prints were all fresh. They were clean, with nothing on top of them. He walked for another hour, pushing hard as the light faded. The prints looked even fresher. He'd figure out how to get back to the road after he found her. And then he'd figure out how to spend his bonus. The money would make the last week worth it, after all.

It was almost dark now. It was hard to see the trail, and he switched on his flashlight, using it to follow her tracks in the mud. It was slower going now, and he worried that he'd lost her trail. Her tracks had vanished. There was nothing but the blank surface of the path, disappearing into the jungle in both directions. He worked his way another hundred meters or so along the path, moving very slowly now. Her tracks had disappeared. He retraced his steps, back to her last print. There was nothing in between, not a single track.

He stood in the middle of the trail in the fading light, listening to the jungle noises, thinking what she would have done. Then he scanned the bushes on both sides of the path with his flashlight. He finally found it on the right-hand side of the trail. A broken leaf, and then a boot print in the mud a few meters off the path. He eased his way through the undergrowth, following her tracks in the dark. She must have left the trail to find a place to sleep for the night.

He tried to move silently, but it was hard. There were too many bushes and branches. It wouldn't matter though. Even if he didn't surprise her, he could run her down. She wouldn't get far in the dark. He hefted the machete, its grip hard in his hand. He'd try and take her alive though. That way, he could play with her for a while, with nobody disturbing him. Then he saw the backpack, lying at the edge of a bush a dozen meters ahead. The jungle was silent. He switched off his flashlight and crept forward. Maybe he would be able to surprise her after all.

The shots came from out of the forest behind him, from an Uzi, like the one that Mikhail had carried. The bullets caught him in the back, and then in the neck, knocking him forward onto the ground. His face was buried in the mud and leaves, as the forest around him erupted with the shrieks and hoots of the jungle birds and animals. He struggled to turn over and get his nose out of the mud. His legs wouldn't move, but he turned himself over with his arms, turning onto his back, searching the curtain of bushes that surrounded him for signs of whoever had attacked him. He found the machete with one hand and gripped it tightly.

Nothing moved. The jungle was a blank wall of green, dark in the night. The sounds of the birds and monkeys began to die down. He could feel the blood soaking through his shirt and starting to fill his mouth. The bitch was going to leave him here, to bleed to death in the mud. He struggled to stay alert and keep breathing.

He almost didn't hear her. There was only the faintest rustle to his left, like a breeze through the bushes. Then she was there, standing over him in the dark. The bullets had paralyzed his legs and severed something in his throat. He could feel the blood pumping out of his neck. But he was still alive. Just barely. When she leaned over to check whether he was dead, he lashed out with his machete. He was still holding it. He somehow managed to swing it at her, in a vicious looping arc, as if he were throwing a ball at her.

She was quick as a cat, and pivoted towards safety, throwing herself back and away, away from the gleaming blade of his machete. He almost got her in the throat. Almost slashed her jugular and left her there dying in the mud next to him. That would have been good. But he didn't. Instead, the blade just caught her at the edge of her collar bone, slicing through her t-shirt and tracing a line of red across her breast, before her momentum pulled her away, out of his reach. She recovered her footing, then took the bamboo spear that she was carrying, lifted it high over her head and drove it down hard into his chest.

He would have tried to slash her again, but she was standing on his hand, trapping the machete against the ground, underneath her boot. He had hardly been able to see her face in the darkness when she struck with the bamboo spear. Staring up at her now, all he could see was her face, teeth bared in a snarl of hatred and triumph, like a tigress, as she drove the spear into his chest with all her weight. That was the last thing he saw as the darkness closed in on him.

Chapter 23
Ivan Petronov

The compound was in the outskirts of Goma, near the border with Rwanda. It belonged to Nahil Mohamed, a Lebanese trader, whose family had managed to survive three generations of civil war in the Congo. That is, the compound used to belong to the trader. Until Ivan's men cut his throat in the bathroom of his house, four days before.

The trader didn't die before he told them everything that they wanted to know about Goma — who he bribed in the local police force, who would help them and who to avoid. The trader tried to resist, and to bargain for his life, but Ivan's men beat him, with their fists and boots, until he finally gave up and began to talk. After he answered the last of their questions, one of the men drew his knife, walked over to where the trader was tied up and casually slit his throat.

The trader felt a flash of searing pain, and then time had slowed down. He was filled with a detached regret. Regret that he never visited his family's home in Lebanon, that he never properly pursued Aline, the nurse who worked in the local hospital, that he hadn't spent time with his three children. And regret that he hadn't trusted his instincts when the Chinese woman appeared in his dusty little office three days before. Regret that her envelope of cash, with far too many bills, awoke a greed that he couldn't resist. He suspected that something was wrong, that something was too good to be true, but he went along anyway — like a sheep to the slaughter. It was justice, he thought, with perfect serenity; it was what he deserved. He was dead when they laid him in his bathtub, on top of his brother's body.

Petronov came in from the compound's courtyard, towards what used to be the trader's living room. A large-scale map of the region around Goma and Lake

Kivu was spread out on a table in the center of the room. The room was window-less and dark, lit by a single metal lantern, hanging from the ceiling. The walls of the room were lined with stacks of cardboard boxes, filled with clothes, canned food, farm tools, DVDs, and other things that the trader sold to the locals.

Yan and Maxim were standing by the table, looking over the map. They both looked unhappy.

"What now?" he demanded.

Maxim shook his head, looked at Yan, and then reluctantly delivered the latest report.

"Gregori disappeared from his checkpoint last night. The soldiers at the check-point saw him in the afternoon, but he left sometime before dark, and didn't come back. The soldiers found his body in the morning, a few kilometers away, hidden in the jungle. Someone shot him in the head, then stuck a spear through his chest. Just like the others."

Petronov swore, then kicked the refrigerator. "Fucking bitch. How did that happen?"

He kicked the refrigerator again, hard, denting the door with his boot.

"Gregori left his weapon at the checkpoint. He probably went for a walk, wanted some fresh air. She must have ambushed him."

"Stupid shit. How can you leave your weapon lying around? No wonder he's dead." Petronov cursed again.

"Where'd it happen?" he demanded.

Maxim showed him where they had found the body, pointing to the map. He squinted at the map, then sat down at the table.

"It's only fifteen kilometers from Goma. She's definitely headed here," he said.

Maxim nodded, and then went on. "The good news is that Gregori wounded her, maybe badly. He apparently slashed her with his machete before she finished him off. We don't know where he got her, but there was lots of blood on the machete."

He thought for a while. If Gregori had hit something vital, then the girl would probably be dead. Even if he hadn't, there would be blood loss, maybe infection. She would need medical help. They were also on her trail again. She had only a few hours lead now, he guessed, but they would be going faster. Losing another man was bad news, but there was a silver lining.

"She'll have to get to town fast now," he said. "And she'll need a doctor. Bring everyone except Dmitri and Alexander back into town. Watch the hospital. And the doctor's offices and pharmacies. That's where she'll go. Have Dmitri and Alexander track her from Gregori's body. She may stop to rest or maybe die. Remind them about the bonus."

"OK boss." Maxim disappeared outside and started making calls.

He sat for a few minutes at the table, staring at the map again. He finished his coffee, then peered around the room. She followed his gaze, then walked to the stove and brought the pot to the table, before pouring him another cup of coffee. She leaned over as she handed him the cup, kissed his cheek gently and whispered "Good morning" into his ear. He nodded back and kept staring at the map.

"She'll come this way," he said, tracing his index finger along the road from the north, along the shore of Lake Kivu. "She'll come along this stretch of the road."

"Maxim," he called into the courtyard.

Maxim hurried back inside and he told him to have the men focus on the hotels and roads in the north of the town, along the lake. That's where they would find her, he said. Maxim left again, to make more phone calls.

Gregori's death wasn't bad news at all, he decided. The girl's options were narrowing, like an animal being driven into a trap. She had to come to town and she had to see a doctor. And she needed somewhere to stay. There weren't many choices, and his men would watch them all. They just had to be patient, wait another day, and she would walk right into their arms.

Chapter 24
Sara West

She sat in a cluster of bushes, across the road from a native hut. It was near the outskirts of Goma, past the last military checkpoint on the road leading to the town from the north. She had bypassed the last three checkpoints, and the local soldiers who manned them, instead staying on the network of trails that criss-crossed the jungle.

She was tired. She had walked all night, putting as much distance as she could between the Russian's body and herself. The soldier had almost surprised her the night before. He must have tracked her boot prints on the trail, and then tried to creep up on her. If not for the noises that he made, and the light from his flashlight, she might have missed him. But the light had alerted her in time to get the Uzi out of her pack, and then to slip out of her sleeping bag and hide in the jungle, waiting in the dark until he arrived.

He had still nearly killed her with his machete. She touched the wound on her breast unconsciously. It ached. She had used painkillers and iodine from the medical pack she took from one of the Russians. But the wound didn't seem to be healing and it hurt a little worse with every passing hour. It needed attention and soon. Or it would start to fester. She needed to get into Goma and find some way to attend to the cut.

The hut she was watching had been hastily built. Its thatched roof was uneven, and the walls were poorly constructed, made from mud and rough wooden planks. The hut's only window had no glass, just a piece of tattered cloth to keep out the insects. There were three children, barely more than infants, and a young girl, in a cleared space in front of the hut. The girl must be their mother, although she could not have been more than a teenager. No one else was in sight.

She had watched the hut for the past hour. There was only a little traffic on the road, mostly local trucks, laden with goods and people, and occasionally, shiny white and blue Range Rovers. The children played games on the side of the road, chasing one another with sticks and tumbling in the dust. The girl fetched water from a makeshift well, pounded manioc, and tended the fire. Neither the girl nor her children had any idea she was watching them.

There were other travelers on the road here. They walked, usually women and usually barefoot, or pedaled impossibly old bicycles. Almost everyone carried something, often on their heads — baskets of fruit or fish, piles of firewood, bundles of clothing, baby goats, everything imaginable. They walked in both directions, heading into and away from the town. In the evenings, when the air grew cold, they would swath themselves in thin, brightly colored cloth — reds, yellows, and blues, all with bold patterns, faded from the African sun, worn from being washed too many times on hard rocks with cheap soap.

She watched the silent procession of figures, wrapped in cloth, balancing bundles and baskets on their heads, walking through the dusk along the road towards the town. The guards at the checkpoints didn't stop these silent figures. They probably had no papers to inspect or money to extort. The checkpoints were for the trucks and cars, which had both.

She waited until dark, and then made her way out of the bushes. The hut was quiet, the children and their mother sleeping inside. No one saw her pad along the road, then across the clearing in front of the house, to where the family's tiny collection of clothes was drying, stretched out on a bush. She walked past the hut, not making a sound. She found two squares of cloth, pulled them down and folded them into her pack. At the door to the house, she picked up the mother's sandals, putting them into her pack as well.

She felt guilty, about stealing things from people who had nothing. She started to leave something, but hesitated, then almost decided not to. Anything of value might attract attention and get reported back to one of the checkpoints, or elsewhere. Then her conscience got the better of her, and she left a cooking pot she had taken from the Russians on the ground next to the bush. When she was finished, she slipped back across the road and into the jungle.

Six hours later, and three kilometers away, an hour before dawn, a tall market woman emerged out of the jungle, on the outskirts of Goma. The woman was wrapped in orange and yellow cloth, wore rubber sandals and carried a large bundle of clothing, balanced on her head. She walked slowly along the road, keeping pace with the villagers who were also making their way to the market, using a bamboo stick to help keep her balance. The woman's face was shrouded beneath the cloth. In the dark, no one could see her features. She was another local trader, taking goods to town to sell.

At the edge of town, the road ran along the lake — Lake Kivu. The waters of the lake were dark grey in the early morning. Along the road was a row of buildings. Most of them were just a single story; the larger ones were two, or occasionally three, stories. They were built out of concrete and cinder blocks, with corrugated metal roofs. Only a few of the structures were painted, usually in white or faded reds and greens. Most of the buildings were stores, selling Chinese household goods, African cloth, local food stuffs, and Hollywood videos. Security guards with thick wooden poles sat on plastic chairs perched outside most store fronts, the better establishments employing men in worn uniforms and boots.

She walked along the road, the sandals chafing her feet. The street was nearly empty, only a few stray dogs and the occasional passerby making his way along the lake. She passed several guesthouses before she reached one that looked promising. It was a three-story building with a sign that said "Hotel Savoy." The lettering on the sign was faded, and the phone number had been repainted what looked like countless times. The front door was open and a tiny Indian woman, dressed in a fluorescent pink sari that was much too large for her, sat behind a massive wooden counter. The old woman was barely visible over the top of the counter, which had been built with someone much larger in mind. The woman was fast asleep.

On a panel behind the counter were a dozen hooks, with a dozen keys dangling like fresh-caught fish on lines. A bare lightbulb hung from the ceiling, illuminating years of grime that had collected in the entranceway. A collage of hand-written signs on the wall behind the woman announced the prices for rooms, disclaimers of liability and rules against farm animals, guns, and whoring.

The tall market woman slipped out of the native cloth as she entered the doorway, easing the cloth-covered bundle off her head and shaking her hair loose. By the time the hotelkeeper had begun to stir, the market woman was gone and an intrepid young Western girl, with long blonde hair and a well-worn backpack, was asking for a room. A room, please, with a lakeside view and a sink.

Chapter 25
Shrati Singh

The blonde backpacker woke her up. She hadn't slept well the night before and was dozing at her desk in the lobby when the girl arrived, asking for a room. She quoted the girl an exorbitant price for one of the rooms on the second floor, the way she did with all the Western backpackers.

The girl negotiated, but without really trying, and ended up overpaying. The girl didn't seem to mind though, just looking evenly at her, then smiling and paying with a worn $20 bill that she extracted from a compartment in her pack. The look and the smile had made her feel guilty about cheating the girl. She considered returning some change, but then decided not to. It would have been embarrassing. And they always needed more money.

So, she pocketed the bill and picked out one of the keys that were hanging behind her, then led the way upstairs. The room had a sink, which the girl had asked for, but no toilet or shower. Those were at the end of the hallway. Hot water cost extra, she pointed out. The girl had only nodded. She also asked the girl for her passport, but she had refused. Mrs. Singh didn't mind. She wasn't going to keep a record of the guest; most of the hotel's business was off the books anyway.

The girl asked if there was anything to eat. Mrs. Singh gave the girl the name of her cousin's restaurant, just a few hundred meters further along the lakeside. But the girl said that she didn't want to go out. Instead, she asked if she could eat in her room. She said she would like fried pork and roast chicken, a whole roast chicken, a large one, with flatbread. And chilies with onions.

"Could you bring the food up?" the girl asked politely, looking right at her. The girl's eyes looked sad, she thought to herself — very pretty, but sad.

This time she gave the girl the price that she would charge the locals. She wasn't sure why. It might have been the girl's quiet politeness, or gentle smile, or her eyes. But she didn't want to cheat her again. She promised to bring the food up to the room, then stood awkwardly by the window and watched the girl for a moment, arranging her backpack on the bed. The girl was different, she thought to herself. Most of the backpackers wanted to eat outside, where they might find other travelers.

Maybe it was because her clothes were so dirty. Mrs. Singh was accustomed to messy tourists, with long hair, unwashed clothes, and bad manners. But the girl's clothes were much worse than any she had seen before. Her jeans were ripped and torn, with dirt and mud worn deep into the creases. They looked as if the girl had slept in them for weeks on end, in the jungle. Her t-shirt was just as bad, stained with dirt and sweat. And her boots were dirty, badly scuffed and caked in thick, dark mud. The girl's clothes contrasted with her manners, which were polite and quiet, not careless or pushy like so many of the aid workers and tourists.

And she was beautiful. Not just pretty, but beautiful, the kind of beautiful that you usually only saw in movies. Grey eyes, set wide over chiseled cheeks, and a full mouth. Blonde hair, still dirty from the road, and very badly cut on one side, but thick and luxuriant, like a lion's mane. It was the girl's eyes, though, that caught Mrs. Singh, as she still stood there, despite her imminent dismissal. Impossibly large and liquid. But also sad, somehow, sad beyond words. They had the same sadness as the eyes of the native women, the women who had seen their husbands and children killed before them in the senseless war that never seemed to end.

The girl looked right at her, watching closely while they stood there. She realized that there was something more than sadness in the girl's eyes. There was also a strength, that she never saw in the tourists or the aid workers or the native women. A cold, hard determination, that made her feel small and uncertain. She played nervously with the end of her sari, and looked down at the floor, wishing that she had swept it properly before the girl had arrived.

Then she realized that she should prepare the girl's food, the way she had said she would, and hurried back downstairs to the kitchen, leaving the girl alone. She wondered about the girl as she prepared the food. There weren't many backpackers these days. The war made it too dangerous for them. And there were never Western women traveling alone anymore. Much less sleeping alone in the jungle. She wondered why the girl would do that. The girl must be very brave, she thought. Or very stupid. But she didn't seem stupid. Just the opposite. She wondered again what the girl was doing by herself in a place like this.

She brought the food upstairs an hour later. She was curious now, and instead of leaving, she sat on the edge of the bed and watched as the girl helped herself to the food. The girl nodded, nearly smiled, as Mrs. Singh sat down on the bed, but then ignored her while she ate. The girl was well-mannered, for a backpacker, especially such a dirty one, but that didn't stop her from devouring everything that Mrs. Singh had brought her. She consumed the entire roast chicken — not a small one, Mrs. Singh thought with a tinge of regret — in only a few minutes. And all the fried pork, plus the flat bread, just as quickly. It was as if she hadn't eaten properly in weeks.

When the girl was finished, the plate was clean, except for a small pile of bones, left neatly to one side, each of them licked completely clean. She folded her napkin and laid it next to the bones on the plate. Then the girl smiled at her and Mrs. Singh realized, with another tinge of regret, that she was going to be dismissed.

"I am sorry, but now I need to rest. I have come very far," the girl said gently.

"Yes. Of course, my child," she said, then stopped, embarrassed at the familiarity that she had blurted out.

The girl smiled at her. Warm, like sunshine on the lake in the afternoon. She hesitated again. Then she told her.

"Men came here earlier, asking about someone. Someone like you." She said this quietly, hesitantly.

The girl watched her intently now, eyes steady. Her smile was gone, the warmth vanished, like the sun behind the clouds.

"They said that they would pay money. And they showed a picture of someone like you," she continued.

The girl watched her, then asked, "What did you say?"

"I said I hadn't seen anyone."

The girl watched her. "Why?"

She looked at the girl. "I don't know."

That was the truth. She didn't know why she had shrugged at the men's questions and looked back to the chicken roasting in the oven. She didn't know why she had ignored the offer of money, more money than the girl would ever pay her. She didn't know why she had lied to the men.

The girl smiled again. Warm and gentle. Like sunshine on the lake. Now she knew why. The smile made her feel alive and strong again.

"You must take care. They were not good men. Very bad ones," she told the girl.

Mrs. Singh knew what she spoke of. She had survived twenty years of Congolese civil war. She had watched successive armies come and go. She had seen the worst of men — white, brown, and black men. Men who had thankfully always ignored her. They would rather have her meals and bed, than an old, skinny Indian woman.

But she had seen them kill each other, and do much worse, far worse. She had seen them kill the farmers and their wives, especially their wives. Seen them stake young men out on the ground and cut them apart like animals. Seen them chop off arms and ears and noses. Seen them kill her own husband, years ago. And she had watched their eyes when they were done. The men today had the same eyes. Cold and evil. Like snakes.

The girl said, "I know, mother. I have seen." Her eyes were hard and distant again, her smile gone.

And Mrs. Singh knew then where the girl's strength came from. Knew where that steady calm came from. She wondered what the girl had seen, wondered what had happened to her out in the jungle. Whatever it was, she knew that it had not killed the girl, had not made her small, the way Mrs. Singh had become, but instead had made her strong. She stood up and walked over to her. She felt braver now. She embraced the girl, her tiny frame pressed against the girl's solid body, hardened by the past month in the jungle, enveloped in her arms. Then she left, before she cried in front of the girl, hurrying downstairs with the plate of little bones, making sure not to spill them on the stairs.

The men were standing there in the dark. Waiting for her in the kitchen when she turned on the light. Eyes watching her. Cold and evil. Like snakes.

Chapter 26
Ivan Petronov

They stood in the hotel's kitchen. He considered sending the men upstairs right away, but then decided not to. Let the girl go to sleep first. She had a gun — one of their Uzis. And probably some of their grenades. There was no reason to give her a chance to use them. Either let her come downstairs, unsuspecting, and surprise her, or wait and let her go to sleep, then take her in the night. In the meantime, they would bring in the other men, and cordon off the roads near the hotel. Maxim went outside and started making phone calls, summoning the team to the hotel.

The Indian woman's body was sprawled on the floor. She had surprised them. Despite the gag, she had lunged across a counter, grabbed for a kitchen knife, and then slashed Alexei's face, almost cutting his throat. He broke her neck then, with a single vicious blow to the head. The stupid bitch. Didn't she know any better, after living in this place for years? He wondered what had come over the old woman. He kicked her body into the corner. It weighed next to nothing, like a small child.

Despite the Indian woman's lies, they found the blonde bitch. A merchant from a shop down the road had seen the girl, or at least someone who might be her, in the hotel entrance that morning. He had eagerly described the girl, as well as Mrs. Singh's hotel, in return for promises of cash. He had also turned his store over to Petronov's men, who crowded into the back rooms with their guns and bags. He had watched greedily, eyeing their watches and equipment. This was too good to be true, he thought. Finally, a gift from God, the chance for enough money to leave this awful place.

He was right. It was too good to be true. His body was lying in the corner of his store. He hadn't felt a thing. As he turned around, to make tea that the men demanded, one of them had cut his throat with a bayonet. He was dead almost as soon as his body hit the ground. He hadn't heard the Russians laughing at the way his eyes rolled up into their sockets and his mouth gaped open as he lay sprawled on the concrete floor. And he hadn't seen them sitting around his table, his father's table, planning how they would kill the girl as well.

It was just before 7:00 p.m. when they heard her door open upstairs. Night was falling and it was nearly dark outside. They were waiting in the dining room and kitchen of the hotel, out of sight. Six men, all former Spetsnaz special forces, with eighty years of combat experience between them. They heard her boots on the floor above them and knew that she was at the top of the staircase, looking down onto the reception desk.

"Come on bitch," he thought to himself.

"Mama," she called out, in a low, resonant voice.

There was no answer. She called again. "Mama."

Silence. They waited for her to come down the stairs. Still silence. The minutes passed, each one slower than the one before. They listened for her footsteps. There wasn't a sound. The men outside watched the hotel's windows now. He had ordered them out of the merchant's shop, to encircle the hotel in case she tried to jump from one of the windows. Nothing moved.

He grimaced. They couldn't keep the street blocked off much longer without attracting attention. They would have to do it the hard way. The fallback plan was simple. First, two men up the stairway, then two more following. The rest of the team would maintain the perimeter.

Pytor and Maxim crept silently up the stairs. At the top of the staircase, they stopped, then headed towards her bedroom. It was the only room in the hotel that was occupied. It was just them and her.

The two men scanned the hall in front of them, eying the doorway, which was half-open, then the other doors on the floor, which were all closed. Nothing moved. They edged soundlessly into the hallway.

They crept across the corridor to the door to her room, and eased it open a little further. The lights inside the room were off. They used their flashlights, but the room looked empty. Pytor kicked the door open wide and waited a moment. Still nothing.

Pytor stepped into the bedroom just in time to catch the full force of the grenade. She had hung it at the top of the door frame, positioning it cleverly, so it couldn't be seen. When the door opened fully, the safety pin was released. Five seconds later, the grenade had detonated, killing Pytor instantly, blowing his head off his body, sending it rolling unevenly along the floor to rest against the opposite wall in the hallway, leaving a wet trail of blood behind it.

Maxim was right behind Pytor and blinded by the blast. The shrapnel from the grenade lashed his face, putting out both of his eyes. He fired wildly into the room. He couldn't see the door to the toilet at the far end of the hallway opening silently and the girl firing two shots into his head, before easing the door shut again. Then the hallway went silent again, suddenly, as if a movie had been stopped in mid-frame.

Alexei and Vladimir were starting up the staircase when the girl shot Maxim. They hesitated when they heard the shots, then rushed up the rest of the stairs. Alexei led the way, his AK-103 spraying shots into the hallway, then into the girl's bedroom. Vladimir knelt at the top of the stairs and waited, his weapon ready, braced against his shoulder. Alexei crouched outside the girl's room, then fit a new magazine into his rifle.

The hotel was quiet again. Outside, neighborhood dogs barked wildly and roosters crowed. They could hear voices shouting in the distance. Inside, nothing moved. The hallway was filled with smoke and the smell of gunpowder. Only one of the ceiling lights had survived the fighting, and it was nearly lost in the smoke, leaving the hall in shadowy half-light.

Alexei turned, then leveled his AK-103 at the door to the bedroom across the hall from the girl's room. He triggered a long burst at the door, ripping the cheap wood apart and wrecking the door handle. He walked to the door and kicked it in effortlessly with one heavy mountain boot, then hosed another burst of bullets into the room. Then he disappeared inside. A moment later he returned. He repeated the same process with the next three bedrooms on the floor. She wasn't in either of those rooms either.

That left two doors, standing shut at the end of the hallway. Alexei turned and faced the doors. He took a fresh magazine from his belt and reloaded his weapon. He fired first at the door to the left, a short burst, and then at the right-hand door, a longer burst. When he was finished, the hotel fell silent again. He crept towards the two doors, half-crouched, keeping against the wall to his right. He moved silently, despite the shell casings and debris on the floor. When he reached the end of the hall, he signaled to Vladimir. The two men directed withering fusillades at each of the two doors.

The instant he stopped firing, Alexei sprang forward, ramming the door on the right open with his boot. The door ripped off its hinges, revealing what remained of a bathroom, the walls pock-marked with bullet holes and the porcelain toilet lying in pieces on the floor, water spraying from a ruptured pipe. He edged inside and then backed away again, nodding towards the door on the left. Alexei was about to kick the second door down when a long burst of gunfire came out of the room from behind the door. The bullets caught him in the neck and face, hurling him backwards onto the floor. He died instantly, his face a bloody ruin.

The hotel was silent again. Vladimir retreated down three stairs and crouched, gun leveled at the remaining door, at the end of the hallway. What remained of the door was pock-marked with bullet holes, both exit and entry marks. Four more of the Spetsnaz soldiers, summoned inside by Petronov joined Vladimir at the top of the stairs. They whispered briefly, and Vladimir scuttled forward through the half-light, slipping into one of the rooms along the hallway. One of the other men crept forward and disappeared into the next room. The last three soldiers crouched at the top of the stairs. They waited for Vladimir's signal.

Vladimir's signal never came. In rapid succession, blasts coming from the bed-rooms and on the staircase sent bodies sprawling into the hallway, uniforms and limbs shredded by shrapnel. At almost the same time, the clatter of heavy machine guns erupted. The noise and gun fire came from outside the hotel, from shiny white Range Rovers that had suddenly appeared along the road, ripping apart the Russians' bodies and what was left of the rooms. Smoke filled the hallway, pouring from one of the bedrooms and from a half dozen metal smoke canisters that rolled noisily along the concrete floor.

After a moment, the gunfire stopped. The hotel went silent again, this time punctuated by the crackling of fire from one of the rooms. Nothing else moved.

Outside, in the dark, he ran along the tiny alleyway that led away from the lake front road. The alley stank of shit. Everything that walked in Goma — hu-mans, dogs, and goats — had shit in this alley. He had been alone, outside the hotel, when his men were attacked. He had sent all of the remaining Spetsnaz soldiers upstairs to get the girl, while he waited outside in the alley.

He had watched silently then, as his men were themselves attacked, from be-hind, by another team of soldiers, who had arrived suddenly in five blue and white Range Rovers. He didn't know who they were, but there were at least a dozen of them, and they were very serious professionals, who had dispatched what was left of his team in barely a minute.

After that, he fled into the night, past the back door of the kitchen and then down the alley, away from the hotel and whoever had attacked his men. He had no idea what had happened. He ran wildly, panting and desperate, through the empty alleyways of the town. He barely knew where he was going. He couldn't do anything more than run as fast as he could into the night, away from the hotel and whoever it was that had wiped out his men.

Chapter 27
Jeb Fisher

He crouched next to Wilson in the entrance to the hotel on the lake front road. Smoke billowed out of the windows of the hotel, while dogs and sirens wailed in the distance. The air was heavy with the smell of gunpowder, burning rubber, and smoke.

"That was fucking awesome," Wilson whispered.

Wilson was right. It had gone exactly as planned, without a single casualty on their side.

Wilson continued. "Listen. Your team goes up the stairs. Now, and fast. The locals will be here soon, if this place doesn't burn down first. The girl is probably dead by now. Get in there, get her files, and let's go home. If she's still alive, she'll be in shock after all this. Take zero chances. If you shoot the bitch, all the better. But get the fucking files."

"Got it," he replied.

Fisher crept through the darkened ground floor reception area of the hotel to Smith and Powell, his teammates.

"So. We go up the stairs on three. Quietly. When we get to the room where she's hiding, I go in, you both cover me."

They nodded and the three men made their way through the wreckage of the hotel that littered the staircase, stepping over the bodies of Russian soldiers. Almost all of the hotel's lights were out and they used flashlights and headlamps, which cast pale shafts of light through the smoke that filled the stairway. When he reached the top of the stairs, he paused, gesturing for Smith and Powell to cover him from there. They knew from their thermal imaging that the girl was in the shower room, on the left, at the far end of the hall.

"When I get to the door, give me thirty seconds of fire into the room behind me. Nothing into the shower but make lots of noise. After that, wait for my signal before you do anything," he instructed.

Smith and Powell nodded. Fisher crept forward along the wall, easing past the Russian bodies strewn along the passage. He avoided the broken glass and concrete, padding soundlessly down the corridor. He wouldn't make the mistakes that the Russians had. Better to use surprise on the girl. If she was still alive.

He paused at one of the bedrooms and waited for a moment, listening for sounds from the far end of the hallway. It was silent, except for the sounds from the streets.

He wondered how it had come to this. How the girl had come so far. It had been nearly three weeks since they had begun chasing her. Two small armies of killers, equipped with some of the world's best weapons, as well as a half dozen helicopters. And here he was, sneaking up on her, with fifteen dead Spetsnaz troops marking the trail she had taken.

He crept back into the corridor and inched towards the door at the far end of the hallway. He knew exactly where she would be — in the shower room, crouched behind a chest-high concrete wall that was what passed for a shower stall in this part of the world. The wall had protected her from the Russians' bullets.

He was sure she would still be there, waiting for the shooting to start again. This time it wouldn't. He slipped silently through the ruined doorway and into the shower room, just as Smith and Powell opened up into the other room at the end of the hallway. The racket was deafening, as two M-16s on full automatic blasted away.

The shower room was mostly dark, with only a dim silvery light coming in from a streetlamp outside the hotel, but he knew where to go. He slipped forward, barely lifting his boots off the floor. By the time the covering fire stopped, he was crouched in the dark on the outside of the chest-high shower stall, his head just beneath the edge of the wall. The hotel was quiet once more, with only the sounds of a fire still burning in one of the bedrooms. He paused for a moment in the darkness, waiting for her breathing to give her away, so that he could pounce on her. The room was completely silent, like a graveyard. Maybe the Russians had finally killed her after all.

She almost got him. She rammed the bamboo spear down from the top of the wall of the shower stall. The tip of the shaft buried itself in his body armor, only barely missing his unprotected neck. If he had been leaning just a little in either direction, he would be dead. Instead, the spear was stuck in his Kevlar jacket, and he turned fluidly, in a single motion, letting the momentum of her thrust pull her down, over the wall, into his arms. He let his M-16 slip to the side of his thigh, then pinioned both her hands effortlessly in one of his and clamped the other hand around her throat. He trapped her legs against the shower wall, using his weight to keep her from struggling.

He could see her in the glow of the streetlight, coming in through the shattered window behind them. Her hair was a golden tangle of curls, radiant in the half-light. Her cheeks were flushed and there was a sheen of sweat on her brow. She was frightened, her breath a little ragged and uneven. But her gaze was calm, taking him in with wary assessment, out of impossibly large grey eyes. He struggled not to stare at her. He also didn't kill her, the way Reid had instructed.

Instead, he said, "You have sixty seconds. What's going on?" It wasn't a question. It was a command.

She didn't scream when he took his hand off her throat. She looked at him and answered in a calm, even voice.

"I don't know. They attacked us. The Russians. Then killed them, all my friends. I don't know why."

"I don't believe you. That kind of stuff doesn't just happen for no reason. They're hunting you for something. Thirty seconds to tell me or I do what I'm supposed to do — kill you, or let them kill you, which I really don't want to do."

She looked at him closely, appraisingly.

Then she told him. "In my backpack. Files. Nazi files from a plane that we found by accident. It was wrecked in the jungle. Files showing where billions of dollars were hidden by the Nazis. And who the Nazis' secret friends were."

He paused. "I still don't believe you. That can't be."

"Let me show you. The papers. In my pack." Her voice was soft and steady.

He laughed. "Sure. And another spear in my neck?"

"You hold me. I swear. I won't try. And I'm out of spears anyway."

He didn't trust her. He was trained not to trust people, especially people in her position. So he held her tight, while letting her reach across him and retrieve her backpack. Then he let her open the pack, take out a thick file of papers, and hand him a sheet of paper from the top of the stack. It was a very old, thin piece of paper, with Nazi letterhead and archaic typewritten font, that he could just manage to read in the light from the window. He looked at what the paper said.

He frowned, then loosened his grip, just a bit. His German was good enough for him to see that she was telling the truth, at least about this paper.

The paper was headed "Freundeskreis" — "Friends of the Third Reich." There was a list of typewritten names. He recognized a couple of the names on the list. They were from well-known European families. He also recognized the first name on the list. It was Franklin Kerrington II, the father of Franklin Kerrington III — Deputy Director of the CIA. The man who wanted the girl dead. The man who had made up lies about who the girl was and what she had done. The man who had sent him out here to retrieve the file — the file with this piece of paper.

He wasn't sure how it all fit together. But he knew that Reid and Kerrington had lied to him. The girl really was a botany student, a scientist, just like the university websites said. She hadn't spied for the Russians, or anyone else, and she hadn't stolen secret weapons plans. Everything Kerrington had told them was a lie.

And the girl's story about the Nazi bomber sounded honest. He'd seen the wreckage of the plane himself. The Nazi documents looked authentic, certainly more authentic than anyone could manufacture, even if they wanted to, in the middle of the Congo jungle. And if the document was real, then Kerrington would have every reason to want to recover the file, and to want the girl dead. Which was exactly what Kerrington had hired him to do. It all fit together. And it was all wrong. Very wrong. The girl wasn't someone bad. Kerrington was the bad guy. And Reid. Not the girl.

"Now what?" she asked.

He didn't know. But he didn't get a chance to answer her. Or even to think about the answer. Smith, followed by Powell and a third man, burst into the shower room, guns leveled at them and ready to fire.

He reacted out of instinct, reinforced by years of training. He swiveled the M-16 away from her, onto Kerrington's three men. They reacted just the way he had, starting to bring their weapons to bear on him. He didn't hesitate then, pulling the trigger and sweeping the men with point-blank automatic fire. All three went down, bullets shredding their vests and helmets.

He didn't have a chance to think about what he did next either. He stuffed the files back into her pack, slung it over his shoulder and then grabbed her arm. He half-pulled her out into the darkened hallway, then into one of the bedrooms facing the back of the hotel. He pulled her across the room to the window, kicked it open with his boot, and stepped up onto the window ledge. He lifted her up, then held her tightly against his torso as he jumped down onto the top of the hotel's water tanks, and then into the alley.

The passageway stank. He pulled her along the alley and then slipped onto a side street a block away. A blue and white Range Rover was parked at the corner. He approached it from the driver's side, then tapped on the window. The driver opened the window and he reached in. A long knife had appeared in his hand and he slashed it across the man's throat, opening a glistening red gash. Blood spurted over the man's shirt and the steering wheel of the car. He opened the door and pulled the man's body out, letting it fall onto the road. He pushed her into the car, across the driver's seat and onto the passenger side, then climbed into the car after her.

"Buckle up," he ordered her. He didn't wait for an answer. His eyes were scanning the street behind them. Making sure that Reid's men hadn't followed yet.

She obeyed wordlessly. She also took the backpack from him, checked the top flap, then clipped it shut when she saw that everything was there. She watched him silently. The keys were in the ignition. He started the engine, pulled the car out of the side street, then drove, fast, heading into the center of town. After ten minutes, they passed another Range Rover, this one painted dark green, parked inside a fenced compound. He turned into the next alley, parking the car in the dark.

"Come. Fast." More commands.

She obeyed again. They hurried onto the street, then into the compound. The security guard smiled at them. He smiled back, an easy, open grin, as if the guard was an old friend. And then he slammed his forearm into the man's face. The guard collapsed without a sound. There were keys on the guard's belt that he used to open the compound gate. After a moment of tinkering with the ignition wires, the engine on the Range Rover sprang to life. He steered the car out of the compound and then back the way they had come, heading out of town this time.

He drove fast. He had to get them away from Reid and his men. It was bumpy, as he swerved to avoid the potholes and piles of trash. He rolled down the windows, and the wind blew her hair across her eyes like a veil. She was beautiful. Dirty, tired, and frightened, but beautiful.

He wondered again how it had come to this. You didn't mess with this kind of people. You especially didn't mess with Reid and Kerrington. He was good, he knew that. Probably the best. But Reid's men would be after them soon. There would always be more of them, an endless succession of replacements that would never stop coming, with inexhaustible resources and eyes everywhere. Someday, somewhere, he would make a mistake. And then it would be over, for both of them.

He tried to make sense out of what had happened, how he had ended up here, along a dirt road in Africa on his way to nowhere. Three weeks ago, even thirty minutes ago, everything had been fine. Then he had met the girl. And now he was as good as dead. He forced those thoughts away and turned back to the road, then glanced at the girl again. She looked back at him through her hair, eyes calm, watching silently as he drove through the dark.

Chapter 28
Franklin Kerrington III

He wore grey slacks, a crisply pressed white shirt, and a maroon cashmere sweater. His loafers were handmade, by the same Italian shoemaker who had supplied his father, and polished to a glossy shine. His hair was neatly trimmed, every strand in place, the same grooming displayed by the more successful members of Congress.

He stood by the French doors, looking into the courtyard. The sun was starting to set, and the neatly trimmed trees around the fountain cast long shadows onto the gravel paths. He listened to Reid's report on the phone while he looked into the courtyard.

Reid briefed him on the raid in Goma. They still weren't sure exactly what had happened. The Russians had been neutralized. A perfect operation. Eleven dead Spetsnaz troops in the hotel and the adjacent store where they had been surprised. In addition, both Russian helicopters had been destroyed on the ground. At best, there were a couple of survivors — two out of the original fifteen or so.

But the girl, and her files, had eluded them again. She had been cornered, but somehow managed to kill three of Reid's men, and then to escape from the hotel, along with the files. There had been a dozen men surrounding the building, but she had slipped through their perimeter. She also apparently then found and stole one of Reid's vehicles, killing another of his men in the process. And after that she vanished, not leaving a trace behind. They were still looking for her trail.

And then there was Fisher. He was missing. Maybe he was dead too, like the other four casualties they had lost. Or maybe she had turned him or taken him hostage. They hadn't found his body at the hotel or anywhere else. He probably was still alive. The working hypothesis was that he had gone rogue, for unknown reasons, and was helping the girl. But it was just as likely that the Russians had gotten them both. Or, that Fisher had been working with the Russians, or someone else, all along. The truth was, they didn't know what happened, either with Fisher or the girl.

He stared into the courtyard and frowned. "This doesn't make any sense. Why would this guy go rogue. He isn't dumb," he said.

"It makes no sense. None at all," Reid agreed.

"What do you know about Fisher? Who is this guy?" Kerrington demanded.

Reid resisted the urge to remind Kerrington that Fisher was his idea. Instead, he said, "Fisher's one of the best that I've ever seen. The training record you sent over was as good as anyone I've ever worked with. And completely straight. Never a whiff of anything crooked."

"A Boy Scout, maybe?" Kerrington wondered aloud.

"A bit of one. But manageable, I thought. And he was fine all the way along this operation. No hints of anything weird." Reid paused.

Kerrington wondered if he had made a mistake. Maybe Fisher wasn't working with the Russians, or anyone else. Maybe Fisher was really just doing what he thought the right thing was. That thought awakened the dark knot in his stomach again. Maybe the girl's files were as bad as he feared. Maybe it was the files that convinced Fisher to go rogue.

Reid continued. "The truth is, we don't know what happened. Maybe the Russians or someone else got both Fisher and the girl."

Kerrington stood for a moment, looking into the courtyard and trying to control his rising anxiety.

He dismissed Reid's theory. "That can't be. You wiped the Russians out, right? Who would have been left to snatch the girl and Fisher? Especially if he's as good as you say."

"Maybe someone got lucky. Maybe they had a look-out who kept his head down until Fisher came by." Reid's voice made it clear he didn't think this was very likely.

"Maybe. But I doubt it," he said.

Reid paused, then continued. "Worst case scenario: Fisher might have sold out. Maybe the Russians turned him."

"Turned the Boy Scout? What would you need to pay someone to do something this dumb? Nobody in their right mind would make an enemy of us," he said dismissively.

"I know. Hard to imagine. But who knows what they can sell her files for."

He exploded at Reid's mention of the files. "What the fuck happened? Reid, this is your fucking mission. Figure it out. Then fix it."

Kerrington hardly ever lost his temper.

"Yes, sir." Reid saw that there was no point pushing back. And he had dropped the ball. He should have made sure that Fisher wasn't alone with the girl. And he should have made sure that the perimeter was tighter. Those were mistakes.

Reid tried to look at the bright side. "We have another dozen men coming in from Djibouti, plus three more copters. We've started patrolling the roads around Goma and we'll step it up in the morning. There'll be ten cars in action by noon. And we'll make sure the police and military checkpoints are working with us. She can't get far, with or without Fisher."

Reid added, "We have people at every airport and bus station in the area. We have a watch on flights from anywhere in the region. We caught her once. We'll do it again. Plus, there's no competition this time. The Russians are out of the game."

Kerrington listened. Reid's arrangements were fine. They were the best damage control they could manage.

Reid continued. "If our friends at NSA can try and find that Range Rover, it would help. I don't see her going back into the jungle. If we find the car, we find her."

"OK. I'll get that going for you." Kerrington's response was curt.

Kerrington hung up and looked back into the courtyard. The shadows were even longer now. He turned away and tried to put Reid and the girl out of his mind, attending instead to the business of the Agency and Washington politics.

But his thoughts kept drifting back to the girl and Fisher, and to the files. In the end, he gave up and poured himself a whiskey, then stood watching the water splashing in the fountain as he sipped it. He wondered where the two of them were and what they were planning. And how they expected to escape his men.

Chapter 29
Sara West

She watched him drive. His face was lit by the light from the Range Rover's dashboard. He was handsome. Short, light brown hair, just beginning to grey at the temples, with high cheekbones and even, white teeth. He hadn't shaved for a few days. With the stubble, he would have fit in perfectly at any of the university towns where she had studied — a slightly rebellious grad student, majoring in philosophy or something similar. His brow was furrowed slightly, not worried, but as if he was thinking his way through a problem that had been posed in class.

He kept his eyes on the road in front of them. He was driving fast — much too fast for a road like this, especially with the headlights turned off. She hoped he knew what he was doing. She didn't have much choice except to go along with him. She doubted that he would have let her leave, and in any case, she would have been dead without him, back at the hotel.

He suddenly swerved the car off the road, without warning, ramming the Range Rover into a cluster of banana palms. He turned off the engine, carefully opened the front door and then waited. He held his hand over the light above the dashboard, and they sat there in the darkness. In a moment, she heard it too: the clattering of a helicopter overhead. It came closer, roared immediately over them, and then moved on. He waited, with the door still half open, as the sound of the helicopter faded, and then was replaced by the jungle noises — the frogs and insects, the village dogs, the wind in the palm leaves. They both listened.

She watched him. She didn't trust him. Not at all. He had said that he'd kill her. That was the first thing he said to her, back at the hotel. She had no doubt that he could have. She had been helpless in his arms after he had grabbed her. She wondered why he had spared her, and instead killed the three men — his three colleagues. And why he was bothering to protect her now.

It had to be the file, with the list of names, that turned him from her killer into someone who pretended to be her protector. He must want the file, the same way that both the Russians and his American friends wanted it. It was what everyone wanted. She wondered why he hadn't just taken the papers from her. Maybe he thought she had hidden the important parts, in the jungle or in Goma. Maybe he thought that he needed her to get everything that he wanted.

She hated the file. It had killed her father and her friends. If she hadn't found the plane wreck, and the file, then everything would be fine. Her father and friends would still be alive. The file killed them, and almost killed her as well. And it probably still would.

But there was more to it now. The file had also become her life insurance policy. It could save her. If she was the only one who knew where the file was, then he would need her. He needed her alive if he wanted the file. He wouldn't hurt her, he couldn't hurt her, if he wanted to get the file.

It took a while for the realization to sink in. She would have to be very careful with him, with how she handled him. She thought about what she needed to do.

"I'm sorry," she said softly, after a while. As softly as she could manage.

He glanced briefly at her. Then he started the engine and backed the Range Rover onto the road. He left the lights off and started driving again, still headed north, away from the town. She wondered again where they were going. He kept his eyes fixed on the road.

For a while, she didn't think he was going to answer her. His eyes scanned back and forth, never resting, sweeping the road ahead of them. He kept his head tilted slightly towards the open window, listening again for the helicopters.

"Why's that?" he finally asked.

She waited just an instant. "You must be in trouble, in danger, for killing all those men. Your own men. I'm sorry that I got you into this mess."

She tried to sound apologetic and sad. Even though she didn't really care about his friends. They had been trying to kill her. And even though it was his fault, not hers, that he had ended up here. She wasn't really sorry about that either.

He laughed out loud. "In trouble. Yeah. You could say that. I am probably in trouble. Actually, lots of trouble. But it's not your fault. It was my choice." His voice was subdued, a little resigned.

That wasn't the answer she had expected. She let him drive. The banana palms flashed past the windows of the Range Rover, ghostly shapes, barely visible in the night. She watched the road ahead.

"You know who's chasing us?" he asked after a few minutes.

"Russians. At least that's who was chasing me before. And now your friends are chasing us. Who knows who else. I thought you would know. That's your job, no? Anyway, who were your friends? The ones who wanted to kill me?"

Her voice was flat. She tried to make it softer, but her anger came out.

He smiled. "CIA. Or that's who I thought they were. Americans, at least. I'm not sure anymore who they are really working for."

"Why?" she asked. "What do they want? Why me? Why my dad?" She hadn't meant to say that. Her voice was angry this time. She wasn't acting anymore.

He looked at her this time, for just an instant, and then back to the road. "Your dad?" he asked.

He sounded surprised. Maybe the CIA wasn't so smart after all. Maybe he really didn't know much about her, at least not much that was true.

"Yes. My dad. He was in the camp. They shot him. The Russians did. While I watched. Because he wouldn't tell them where I was. He's dead."

It hurt just to say it out loud. It made his death more real. More final. She spit the words out this time, like little round stones, one after another, hard and cold, into the warm jungle air. She still wasn't acting.

"I'm sorry," he said. "I didn't know that." He sounded surprised. And apologetic.

He slowed the car and glanced at her again. She stared ahead, watching the palms roll past in the moonlight, like some endless black-and-white film. She struggled to control herself. She didn't trust him. He was a killer, who had signed up to hunt her and then to kill her. And he would have done that, until he decided to betray his friends, probably to take the file for himself. She sat in silence for a while longer, thinking as the palm trees flashed by, thinking what she would have to do to stay alive, to keep him from killing her.

Then she told him a story about what had happened out in the jungle. She didn't tell him much, just the timeline — the attack on the camp, her flight through the jungle for the next two weeks, her arrival in Goma. She didn't tell him about most of the things that she had seen, or most of the things that she had done.

Then she told him some other things as well. Things that hadn't happened. She told him how she hid some of the most important papers of the file that she had found in the German plane. How she had hid the most important parts of the file in the jungle, and in Goma. And how she sent a letter from Goma to a friend, telling him how to find the file if anything happened to her.

Then she finished. "Nobody can find it without directions. If something happens to me, my friend will get the file. And he will tell the world, the whole world, what I found."

She stopped, and wiped her eyes, then looked away, at the palm trees, and waited for him to answer.

"I'm sorry," he said again, as if he hadn't even heard her story about hiding the file, "I'm sorry about your dad."

She kept staring out the window, then answered before she could stop herself. "He died for me, because of me," she said. It hurt again just to say it out loud.

He didn't answer. He drove for another ten minutes, both of them silent, lost in their thoughts. Then she saw that he was watching the road intently again. He slowed the car. He reached into the pocket of his vest and took out a small pistol, slipping it into his jeans, in the small of his back. He kept his eyes on the road.

"What is it?" she asked.

"A police checkpoint. Ahead of us. Just be quiet. I'll do the talking. If I start shooting, stay down."

The "checkpoint" was just a few rocks the size of shoe boxes, laid haphazardly across the road. He eased the Range Rover slowly to a halt, next to the thatched shack where two local soldiers stirred. They were teenagers, half-asleep and bleary-eyed.

He stepped out of the car and walked over to them, checking whether they were alone. One of the soldiers shined a flashlight at him. He smiled broadly at the soldier and handed over an ID card. It looked like a UN pass. He must have taken it from the man who had been in the Range Rover. One of the men he killed back in Goma.

The soldier inspected the pass, then smiled and said something, too low for her to hear. Jeb laughed again, then reached into his pocket. He found his wallet and handed over a couple of bills, then laughed once more, before he surrendered another bill. The flashlight's beam shifted to the rocks and then back to him. He returned, started the car, and then pulled away, skirting the make-shift barrier. The thin beam of flashlight disappeared behind them as the Range Rover picked up speed. They drove in silence for a few minutes, the trees of the jungle flashing past again, black and white in the lights of the car.

"Here's the plan," he said, a few minutes later.

"We don't have any good options. But there's a UN air base about a hundred kilometers ahead of us. It's a logistics center for the UN humanitarian and peace-keeping missions in the Congo. They do five flights a day to Europe. That's where we're going. When we get there, we're breaking into it. I'm not sure exactly how, but it should be doable. Once we're inside the base, we hijack one of their planes, or maybe stow away on it. A big enough plane to get us to Europe. We take that plane — I can pilot it — and land somewhere, anywhere, with an airfield. Once we're in Europe, we can disappear. New identities and all that. You go your way. I go mine."

He looked at her, waiting for a reaction.

"It's up to you, of course. You don't have to come. We may not make it. It's dangerous. Lots could go wrong, really wrong. It's actually not a very good plan.

But I can't think of anything better, and we're running out of time. If you want to stay, don't want to come, that's okay."

She looked back, watching him drive. She didn't believe him. He wouldn't let her go. Not without getting the file. And she also didn't like his plan. It sounded crazy.

"Why that? Why steal a plane? Even if we could."

"We can't stay here, in the jungle or on this road," he said. "They'll eventually find us. And we can't cross borders or use airlines. They'll find us the moment we do. We also can't use credit cards, even if we had them. And I'm a bit short on cash just now. So we're stuck here. Where they're going to find us, probably sooner than later. Trust me. I know what they can do. So, there's no other way. Except we steal a plane and get away."

She watched the palm trees rolling past. In the dark, they looked like scarecrows. Or bodies staked along the road, a forest of death.

Maybe he was right. Maybe it wasn't so crazy. She didn't even have a credit card, much less any cash, apart from three more $20 bills. That would last another couple of days. At most. She didn't even have a passport or a phone. She had left them back in the camp, along with everything else she owned. She didn't really have a choice.

"OK. What do I need to do?" she asked in a flat voice.

He glanced at her and smiled broadly. "Buckle up, girl. This may be bumpy."

She wanted to smile then too, just at that moment, because of his boyish grin and easy confidence, notwithstanding all their problems. His smile started to lift the sadness and the anger, as if she'd taken off her pack.

But instead of smiling, she turned away and looked back at the trees rolling past the windows of the car in the dark of the night. And the fear and anger came back. She didn't trust him, and she still didn't like his plan. But she also didn't really have a choice. She had never felt as alone as she did now, not even when she had been out in the jungle.

Chapter 30
Yan Wu

They sat facing each other in the dining room, the teak table bare between them. It was night and the room was dark, except for the light from a single lamp hanging from the ceiling, casting a golden circle onto the surface of the table.

When he had been planning the mission, she suggested that they rent the villa and have it waiting, in case they needed somewhere to escape to. She had been right. They needed the villa.

They had fled in the night, across the border from the Congo, into Kigali in Rwanda. Goma was a catastrophe. They lost their entire team, every single man, to the Americans. And the Americans probably got the girl as well. But the two of them managed to survive. She had driven the escape car away from Goma, up through the hills and past the border controls into Rwanda.

He couldn't have done it. He had stumbled into their safe house in Goma that night, after the Americans' attack, panting and nearly hysterical. She talked him down, quietly and patiently, and then drove them across the border. Once he calmed down, he had been in shock, staring blankly out the windows of the car while she drove. And when they reached the villa, he drank himself into a stupor. In the space of an hour, he finished an entire bottle of vodka, then part of another, which left him comatose, curled up like a child in the bed, for the entire next day.

While he slept, she sat in the garden at the back of the villa by herself. She thought about how to handle their defeat, what to do next, where to go. Maybe it was time to quit, she thought. Before things got any worse. But she realized that wasn't what she wanted. The Nazi file was too much to walk away from. It really

did exist. And it was worth billions of dollars, maybe more. It was enough to protect her, to buy her safety, for the rest of her life. She couldn't walk away from
that. Not after coming this far.

She was sure that they still had a chance to retrieve the file. She didn't think
that the Americans had got the girl. She wasn't sure, of course. But the girl was
very clever. It would be hard to catch her. And she had seen the Americans' helicopters over the roads out of Goma during the night, searching for something, for
someone. It must be the girl. And if the Americans already had the girl, they
wouldn't still be searching for her. She must somehow have gotten away again.
And she probably still had the file.

It was still just a question of finding the girl, before the Americans did. So she
sat quietly in the garden, all through the day, thinking what they needed to do to
catch the girl again — who they would need to get help from, and how to get Ivan
to make the plan work.

As night was falling, she finally awakened him, and then nursed him into con-
sciousness. She filled him with aspirin, fresh-brewed Rwandan coffee, and half a
glass of orange juice. She left him to shower and then to grope his way back to
something approaching normality. It had taken another few hours before he made
his way out of the bedroom, shuffling down the hallway in his bathrobe and slippers like a hospital patient. He sat silently at the table, staring into the dark. He
was a broken man.

She hadn't allowed him to give up. Softly, patiently, she calmed his fears,
coaxed him back to rationality, flattered his vanities, all the while planting the
seeds for a new start on their project. He wanted to run, to hide, to let the CIA
have the girl and the files, to let them have whatever they wanted. Just leave him,
leave them, alone. He was still rich, rich beyond what most people would ever
want. They could do anything and go anywhere they wanted to. He swore that
this place, the file, this whole project, was cursed. They had to leave, just get up
and go, and cut their losses.

It had taken her the entire night, but she hadn't given up. Never disagreeing
with him, never confronting him, and instead just using quiet flattery and subtle,

patient hints of bigger dreams, more power, richer treasures. She told him about the American helicopters, and how they were still hunting the girl. She convinced him that the girl, and the files, must have escaped the Americans.

Slowly, after she fed him — with Russian pickles, black bread, herring, caviar, and vodka, just a little vodka — he started to turn. And then, an hour after midnight, facing each other in the dark across the dining table, he declared that she was wrong, that they couldn't run away. This was too big, and the prize was too precious. But they needed help. The Americans were too numerous, too well-prepared, too well-informed. He would have to strengthen his hand, to even the odds.

She knew all along that this was what he would eventually say. She knew that he would want help — more resources, more firepower — and she knew where he would turn. He would look home, to Moscow, to his former KGB friends, and his new friends at the FSS. He always did.

"Alexei. Alexei Roganov. He's the answer," he declared. "Alexei's the man for this. Just the one."

He nodded his head vigorously, in agreement with that pronouncement. He was excited now. Excited by the new possibilities. He took another drink of the vodka.

She waited. She let him find the solutions that she had hinted at earlier in the evening.

"Alexei. He can use his friends. His friends, my friends, in the FSS."

"Yes," she said. "What will they do? What can they do that you can't?" she asked. She knew the answer, but wanted him to say it, to think it through.

"Alexei and his friends can track the girl, if she got away. Better than I could do it at this point, especially if she gets out of Africa. And they can track the Americans, if they got the girl, and fight them, better than we could. They have more guns, more men."

"Yes." She nodded.

She had hinted the same thing, hours ago. It had taken him longer than usual. It must be the shock. And the vodka.

"Why track the Americans?" she asked. She knew the answer to that question too, but she let him explain.

"The Americans follow the girl. We follow the Americans and let them lead us to her. And to the file."

She poured him another shot of vodka, just a small one.

"What if Alexei, what if your friends at the FSS, take the girl for themselves? Can we, can you, trust them?" She knew the answer, of course.

He laughed. "Of course not. I can't trust them. I can't trust anyone. Not anyone but you. So I will control them. Just give them bits of information. Enough to let them work. And then we watch, we watch them all the time and, when they get close, we grab the girl and the files, before they do."

She nodded again, took his hand, held it softly against her cheek, and smiled.

"Call Alexei tomorrow then. Not tonight. You rest now, think about what you tell them. Then we talk. And you call him afterwards."

She watched him closely for a moment, then stood up and walked around the table, put her arms around him, and rested his head against her breasts. She held him that way, gently cradling him, while he finished the vodka, sitting at the table, as morning began to break.

Chapter 31
Jeb Fisher

They could see the light from the UN air base to the south for almost half an hour before they reached it. At first, there was only a pale glow, just above the treetops. Later, the glow brightened and, by the time they reached the security fence around the airstrip, the sky above the base was silver-white, illuminated by the glare of the airfield's lights.

The base was surrounded by a three-meter-high security fence, topped with multiple rolls of barbed wire. Every few hundred meters, a pair of security cameras was fixed on a post, set back from the fence. At the far end of the runway, parked in front of a large hangar, were two white planes with light blue UN markings. The hangar doors were open, but both the hangar and the area around the planes were deserted.

There were more cars on the road now and he turned on the Range Rover's headlights. They reached the main entrance to the base, and he slowed the car as they passed the security gate. He could see three uniformed guards — two Africans, one white — all inside a concrete guardhouse with a large glass window. The tinted glass was thick, and almost certainly bullet-proof. He kept driving.

It was nearly morning — 4:45 a.m. — and the huts scattered along the road were beginning to show signs of life. They probably had only an hour or so before workers began to arrive at the base. Once that happened, any hope of making his plan work would be lost. He needed to get them inside the base now or come up with another plan.

He focused again on the airfield's security fence. There were no other entrances to the base, at least none that he could see. Inside the barbed wire security fence, a dirt track ran parallel to the road. There would be patrols along that track, in addition to the cameras. It would be next to impossible to get over, or through, the fence without being detected. He turned his thoughts away from the fence and back to the entrance gate, pondering how to get them through it.

The opportunity appeared suddenly, out of nowhere. Just over a gentle hill, a white UN Range Rover was stopped at the side of the road. An overweight white man in his early fifties struggled in the half-dark with a spare tire. The man wore khaki shorts, a white linen shirt, and a baseball cap. He was drenched in sweat.

The road was empty. Jeb eased the car slowly to a stop alongside the man's Range Rover, then smiled broadly. She looked puzzled, but he ignored her, all of his attention on the man with the spare tire.

"Bad luck there. You look like you could use a hand."

The man's face was red from exertion. It lit up at Jeb's offer.

"*Oui*. Zhat is just what I need. *Merde*. Stupeed, stupeed roads," the man said, shaking his head in frustration, and gesturing at the flat tire.

Jeb laughed easily and pulled their car off the road, parking it just behind the Range Rover.

"Come. But leave this to me," he whispered to her.

She followed him out of the car.

"Let's see what's wrong here. My dad was a mechanic," he told the man. Then he offered his hand. "Matt. Matt Williams."

The man smiled again. "Rene Fourtou. Zhee second time zhis month. Awful luck. I don't believe eet."

"No worries. We'll get it sorted. You with the UN here?" he asked.

"Of course. We all are, no? Just driving to zhee base," the Frenchman said.

"Yep. That's right. Let me check the jack."

He walked to the side of the car and checked the jack, then picked up the jack handle and used it to lift the chassis of the Range Rover an inch or so higher.

He surveyed the work and then turned, scanning their surroundings. The road was still empty in both directions. No one else was in sight.

Rene never saw the jack handle coming. It made a dull thud against the side of the Frenchman's head. Sara stifled a gasp.

He picked up Rene's body, maneuvering it into the rear seat of the Frenchman's own car. He found a roll of tape and rope in the toolkit at the back of the car. He used the rope to bind the Frenchman's hands and feet, and then taped the man's mouth shut. He went through the man's pockets, taking his UN pass, wallet, and phone. He also took the Frenchman's baseball cap and sunglasses, then tried them on.

"*Oui*, madame. Zhis road ees awful, no?"

She smiled. She was just being polite, he could tell, but she still smiled.

He told her what to do. "We need to hustle. Use a rag and wipe down the inside of the other car. The one we came in. Anything we might have touched. Wipe it completely clean. Then bring me the rag."

She looked at him for a moment, then left without a word, heading back to their car. He worked quickly, changing the tire on the Frenchman's car in the space of a few minutes. His father hadn't really been a mechanic, but he still knew how to do this. He found a blanket in the rear of the Range Rover and arranged it over the Frenchman's body. Then he walked back to the other car, where she was finishing her tasks.

"So. My name isn't Matt."

"I figured that. Anyway, you probably know, but I'm Sara, Sara West."

She held out her hand.

"Jeb Fisher."

They shook hands. Her hand was cool and soft. He let it go after a moment and then they stood there awkwardly by the side of the road. The sun was just beginning to light up the sky to the east.

"Right," he said. "We really do need to hustle. Here's the plan. It isn't great, not even good, but like I said before, it's all we have. I hide our car in the jungle now. Then I drive us onto the base with Rene's car, using his pass. You hide in the back. If all goes well, the guards have waved him, and this car, past the gate the last hundred days in a row. And they do it again today. But if they don't, and something goes wrong, then we drive out, drive out fast and hard, probably with them shooting at us. If that happens, you hang on and keep your head down. Whatever happens, don't try and help me. I'd appreciate the thought, but it wouldn't help."

She waited for him to finish, then nodded. "OK. I can do that. How do we get the plane?"

"Not sure yet. We'll know when we're inside. Hopefully, we just drive up to it and climb on board with nobody around to bother us. We both deserve a little good luck."

He got into their Range Rover, started it, then drove the car off the road into the jungle, plowing through the thick underbrush. In a moment, the vehicle was gone, swallowed up in the jungle as if it had never been there. He returned in another couple of minutes, the rag tucked into the pocket of his jeans.

"OK. Showtime," he said.

He helped her find a place to curl up on the floor in the backseat, next to the Frenchman's body. The man was still out cold. Then he closed the door, climbed into the driver's seat and started the engine.

He wondered if he could trust her. Probably not. Especially if things went wrong. But he didn't have much choice at this point. Every minute they waited gave Reid's men more chances to find them.

In ten minutes, he was at the security entrance to the airbase. He kept the Frenchman's baseball cap pulled down low, and his own pistol on the seat beneath his leg. The window on the driver's side was rolled down, just below eye level, so it was harder to see his face. There were no other cars at the gate. He pulled forward and held up his pass, waving it casually at the guards, as if he did this every day.

Nothing happened. He waited another moment, fighting back rising unease. Still nothing, the seconds crawling past. Still nothing. And then the gate opened. He never saw who waved them through. He breathed a sigh of relief, then drove slowly into the base, just as if he knew exactly where he was headed. The grounds were well-lit and neatly gardened. Signs pointed helpfully towards various buildings. He headed towards the "Cargo Terminal."

"Almost there," he said, loudly, so that she could hear. "All good so far."

She didn't reply. He assumed that she was fine. In less than five minutes, they were at the cargo terminal. At this time in the morning, it was still deserted. He drove around the side of the building and parked in the shadows next to the terminal.

"OK. Let's do it," he said.

He got out of the car, using the rag to wipe down the surfaces they had touched. By the time he was finished, she had crawled out of the rear compartment and was waiting next to the car. He checked that the Frenchman was still breathing and then led her to the building. They had to hurry now. If something went wrong, they would be trapped inside the base.

"Same game plan as before. I lead. If anything happens, keep your head down. No matter what, don't try and help. Got it?"

It wasn't really a question, but she nodded.

Dawn was just breaking as he forced the door to the terminal open. The building was deserted, just as it had appeared from the outside. It smelled of floor wax and aviation fuel. Their footsteps echoed off the bare concrete walls as he led them down darkened corridors to the far side of the building, where floor-to-ceiling windows opened out on the airstrip. Through the windows they could see two Boeing 727s standing wing tip to wing tip, twenty-five meters away from the terminal, brilliant white against the grey concrete and brown grass of the airstrip.

"Wait here," he ordered, and headed to the glass doors opening out onto the runway.

It was bad luck. Very bad luck in fact. The security guard was huge, weighing at least 110 kilos, and built like a prize-fighter. His uniform was a couple sizes too small. He must have been asleep, head down on a desk next to the door to the runway, shielded from sight by a room divider.

As Jeb eased the door to the runway open, the guard rose, silently, picking up his security baton, then swinging it in a vicious arc. He heard the man at the last moment and half-turned, then almost ducked under the blow. But he didn't, and instead it caught him on the side of the head and knocked him onto the floor. The guard followed, moving lightly for someone of his size. The man was a local Hutu tribesman, a solid block of muscle from head to toe. The guard swung the baton again, like a club, catching him on the left arm this time, then raising the baton again. He braced himself for the next blow, pulling his feet underneath his body and trying to avoid the guard's attack.

She wasn't very good at following orders. The guard didn't see her come out from behind the room divider. He also didn't see the jack handle as she swung it, with all her might, against his head. The resulting thud was just like the sound that the Frenchman's head had made, and all 110 kilograms of muscle collapsed onto the floor.

She looked down at him, still crouched on the floor. "So. What's the game plan now?" she asked, raising one eyebrow just a little.

He smiled, massaging the side of his head with one hand before answering. "Thanks for that. I messed up."

He really had, as well. He was embarrassed that he'd screwed up in front of her, and almost got them both killed.

Then he nodded at the plane. "That's our ride. All we need to do is buckle up."

"Sure. But I need a minute," she said.

She left him nursing his head and disappeared down the hallway with her backpack in the direction of the restrooms. While she was gone, he massaged the lump on his head, then checked his HK416. The magazine wasn't seated properly, instead tilted off to the left. He must have fallen on it when the guard had surprised him. He leaned against the clip, trying to ease it back into place. It didn't work. Instead, it broke the seating mechanism. He checked to see if the guard had a gun. He didn't. He hoped that she still had a weapon.

He was at the door to the terminal, still rubbing his head, when she returned almost ten minutes later. She carried her backpack in one hand. She had taken a long time, almost ten minutes.

"I thought you got lost," he said, looking at his watch. "We really need to hurry now. Staff will start arriving before long."

"No worries. Just needed a moment," she said, closing the top of her backpack and fastening it.

"You figured out our ride?" She smiled at him.

He laughed. "Yep. That one there," he said, pointing to the nearest cargo plane. "Let's see if it's ready to go."

They walked out of the terminal, next to each other, onto the concrete runway. It was still deserted. The sun was just beginning to show through the tops of the trees in the distance, and it caught in her hair, golden in the morning light, as she climbed into the cargo hold.

Chapter 32
Franklin Kerrington III

Kerrington took the telephone call from Reid on the encrypted phone in his bedroom. He was alone, in a dressing gown, at the desk in one corner of the room. It was nearly 3 a.m. and the house was silent. His wife was at their country estate, in Virginia, where she had spent the week.

Reid had more bad news. The latest developments were not disastrous, but they weren't good either.

"We know a lot more now, sir. Fisher has definitely gone rogue. He's either helping the girl or the other way around. Bad news is, they've hijacked a plane. Fisher is a trained pilot, thanks to the Agency. They're apparently on a cargo plane, a converted Boeing 727, that they took from a UN base south of Goma this morning. So far as we can tell, it's just the two of them. The transponder has been disabled and there's been no contact with the aircraft for the last three hours."

Reid described what his men had found — the two abandoned Range Rovers, the unfortunate French aid worker, and the UN guard. They also had camera footage from security cameras at the UN base. That all left no doubt. Fisher and the girl were working together. They had driven through the night, somehow evading Reid's men and their helicopters on the road heading south from Goma, then slipped through security at a UN airstrip 250 kilometers away. At the airfield, they found a fully fueled cargo plane, prepped for a morning flight to Cyprus. Fisher had taken off, presumably with the girl on board.

Kerrington swore and got up from the desk in frustration. "God damn it, Reid. That's fucking perfect. What's the range on a fully fueled Boeing 727? Four thousand miles? Maybe I should go wait for them at the arrival gates at Dulles."

Reid knew better than to try to sugar-coat things at this point. "It's got a range of 2,700 miles give or take a bit. I know it's not great. We know they're heading north. We got a couple radar sightings of the plane from Rwanda. But they could be going to lots of different places."

Kerrington swore again. "That's a fucking nightmare. You can't lose them. I told you that."

"I know. We're on it," Reid said quickly. "We've been watching radar everywhere possible. They can't get across the Mediterranean, can't get across Egypt or Israel, can't go most places, without us spotting them."

"Where are they going? Fisher's flying the plane. What's he thinking? Where's he going?"

"Our best judgment is that they'll be trying to get to Europe. They'll stand out like sore thumbs anywhere else. They'll probably be headed for Italy, maybe Greece. That's our assumption," Reid explained.

"What about Fisher's contacts, resources? Anywhere he might run to? Anywhere that he thinks we don't know about?" Kerrington asked.

"Nothing in his records. Nothing at all so far. We're doing a full review. If you could expedite at the Agency, it would help."

"Fine. It will happen right away. What about her? What do we know?"

Reid didn't know much. "Basically nothing of value. She's just a normal university student. A plain-vanilla upbringing, other than lots of foreign travel with her father. Nothing else out of the ordinary. No close family or friends in Europe. Her mother passed away a few years ago. So far as we can tell, there's nowhere in Europe that she might run to."

"Get me a full study of both of them. ASAP. We need to figure out where they're headed. And lock down every fucking airport and train station that you can in southern Europe. Tap into computers and security cameras at the border crossings too. Everywhere in Europe. They have to use their own passports, right? We'll know if they try and cross an EU border."

"We're on it," Reid said.

Kerrington hung up. He didn't bother to repeat himself. He had told Reid once that this was unacceptable.

He got up from the bed and poured himself a whiskey, a double. He needed it, or he wouldn't sleep tonight. This wasn't how things were supposed to go. He took a long swallow, feeling the warmth a moment later in his stomach. Then he walked downstairs, to the breakfast room. It was dark. He stood by the French doors and watched the moonlight on the waters of the fountain in the courtyard.

Things weren't under control. Not even close. With Fisher helping her, the girl and whatever files she had found were a bigger threat. A much bigger threat. And who knew where they might be headed or what they might do next. He felt the panic rise again in his gut, then forced it down and tried to think constructively. He made a note of the items that he had told Reid that he would take care of. And then he thought about what else he should do.

He needed more intensity, more creativity, on the ground. Reid was good, at least he always had been before now. But Reid was a lieutenant, not a general. He didn't have the ability to think five steps ahead, to think outside the box. Dealing with Fisher and the girl demanded that. They were smart and unpredictable. He needed someone who could anticipate the next unforeseen alliance, the next plane hijacking.

It took another hour watching the moonlit waters, and another whiskey, before he found the answer. He reached it reluctantly, but at the end of the day, it was clear. He called the Agency's travel bureau on his secure CIA phone and made arrangements to charter a private jet to Europe at the end of the week. He would eventually end up in Zurich. That's where the bank was, and that was where the files would lead. That was where Fisher and the girl would go. He might as well start preparing to go there as well. To finish this himself.

Chapter 33
Sara West

She sat in the co-pilot's seat in the cockpit of the UN plane, watching him at the controls. He was calm and meticulous, as if nothing could faze him. The same way that he had been ever since they climbed on board three hours ago. The same way that he had been when he killed the three men at the hotel in Goma, and the driver of the Range Rover.

After they boarded, he had checked the plane's systems, disabled the transponder, readied the engines for take-off and then taxied out onto the deserted airstrip, ignoring the shouts of four more native security guards, who chased helplessly after the plane. The Boeing 727 had barreled down the runway, and then lifted off into the rising sun over the African jungle, dark green beneath them. He looked at home in the pilot's seat. He never reached for the wrong switch, never stopped to think, never wasted a moment. It was as if he were out for a weekend drive in his car.

He flew low at first. Very low, just meters above the treetops. She could guess that he wanted to stay beneath whatever radar there might be. After an hour or so, he ascended, until they were at a normal cruising altitude, above the cloud cover. Then it was just the two of them in the cockpit surrounded by sky and clouds, the rhythmic sounds of the plane's engines in the background.

After they were above the clouds, he put the plane on autopilot and excused himself. He returned a few minutes later. He had washed his face, and also found a refrigerator, stocked with soft drinks and snacks. He offered her a Coke and a candy bar. Her mouth watered. She realized she hadn't eaten in more than a day, since the roast chicken at the hotel in Goma. It seemed a lifetime ago. She devoured the Snickers in three bites. He laughed at her and disappeared again, returning in a moment with a large box of assorted junk food. She balanced the box on her lap, and they attacked the snacks like hungry children.

"So. Here's the plan," he started after a few minutes.

She looked evenly at him when he said that, then blinked and leaned back in her seat, watching him coolly. She had been thinking how to handle this. She let him continue.

He went on, his voice serious. "I'll need to see the file again. I need to figure out how you go to the authorities."

She didn't answer. She kept looking at him, and then smiled ever so slightly.

He looked puzzled, then gently repeated the request. "So... Can I have another look? It's important."

"I don't have the file. It's gone," she said. She wondered how he would react.

He stared at her for a moment, then replied, impatiently now. "Don't play games. I just saved your life. And took a massive whack on the side of my head. I need to figure out what your stupid file is. What it means. I need to do that to save your life. And mine too, by the way."

She looked back at him calmly and took a sip from her Coke. "Listen to me. For a change." She made sure he heard the emphasis on the final phrase.

She put the Coke carefully into one of the cup-holders on her seat, then continued. "The file is gone, like I said. Thanks for saving my life. But most times I checked, you and your CIA buddies were doing your best to hunt me down and kill me. Don't forget, if it weren't for you, and your American and Russian friends, I wouldn't be here. And my dad wouldn't be dead. Sorry about your head, too. But I didn't miss the guard. You did. After you told me to stay out of the way, remember? In fact, I think you owe me a thank you. For saving your life, Mr. Secret Agent."

He smiled at the last quip. "You're right. Thank you. You did save my life. I was careless."

He paused, then continued, serious again. "I know it doesn't help, but I'm sorry. I'm really sorry about your dad." He looked as if he really were. She wanted to believe that he was. But she still didn't, couldn't, trust him.

She nodded anyway, then looked back at him, and waited.

"But I still need to see the file," he said, after a moment.

She laughed and rolled her eyes. He'd see soon enough. Then she peered out of the cockpit window, trying to catch a glimpse of the ground between the clouds. He stood up in exasperation and picked up her backpack. She wrinkled her brow slightly, while she studied the clouds, but didn't protest. He unfastened the clip and inspected the contents. On top was what was left of her clothing. It hadn't been washed in weeks, and smelled just that way. He found her spare t-shirt, still stained and stiff with her blood. He looked at her quizzically.

She ignored him, still studying the clouds below. He found the Uzi, its magazine empty. Her toothbrush. The Russians' medical kit. Her windbreaker. And nothing else. The pack was empty.

"OK. Where is it?" he demanded.

She looked over at him, away from the window, eying him coolly. "So. Here's the plan. The game plan," she said, with a hint of a smile.

She went on. "No more orders. You don't tell me what to do. Not anymore. We talk about what we're going to do. Then we decide, together. We both decide, not you decide." Her voice was soft, but firm.

He smiled and nodded. "Sure. That's fair."

She continued. "Like I said, the file is gone. It's back in Goma."

She didn't explain where the file really was. She didn't trust him. So she didn't tell him that she had found the mailroom at the UN airbase, when she pretended to go to the bathroom, and the laundry cart full of brightly colored DHL courier packages, destined for locations around the world. She also didn't tell him how she had substituted the file for the contents of one of the packages along with a short handwritten note, then readdressed the package to an address in Italy — an address in Italy that she was sure no one would ever discover. And she didn't tell him that she'd hidden that package, and the file, among all the other packages headed to Europe on the next UN plane, before hurrying back to rejoin him in the terminal.

She didn't tell him any of that. Instead, she smiled at him. He looked back and waited.

"It was probably risky. A big risk, hiding the file back there," she admitted. That part was true, she thought. It was a risk. Maybe the package would be discovered. Or get lost along the way. But it was a risk she had to take.

"But I didn't trust you. I don't trust you now. I don't even know you. For all I know, pretending to help me is just a trick, to make sure you get your hands on everything I found." That part was true too.

She took another sip of her Coke, surveyed the clouds again, and then looked back calmly at him.

"So," she continued. "Here's the plan. You are going to protect me. You're going to take me where I need to go. If anything happens to me, you lose the file. Once we get to where I want to go, I decide what we do. That's the game plan."

His reaction wasn't what she had expected. He didn't look angry. He just carefully closed her backpack, clipped it shut, and returned it to the floor, next to her seat, where it had been before. Then he looked back at her and smiled. She wondered why he wasn't angry. He didn't seem very surprised either. Almost relieved. That didn't make much sense.

He didn't ask about the file, didn't even mention it. Instead, he asked, "What's with the t-shirt? That's your blood?"

She nodded. "Yes. I was careless too. And you weren't there to protect me yet. The way you are now." She smiled again, mocking him gently.

"It looks like a lot of blood," he said. "If it came from you, I should have a look. My dad was a doctor." He smiled.

She considered that for a moment, then nodded and pulled down the top of her t-shirt. She turned in the co-pilot's seat so that he could see the wound. It was still an angry red. The stitches were fresh and white against her skin. He looked worried and moved to the edge of his seat, then slipped onto his knees in front of her. He lifted up her shirt and inspected the gash more closely, touching it gently, brow still furrowed.

"I guess the CIA trained you as a doctor too," she said, trying to ignore how close he was now.

He nodded. "Sort of."

He didn't look up from what he was doing. He still looked worried.

"I'll be back," he said, and disappeared into the cargo hold.

He came back with a medical kit. A real one. He sorted through its contents and found antibiotics and bandages. He cleaned her wound, with soft, patient strokes, then smeared the antibiotic cream over it and applied a bandage. His touch was careful, expert — like the way he flew the plane. When he was finished, he gave her two tablets to swallow, then pocketed the plastic container with the rest of the pills.

"Who sewed that up?" he asked, looking at the wound across her breast.

"I did. At the hotel."

"Seriously? With no painkillers?"

She nodded, then explained for him. "I did a year and a half in medical school, before I realized that I like plants a lot more than people. And I didn't have much choice. These guys were chasing me and I figured they'd have the doctors' offices all staked out."

She smiled. "I've seen lots of spy movies."

He laughed, then turned serious again. "That's not so easy. Maybe a little scary. I don't know many folks who could do that."

"I guess it's not so pretty. I never got a tattoo. This will have to do, I think."

He nodded, then put away the medical kit. It was strange, she realized, after weeks alone in the jungle, to be together with someone else. They were quiet for a while, each one of them watching the clouds drift by beneath the plane. Then she told him the story, the whole story of the past three weeks. She hadn't planned to, and he didn't prompt her, but it started to come out and once she started, she couldn't stop.

She didn't leave out hardly anything this time. She just told him what had happened since the day that Jackson found the plane wreck in the jungle. She described each day, every night, in a quiet voice, as she looked out at the clouds.

She told him how she watched her father die, as she sat up on the ridge. How Robert betrayed her. And how Jackson had told her goodbye. She told him how she ran and hid herself under the tree trunk in the swamp. And then how she had run again, day after day, night after night, and finally how she stopped running, and fought back instead. How she had found them in the night, alone in their tents. What she had done. How it felt to kill someone, to watch a man die, bleeding in the mud, with her spear in his chest. She almost left that out, but then she didn't. She told him everything that had happened out in the jungle.

When she was finished, she looked at him. She realized that her eyes were glistening. But she didn't let herself cry. Not now. She wasn't sure why she told him. Maybe it was to make him like her, to make him want to protect her. Maybe it was because she needed to tell someone, and there was nobody around but him. Maybe it was really just for her.

He watched her, eyes locked on hers, as he leaned close to hear her voice over the sound of the plane's engines. He didn't say anything for a while, instead just staring at her as if he hadn't seen her before. Then he looked out of the cockpit window at the clouds moving silently beneath them, before turning back to her, closer now than before.

She pulled away then, before he could say anything, turning business-like and asking, "So now what? How do we get to Europe? To Switzerland?"

After a while, he answered her question. He didn't mention her story, just answered what she'd asked. "The next bit won't be easy either," he said. "But it's doable. In fact, a whole lot more doable than a few hours ago."

He took another drink of Coke and checked the autopilot.

"We probably can't land this thing. I could actually do it, land it, without much problem. That's not the issue. The problem is that we can't land unannounced at some airstrip. And if we announce ourselves anywhere, then our friends, either the Americans or the Russians, or both of them, will find out. Then it's game over."

He continued: "And we can't fly into NATO airspace. Turkey, Greece, Italy. Probably even Egypt. If we do, their radar will spot us. Odds are, they'd send planes to force us down. Then we'd be dead too."

"So. Then what? Where do we go?" she asked.

"It's complicated," he said. Then he laughed. "Actually, it's really simple. We don't have a choice. But you probably won't like it…"

"Try me," she said.

"We fly into Libya, over Libya. It's no-man's land. No radar. No air force. No nothing. And when we reach the Mediterranean coast, we exit. We parachute out. We can't land this thing, so we don't. Once we're on the ground in Libya, we figure out how to get to Europe. We smuggle ourselves in, and then we disappear."

She smiled. "I like it. I always wanted to learn how to sky-dive." That wasn't exactly true, but she wasn't going to let him think she was afraid.

He laughed again. "Put your clothes on. We have work to do."

Then he went back into the cargo hold, leaving her alone in the cockpit, surrounded by the clouds and sun, wondering what he was thinking. Wondering whether he had believed her. And wondering how they were going to survive the next few days.

Chapter 34
Yan Wu

He woke late. It was long past noon. She had been up for hours, sitting on the veranda in the back of the villa. She hadn't left the house. There was nowhere to go, and the Americans might be looking for them. After he woke up, she came back inside and kissed him gently.

He hadn't showered. He ignored her kiss and went into the kitchen, helped himself silently to the coffee she had made, then checked his computers and phones. He didn't speak to her. His face darkened as he checked his emails. He cursed under his breath, frowning at his laptop. He turned the computer off, then logged into it again, scowling at the screen. She suppressed a wave of anxiety. She had seen that expression before.

"Fucking Alexei," he swore. Then more curses, now in Russian.

She didn't reply. It was important to stay out of his way when he was like this. Let him calm down, then try and comfort him. That usually worked.

It didn't work this time. He didn't calm down. He slammed the laptop shut and then kicked the table in anger. He kicked it hard, with his bare foot. It must have hurt. He cursed again, shouting now in Russian. He disappeared into the bedroom. Her heart leapt. Maybe he would shower, cool off, and emerge as if everything were normal again.

He didn't. He came out of the bedroom, face red with anger. His belt dangled ominously, from one meaty fist. She braced herself.

"Stupid bitch," he swore at her. "This is your fucking fault." He was crazy now.

She avoided his glare. He took her by the arm and half-dragged her off the sofa. He gripped her hard, nails biting into her flesh. She let him pull her across the room. It wouldn't help to fight. She had learned that the hard way. He dragged her into the bedroom and pushed her onto the bed. He cursed again, in Russian, froth on his lips, his eyes squinted and dark. She rolled onto her stomach, protecting her face and breasts. He cursed again and snapped the belt. It made an ugly crack.

She ignored the sound. She tried to let her mind drift, away to that place she found in her exercises. The place of calm and peace, detached from the fear. Detached from the pain. He lashed her viciously across the buttocks with his belt. Again, and then again and again. Hard, brutal blows that made her gasp, made tears leak out of her eyes.

She didn't resist, didn't scream, just tried to stay in that faraway place. It was an ancient temple, in the mountains, silent and serene, with a row of willow trees along a stream, and a tranquil courtyard. She forced his grunts and the belt away, out of her mind. And tried to let the beauty of the willows wash over her. Soft, swaying in the wind above the streambed and the mountain waters, beneath distant peaks, covered in snow.

He threw the belt against the headboard. He clambered onto the bed, between her legs. She forced herself to concentrate on the temple and the courtyard. He ripped her panties off. She couldn't help herself, but the fear had started to make her wet. He grunted and rammed into her. It hurt, hurt badly. She wasn't that wet. He fucked her crudely, like an animal. He picked up the belt and whipped her again, then looped it around her neck, pulling her head back towards him.

"You like that? You like it, bitch. Don't you?" She could feel his spittle on her shoulders.

"Answer me, bitch."

She knew what to say. Knew what he wanted. She forced herself to say it.

"Fuck me, fuck me harder. Please."

And she started to moan. She knew how to make it sound real. She ground her hips against him. It worked. Faster than she had hoped. He came with loud grunts and panting, before he collapsed on the bed. In minutes, he was asleep again, snoring with his mouth half open.

She waited until he was sound asleep. Then padded to the bathroom and cleaned herself. She checked to make sure he hadn't damaged her, and then showered. Long and hot. She stood there for twenty minutes, the water as hot as she could bear. And then she went silently back out onto the veranda, as far away from him as she could get. It was nearly dusk. She left the lights off and sat on the stone floor, legs crossed, and let her thoughts drift away. But she couldn't find the temple or the mountains. All that she could find was the past. Her own past.

She remembered all the other days, all the other nights, when other men had done the same things, and worse, to her. When she had been barely a teenager. Just a girl. She was cursed with beauty, as well as poor and weak parents — a father and a family who couldn't, or wouldn't, protect her.

First, it had been the local police, later the Beijing officials and then the spies. They had all used her as their plaything, first in their village, for themselves, and then loaning her to their friends and clients. After that, they had trained her, trained her to work for them, a spy whose job was to fuck. To fuck foreign businessmen, diplomats, and spies. Arabs, Africans, Chinese, Japanese, Europeans, everyone. First to fuck them and then to steal their secrets, to persuade them to talk, to leave their computers in their hotel room. They used her as a honey-trap, a child-like beauty, who lured men, and sometimes women, into bed.

She couldn't count how many nights strangers had used her, leaving her curled up in a ball, covered in their saliva, sweat, and semen. And then the knowing stares and smirks. The people she saw in the hotels, or the streets, who knew that she was a whore. A dirty whore. She remembered the days when she had been ashamed to leave her room, ashamed for anyone to see her, embarrassed that she was alive.

Somehow, she had survived. Most of the other girls like her hadn't. But she had. She had never given in, never let it break her. And she had sworn to herself that she would escape. She wouldn't just survive, she would escape.

She waited, watching and learning. She learned how to use her beauty, her body, and her mind. She persuaded her handlers to begin to teach her what they knew. First to send her to school, then to teach her their spy craft, and finally their secrets, everything they knew. She had learned well, absorbing what they could teach her, with a single-minded determination. Then asking for more, always more, until she knew more than the men and women who were assigned to teach her.

And she also swore that she would make her masters pay for what they took from her, for what they made her do. After eight long years, when she was twenty-six, she was ready. They had nothing more to teach her. And she had stolen, borrowed, and saved enough money to run, and to hide, so that they would never find her.

Even more important, she had found Ivan Petronov — one of the foreigners she was assigned to seduce, to pump for his secrets. But she had other ideas. He told her about his wealth, his connections with his former colleagues at the KGB and his ambitions. But she hadn't told her handlers about that, instead distracting them with trivia and petty complaints. She knew Petronov had the money and the power to protect her, the way her family hadn't. And she knew she could control him. Usually. Most of the time. Except on days like this one.

She escaped, silently, one night, disappearing with a new passport, that nobody knew about. She left behind a collection of mementos for her former masters — a bottle of poisoned whiskey, a booby-trapped car, a computer virus, a file of photographs delivered anonymously to a rival. Those few who survived had chased, but they never found her. She had escaped. And she had found Ivan.

She was waiting again now. Waiting for the right moment to escape again, once and for all. She re-crossed her legs and took another breath. This time it worked. The temple came to her. Stately and solemn, surrounded by willows, glittering silver in the moonlight along the stream. And a silent courtyard, with graceful arches along the sides. Somewhere safe, where nobody would hurt her again.

Chapter 35
Jeb Fisher

He checked the plane's instruments again. They said that the fuel tanks were nearly empty. That wasn't what he had expected. He had expected that they would have enough fuel to make it to the Mediterranean coastline. But they were still hundreds of kilometers short, over the desert in eastern Libya. The sky was almost cloudless, and they could see the desert beneath the plane. It was empty brown and grey sand, without a hint of life, apart from a long, straight road, cutting through the desert.

They needed to exit now, in order to be sure that the plane would end up crashing nowhere near them. He took her to the cargo hold in the back of the plane and showed her the parachutes, that he had already laid out and checked. Then he strapped her into one of the chutes, triple-checking the fasteners. He reset the autopilot, turning the plane around and sending it back the way that they had come, across the Libyan desert and hopefully into Egypt. With good luck, the Egyptian air force might shoot the plane down, maybe trying to keep it secret, leaving Kerrington and everyone else guessing even more.

He put what remained of the snacks from the plane's pantry, together with four plastic bottles of water, into her backpack. That was all there was. He added the remaining soft drinks — six cans of Coke — and then slung the pack over his shoulder.

He led her to the emergency exit at the rear of the cargo hold and made her hold onto one of the internal supports, alongside the external door. It only took him a moment to disarm the safety mechanism and unlock the external door. He had slowed the plane's air speed, but when he released the emergency door, it would still be bumpy.

He held onto her, one arm around her neck, and then pulled up hard on the emergency release mechanism. He couldn't help but notice that she smelled good. Warm and fragrant, like she was wearing perfume. He forced himself to concentrate on the door. The door's latch finally engaged and he pushed it out, holding her tighter.

The emergency door was ripped away from the fuselage of the plane. The wind rushed past them, howling like some kind of animal, clawing at their clothes and hair. He moved her to the edge of the airframe, holding her hand tightly, standing right behind her, his body very close to hers. Her hand was cool and dry. She looked around at him and smiled. He'd told her that they would jump on three.

He squeezed her hand once, then twice, and on three he pushed her out of the plane, jumping after her a heartbeat later in the same fluid motion. The wind threw them back, away from the plane, which disappeared in seconds. And then they were falling, plummeting down towards the sand.

He fell feet first, controlled. At first, he couldn't see her, then spotted her behind him, and a bit higher, tumbling wildly through the air. He maneuvered then, through the empty space, until he was alongside her. He reached out, then grabbed her, and fought the momentum, helping her stop tumbling. In a moment, they were falling together, at two hundred kilometers per hour, the ground racing up towards them. He caught her eyes, and she smiled again. He held up one finger, then two, and then three. She followed the instructions he had given her on the plane and their chutes blossomed together above them, orange and white against the blue of the cloudless sky. They drifted down, hands linked, the way he had told her, towards the empty desert.

Their luck held. They landed in a dune, fifteen meters high, a miniature hill of powder-soft sand. Nothing broken and nothing twisted. Just shoes and clothing filled with tiny grains of sand. Better yet, the road that they had seen from the plane was less than a kilometer from where they landed — a long, impossibly straight road with occasional bushes alongside it. They couldn't have planned it any better.

He buried the parachutes in the sand, as deep as he could manage. She helped him, scooping handfuls of sand out of the hole he dug.

She was smiling broadly. "Thanks. That was awesome."

He couldn't help but laugh. She had survived a hellish three weeks in the jungle, then a firefight with Russian commandos, before their plane ran out of fuel and she had to parachute into the middle of an empty desert. And she thought it was fun. He could tell, as well, that she really did.

"Anytime. Let's hope the next part of the plan goes as smoothly."

She smiled again. "So, what do you steal now? Another plane?"

"Nope, just a car, I hope. We'll need to hike over to the road, then figure out how we persuade someone to give us their wheels."

"I can help on that, I imagine. Scantily clad maiden in distress alongside the road should do the trick."

He laughed again. "My thought exactly. Let's figure out where we do this. And get out of the sun. We won't last long in this heat."

It took about an hour to get to the road. The sand dunes were beautiful, and luxuriantly soft, but next to impossible to walk on. For most steps that they took, they lost three-quarters of the ground they covered, slipping back down the dune or sinking to their knees in the soft sand. The sun was relentless, brutally hot and nearly blinding when they faced it. The wind cooled them a bit, but also sucked the moisture off their bodies. His mouth was dry long before they reached the road. He wasn't sure, but the temperature couldn't have been less than 45°C.

The road was only a kilometer or so from where they landed, but when they reached it, they were both dripping with sweat and exhausted. They emptied out their shoes, and pockets, and then he scouted for a place to wait. There weren't many choices. They ended up under a scraggly bush, the most substantial one in sight. It shielded them from the sun, but only barely.

"This may be tricky," he said. "Ideally, we get a car with only one person in it. And not someone with weapons. You flag them down, then I come out from behind the bushes and play the heavy. Hopefully, they're not stupid and no one gets hurt."

"That sounds good," she nodded. "And what about not so ideally? Then what?"

"Then things get ugly. Then you get out of the way."

"Oh. I know. Like last time? In the terminal?" She smiled at him. "Don't worry. I'll behave."

He turned serious. "I don't have a weapon," he said. "At least not one that works."

Her Uzi was out of ammunition and he hadn't been able to repair his HK416. He hoped that the occupants of the vehicles on the road wouldn't be armed.

They found the least uncomfortable place underneath the bush. The road was empty. And it stayed empty. It stretched as far as they could see in both directions, a thin, shiny black ribbon cutting straight through the desert, heat shimmering in waves above its surface in the afternoon sun. They drank two of the cans of Coke that he had stowed in her pack. The liquid was warm and sickly-sweet, but they were both parched. They watched the sun creeping towards the horizon, above the empty road.

After an hour, she curled up, leaning her head onto her knees. It had been nearly forty-eight hours since she had slept. After a few more minutes, she leaned up against him, fast asleep. He eased her head onto her backpack, and when she stirred, onto his fleece, pillowed in his lap, and settled in to watch the road.

He tried to make sense of the last twenty-four hours. He knew he was as good as dead. He was in the middle of Libya and didn't even have a weapon or a vehicle anymore. Even assuming that Libyan militia or bandits didn't get them, Kerrington and Reid would be on their trail right now, with everything the CIA and NSA had to offer at their disposal. Reid's men would be here before long. And then they'd be dead.

Despite everything, he didn't regret what he'd done. Kerrington and Reid were evil, plain and simple. They were happy to kill innocent people to protect their dirty secrets, whatever they might be. He had done what he had to. And he felt more alive, more complete, than he had for years.

It was her, of course. He didn't understand her, much less trust her, but she had caught him even more tightly during the last few hours. She had caught him with her story on the plane, her sadness and her laughter, her eyes and her smell. He knew that this wouldn't last much longer, that Reid's men would find them soon. But he realized that he didn't care, that he had made the right choices, that this was worth it. Whatever it was, and however long it lasted. It was worth it.

He turned back to the road, watching the thin black line disappear into the dunes where they met the horizon. He was still watching when the sun set to the west, into the darkened dunes, while she slept, her head cushioned on his lap.

Chapter 36
Reginald Reid

He stared out of the window. The rain hadn't let up for most of the day. The potholes in the road had turned into small ponds and the ditches along the streets into frothy streams. Night would fall soon, but it had already been grey, as if dusk had arrived, for hours.

The latest reports were bad. There was no other way to spin it. The crash of a UN cargo plane had been reported, near the Egyptian border with Libya. There had been no fire at the crash-site; the plane's fuel tanks were apparently empty. There were no bodies in the plane and the emergency exit door was missing, along with two parachutes. The plane's black box was being analyzed, but it had been disabled. The plane seemed to have been set on autopilot, but that wasn't certain.

A needle in a haystack, he thought. He had a working hypothesis of what Fisher had done, but it was mostly guesswork. Fisher and the girl had flown north, out of the Congo, and across South Sudan, Sudan, and Libya. After crossing the Sahara, they parachuted out of the plane, somewhere in Libya, or maybe Egypt, leaving the empty aircraft to fly on autopilot until it crashed somewhere. They could be anywhere within a thousand-kilometer radius in Libya — possibly Egypt, or maybe Tunisia — even assuming that the basic hypothesis was right.

He looked at the map of North Africa, plotting what he imagined their flight path would have been, thinking what they would have wanted to avoid, where they might want to end up. He swore again. It was all guesswork, and even then, an impossibly large search zone.

Still, they needed to start somewhere. And, through a process of elimination, he ended up with a handful of roads, running north to south through Libya. Fisher and the girl would head for Europe, and they probably wouldn't have flown over

Egypt. They would have worried about radar and the Egyptian air force. They would have headed into Libya; he was fairly certain. It was a no-man's land, both in the air and on the ground. They would be most likely able to avoid detection there. It would be dangerous; the country was a mess, divided between warring militia, fighting over oil and the scraps of Qaddafi's regime. But it was still the least bad choice for them. Fisher would know that.

Once Fisher and the girl were on the ground, they would need transportation, almost certainly by road, north to the Mediterranean. Libya had only a few major roads, and a handful of other smaller ones, that were all visible from the air. They would have parachuted out of their plane near one of these roads and would then have tried to find transport headed north. Perhaps it wasn't such a needle in a haystack after all, he thought. He could arrange checks along a half dozen roads, which Fisher and the girl would have to use. Maybe this wasn't much worse than the Congo. Maybe it was even better.

He thought for a while, and then called Kerrington. Kerrington was still furious that Fisher and the girl had escaped again. Despite that, his mood improved slightly when Reid walked him through their hypothesis. He agreed that Fisher was probably in Libya and would have to make his way north, along one of the few roads running across the desert. Kerrington also agreed that they should try and block those roads, to find Fisher and the girl as they headed north.

"The Libyan militias. They're the ones that can do this," he said. "Can you get them to run some checkpoints for us? On the north-south roads."

Kerrington's answer was brusque. "Of course. I'll have them do your job. What else?"

"I'll get the team to the Mediterranean. Probably Malta. Where they can move fast when we pick up the trail again."

"Don't disappoint me again. This isn't what I expected." Kerrington's voice was cold.

"Yes sir."

He hadn't heard Kerrington this angry or distant before. Whatever the girl had must be seriously important. He gave Kerrington a summary of the other steps they were taking. He walked through the alerts at every border crossing in Southern Europe, Egypt, and Tunisia, as well as every airport in Europe, and the lookouts on charter air travel companies and shipping companies. It was an impressive list.

Kerrington was unimpressed. "Fisher isn't stupid. He knows we'll do that. What will he do then? What's his next step? That's what your job is. Figure it out."

"We're working on that, sir. We're watching harbors. In Egypt and Tunisia. As well as smaller aircraft. We also have a special watch out for stolen and lost passports."

Kerrington was silent.

"One more thing, sir. Can you arrange a review of all the girl's contacts? Everything we can find out about who she knows, especially in Europe?"

"You're thinking of places she may head in Europe?" Kerrington asked.

"Yes."

"We'll get that done too. As well as Fisher's. I'd imagine Fisher's are more likely. He must be running their show now." Kerrington's voice was only marginally less hostile.

He continued. "Keep me updated with all new information. And don't forget. Don't disappoint me again."

Then Kerrington hung up.

Reid looked out the window again, at the rain falling on the potholed road. The call could have gone worse. But things still weren't good. Maybe the girl and Fisher weren't even in Libya. Maybe they wouldn't use one of the main roads. There was an endless list of other maybes, in addition to those. He watched the monsoon rains, wondering how many million raindrops had fallen in the Congo that day. He turned his mind back to the girl and finding her. Like finding a raindrop in the monsoon season, he thought darkly.

Chapter 37
Sara West

The cold woke her up. It was freezing. He was sound asleep, one arm curled around her waist, the other around her backpack, his head resting on her shoulder. The night was bright with stars, more stars than she had ever seen before, covering the entire sky, lighting up the dark. It was so different from the jungle, where trees and clouds hid the sky. She stared at the stars, trying not to wake him.

"Awesome, no?" he asked. She hadn't succeeded.

"Yes, it is. I've never seen anything like it," she said.

They watched in silence for a moment. Then she started to shiver. He reached into her pack, found her fleece and rain jacket, and handed them to her. She pulled them on, teeth chattering in the desert night.

"There hasn't been a car all night long," he said. "Maybe there won't be one for a few days."

"Ugh. We'll run out of water. Out of the frying pan, into the fire, as they say."

She realized that they were still in danger. In fact, they might be in more danger than ever. They couldn't survive more than a few days without water. The desert would kill them, just as surely as the Russians, or Jeb's CIA friends, would. Assuming that Libyan bandits or soldiers didn't get them first.

"Yep. Fingers crossed. You try and get some sleep. I'll watch. I can keep playing pillow. It's better than the alternatives."

She laughed. And curled up on his lap, one of his arms cushioning her face, the other close against her body. It made her feel safe. Even if they weren't safe at all. And even if she didn't trust him at all. It still felt good. She was asleep again in minutes, breathing slowly but deeply, while he watched the road.

She woke hours later, the sun already well above the horizon. It was a blinding white disc, hanging motionless in the cloudless sky. The cold of the night was gone, replaced by dull, innervating heat. She realized that he was gone as well, leaving her head cushioned on her backpack. She sat up and looked around. He was nowhere to be seen. She wondered where he had gone, and when, maybe whether, he'd be back. She realized she was sweating and pulled off her fleece, then settled in to wait for him.

She could see their surroundings again now that it was light. The desert stretched out, flat and almost featureless, in every direction, punctuated only by occasional clusters of dunes or bushes. It was unbearably hot. Even without her fleece, she continued to sweat. The air was blistering, as if she was sitting next to an open fire. It burned her throat when she breathed. Sweat from her forehead stung her eyes. She looked for the shadiest patch of ground underneath their bush, and then settled down to watch the road.

He returned half an hour later. The sun was halfway across the sky. His t-shirt was soaked through and beads of perspiration dripped down his face and arms. He had tied his fleece around his head, like a turban, to protect his face from the sun. He sat down next to her in the half-hearted shade of the bush.

"Well. There's nothing much to the south," he said. "And no signs of anything on the road."

"How long can we last, without more water?" She didn't think she wanted to hear the answer.

He wrinkled his brow. "I'm not sure. We've got three liters or so of water. That won't last long. Maybe two, maybe three days." He paused. "We'll weaken too. That will make us easy targets, before too long." He looked somber.

He continued. "I looked for places we might dig for water. There's nothing. The best thing, the least bad thing, is to stay here, and not exert ourselves during the day. The more we sweat, the more we'll dehydrate."

She nodded. "I don't think I can move anyway."

Unfortunately, it wasn't much of an exaggeration. The heat was overpowering.

He continued. "And we probably shouldn't talk much. That uses up moisture too."

She nodded again. They sat together under the bush, watching the heat shimmer on the black surface of the road. The wind blew continuously, a constant stream of heat against their backs. Otherwise, the desert was empty and silent.

Nothing moved for the entire day. Each one of them got up twice, looking for a nearby bush to use as a toilet. The second time that she got up, it burned when she urinated. She was dizzy when she stood up as well. By the end of the day, her throat was parched, and her tongue was thick in the back of her mouth.

Towards evening, they shared another Coke, together with a few swallows from one of the bottles of water. She had trouble swallowing at first. The can of soda was empty in a moment, leaving her as thirsty as before. Her throat hurt when she swallowed.

They sat in silence again as the sun began to set. When it was dark, they talked for a few minutes. She was still exhausted, from the last three weeks and the heat of the sun. They finished one of the bottles of water, then curled up around each other, underneath the bush, before they went to sleep. She dreamt of water — icy pitchers of clear, cold water and gurgling mountain streams. When she woke up in the middle of the night, her mouth was parched again. She forced herself to go back to sleep without taking another drink.

It was almost dawn when he gently shook her shoulder. "Wake up call. We may have company."

She woke instantly, rubbing the sleep out of her eyes and sitting up. She was still dizzy.

"Over there. Still a long way off." He pointed north, towards the horizon. She almost missed them, but then saw the lights in the distance, almost blending into the stars.

"Yep," she said. "What's the plan?"

"It's what we said before. You flag the car down. If we're lucky, it's a driver with no passengers, and no weapons. You get him to stop, and I take care of him. If we aren't lucky, I improvise. Just keep your head down."

She thought for a moment, then nodded. She wanted to mention that he didn't have a gun, at least not one with bullets, but decided not to be negative.

He stood and walked across the road, then disappeared into the shadows. It was another fifteen minutes before the car reached them. Dawn was just beginning to break by the time the car arrived. It was an old Land Rover with faded grey paint that bumped along noisily over the corrugated desert road. Dark smoke poured out of its exhaust pipe.

"Ready, now," he said, just loud enough for her to hear.

He was crouched behind a bush on the other side on the road, across from where she waited. She had taken off her fleece and undone her hair. The car slowed when it reached her. It had to slow down, and pull to the side of the road, in order not to hit her. Then it stopped, five meters from where she stood. The driver's door opened.

Her heart leapt. An old man, with no weapon visible, stepped out. He had white hair and dark brown skin like a hazelnut beneath an untidy, dirty white turban. He wore loose white trousers and badly worn leather slippers that looked several sizes too large. His face was friendly, like someone's grandfather. He smiled and said something to her in Arabic.

She replied, "Help me. I don't understand. I'm lost." She tried to look lost and afraid.

The old man smiled and answered, still in Arabic. Still friendly. And then the other three doors of the Land Rover opened, one after another. Five more men climbed out, wearing what looked like military uniforms. They were all armed with pistols, and one was also carrying an AK-47. The soldiers were big, tall and heavily built. They wore sturdy military boots and looked like they worked out daily. Her heart sank. This wasn't good. She had no idea how Jeb would deal with two of these men, much less all five. Most of them were bigger than he was. Even putting aside the fact that they all had weapons and he didn't. Maybe, she thought, they would be friendly, happy to help two lost foreigners.

She moved into the center of the road, into the glare of the headlights, so Jeb could see her. She forced herself not to glance across the road, towards the bush where he was hidden in the half-light. Several of the soldiers came forward. More comments in Arabic, and some laughter, a bit nervous at first. One of the men picked up her pack from the side of the road and began to look through it. Two other men walked behind her.

The man with her pack said something in Arabic, then laughed. More Arabic and more laughter. This time the laughter wasn't nervous. One of the men behind her circled back in front of her. He was in his mid-40s, with oily skin, heavily pocked-marked, and badly shaved. He had silver bars on his shoulders and looked like he was in charge. He stepped up close and eyed her for a moment, then said something else in Arabic. The driver replied in Arabic, provoking a sharp retort from the uniformed man, and more laughter from the others. She could smell the man's breath, heavy with garlic and tobacco. The others circled her now, all of them staring at her.

"I'm lost. Can you help me?"

It was a lot easier now to sound lost and afraid. All of a sudden, she wondered where Jeb was. And what she would do if he just disappeared. If he decided that these odds weren't so good.

The man with the silver bars didn't reply to her question. Instead, he grabbed her by the hair, and dragged her towards the bushes. The other men laughed and followed. She fought back, kicking at the man's legs, and trying to get his hands out of her hair. He slapped her, hard, with his free hand, kicking back at her legs and continuing to drag her into the bushes. Two of the other men followed, one of them starting to unbuckle his belt. There was no sign of Jeb. She started to scream, and the soldier hit her again.

She didn't see what happened next. One second, the soldier with the silver bars and pock-marked face had a hold of her hair, dragging her into the bushes.

The next second, the man was lying in the sand next to the road, neck twisted at an impossible angle, eyes staring vacantly at her, one side of his face an ugly, red mess. She hadn't seen what did that to him. Then she saw Jeb step into the headlights of the car from behind her, facing the remaining four soldiers. His body was relaxed, at ease, poised lightly, almost as if he was a ballerina. He had a large rock the size of a grapefruit in one hand. The bottom of the rock was dark and wet, blood dripping onto the sand.

Two of the remaining men reached for their pistols, while the others moved towards Jeb. He waited for a heartbeat, and then he was on them. Crouched by the bushes at the side of the road, she could barely follow what happened. Instead of retreating, the way the men must have expected, Jeb attacked. His hands and boots, and the stone he carried, cut a path of ruin through the soldiers. He kicked and punched, moving with fluid grace, leaving broken faces and limbs behind. For an instant, as he spun around between two of the soldiers, she caught a glimpse of his face in the glare of the Land Rover's headlights. She hardly recognized him. His eyes were fixed on his next victim, his mouth locked in a half-snarl, teeth bared like a wolf. It scared her, even though he was on her side, protecting her.

One of the men raised his gun, managing to point the weapon in Jeb's direction, but Jeb stepped smoothly past the barrel, headbutted the man in the face, and then, as if in slow motion, ripped out the man's throat with his bare hand, leaving the soldier making wet noises on the ground as he moved on to the next man. Another of the men was still trying to unholster his pistol when Jeb got to him, delivering a flurry of kicks and then a blow with the rock that left the soldier's face bloodied, neck broken, and body limp in the sand.

In less than a minute, all five of the soldiers lay on the road. She was sure that none of them would ever get up again. Jeb surveyed them coldly. None of the men had scratched, or even touched, him. Blood dripped off the fingers of one of his hands, from the throat of the soldier he had killed. His other hand still held the rock, also wet with blood.

The elderly driver tried to clamber back into the car. He didn't succeed. Jeb pounced on him, slapped him, brutally, across the face, then searched him for weapons. He dropped the rock by the side of the road. It was shiny in the car's headlights, slick with the soldiers' blood.

"Get their guns," he ordered.

Then he thought better of it. "Forget that. Come over here. Watch this guy."

She did what she was told. He handed her a pistol, which he had apparently taken while he was dispatching the five soldiers. "Just point it at his chest," he said.

He stripped the five bodies of their pistols, checking for additional weapons. He also collected the AK-47s, then deposited the guns in the car. He returned and looked at the driver, lost in thought.

"You can't just kill him," she said.

He looked at her dismissively and continued to eye the driver. His face had the same look that it had when he was killing the five soldiers. The old man's lips started to quiver.

Jeb said something, apparently in Arabic, in a low, menacing voice. The old man started to cry. Jeb slapped him, hard, across the face again, and said something else in Arabic. The old man looked at him and struggled to take a breath. Then the man tried to steady himself, leaning against the front of the car.

After the old man pulled himself together, he and Jeb talked for a few minutes in Arabic, while she waited by the side of the road, still holding the pistol. She hadn't expected that Jeb could speak Arabic, but it made sense when she thought about it. Given who he was. The old man was answering Jeb's questions. At one point, Jeb snarled and took a step closer to the man. The driver started to quiver again, then answered, stammering, and fighting back tears. She could understand why the man was afraid.

When he was finished, Jeb had her stand guard over the old man again. He found rope in the car and used it to bind the man's hands and feet, then loaded him into the luggage compartment. When he was finished, he dragged the five bodies off the road, into the bushes. She realized with a chill that he had killed all five of the soldiers — with nothing but his hands and a rock. The men had never really had a chance against Jeb, notwithstanding their numbers and their weapons. She also realized that she was afraid again, afraid of him.

He returned a few minutes later. The road was empty now.

"Let's go then," he said.

They got into the Land Rover. It smelled of dust, stale tobacco, and sweat. The windshield was cracked and covered with dust. The ancient seats were dirty and uncomfortable, their springs broken years before.

He started the engine, listened for a moment, then turned the car around, and they headed north. Neither of them said anything for a while. He drove in silence for fifteen minutes.

"They would have killed you. After a while," he said. His voice was hard and flat. He sounded angry. She knew he was right. She nodded and tried to find her voice. It took a moment.

"I know. I just wasn't expecting it. It was so sudden."

He was quiet for a moment. "I'm sorry. We should have talked it through more. It's my fault," he said.

He was quiet again. She watched him driving out of the corner of her eye. He was calm now. And scary. Even scarier than the Russians.

"It's my job, you know," he said after a while. "It's what I do. Or did."

She looked at him. He looked troubled, almost embarrassed that he had frightened her. She thought for a few moments, trying to process what had happened.

"I know that," she said quietly, after a while. "Don't forget, I'm the one with the bamboo spears," she laughed wryly. "I know you had to do it."

"They weren't any different from the Russians," he said. "They had worse luck but were just as bad."

He continued after a moment. "Maybe I didn't have to do all that, maybe not to all of them," he admitted finally. "I was angry, worried."

He paused again, then finished: "I could hear what they were saying, what they had in mind, what they had in mind for you."

She looked at him again. She wondered if he was telling the truth. There wasn't any reason to trust him. He could say whatever he wanted, whatever he wanted her to hear. They drove in silence after that for the rest of the morning, each one lost in thought, the road stretching out in front of them like a black ribbon across the desert.

Chapter 38

Ivan Petronov

He woke late. Light was streaming into the room through half-opened curtains. His head pounded from last night's vodka. He struggled upright, leaning against the headboard, knees up in the bed, looking around the room. He didn't recognize it. It took a moment to remember. Then he recalled. The villa in Kigali. The night before, when he had used her, rougher than ever before. And he was sure that she had loved it. It made him feel strong, powerful, notwithstanding the hangover.

Then he recalled the days before that. The fiasco in Goma, their desperate flight to Kigali, Alexei's silence. The darkness closed in around him again. His head continued to throb, one wave of pain after another. He stared out the window, trying to summon the energy to climb out of bed. He felt lost again.

Yan came silently into the room. She wore a light pink silk dress, simple and thin, and a single string of pearls, white against her skin. Her feet were bare on the dark wood floor. She carried a mug of coffee, steaming and strong, with hot milk, foamed the way he liked it, along with three aspirin. She sat on the side of the bed and kissed his cheek, handing him the coffee.

"My little Russian monster. Did you sleep well?"

She smiled shyly at him, then blushed slightly and looked away, as if she were flustered. Despite his gloom, he smiled to himself. She always amazed him. How she wanted him, so badly, no matter how rough or drunk he was. And then, how she was so sweet, so innocent, afterwards.

"My little girl. I slept like a child," he answered.

He didn't mention his rage the night before, the beating or the belt. She waited until he had taken a drink of the coffee.

"Your phone's been ringing all morning," she said.

She had his phone in her hand.

He scowled. "You should have woken me."

He took the phone from her and looked at the missed call list. "It's Alexei," he said.

He got laboriously out of bed and crossed the room to the table where his laptop stood. His paunch was larger than ever. He put that thought out of his mind and stood there, naked and barefoot, as he went through the computer's log-in procedures. She watched him, her eyes expressionless. Once he was logged in, he knelt before the computer, checking his email accounts. After a moment, he smiled expansively, his face beaming. It was excellent. Just as he had expected, just the way he had planned things.

"Alexei. I knew it. The man is a prince," he declared.

She watched him as he went on. "He can send another team. A better one. They can leave right away. The same price as the first one. And he already arranged for his friends in Moscow, at the FSS, to watch for the girl, and to watch the Americans."

He continued peering at his emails. And smiled again.

"Alexei has a lead. A UN plane. It was hijacked, from an airfield near Goma. Then crashed in Egypt, near the Libyan border. It must be the girl. The Americans didn't get her after all." He paused. "And something else. She may have help."

She narrowed her eyes. "Who would help her?" she asked.

"Don't ask me."

He paused. "Maybe Alexei is playing with me," he mused.

She remained silent, watching him.

"Maybe one of the Americans played a double game," he said, after another pause.

"Yes," she said quickly. "Maybe a double game, or triple, by one of the Americans."

She took the coffee mug over to him and put it beside the computer. He drank again, absent-mindedly, while he stared at the screen.

"You could speak with Alexei," she suggested. "Let me make you breakfast first though. Better talk to him on a full stomach."

He grunted and looked back at the screen. She left the room silently. After a few minutes, he turned off the computer and went into the bathroom. He showered quickly, thinking about their next moves. They would go to Europe. Maybe Italy, maybe Spain, or Greece. The girl couldn't stay in Libya, either with or without help. She could disappear in Europe, blend in with the crowds of tourists and students. That's where she would go. And that was where they would follow.

They really needed Alexei's help, he thought as he stepped out of the shower. There was a fresh mug of coffee waiting next to the bathroom sink. He could hear her cooking him eggs and bacon in the kitchen. He smiled.

He ate heartily while she watched from across the dining room table, where they had sat three nights ago. Afterwards, he sat on the veranda at the back of the villa and called Alexei. The call was friendly and very productive. He had forgotten how long they had known each other and how much the man owed him. As nearly as he could tell, the full services of the FSS and Russia's other intelligence agencies were at his disposal. For a price, of course. They discussed how to put those services to best use. Alexei even apologized for the quality of the men he had supplied previously. What happened in the jungle, and then in Goma, was inexcusable, he said. He promised that the new men would be better.

Ivan came back into the house smiling broadly. He was in a jovial mood.

"Let's pack. There's a flight to Rome tonight, just after midnight. It's the first flight to Europe."

She smiled. "Breakfast in Rome. That sounds perfect."

He watched her go, then turned back to the remnants of breakfast, sopping up the pools of egg yolk and bacon grease with the last piece of toast. Then he pushed his chair back from the table and looked into the garden, savoring his success. He was back on the girl's trail, with a new team. This time, they would get her, and the file. He was sure of it.

Chapter 39
Sara West

They drove most of the day, along the empty road. The desert stretched out on either side of the track, flat and featureless, like an endless parking lot, interrupted only by scattered bushes and occasional sets of dunes. They had passed no other cars, no villages, no checkpoints. Just 450 kilometers of broken road and empty desert.

They ate dates and bread, which they found in a bag on the rear seat, together with a few plastic bottles of water. The water was warm, tasted slightly metallic, and the bread was stale and dry. But the dates were sweet and bursting with thick, golden syrup. After a diet of Snickers and potato chips for the last two days, they finished the soldiers' rations greedily, licking the sticky syrup off their fingers, as the Land Rover bounced along the road.

They were closer to the Mediterranean than she expected. It would only be another hundred kilometers or so before they reached the coastline. They would also be coming to populated areas soon, with villages and checkpoints. In the middle of the afternoon, Jeb stopped the car and pulled its former driver out of the luggage compartment. The old man was disoriented after spending ten hours tied up in the rear of the car. Jeb questioned him again in Arabic, sharply grabbing him once by the throat when the man failed to answer to his satisfaction.

The man came from the coastal region near the Egyptian border, where the road was headed. He knew the villages, militias, and roads. He also wanted to live. Jeb had frightened him, and he talked freely, his voice breaking from time to time, but answering all of Jeb's questions and occasionally volunteering information. He told them about the checkpoints along the road, where the militia that controlled the area demanded tolls and blocked the route. He explained how to avoid the checkpoints, the tracks that the locals used when they wanted to bypass the guard-posts. He described the villages along the road, further to the north, along the coastline.

The old man also told them about the smugglers, the Italians and Greeks, who controlled the ships that took the refugees north, across the Mediterranean to Europe. He described where the smugglers could be found, what they charged, where their ships would wait and where the refugees would be kept, before their voyages north. Jeb interrupted him from time to time, breaking off occasionally to summarize the conversation for her.

After an hour or so, Jeb gave the old man more water and allowed him to walk away from the car, to stretch his legs and to pray, on a tattered square of carpet that the man kept in the back of the car. When he returned, Jeb questioned him again, more closely, about the checkpoints, militias, and smugglers. He let the man sit in the shade of the car now, comfortably, and gave him a handful of dates and more water. The man told them that his name was Ahmed, and then ate greedily, continuing to answer Jeb's questions.

It turned out that Ahmed was related to a local militia leader. One of his nephews was the commander of militia forces further along the coast, to the west, in the direction of Benghazi. Jeb and the man talked freely now in Arabic, while she found a place to sit in the shade of one of the acacia trees growing alongside the road.

It took a while, but after an hour of meandering conversation, Ahmed suggested a deal — that they release him, rather than killing him like the others, and in return he would make sure they received safe passage to one of the smuggler's camps and then on to Europe. Ahmed's nephew could arrange both and would do so in return for his uncle's safety. Ahmed enthusiastically outlined the exchange. His voice was steadier now, and he gestured expansively with his hands.

Ahmed's face fell again when Jeb produced the leather briefcase that they had found beneath the driver's seat, wrapped in an old canvas sack. Inside the briefcase, in neat stacks bound by rubber-bands, was $150,000 in new $50 bills. The money was intended for southern tribes working with Ahmed's nephew. After a moment, though, Ahmed's smile was back. If the money was returned, he assured them, then there was no doubt: his nephew would make sure that they were delivered safely to the Italian coast. This was certain, a matter of family honor.

Jeb had looked appropriately skeptical and mulled the proposal, as if it were a surprise to him. He had also questioned Ahmed sharply about his family relations, how well he knew his nephew, his nephew's position in the militia and the number of fighters he commanded. Then he left Ahmed to enjoy more dates and a cigarette, while he joined her underneath the tree. He described his conversations with the old man and said that it might be their ticket out of Libya. At least assuming Ahmed was telling the truth and that their luck held. Then he went back to finish their negotiations with the old man.

Half an hour later, the Land Rover pulled onto the road again, heading back south, the direction they came from. This time, it had three occupants, including an elderly local man, sitting next to the driver. The driver was light-skinned and wore a dirty white turban above mirrored sunglasses. The old man looked nervously, from time to time, at the bulge in the waistband of the driver's jeans, where one of the soldiers' pistols was tucked, but for the most part he was all smiles, like someone whose life had just been spared.

After twenty kilometers or so, they turned off the road onto a faint dirt track that the old man pointed out, and then followed it, across more empty desert. It took another couple hours, but by the end of the day, having encountered no checkpoints, they had reached the coastline. They passed two villages along the way, tiny collections of one-story stone buildings, clustered around the crossing of dirt tracks in the middle of the desert. Children and an old man waved to Ahmed in one of the villages as they drove past, but otherwise the road was empty, just as Ahmed had promised.

When they reached the shore, they left the car parked in the shade of a tree and climbed up to the top of a ridge that looked out over the water. They could smell the salt of the sea, fresh and tangy in the breeze. The ridge was set back a couple hundred meters from the shoreline and looked down onto a compound of a dozen or so buildings and another handful of tents, hugging the curve of a rocky cove. A scattering of lights glowed in the twilight. A few dogs wandered lazily around the compound, in search of scraps or shade.

Ahmed smiled broadly and reminded them of his promise that they would be able to avoid the checkpoints and that he would bring them to the camp of one of the human traffickers. He pointed to a brand-new SUV, parked near the largest of the stone buildings, and assured them that this was a good sign, that the Italians were there. He also pointed out a rusty fishing vessel anchored five hundred meters or so offshore, further to the east. That was the smugglers' ship, which they used to transport their human cargo across the Mediterranean.

They debated how to approach the Italians. There weren't many options, and they ended up driving straight down into the compound. Jeb kept one of the soldiers' pistols in his waist band, and an AK-47 on the floor, next to his feet, beside the briefcase they had found beneath the driver's seat. Ahmed assured them that he would handle everything, that he knew the Italians and that they trusted him. Jeb was skeptical, but couldn't think of any better alternative, so the three of them drove up unannounced to the smugglers' compound.

When they reached the compound, two men in jeans and dark t-shirts, carrying AK-47s, appeared from one of the buildings. Ahmed greeted them in Arabic and the men replied. It went just as Ahmed had promised. The two men lowered their weapons, smiles breaking out after Ahmed's greetings. One of the men walked back into the compound, disappearing into the largest of the stone buildings. He reappeared a few minutes later, directing them to park the Land Rover next to the building.

The two men stood watch as Ahmed, followed by the two of them, exited the car and entered the stone building. Jeb brought his pistol, tucked into his waistband, and the briefcase filled with the $50 bills. The interior of the building was rustic, but comfortable — bare stone floors and walls, traditional wooden furniture, a brass lantern hanging from the ceiling, and tribal carpets on the floor. A large fireplace dominated the entrance chamber, its sides darkened by soot.

Antonio Allesandri was a big man — a bit taller than Jeb and more than thirty kilos heavier, with dark brown hair slicked back from his forehead and a bushy beard. He was dressed in neatly pressed grey trousers and a baby blue polo shirt. A pair of designer sunglasses were perched on the top of his head, and he wore a chunky gold ring in one ear, like a pirate, was well as a thick gold necklace. His

English was heavily accented when he greeted Ahmed. Ahmed smiled uncomfortably, before Allesandri nodded at his guests. Jeb responded, first in English, then switching to Arabic halfway through his greeting, and then back to English again when he saw that Allesandri didn't understand.

"Like Ahmed said, we're old friends. He's been a great help. Probably saved our lives. We promised to return the favor. We wouldn't want anything to happen to Ahmed. Not on my watch."

Like Allesandri's men, Jeb had his pistol tucked in the front of his jeans this time. He kept his hands away from the weapon the entire time.

Allesandri laughed out loud. "Oh, my friend. Excuse me. I missed your name. And your lovely friend's name," he said, nodding at Sara.

Jeb responded with a smile, offering his hand. "You're quite right. We haven't been properly introduced. Matt. Matt Lake, and this is my wife, Karen."

She smiled as well. Allesandri laughed again. His security guards chuckled as well.

"No doubt. I am delighted to meet you. A real pleasure," he said, taking Jeb's hand warmly. He had heavy gold rings on three of his fingers.

Allesandri continued. "So, Mr. and Mrs. Lake, what brings you to my humble abode? What can I do for you and your friend, Ahmed?" His smile was even broader.

"We want to visit your country, Mr. Allesandri. Naples. Or Bari. Somewhere in the south."

Allesandri laughed again. "Of course. Such beautiful places. I am from Naples. A lovely city. And you wish to go by sea, I suppose. A cruise, perhaps?"

"Just that. Nothing too fancy. But a quick voyage, for the three of us. That would be perfect," Jeb replied.

"The three of you? Your friend, Ahmed? Are you sure? His Italian is not so good, I believe."

"We have promised to show him your country, my friend. As much of it as he wishes. We'll make sure that he is safe. That nothing happens to him."

Allesandri glanced at Ahmed, then asked him, translated by one of the guards, whether this was true, that he wished to visit Italy. Ahmed swallowed nervously, then nodded, explaining that he had wanted to visit Rome his entire life. The guard translated into English again. Jeb stepped slightly closer to Ahmed as the old man spoke, still smiling at Allesandri, like they were old drinking buddies.

Allesandri hesitated for a moment after Ahmed replied, then smiled back. "Excellent. Whatever Ahmed wishes, I am pleased to arrange. I am only your humble servant."

He paused again, stroking his beard, then continued. "Then there is the question of money, I am afraid. This is not cheap, what you ask. Not at all. My boats are booked months in advance. This is difficult, even for friends of Ahmed."

Jeb held up the briefcase. "We understand. Completely. But this should be enough, I am sure."

He opened the briefcase, letting Allesandri see the stacks of $50 bills, lined up neatly like peas in a pod. Allesandri looked into the case, then selected one stack and inspected it for a moment, before nodding.

"Well, then, Mr. Lake. You are right. That will do. We have a deal. A friend of Ahmed's family is a friend of mine. Our next ship leaves tomorrow, just after sunset. Don't forget the briefcase." He smiled even more broadly.

"We'll be there. Tomorrow evening. All of us," Jeb replied. "We'll see you then."

Jeb nodded to her, then looked towards the door. They left, with Ahmed exiting first. Jeb made room for her to walk ahead of him, then followed, close behind. Allesandri's guards came out with them, then waited in front of the house as they climbed into the Land Rover.

Jeb drove them back onto the ridge, then further along the desert track. Ahmed didn't say a word. They drove back through the desert villages they had passed earlier. Both villages were deserted this time. A dozen kilometers later, Jeb turned the Land Rover off the track and into the scrublands that surrounded the road. He drove for twenty minutes or so, swerving to avoid bushes, rocks, and gullies. Finally, in what looked like the middle of nowhere, he eased the car to a halt in a shallow dip, concealed from view by bushes and rocks. He turned off the Land Rover's engine. The desert was silent around them. The only sound was the bushes rustling in the wind. They could still smell the sea.

Ahmed looked at Jeb. After a moment, he asked, in Arabic, what would happen next. Jeb explained that they would spend the night here, in the car. It wouldn't be comfortable, but it was safe. Tomorrow they would return — all three of them — to Allesandri's compound. They would depart — all three of them — that night for Italy, on Allesandri's ship. Ahmed could return with the same ship, if he wanted to. But he would have to come with them. Jeb said he was sure that Ahmed understood.

Ahmed nodded. He wasn't happy. But he understood. A hostage, he said, in Arabic. Jeb nodded. "But remember my promise. I gave you my word. I won't hurt you."

Ahmed nodded again. Then turned towards the window, leaned back against the seat, and closed his eyes.

Jeb glanced at her, then suggested she settle in as well. She stretched out on the rear seat, rolling her fleece into a pillow. Jeb turned sideways, then leaned back against the door, his feet up on the seat. He kept the pistol tucked into his jeans.

She didn't fall asleep for a long time. She lay awake and watched the two men, first Ahmed, and then Jeb. She would have been dead, again, without Jeb. But she still didn't trust him. He had to be using her, almost the way he was using Ahmed and Allesandri. That was true no matter how many times he saved her life, no matter how infectious his smile might be, no matter how good or how safe she felt with him. She looked away and watched the stars rise above the horizon, out of the window of the car. She finally drifted off to sleep late in the night, after the stars had come out and lit up the sky again.

Chapter 40
Maximilian Staehelin

The bank's offices were just off Bahnhofstrasse in the center of Zurich. They were only a few hundred meters away from the headquarters of UBS, in the heart of Switzerland's financial district. Staehelin & Co. was one of the most respected private banks in the city, which was crowded with dozens of exclusive and very well-respected private banks.

The bank was founded in the eighteenth century and, for the past seventy years, it had been the banker for the political and economic elite in much of Europe and a scattering of other countries around the world. It had a reputation for avoiding the corrupt dictators, generals, and politicians who frequented other Swiss private banks. Staehelin & Co. had put principle before quick profits, shunning deposits of bribes, drug money, and other ill-gotten gains from Africa, the Middle East, China, and elsewhere. Instead, the bank built a reputation for rectitude and honesty. Even its competitors respected the bank's integrity.

The bank's offices overlooked the Limmat River, across the street from the Swiss bank regulatory authority. The building was an architectural masterpiece, designed by a world-famous architect from Brazil. The exterior was severe, covered mostly with rough stone, with scattered windows, while the interior was sleek and open, with floor-to-ceiling windows on five floors of an enormous internal atrium.

Staehelin & Co. was known for its refusal to advertise, no matter what its rivals chose to do, but it had proudly announced the building's selection as one of Switzerland's most environmentally friendly offices. The bank also donated 5% of its profits each year to charities, focused on improving labor standards around the world. The bank adopted the policy in the 1960s, with the full support of its major shareholders, the Staehelin family trust.

Maximilian Staehelin's office was on the top floor of the building. The office was impressive, but not over-awing. It looked over the river, with panoramic views to Lake Zurich and the Swiss Alps in the distance. The furniture in Staehelin's office was modern and minimalist. A sleek black desk, with no drawers, stood to one side of the room, with an elegant desktop computer resting on top of it. Apart from a telephone, also sleek and modern, there was nothing else on the desk. Four chairs, black leather and matte metal, stood in front of the desk, arranged precisely on the dark grey carpet.

There were no files, and no other furniture, in the room. Two brightly colored oil paintings, both Picassos, hung on the walls, but otherwise the office was unadorned. Recessed lighting, and sunlight from the floor-to-ceiling windows, gave the room an open, airy feel. Classical music played softly from a concealed sound system.

Staehelin was the Chairman of the bank's management board, as well as its largest shareholder. He had held the position for the past twenty years, taking over from his father, who had served for almost forty years before him. Staehelin sat behind the desk, reading a report on the computer screen. He was dressed formally, in a dark grey, almost black, suit, and dark blue tie. His hair was black, grey at the temples, combed straight back from his forehead. He was handsome, with a long, straight nose, thin lips, and dark brown eyes. His brow furrowed as he read. He leaned forward in his chair, one hand holding the computer's mouse. He wore a pinky ring with the Staehelin family crest and an elegant Swiss wristwatch.

The report had been produced, at considerable expense, by a private investigative firm known for its contacts in intelligence services and governments around the world. The firm had been tasked by Staehelin & Co. for years with reporting on discoveries of Nazi archives and files, particularly in relation to banking. The cost was justified as part of the bank's campaign to ensure that it accepted no illegal or unsavory funds.

The dossier reported on rumors in Moscow and Washington. The rumors were unconfirmed, but emanated from highly placed informants, who said that large amounts of money and activity were being directed towards the subject of the rumors. The informants reported that a plane wreck had been discovered, somewhere in East Africa, containing a trove of Nazi documents. The documents supposedly included details of a secret Nazi fund, allegedly deposited in unnamed Swiss banks during WWII.

Russian intelligence services were reportedly making efforts to find the wreckage and recover the files. There were reports that other spy agencies were also involved, but these were unconfirmed. The reports were all linked to a mysterious series of shootings and explosions in Goma, not far from Kigali, that left a couple dozen bodies scattered around the town.

Staehelin read the dossier twice. It was an odd report and there was no particular reason for alarm, but the rumors still worried him. The investigative firm was tasked to ferret out exactly this sort of information, so that he could take protective measures if they became necessary. He told himself that those measures weren't needed now. That the report contained nothing more than unconfirmed rumors. Even if true, the alleged plane wreck, and "Nazi" files, might contain nothing. Even if the files existed, and concerned secret Nazi funds, there was no hint that the bank was mentioned in the files. There was no reason to be concerned.

Still, he felt his throat tighten at the thought of reports about Nazi assets hidden in Swiss banks. Staehelin & Co. had survived previous scandals over dormant Jewish accounts and assets looted by the Third Reich and hidden in Swiss banks without incident. The bank had always served a small, elite clientele, and had invariably exercised discretion in choosing whom to do business with. Staehelin & Co had encountered virtually none of the problems that most other Swiss banks had faced from their WWII dealings.

But Staehelin knew very well that the regulators and lawyers had missed things at Staehelin & Co. that were much more important than what they had found in other banks. He hated even to think about it, but he couldn't help remembering the accounts that the bank had held since the last days of WWII — enormous deposits of Nazi money that had been kept off the bank's accounts, hidden from the accountants, lawyers, and regulators. Hidden even from the bank's supervisory board, and instead, known only to Staehelin, like his father before him.

He shuddered at the thought that the deposits might be discovered. If they were revealed, he and the bank would be ruined: the secret accounts were improper, violating dozens of Swiss banking regulations. It would be a disaster if they were ever revealed.

He calmed himself. This report was no doubt a false alarm. It had been seventy-five years since the Second World War had ended. There weren't any secret files floating around Africa linking Staehelin & Co. to the Nazis. That was nonsense. Staehelin chided himself for letting his imagination get the better of him, conjuring up demons for no reason.

The phone rang. It was the Speaker of the Swiss Parliament, confirming dinner and the opera that evening. Staehelin answered cheerfully, congratulating the man on his birthday and describing with enthusiasm the restaurant where his secretary had booked dinner. It was a new establishment but had already earned two Michelin stars. It would be a real treat. He gave no hint of the worries that had weighed on him a few minutes before.

After he hung up, Staehelin left his office. Frau Schmitt, his secretary for the past twenty years, wished him a pleasant evening. She used the formal mode of address, as befitted his station. He took his private elevator to the underground garage, where his chauffeur was on call. With luck, he would be home in time for a glass of champagne on the patio before they left for the opera. As his Mercedes pulled into the traffic along the lake, Staehelin opened his elegant leather briefcase, a Christmas present from his wife, put on his reading glasses and began reviewing the bank's draft accounts. He was the picture of Swiss propriety.

Chapter 41
Sara West

The sun woke her up. It was streaming in through the windows of the Land Rover. She had slept nearly ten hours, waking up cold at some point in the middle of the night and wishing she still had her sleeping bag. She snuggled further into her fleece instead and managed to sleep through the rest of the night in the back seat of the car. The Land Rover was empty — Jeb and Ahmed must have left at some point. She sat up and peered out of the dusty windows, finally spotting the two men seated under a tree fifty meters away. They were talking like old friends.

Ahmed had made tea using a battered aluminum tea pot on a small butane stove, which he had produced from the rear of the Land Rover. She walked over to them, then shared the mug that Jeb had been using and watched the wind in the bushes as it swept across the desert, blowing north out of the Sahara. The day was already hot, even though it was only 9 a.m. in the morning.

She sat next to Jeb on a large, flat stone, the two of them handing the mug of tea back and forth. Ahmed was in the middle of what seemed to be an endless Arabic story, accompanied by elaborate hand gestures, which periodically prompted Jeb to chuckle appreciatively. There was no sign that the story was anywhere close to ending. When she had finished two cups of tea, plus the dates and bread that they saved for her, she excused herself and left Jeb to Ahmed's narration. He winked as she left, as if to say that it was going to be a long day.

She spent the afternoon in the car, trying to make sense of the past four weeks. She still hadn't fully digested what had happened. She wondered if she ever would. Her life had been ordered and comfortable — a fiancé and a promising career. She had been a relatively normal, well-adjusted graduate student, with a predictable, reasonably settled life. Exotic treks in obscure jungles were a little out of the ordinary, but tenure at a good university, marriage, and kids lay reliably ahead. And she had been happy. Or at least content.

That was all gone now. Two teams of trained killers were probably still hunting her, willing to stop at nothing to get their hands on the files that she had found in the jungle. She was having tea with another killer in the middle of the Libyan desert, and she was about to be smuggled into Italy by yet other killers. And, truth be told, she was not that different from any of these men, not anymore, as her bamboo spears and the grenades had revealed. She realized, with a sort of clinical detachment, that she didn't know herself anymore, that she didn't really know who she had been or who she had become. Which of the people was really her — the geeky botanist and happy girlfriend, the terrified victim, running for her life, or the killer with the bamboo spears and machete? She wasn't sure anymore.

She was even less sure about Jeb Fisher, if that really was his name. He was a killer. A savage, ruthless killer. She had seen it on his face in the desert two days ago. He had also been a heartbeat away from killing her in the hotel in Goma — she saw that in his eyes as well. Or at least from turning her over to his CIA friends, which was no different. He hadn't done either though, and instead he saved her life — at least twice, and probably more times than that.

And she was still certain to be dead without him. She had managed to survive, for a few weeks, in the jungle. But she had been more experienced than her pursuers in the wilderness, and all their resources — their helicopters and guns — had been mostly useless out there. It would be different in other places. In the deserts, in cities, just about everywhere else, they would be in their element. And their equipment and resources would be lethally effective. Not to mention the fact that she had virtually no money, much less a passport or credit card. She would be hunted down and dead before she knew it, once they got back to civilization.

Jeb could protect her now. If anyone could save her, he could. She hated the thought of being dependent on him, but it was the reality. He was trained at all the things she needed — flying planes, smuggling himself across borders, avoiding detection, and killing people who tried to hurt them. She remembered the five bodies in the desert, and the bloody stone, again. If she was going to survive, she needed him.

But she was just as sure that she couldn't trust him. It wasn't just that he had been about to kill her. More important, there was no good reason for him to have turned on his former comrades, his friends, and to have killed them, just the way he killed the five men on the desert road. The only explanation for his actions must be that he wanted the same thing that the others did, that he wanted the files that she had found, just like everyone else did. It was just that he was smarter and more ruthless than the others. He would persuade her to hand the files over to him, freely, and then kill her afterwards, instead of killing her first.

She wished it were different. Not just because it would be a whole lot safer. But also because she really wanted to trust him, because she liked the way he had responded when she told him about what happened in the jungle, and to her father, the easy way he laughed, and his confidence when the odds looked hopeless. And he was attractive. Not like the men she had known in the past, like Robert or the handful of university tutors and students before him. Instead, he was attractive in a raw, physical way that stirred something deep inside her, drawing her to him when she watched him move and when he had held her through the desert night. But she forced herself to put those thoughts aside, and to focus on staying alive. And that meant not trusting him. It meant using him, using him to protect herself.

"Planning something else sneaky?"

She started, feeling half-guilty. He had walked over next to her. Trim and tanned, looking well-rested.

"Here. You must be thirsty," he said, handing her a water bottle, still cool from the cold of the desert night.

"Thanks. That's nice." She took a long drink, then shifted into light and easy mode.

"Sorry I slept so late. I hope Ahmed was good company," she said with a smile.

He laughed. "Not as good as you. But I did learn the history of his family, and his village. He likes to talk."

He paused for a moment, then continued. "I think I've worked out the next step in our little world tour and wanted to run it past you. Tell me what you think," he said with a half-smile.

He outlined a simple, but clever, plan. They would travel with Allesandri's other passengers, the refugees, on his vessel. They would take Ahmed with them, all the way to Italy, and release him when they arrived safely on the Italian mainland. Ahmed would be their insurance policy, against either Allesandri or Ahmed's family trying something stupid.

She wasn't sure. "What if something goes wrong? We can't hurt Ahmed, or we lose our insurance policy. Won't they know that?"

He laughed and said that she should have been a spy. That was a problem. But neither Allesandri nor Ahmed's family had any reason to put Ahmed in danger and, in any case, there wasn't any better option. Letting the two of them go was easy, and a good trade for Ahmed's safety. The really important thing though, was for her to stay very close to him, the entire time. The biggest risk, he said, was that someone would try to grab her, as a hostage, to trade for Ahmed. That was a scenario they needed to avoid.

She didn't know whether to be touched at his protectiveness or to think that he was using her, making sure to protect the value of his captive. But she nodded and said that the plan sounded fine. Or at least the best they could do. Then she excused herself, leaving him to explain the plan to Ahmed and reassure the old man that he wouldn't be harmed.

He apparently succeeded. After a long talk, the two men shook hands, then embraced like old friends. After that, they settled in for another chapter of the family history. When dusk arrived, they departed in the Land Rover, Ahmed smiling and still chattering away in Arabic.

"His first crush," Jeb commented to her during a pause in the narration.

They reached Allesandri's compound without incident. The villages were dark again, except for a few howling dogs, and the roads were equally empty. The compound by the coast was bustling though. A dozen vans and cars were parked hap-hazardly along the track that led down to the sea and clusters of men and women, a few with young children, waited in the vehicles' lights by the side of the road. Young Libyan militia men, swathed in white or tan lengths of cloth, all of them carrying weapons of some sort, stood watch over the various groups of refugees. Six inflatable life rafts were beached on the shore of the cove. More armed men guarded the vessels.

They left the Land Rover along the side of the road and walked down into the compound in the dark. Jeb positioned Ahmed squarely in front of him as they walked among the buildings and tents, his pistol tucked in the front of his jeans. He also brought the AK-47 this time, carrying it casually in one hand. She walked next to Jeb, their arms almost brushing, with one of the weapons that Jeb had taken from the Libyan militiamen in her waistband as well. She also carried the dirty canvas bag, containing the briefcase and the stacks of $50 bills.

Twice, they were stopped by the young men with guns and flashlights. Each time, Ahmed answered, with Jeb watchfully observing. Each time as well, they were waved along.

The refugees were from every part of the African continent and Middle East. Tall, dark East Africans, shorter Congolese, light-skinned Ethiopians and Eritre-ans, Arabic-speaking Syrians and Libyans — all waiting anxiously in little groups. They had spent their life savings, or that of their families, to get this far. These were the lucky ones, as well. Countless others were cheated, paying for transport that never arrived or disappearing in mass graves in the Libyan or Egyptian deserts. They had all risked everything for the chance to try and start a new life — scrub-bing floors or butchering chickens in Europe, taking the jobs that Europeans weren't willing to do. Now, they were on the doorstep to the promised land, only a few hours of sea lying ahead of them.

The three of them made their way along the darkened road to the stone build-ing in the center of the compound, where they had met with Allesandri the night before. Jeb kept Ahmed in front of them and a shoulder-high stone wall to one side. He pulled the pistol even further out of his jeans and kept the AK-47 out and ready. He made sure, as well, that they avoided the light that spilled out of a few of the buildings along the way, keeping the three of them hidden in the shadows most of the way.

When they reached the stone building, they waited in the darkened alleyway, as Allesandri's guards disappeared inside. The guards reappeared a few minutes later, flanking the smuggler. Allesandri stood on the porch of the house, smiling broadly. She noticed this time that one of his front teeth was capped, the gold glinting in the lights of the compound.

"My friends. Ahmed. Welcome. Welcome to my home."

He gestured for them to come in. "Come. Share a glass of wine with me. It's Algerian, but very good. As good as any Chianti, you can be sure."

Jeb smiled just as broadly. "Thank you. Thank you so much, Antonio. But we do not drink."

He stepped slightly to the side of Ahmed, in front of her, making sure that his AK-47 was fully visible.

"Well then. Of course. But please, some tea, mint tea, after your journey. You must be thirsty." Allesandri's smile was fading.

"We would love to. Thank you again, Antonio, my friend. It is most kind. But we have just eaten. And we wouldn't want to delay the ship," Jeb said, nodding at the lifeboats.

Allessandri's smile disappeared entirely. "Mr. Lake. That is what you call your-self, I believe. You and your lovely friend are free to go. My ship is your ship. But Ahmed is another matter. I have been in touch with his nephew. He tells me that Ahmed has never wanted to visit Rome, or my beloved Italy. I cannot understand that, not at all, but I am assured that it is true. So, Ahmed will remain here, while you and your friend are free to go."

As Allessandri spoke, two more men, in traditional tribal garb, came out of the house to stand beside him. They both nodded to Ahmed — second cousins most likely, she thought to herself. She tried to ignore the wave of panic that rose in her stomach. This wasn't what they'd planned.

Jeb just smiled again, a little lazily, like this was just what he had expected, and as if he didn't have a care in the world.

"My friend. Thank you for your assurances. They are most kind. And fully accepted. But Antonio, my friend, you must ask Ahmed, not me. Ask him whether he wishes to visit your country. And his nephew, he should ask the same questions." Jeb nodded at the two men in traditional garb.

The furrows on Allesandri's brow deepened. She realized that he probably did not speak Arabic well enough to ask the questions.

After a moment, Jeb spoke again, this time in Arabic, addressing both Ahmed and the two new arrivals, inviting Ahmed freely to declare whether he wished to visit Italy or not. Hurried translations then ensued, with Allesandri and his guards whispering to the two cousins. Ahmed answered immediately, declaring his firm intention to visit Italy, if only to set foot on its shores. He needn't visit Rome, or even Bari, but to set his feet on the Italian coastline, if only for a moment, this would fulfill a life-long dream. He nodded vigorously, one hand on his heart.

Before Allesandri could speak again, one of his security guards reached towards his weapon. She hadn't noticed, instead intent on Ahmed and the dialogue. But Jeb reacted like a cat, his right hand pulling the pistol out of his pants and leveling it at the guard, his left arm around her waist, drawing her body close to his, keeping Ahmed between them and the guards. The same arm held the AK-47, now pointed directly at Allesandri and his men.

Jeb spoke calmly to Allesandri, as if he were asking him about the menu at an up-market deli in New York.

"You can see that Ahmed wants to travel with us, at least to the Italian shoreline. Antonio, I know you are a man of your word. Please don't allow any of your men to spoil that reputation, or worse. Ahmed will be back with his nephew by noon tomorrow, with his dream satisfied, if you keep your men under control. You have my word on that. And if something happens tonight, if something happens to Ahmed, because your men do something stupid, you will have to explain that to his nephew."

Then Jeb repeated the message in Arabic, for the benefit of Ahmed's relatives. When he was finished, he looked to Ahmed, who declared that Mr. Lake was indeed a man of his word, a man he would trust with his life.

Allesandri frowned, then barked in Italian at the security guard who had reached for his weapon, sending him back into the stone building. When the man was gone, the smuggler conferred with Ahmed's two cousins and the remaining members of his retinue. After what seemed like interminable exchanges, Allesandri's smile returned.

"So, my friends. Mr. Lake. This is perfect. Ahmed will accompany you to Italy, and then he will return immediately. One of his cousins shall travel with you, together with my guards. And if anything should happen to Ahmed, any accident, then it will be most tragic for you and your beautiful friend. My men will have orders to bring you back here, alive, for Ahmed's nephew to decide what punishment you deserve. I can tell you, he is not a gentle man, so you should take very good care of his uncle."

Jeb smiled easily. "No worries. I shall protect his uncle with my life."

Allesandri nodded. "Very well. Let me suggest that you go now to the ship, immediately. There will be room with the captain, on the bridge. You should stay there. That is better. You can be sure."

"Agreed."

And they were done. Or almost done.

"One more thing, Mr. Lake. The briefcase," said Allesandri with a smile. "Let's not forget that."

"Of course not," Jeb replied, handing the smuggler the leather briefcase.

One of Ahmed's cousins stepped forward then, in front of Allesandri, nodding at Jeb and taking the briefcase. Allesandri's face darkened and he started to protest, then thought better of it. The tribesman disappeared back into the house and returned a moment later, without the briefcase. He nodded again at Jeb, then said something in Arabic to Allesandri's guards.

Allesandri scowled again, then nodded curtly at Jeb, and disappeared back into the stone building, accompanied by his guards. One of the tribesmen came down off the porch to stand next to Ahmed, and the four of them then made their way along the cove to the inflatable boats. Jeb kept the AK-47 out and ready, walking behind Ahmed and next to his cousin, keeping to the side of the trail. He made sure that she was right next to him, his shoulder touching hers as they headed to the beach. She could see that his eyes swept the path continuously as they walked, and that he kept the two of them in the shadows, making them nearly impossible targets.

When they reached the beach, Jeb pointed to the lifeboat that lay closest to the cliff at the side of the cove, in the shadows of a large rock, then directed Ahmed and his cousin to sit apart, one in front and the other behind the two of them. Then he ordered the boat's pilot to take them out fast, through the waves and surf. He sat facing the shore, the AK-47 on his lap, his eyes fixed on the coast. The journey in the little boat was bumpy and they were drenched in spray in less than a minute.

Despite the waves, they arrived at the smuggler's vessel in barely fifteen minutes. Allesandri's ship was an ancient wooden fishing boat, thirty meters long, less than five meters wide, its hull coated in barnacles and seaweed, with its engine belching dirty black smoke. The captain's bridge sat near the front of the vessel, a squat metal box with small, dilapidated windows on all four walls, facing in every direction. A late-model radar unit was mounted on the top of the cabin, its sleek modern lines contrasting with the disrepair of the rest of the boat.

The captain greeted them coldly. His English was broken and heavily accented. He directed them to sit inside the cabin, on one side, away from the wheel. The interior of the bridge was in no better repair than the boat's exterior. The windows were scratched, dark with grime from the ship's engines and tobacco smoke. The floor was cheap linoleum, squares missing in a few places, revealing badly worn timbers beneath. Two ashtrays sat next to the wheel, overflowing with the butts of hand-rolled cigarettes. The room reeked of stale smoke and unwashed clothes. There were only two chairs.

Ahmed sat in one of the chairs, with his cousin hovering next to him. Jeb stood, a meter or so away, the AK-47 still out, pointed towards the floor. The captain's first mate started to protest about the weapon, but Jeb silenced him with a curt direction to take it up with Mr. Allesandri.

Ahmed and his cousin chatted quietly, as if they were gossiping at the barber shop. She wondered idly what they were talking about. Jeb read her mind, leaned over with a smile and whispered, "Family politics, you aren't missing much."

Half an hour later, the refugees began to arrive on the ship. They were dressed mostly in worn Western garb, jeans and shirts, bundled in cheap sweaters against the wind on the open water. They carried virtually nothing, just one small bag per person. Each group of refugees was accompanied by one or two young Libyan men, who used their weapons to direct the passengers onto the ship, and then to sit in rows on the deck. Nobody spoke, other than the guards. A bank of lights, mounted on the pilot's cabin, illuminated the deck, casting ragged shadows onto the timbers and the waves beyond the railing.

It took an hour to load the vessel. When the last lifeboat had departed, the ship was packed, like a subway car at rush hour. Every square centimeter on the deck, apart from narrow passages to the bow and stern, was taken up by anxious brown and black faces, most eyes wide in fear or anticipation. The guards issued a brief set of orders in Arabic, French, and English — no talking, no standing, no eating. There were no toilets, and there was no water or food, so there was no reason for anyone to stand or move. Then, the captain turned off the lights, leaving the deck, and the vessel's cargo, in darkness.

A moment later, the ship was underway. The captain peered out of the windows on the bridge, through a haze of cigarette smoke. The sea was choppy, with two- and three-meter-high waves rocking the boat as it left the Libyan coastline behind. The engine groaned angrily, laboring to drive the vessel's hull through the swells. There were no lights on the ship, except two dim bulbs over the wheel in the cabin, and the illuminated display of the radar system. The captain consulted the display repeatedly, adjusting the settings from time to time. He listened intently to the marine radio as well, flipping between channels, but never spoke into it.

The crossing took nearly a day. After five or six hours, the sun rose, at first casting a gentle, soft light that warmed the cabin and the rows of migrants huddled on the deck. By mid-morning though, the sun had become a blazing white ball, hanging motionless in the sky, and blistering the refugees. The cabin was just as uncomfortable, an almost airless metal box that baked in the heat of the day. She found a corner, next to the doorway to the cabin, where an occasional breeze brought momentary relief. Jeb continued to stand, AK-47 always in hand, sweat beading on his forehead, but his eyes never leaving the captain and his guards. By noon, she was exhausted, and dozed fitfully, lulled by the throbbing of the engines.

At some point she fell asleep and, when she awoke, it was nearly dusk again. Jeb was still standing in exactly the place he had been hours earlier, his AK-47 still out and eyes still scanning the room and the deck. Ahmed and his cousin were sound asleep, heads buried in their sweaters on the floor of the cabin. Jeb handed her a bottle of water, ice-cold from the captain's cooler, and smiled as she drank nearly half of it. Their t-shirts were dark with sweat. She wondered how many times she had sweat this shirt through in the past four weeks.

"Another hour or so," he said, nodding in the direction they were headed.

"Then what? How do we get ashore?"

"Should be easy. We just worked it out. Another inflatable meets us, close to shore. We take Ahmed, then say our good-byes when we reach the shore, and he comes back. Everyone is happy with it."

It made sense. And there was no better option.

"And the refugees?"

"They get off further up the coast. Where the boat can get in almost to the shore."

In twenty minutes, the lights of the Italian coastline came into sight. Half an hour later, the boat's engines slowed, then stopped. Minutes later, a flashy new

Zodiac inflatable pulled alongside the vessel. The captain waved them towards the Zodiac, glad to be rid of them.

They climbed down off the bridge, Jeb still watching every move that the guards made, and then found their way between the rows of human cargo. The deck was slippery and stank of vomit and human waste. Many of the refugees were hollow-eyed and gaunt, after a sleepless night and day of sea sickness. She realized that her clothes probably smelled no better, after weeks in the jungle.

Ahmed's cousin led the way. She followed, with Jeb and Ahmed right behind her. Jeb's AK-47 was out again, his eyes still continuously surveying the refugees and guards. He directed her into the Zodiac, following Ahmed, and then climbed lightly aboard, scanning the fishing vessel the entire time.

He nodded at the pilot of the Zodiac and then they were away, the inflatable skimming over the swells. The sea air was intoxicatingly clean after the stench of the boat. She filled her lungs with the air, letting the wind and the spray wash the dirt and sweat off her face.

The shoreline was dark for kilometers in both directions, and she could just make out the sandy beach in the light of the moon. The pilot guided the Zodiac through the gentle surf, heading towards the deserted coast. Jeb directed him towards a stretch of the shore where low scrubs and sand dunes marched down almost to the waterline.

The rubber bottom of the Zodiac rasped over the sand and pebbles of the shoreline as the pilot beached the boat. Never taking his eyes off the other three men, Jeb helped her clamber ashore with one arm. His other arm still held the AK-47, out and ready. He smiled then, whispered quietly in Arabic to Ahmed, who beamed and embraced him briefly. Then he sprang ashore as well, leading her quickly into the vegetation, and out of sight.

A moment later, the growl of the Zodiac's engine disappeared into the sound of the surf, and they were alone on the shore. The moon was bright, still high in the starry sky. The air was sweet with pine and sea-salt, and the sand was warm beneath their feet.

When she asked what next, he smiled. "We won't get very far in the dark. And we're both beat. Let's put some distance between us and this place, and then it's naptime."

She didn't need any persuading. He led them a hundred meters or so through the bushes and pine trees, until they found a deserted beachfront road that ran parallel to the coast. They followed the road for about an hour, the two of them walking silently, side-by-side in the dark, through the dunes and scrub pines. When he found a stretch of forest that looked particularly dense, he led her by the hand through the trees to a sandy bowl, underneath a gnarled old pine tree. They curled up out of the wind, huddled together with the fleeces and each other for warmth, too exhausted to talk. They were both asleep in the sand in a matter of minutes.

Chapter 42
Reginald Reid

Reid sat in what remained of Antonio Allesandri's living room. He listened to the sound of the surf in the distance. His men had ripped down the ornate Egyptian lamps, which hung from the vaulted stone ceiling, leaving only bare light bulbs dangling in the air. They had also pushed the two sofas out of the living room into the hallway, leaving just a single wooden chair standing on the stone floor in the middle of the room. Four finely woven tribal kilims had been pulled down from the walls and bunched up around the legs of the chair. They needed to do that to keep Allesandri's blood from soiling their shoes.

At last, things had started to look up. Two days ago, they received a report of five dead Libyan militiamen found on a road heading south from Benghazi into the desert. The bodies belonged to men from a local militia, whose leader was on good terms with the CIA. They also received reports of two Westerners, a man and a woman, who had supposedly abducted a relative of the same militia commander.

They followed up quickly and, yesterday evening, had been pointed to Allesandri and his compound. Provided that the CIA made it worth his while, the local militia leader was happy to deliver Allesandri up to Reid's tender mercies. The CIA paid handsomely for the information and, just after noon, Reid and his men had descended on Allesandri's compound, together with a complement of Libyan militiamen, riding Toyota pick-up trucks and wielding Russian machine guns. They made short work of Allesandri's security, and the Libyan militia departed, leaving Reid and his men to their work.

Allesandri's body was tied to the chair in the middle of what used to be his living room. He was shirtless, his flabby white flesh bruised and sweaty in the harsh new lighting. It was such a shame, Reid thought, how the man allowed himself to go to seed. He must be twenty-five kilos overweight and reeked of cigarette smoke. Still, he had been tough, refusing for nearly an hour to provide the information that Reid demanded.

It was only after one of Reid's men had brought out a pair of pliers, and begun removing the Italian's teeth, one by one, that the smuggler finally broke. It was after the fifth tooth had been deposited in a neat little collection on the tea tray next to the chair, along with the man's other four teeth, all badly stained with tobacco and red wine, plus one with a gold crown, that Allesandri finally broke down.

Once he had broken, the smuggler explained where his ship had gone, where its captain could be found and what he remembered of Fisher and West. They wiped the blood off his mouth, gave him water to drink and loosened his hand-cuffs, so that he could finish answering Reid's questions. And when he was finally done, his men had ignored the smuggler's sobbing and slit his throat. The blood was still oozing out of the wound, dripping down the man's body and soaking the kilims in a rich scarlet red.

Reid retreated from the living room to escape the flies and thought through the things he needed to do. Most important, was to find Allesandri's ship and its captain. That should be easy. They were both in a fishing village, off the tourist track, not far from Bari in southern Italy. It would be no more than a day or so and they would have the exact location where the smuggler had delivered Fisher and West into Italy.

Reid also ordered a full-court press on southern Italy — men watching train stations, airports, hotels, and hospitals. He could focus the search when he had more information, but he thought that this dragnet was a good start. He assumed that Fisher and the girl would try to return to the United States. So, he also arranged for U.S. embassies and airlines to be on alert for travelers matching the couple's description.

He was pleased with what they had accomplished in the last three days. They had gone from a needle in a haystack to being right on Fisher's trail. That was before he spoke to Kerrington. Kerrington wasn't pleased. He wasn't pleased at all that the girl had managed to get to Italy. Now, he said, it was a whole new ballgame. Fisher and the girl would be able to blend in with their surroundings, to disappear into the Italian countryside, or a city. Especially if they had a head start. The way they did now.

Kerrington demanded faster action to locate the fishing vessel's captain. Waiting another day was out of the question. In another day, Fisher and the girl could be long gone. Did Reid expect them to leave a trail of breadcrumbs for his men to follow? Did he really think Fisher was that stupid? And why hadn't they put out a search for all reports of stolen cars? Kerrington slammed his phone down after ordering him to get to Italy that night, and to track down Allesandri's vessel immediately, no matter what it took.

Wearily, he directed two of his men to take care of the mess they had made in Allesandri's house. He told them to arrange a fire later that night, after they disposed of the body. Then he sat down on the porch of Allesandri's house to figure out how to get his team from Libya to Italy in the middle of the night.

He felt a flash of anger at Kerrington. After all, Fisher was his fault. None of this would have happened if Kerrington hadn't insisted on including Fisher on their team. He wondered again why Kerrington hadn't trusted him. Why he'd insisted on someone else joining the team. But he put that aside and picked up his phone, then began making arrangements for a plane that would get him and his men to Italy by morning.

Chapter 43
Jeb Fisher

He woke with the dawn, his arms tangled around her, on a bed of pine needles. He let her sleep for a few minutes, watching her eyelids flutter in the early morning light. He was half-afraid to imagine the scenes that were playing out in her dreams, the images from the jungle and the desert. He eased his arm from around her neck, trying not to wake her, letting her head gently down into the needles.

She was awake instantly, eyes wary. Then she smiled.

"One cappuccino, please. No sugar."

He laughed. "Coming right up. In fact, go back to sleep for a bit and we'll make it breakfast in bed."

"That sounds perfect. You won't forget me?"

He laughed again. "That will never happen, honey. It may take a couple of hours. I need to go shopping. But I'll be back."

She smiled and snuggled into the pine needles. He resisted the urge, just then, to go to her. She was beautiful, curled up lazily on the sand, eyes sparkling in the morning light, her smell still around him. But he forced himself to turn away, and then made his way up the soft, sandy slope, through the scrub pine trees and back to the dirt road.

The dirt road was still deserted. He wasn't really going shopping. They didn't have any money, and he didn't dare use his credit cards. So he needed to be creative. He started off in the direction that they were headed last night, walking fast along the road. After a couple of kilometers, he found what he wanted.

It was a vacation home, closed up for the off-season. The old stone farmhouse had been redone with decorator touches — flower baskets hanging from the eaves, a gravel drive and landscaped garden, brightly colored shutters, plus a gleaming skylight in the roof. There was no car in the driveway and the windows were shuttered. An alarm on the front of the house was meant to warn off intruders.

He walked briskly through the front yard, as if he owned the cottage. At the rear of the house, he found a drainpipe and climbed to the roof. As he hoped, the skylight was unprotected. He pried it open and dropped to the floor of the bedroom.

The house was empty. He took stock of what the owners had left behind. It didn't look like much. There was a local map, with the cottage's location helpfully circled, a tin with 100 Euro or so, and a toolbox with everything that he would need when he found a car that suited him. That would be the riskiest part of his plan. Reid, and maybe the Russians also, would be monitoring reports of car thefts in the region. The sooner the vehicle he took was reported stolen, the greater the risk that they would be tracked.

He was about to leave when he noticed the motorcycle helmets in the front hallway. There were four of them, hanging from pegs on the wall, together with two heavy nylon jackets. He scanned the back of the house and saw the garden shed. Five minutes later, he had climbed out of the farmhouse the same way he had entered and was forcing the lock on the shed. Inside was a barely used 750 cc BMW motorcycle. It was no doubt part of the cottage owner's mid-life crisis, but exactly what they needed.

The bike was fully fueled, tires inflated and keys in the ignition. It started on the first try. After stashing the most useful tools in one of the panniers, he returned to the cottage. He collected an assortment of clothes — male and female — from the bedrooms. He smiled at the designer labels. He had never owned any of these brands. And, he suspected, she hadn't either. Then he checked the kitchen for food. There was none. Nothing but long-life milk and an espresso maker. Very Italian.

Twenty minutes later, he eased the bike into the bushes along the dirt track. He found her a few minutes later, stretched out in the sun, eyes closed. She smiled as he made his way carefully down the incline. And then laughed out loud when he delivered her a homemade cappuccino.

"Wow. Awesome. I can't believe you really did this," she said.

They sipped their coffees from the mugs he had brought, sitting on the edge of the dune, watching breakers roll across the blue of the Mediterranean.

"The best I've had in weeks," she said with a smile.

He returned the smile. "Ingrate. You probably won't be satisfied with your new wardrobe either," he said, handing her a shopping bag filled with clothes.

She sorted through the bag. "Wow. These are gorgeous."

She held up an elegant cashmere sweater and a pair of designer jeans. The sweater was light grey, almost like her eyes.

"I thought we could do with a change of clothes. There's underwear as well."

She smiled again, eyes playful. "Sure. It's only been a month," she said, looking down at her jeans and wrinkling her nose. "Shall we get changed?"

He laughed then and said, "I have a better idea. Let's not change right yet. I'll drive us north and we'll find another quiet beach and have a real bath. We could do it here, but let's put some more distance between us and where we landed."

"Drive?" she asked. One eyebrow was raised slightly.

"You'll see. It's a beauty."

"Whatever you say," she said, and then rose gracefully from the dune, heading back in the direction he had come, sure-footed on the sandy trail.

He led them to the road. "This is ours," he announced, pointing proudly at the BMW standing in the shadows.

"Ours?" Her eyebrow was raised again.

"Well. It's on long-term loan. Like the clothes."

"Aren't people supposed to pay for stuff like this. Or is this another secret agent thing?"

He was about to protest, and to say that nothing would be missed, or that there wasn't much alternative, but then he didn't.

So instead, he said, "OK. You're right. How about this? We take their name and address and, when everything settles down, we send them enough money to replace all this?"

She eyed him with that cool, wary look again. Then smiled. "That's sweet. I don't know when everything will settle down, or if it will. We should talk about that. But let's get their name and address. It's the least we can do."

"Fair enough. Now, did you ever ride on one of these things?" he asked, handing her the helmet.

"No.... They weren't really the thing at university."

"Well, it's easy. A bit like skydiving. You'll love it."

She had to laugh again. "I can't wait."

It sounded like she meant it. She put on the helmet, tucking her hair underneath it, then climbed onto the back of the bike.

"Just hold onto me. Arms around my waist."

She leaned forward and wrapped her arms around him. And they were off. He stopped, like he promised, long enough to memorize the name and street number on the mailbox of the cottage. Then he drove north, along the coastline, for another ninety minutes. It was beautiful. Tiny fishing villages, rolling hills, and the sweep of the Mediterranean. With her clinging tightly to him, he gave the bike more gas, letting the wind and the scenery start a new day for them.

Chapter 44
Sara West

The coast was breathtaking. Arms wrapped around him, swaying with the rhythm of the motorbike, she watched the pine trees, sand dunes, and water flash past. After an hour and a half or so, he found another secluded stretch of coastline, and pulled the bike off the road, into the trees.

They picked their way down to the deserted beach, then looked at one another awkwardly for a moment, before she shrugged her shoulders and stripped down to very worn and dirty underwear. She would have been embarrassed, but he had seen her filthy bra already. He followed suit, pulling off his jeans, and then they raced across the sand, into the waves.

They had the sea to themselves. It was cold, but perfect. The surf was just heavy enough to ride and the water was crystal clear. They played like teenagers in the waves for nearly an hour, before he signaled towards the shore.

"I could do this forever, but we better be going. The bike isn't locked."

She made a pouty face. "I can't believe there are thieves around here."

Then she smiled at him and raised her eyebrow again, before heading back to the shore. There was a freshwater shower not far from where they came out of the sea. They washed off the salt water, scrubbing themselves for the first time in days. He produced shampoo from the shopping bag, and they took turns washing the dirt out of their hair.

When they were done, he checked her wound again, as he had on each of the last four days, then gave her more antibiotics. He stood very close, staring intently and gently touching the sutures. She could feel the warmth of his body, and smell him too, rich and masculine, underneath the tangy salt of the sea.

She forced herself to step away when he was done. She didn't trust herself, standing there like that with him. She turned around to look for the clothes they had brought, before turning back to him, his eyes following her. Then the moment stretched out, as she stood in the sunshine, hair glistening golden, nipples erect through the cotton bra, holding the bag in front of her. But she broke it again, taking her new outfit and stepping behind a bush to change. He disappeared in the opposite direction.

They both emerged a few minutes later, wearing the most expensive clothes that either of them had ever owned, together with large smiles. Fancy jeans and cashmere sweaters. They looked like an Italian power couple — lawyers or bankers down from Milan for the weekend. Stylish black motorcycle jackets completed the picture. They deposited their old clothes in a litter basket near the beach, then walked back to the motorbike. As they mounted the bike, she suggested that he head for Florence. He agreed with a smile. Putting her doubts aside, for just a moment, she wrapped her arms around him again and cushioned her face against his back.

She let herself imagine that the picture was true, that they really were a settled, happy couple, returning home after a weekend away in the country, whose only trouble was where to stop for lunch. But that wasn't real, the truth was so far away from that, she thought somberly.

In truth, they weren't a couple and they didn't have either a home or jobs; instead, they were running, again, for their lives, in stolen clothes on a stolen motorbike, with goodness knew how many people chasing them. And she was holding onto a stranger whom she didn't know and didn't trust. Someone who probably wanted to steal the file that she had hidden from him. And then to kill her, the way he had killed all the others in the last few days. Unless, she thought darkly, she killed him first, using the lessons she had learned out in the jungle. Then she forced those thoughts out of her mind and wrapped her arms around him a little more tightly, letting the wind dry her hair as he powered the bike along the Mediterranean coastline.

Chapter 45
Ivan Petronov

He sat on the balcony of their suite on the top floor of one of Rome's grandest hotels. The hotel stood at the top of the Spanish Stairs, an oasis of faded elegance, away from the city's heat, and crowded streets. She had persuaded him that they deserved a break, and some creature comforts, after four weeks in Africa. Once he agreed, she took over, choosing the hotel, and arranging for their relaxation. She had chosen brilliantly.

They had eaten fabulously last night, in a world-famous restaurant, gorging on baby artichokes, tiny fried squids, spaghetti with fresh clams, and then steak, served rare, dressed with nothing but olive oil and coarsely-ground black pepper. All accompanied by two bottles of vintage Montepulciano, each of which cost as much as some cars. It was good to be back to civilization.

Flying to Rome wasn't entirely a vacation though. His friends at the FSS in Moscow had reported a sudden show of interest by the CIA in southern Italy, with local informants watching airports, train and bus stations, and larger hotels. The Americans were apparently paying equal attention to local police reports for much of the country. It looked as if the CIA had somehow found a trail leading to Italy. The most likely conclusion was that the girl had made her way to southern Italy, probably by boat, and then disappeared again.

She persuaded him that they could only wait and watch — wait for the CIA or their friends in Moscow to pick up the girl's trail again. Rome was as good a place as any for them to do that.

There was one more thing that she suggested. They asked his friends at the FSS to identify and trace every conceivable contact that the girl might have in Italy. They searched through university classmates, family friends, old professors, travel companions, roommates, and Facebook friends. And then they checked all those thousands of people to find anyone living in Italy. When that list seemed to lead nowhere, they widened the search, to the contacts of the girl's father and mother, repeating the process. A team of analysts in Moscow was scouring these names for clues about where the girl might run. So far, they had found nothing.

After his nap, he joined her on the balcony, and they ordered a bottle of the hotel's best champagne. It was the price of another small automobile, but with his money it didn't matter in the least. They sat in silence, sipping the champagne, as the late afternoon sun began to set, filling the square below the hotel with liquid gold.

"She can't be alone," Yan said softly. "We underestimated her before, I know, but still, she couldn't cross half of Africa, and then the Mediterranean, without help. Especially not from Libya. Someone must be helping her."

He nodded, then thought for a moment, surveying the square below, over the top of his champagne glass.

"That must be right," he said. "And she doesn't have a passport or credit cards. We know that she left those back in the camp. She can't get anywhere without those."

"But she did. Or so our American friends must think," she said. "Someone must be with her. Someone with money and training. It must be someone who knew enough to avoid the airlines and border crossings. And who could still get them out of Libya and into Italy. That's not so easy."

He toyed with the possibilities. Yan was right. There must be someone else with the girl, someone helping her. "Maybe one of the CIA's men," he mused. "One of the men who hit us in Goma."

"That was my thought too," she said. "But why would one of them betray the Agency? That's a very risky choice."

He laughed. It was obvious. He explained it to her. "It's the money. The money in the accounts," he said with certainty. "Nothing else would make sense. She offered to split it with him."

He was sure of this. Somehow the girl had worked out what the files contained, and then convinced whoever was with her that she would share the money in the Nazi bank accounts. He smiled to himself. If his hypothesis was correct, that would be a very expensive promise. He doubted any rescue mission had ever cost as much. Tens of billions of dollars. Maybe more.

But then, she probably didn't have many alternatives. And she would probably lose it all, in any case. Whoever was protecting her would be on her side only until he got his hands on the file and the money. Then her protector would leave, probably after killing her, taking the money with him. He explained that to her. Then they sat in silence for a while longer, the last rays of the sun reflecting off the water in the fountains in the square.

"A strange couple," he said again, after a while. "They must not trust each other."

She was still for a moment. She didn't look at him, and just nodded. Then she stood up and carefully refilled his champagne, leaning over to kiss him softly as she handed him his glass. She sat down again, moving her chair closer to his.

Then she changed the subject. "I know I shouldn't, but I feel a little sorry for the girl. She didn't choose this."

He laughed coldly and shook his head. "She took the file. And she still has it. It's her choice."

They were silent for a while again. She watched the light fading in the evening sky.

After a long pause, she said: "She's never going to give it up. After what the men did, to her father, her boyfriend, she'll never give up now. She must want revenge, as well. After everything that happened."

He laughed again. "You're right. You seem to know her well, my dear. Now just figure out where they're going."

"I'm working on it love."

She smiled and took his hand, holding it to her lips. He could feel her breath, warm and moist. It was a small thing, but it made him feel good when she did that. So young and beautiful, so devoted. He felt so much better, so much more secure, now that they were back in the civilized world. He sipped the champagne contentedly, watching the square below them, holding hands with her on the balcony, as the sun set over the city's rooftops.

Chapter 46
Jeb Fisher

He drove hard all through the day, and well into the night. They stayed off the main highways, with the Autostrada's police, tollbooths, and security cameras. Instead, with the help of the map that he took from the vacation cottage, they followed secondary roads along the coast, heading north, past Naples. He avoided the city, taking the ring road that skirted the urban center, where he thought that Reid, and maybe the Russians, might have their men looking for them.

About an hour later, they stopped to eat in a local pizzeria. It was a hole-in-the-wall, on the side of the road, with no tablecloths or placemats. But the pizza was delicious — their first real meal in weeks. Thin, crisp crust, homemade tomato sauce and freshly grated cheese, hot and oozing and oily. The restaurant owner laughed out loud when they ordered a second round of pizzas, both of them wordlessly devouring everything that he brought.

He forced himself not to stare while she ate. Her face was flushed from the sun and the wind, her hair thick and golden, with curls tangled around her face. He concentrated on the food and her banter, letting her tease him about his driving and appetite.

When they finished the food, she told him where she wanted to go. She said she was sorry, that she couldn't tell him more. And she looked sorry, as well as torn, as if she were tempted to tell him everything that she was holding back. But she hadn't. Instead, she asked if he would drive her to a town further to the north, not far from Florence, named Lucca. Then leave her for a few hours. And she would need money, several hundred Euro or so. She wouldn't tell him why.

He looked puzzled but said he would. He didn't have much choice and he understood her suspicions. He would have been at least as mistrustful if he were in her place. But he also pointed out that her plan had some logistical problems. They would need a place to stay in Lucca, or nearby, which would cost money. And he had barely enough cash to pay for the pizzas, not to mention the money that she wanted, plus what they would need for gas.

So, he suggested that they stop just south of Lucca, in Pisa, and let him do a little more shopping amidst the crowds of tourists. He promised to keep track of the amounts and the donors, like they did with the bike and clothes. She had looked unhappy, and thought for a moment, before relenting. And then they set out again, driving through the night on country roads that were mostly empty.

He thought about stopping somewhere along the way, so they could rest. But that would have meant more risks, which he didn't want to take, and would have required money, which they didn't have yet. He wasn't tired, so they continued on, cruising into the night through the darkened countryside and past deserted towns. They had circled Rome well past midnight, the glow of the city lighting up the sky to the east, as they headed further north.

She held onto him the entire time, occasionally shifting her grip, moving her arms up around his neck or shoulders. They stopped a few times along the way, for water, or a bathroom, or just to stretch their legs. On the last stop, at a gas station an hour past Rome, she missed her footing, legs stiff from the long ride, and stumbled up against him. Her smell, warm and feminine, swept over him, and he caught her, arms instinctively steadying her, then both of them held onto each other, for just a heartbeat too long, before she turned quickly away, headed for the toilets. She kept her distance when she returned, and neither of them mentioned that moment the rest of the night.

They arrived in Pisa in the middle of the morning. He parked the motorbike in a quiet street, not far from the city center, leaving her in an outdoor café with enough money for coffee. He bought a guidebook from a tourist stall, using the last of their cash. Then he made his way to the city's sights, looking like someone who belonged to one of the tour groups that circled the Leaning Tower. It was a world apart from either the rainforest or the desert, crowded with people and noises, surrounded by Renaissance masterpieces and fashionable shops.

He circled the most crowded sights, taking his time, checking for police and plain-clothes cops, as well as for other pickpockets. After an hour, he was satisfied and went to work in earnest. In the space of twenty minutes, he had taken a backpack, which he emptied of its most valuable contents, and then six purses and another backpack. He kept the passports with the owners' cash neatly folded inside. His final hit was a flashy blonde Russian woman, who was paying more attention to her makeup than to her Bottega Veneta handbag. It yielded a few thousand euros, and he decided to retire while he was ahead.

He found her lost in thought back in the café, looking up at the façade of a Renaissance chapel across the cobblestone street. He paid the bill, with a crisp new 100 Euro note, winking at her as he tipped the waitress generously. Then they walked in silence back to the motorbike, before heading out of the city, up the coast to the north.

They reached Lucca in the afternoon. It was a walled Medieval city, ringed by massive fortifications. She told him that she knew where they could stay, and directed him into the city, onto a street just outside the old city center. She told him to stop off a tree-lined square, along a quiet canal, not far from a small hotel. He scouted the hotel before they went inside, concluding that they wouldn't attract the attention of Reid or anyone else if they stayed there. Then she disappeared into the lobby, telling him to wait by the motorbike. She was back in a few minutes, with a room key and a mischievous smile.

"Just look slightly guilty and come with me." Her smile didn't go away as they walked to the hotel.

She took his hand, as they walked through the lobby, followed by knowing glances from the receptionist and concierge, then up a medieval stairway to the first floor. The room looked out over the canal. It was furnished with antiques, including a large, canopied bed that stood against one wall.

She smiled, then said, "I couldn't very well insist on discretion and then ask for single beds, no?"

He laughed, then praised her tradecraft. "If that botany thing doesn't work out, just let me know. You could have a real future in my line of work."

She laughed as well. "I may take you up on that. My career has hit a bit of a bump in the last month."

Then she abruptly went silent, lost again in her own world for a moment. He was sure she was back in the jungle, either running for her life or watching the massacre at the camp. He started to go to her, to try and comfort her, then hesitated, and instead let her be, busying himself with sorting through the items he had taken in the morning. He collected a pile of things that he needed to dispose of, then made separate piles of the money and the passports. He sat at the antique desk, in front of the window, and used the hotel stationery to make a list, carefully entering each name and passport number next to the amounts he had taken.

After a few moments, she came over and stood next to him, watching as he wrote.

"Thank you. That's really sweet," she said finally.

He looked up at her. "I hope I'm getting it right. This wasn't part of my training..."

"That's why it's sweet," she said, resting her hand on his shoulder for just an instant.

Then she had turned business-like, sitting down facing him. She was going out, she told him. She needed 400 Euro or so, like she said before, and would be back for dinner. Maybe he could find somewhere nice where they could eat, she said with a smile. And then they could talk. He nodded and said of course, giving her half the money he had taken that morning. She left then, taking her backpack and pausing at the door, with an awkward smile, before leaving him sitting alone in the room.

He waited a minute, and then left the room himself. He moved soundlessly, so the receptionist didn't notice as he came down the stairs and left the hotel. He followed her silently down the street, keeping in the shadows, so that she wouldn't have seen him even if she turned around to look. But she hadn't. She headed towards a cab rank in the square near the hotel. He sprinted to where they left the motorbike, then waited for her to get in the cab. When it drove off, he followed on the bike, maintaining a careful distance.

He felt guilty, to be spying on her. But he had to. No matter how attracted he might be, he couldn't let himself trust her. Especially when she had insisted on going out alone. She must be doing something connected to the file — either collecting it or giving it to someone. She might need protection, even if she didn't want it.

And he might have misjudged her; she might be planning to just leave, with the file, and never come back. He wondered, if you assumed that her story about the Nazi file was true, how many billions of dollars the file would be worth. It was a pretty big temptation, any way you looked at it. Even worse, what if the file were something else, something like the weapon designs that Reid had said. And so he followed the cab out of Lucca and into the countryside.

The sun was setting, and most cars had their headlights on. He fell back a few hundred meters behind the taxi, occasionally switching off his own headlight, so they wouldn't see him. The cab wound its way along the country roads and then finally stopped after twenty kilometers or so in front of a farmhouse, standing alone in a grove of cypress trees. He watched from the shadows along the side of the road, where he couldn't be seen. Sara got out of the cab and an elderly woman came out of the house to greet her. The women embraced like mother and daughter, hugging each other for a long moment, and then went into the farmhouse together.

He left the motorbike in the trees beside the road, about fifty meters away, and crept up on the house. Thankfully, there was no dog. He slipped into the garden, then watched them through the windows from the bushes.

The woman had grey, almost white, hair, and a grandmother's smile. She must have been in her seventies. After a few minutes, she disappeared into another room and then returned with a DHL package, brightly colored and bulky. Sara and the woman spoke for a while, and then Sara opened the package. Inside was an envelope, which contained a thick stack of papers. Sara took the papers out of the envelope and leafed through them.

The two women talked for another thirty minutes, before the older woman took the stack of papers and disappeared into an adjoining room. The lights in that room went on and he shifted positions in the yard so that he could watch what the woman did. She was standing in what looked like a home office, complete with a desktop computer, a printer, and a copier. She turned the machines on and started copying the papers from the DHL package.

Sara came into the office halfway through the copying and the two women continued to talk. At one point, the woman stopped and showed Sara a page from the copy she was making. They held it up to the light, then laughed together, as the woman shrugged.

When the copying was finished, the woman handed the originals back to Sara and placed the copies in a thick envelope. Then they sat together in the living room talking for another hour, before the woman picked up her phone and made a call. Twenty minutes later, a taxi arrived at the front of the house. The two women embraced tightly as Sara walked to the cab, both wiping away tears and laughing.

He stayed in the bushes for a moment, then ran to the bike, wheeled it onto the road and followed the cab back towards Lucca. When they neared the town, and began to encounter traffic, he opened up the gas and roared past the taxi. He left the motorbike exactly where they had first parked it, then hurried to the hotel and went silently back up the stairs to their room. He just had time to reserve a table at a nearby restaurant, promising regional specialties, before she returned. She looked pleased when he told her about the restaurant, then apologized for leaving him alone for a boring evening. He felt guilty as he told her not to worry and said that it hadn't been so long.

They walked to the restaurant, which turned out to be an inspired selection. It was rustic and dimly lit, with a huge open fireplace along one wall, where skewers of meat roasted over glowing coals. They sat at a table in the corner and ate juicy cuts of beef, accompanied by earthen pitchers of rich local red wine and slabs of freshly grilled polenta.

It was like a date. They talked, for the first time, about themselves. They traded life histories, starting at the beginnings and working their way forward, with lots of detours and questions along the way. There were overlaps in their backgrounds; they both attended premier universities, studied hard, were high achievers and loved sports. But, for the most part, they were from completely different worlds. He told her stories about the CIA and his favorite operations. She told him about growing up in college towns and jungle camps. And they laughed about their taste in movies, music, and food along the way.

They were just finishing his career at the CIA when they realized that the restaurant was empty, and the owner was hovering impatiently at the door. They had talked until nearly 1 a.m., not noticing the other customers leave or the lights in the restaurant go down. They thanked the proprietor profusely, and paid in cash, with a healthy tip, which repaired relations.

They walked in silence back to the hotel along the cobblestone streets, past medieval churches and deserted piazzas. The hotel was dark, and they slipped up to their room without waking the night receptionist, who was asleep at his desk.

He closed the door, then crossed the room to shut the curtains. She put the backpack on the desk by the window, turning towards him, just as he finished drawing the last curtain. They stood there for an instant in the silence, the room still, except for her breath. Then they each reached for each other at the same moment, still without a word, her hair golden in the light of the lamp.

He took her hard and fast the first time, their mouths and hands locked together, their breaths and bodies entwined, his weight heavy on her body. She came along with him, one hand on his waist, her moans smothered by his chest. The second time was soft and tender, each of them exploring the other, slowly, lost in the dark, and in each other's touch and taste. She came again, his tongue driving her over the edge, then burst into laughter, holding him tightly as the aftershocks subsided. After she came the third time, they collapsed into each other's arms, legs tangled together, and then slept soundly, like children, for the first time in weeks.

Chapter 47
Sara West

She awoke to sun shining, through the open curtains, onto the bed. She could hear the sounds of a market, vendors hawking their produce, outside the windows of the room. She looked at the bedside clock — 2:15 p.m. — then picked the clock up and checked it again. She hadn't slept for twelve hours in years, not since she could remember. She stretched lazily under the down comforter.

Then she remembered last night and sat upright in bed with a start. Where was he? Where was the backpack with the file? How could she have left it unattended, lying out in the open? She looked around the room, and couldn't see it, then jumped out of bed, and rushed, panic rising in her stomach, leaving a sudden metallic taste in her mouth, to the desk, in front of the window.

The backpack lay there on the desk, exactly where she had left it the night before. She opened it up. The file of papers was inside as well, exactly where she put it. Nothing had been disturbed.

She breathed a sigh of relief, then sat down on the side of the bed and began a prolonged session of self-remonstration. She had just had unprotected sex, two times, or maybe three, she wasn't sure which. With a man she didn't really know and didn't, couldn't, trust. Then she had left the file lying there for him to walk off with. This was Thelma and Louise on a whole new level. How stupid could she be? She tried to work out the answer to that while she brushed her teeth and showered.

She didn't find his note until she finished dressing. It was on the desk, right next to the backpack. She frowned at the little surge of elation that followed just from seeing it. He was short and to the point, but very sweet. "Big kisses baby. I didn't want to wake you. I'm out shopping and will be back around 5. Miss you already."

She smiled, then decided that she needed to talk with him about the file, and what she wanted to do next. First, though, coffee, and finally working out how much she could trust him and how their conversation should play out. She headed downstairs for an expresso, smiling to herself at the achy feeling between her legs. She might not be able to trust him, but she didn't have any regrets about last night. Not at all.

He came back to the hotel a little after 5 p.m., just as his note had promised. He carried a leather suitcase, large and well-made. It was full of more clothes, also tastefully selected, for both of them. He had also purchased underwear and toiletries, again, for both of them.

"Hi honey. Santa Claus. And I kept a list. Did you miss me?"

"I did. Actually. Once I finally woke up…"

He held her tight. Silently for a moment. Then, slightly awkwardly, thanked her for last night and said he had scouted out another very nice restaurant.

She looked up at him. Then, still holding him, said, "Jeb. We need to talk."

She'd spent the afternoon thinking how to do this.

"Uh oh. So soon? That sounds serious," he replied.

"No, baby. It's a good thing. But no restaurant tonight. Let's order from room service instead. You have some reading to do. I can help. Then we talk."

"Sure. Maybe movies after. 'Game of Thrones' or something."

She laughed. "What's wrong, sweetie. Not enough blood and sex in our lives?"

He rolled his eyes at her. She hadn't expected an answer.

She walked over to the desk and retrieved the file from the backpack — a large stack of old papers. Then she handed the entire package to him and nodded at the easy chair. She asked him whether he could read German. Passably, he told her, although in truth he was nearly fluent.

She felt guilty that she hadn't given him all of the papers in the file. There were four dozen or so papers, legal documents with signatures, witnesses, and seals, which had been in a separate embossed leather folder, sealed with a faded red ribbon, which she hadn't looked at carefully before. As she worked through those during the afternoon, she concluded they were especially important.

The papers were written in complicated lawyer's language, which was hard for her to follow. But despite the difficulty, she could tell that the documents in the leather folder were powers of attorney and transfer deeds, all signed by both H. von Wolff and A. Hitler, and witnessed by yet others, then stamped and sealed. The papers said that they granted all rights, title, and authority over a series of bank accounts to the person named in each of the documents.

All of the documents were blank, though, with a space left for a name to be inserted. As far as she could tell, she could put her own name, or anyone else's name, into those blanks, and then would be the owner of whatever was in the accounts they referenced. At least, that's how it looked to her. She wasn't a lawyer, but that's what the papers said.

She gave Jeb everything else in the file, but she left out that folder, and all of these documents — the powers of attorney and transfer deeds. She also left out another document, listing a few dozen bank accounts and setting out a detailed protocol with code words and account numbers, for accessing the accounts. The account numbers on the protocol matched those on the powers of attorney and deeds of assignment.

She carefully kept all of these documents in the leather folder concealed in the bottom of her backpack, in a compartment that held the pack's rain shield. She wasn't sure why she did this. It felt wrong, a bit like she was cheating on him. But some part of her still insisted that she didn't really know him, even after the last week, even after last night, and that she still couldn't really trust him, either. In fact, after last night, she couldn't really trust herself. She needed to do it this way, to protect herself.

She also didn't tell him that she and Maria had made another copy of the entire file, and that she left it with Maria, at her house outside Lucca — a place where nobody would ever look. She decided that she needed the copy as insurance, in case anything happened to the originals. She trusted Maria with her life. Maria was her former nanny, who had raised her for almost ten years, both before and after her mother died. She loved Maria like her own mother. And she knew that Maria would keep the copy of the file safe, no matter what. She felt guilty, again, not telling Jeb about Maria or the copy, but she couldn't, in case she was somehow wrong about him.

He spent nearly three hours sitting by the window, working his way through the papers that she gave him. He occasionally asked her to translate German words. When he was nearly finished, he looked up and suggested pizza from room service. She ordered and by the time the food arrived, he was done with this reading.

They sat on the bed, barefoot and cross-legged, and shared the pizza and a beer from the minibar. While they ate, he started to talk.

"So. … It's pretty hard to believe. A Nazi war chest, hidden for seventy years in deepest Africa. Billions of dollars, probably more, in secret Swiss bank accounts. That nobody ever knew about. Plus, a list showing that some very powerful people, and their families, were Nazi spies. That all sounds a bit crazy."

"So, do you believe it?" she asked.

"Well, it may be crazy, but I believe it. I do now. The documents must be authentic. I'm no expert, but those sure look like seventy-year-old Nazi documents. And we both saw the place where they were hidden, plus the Nazi plane and the bodies of the German soldiers. There's no way that could all be faked. Plus, the reactions of Kerrington and the Russians. Those guys must think the documents are real. Again, I'm no expert, but I'm as sure as I can be that this stuff is all real."

She was relieved. That was one point of showing him the file — to figure out whether she had misunderstood it, because she was just an amateur or because of her shock at what happened to her father and the others. She wanted to be sure that she hadn't overreacted or missed something. Jeb had no reason to lie, or even to fudge things, on this issue.

"That's what I thought too," she said. "That's why they killed my dad and everyone else. And why they're chasing us. They're either after the money in the Swiss bank accounts, or they're trying to hide their histories, or both."

"So, what next? What do you want to do now?" he asked.

This was the question she was expecting. It was a question that she had been asking herself. What did she want? That question was another reason for showing him the file. She was going to be honest with him about this part. Not to trust him, at least not completely, but to tell him exactly what she wanted and see what he said.

"I'm still working that out. I'd like to hear what you think I should do, what we should do," she said.

She paused for a sip of beer, then continued.

"This is what I think though. This is what I want. Two things. Two things that I know right now that I want. First, I want justice. Or maybe vengeance. I don't care much which anymore. Justice, for my dad."

She paused to steady her voice. He moved closer to her on the bed, his shoulder brushing hers.

"Justice for my dad, and for my friends. Payback for what those men did to them. And for whoever was behind those men. Whether they were Russian or American or whoever. I don't care who they are. I want every one of those people dead and destroyed. Completely."

She was surprised at her fury. She had planned this part of the talk, what she would say. But it came out differently than she imagined, with a venom that made her pause. She never would have said these things, thought this way, before those weeks in the jungle. She had changed out there. She was someone else now. This new person surprised her, scared her a little.

But what she said didn't scare or surprise Jeb. He just nodded.

"I get that. I see it," he said. "It's not so easy. But I understand."

"You said two things," he commented, after a pause.

"Second, truth. I want the truth of all this to come out. I want to understand what this file means, what really happened with all the money. Where it came from and where it went. And I want to know who this circle of secret Nazi spies and supporters is, and what they did, what they're doing. What they did in the past and what they're doing today, aside from trying to kill me. And I want the world to know as well."

He nodded again. "OK. I get that too. I get both of those things."

He leaned closer.

There was one more thing. This was the important part now. She took a breath, then looked at him, her eyes locked on his.

"I need your help. I can't do this alone," she said.

He answered right away. "You know I'll help you, no? I'm not sure what I can do, what we can do. But there's no point to my stopping now. Even if I could."

She hadn't fully expected that. She thought that he might help, but not this way, unhesitating and unconditional. She wondered if she could believe him. If he wasn't really just after the money.

But she continued anyway. "Wow. That's something."

He laughed. "Yeah. It is. But like I said, I can't stop myself now."

She looked at him again, still not sure whether to believe that it was real. Not sure whether she could trust him. In fact, she was pretty sure that she shouldn't. She kissed him anyway, softly, on the cheek, looking into his eyes, as if she had no doubts. Then she launched into the next part.

"I have some ideas. Ideas about what you can do, about what we can do. They may be stupid. But they're a start."

She took another drink from their beer and continued.

"So. We go to Zurich, to this private bank where the Nazis put their money. Staehelin & Co. or whatever it's called. We give the bank the account details, and demand access to the accounts. We try and find out what's in those accounts. That takes us a long way towards truth. And it probably draws our American and Russian friends right to us. In a place we choose. Where you can surprise them. Then we kill them. Kill all of them."

Again, it came out differently than she had planned. With more fury. It scared her again.

It still didn't scare him. He thought for a while.

"It's a real long shot, honey. Who knows what the bank says. Maybe it says the accounts are gone, or never existed, or whatever. Maybe it says that the papers in your file don't give us have access to the accounts. And me, us, taking out two teams, probably big teams, of fully equipped professionals. Both Americans and Russians. That's tough. Really tough."

She answered right away. "You could do it. I've seen you. You're the best there is. You told me as much last night. And I can't do it. I can't do it myself. I need you." Her voice was low, her eyes locked again on his.

"What's our alternative?" she asked. "If we don't kill them, they'll chase us. No matter where we go. They'll chase us to the end of the world."

She caught herself, half-surprised, half-embarrassed at how the "we" and the "us" had come out so naturally. That hadn't been part of the script. He heard it too, and held her gaze, for another long moment.

"I'd like to run," she continued. "Find some eco-farm in California or a vineyard in Italy. Put this all behind us. But they'd find us. You know they would. And even if they didn't, I wouldn't get justice or truth. I don't want to keep running and hiding. I wouldn't be me. Not the me I am now."

He looked at her, then off into the distance, before he answered. "You may be right," he said at last. "They will chase us. That's for sure. Maybe we don't have a choice anymore. But I just don't know how we make your plan work. They'll have thirty, fifty, a hundred agents, endless money and weapons, and intelligence. I don't know how to beat them. I just don't see how to make it happen."

"I know. But we can figure that out. We're just starting. Maybe it can be like the hotel in Goma," she said. "Only this time we plan it. We play the Americans and the Russians off against each other. We lure them all somewhere, at the same time, using the files, and me, as bait, and then we let them do most of the work for us. They go after each other, like World War III. And then you finish it, we finish it, finish all of them, and walk away. And live happily ever after."

He thought for a while longer, then smiled, shaking his head.

"Maybe." He laughed then. "You are a very dangerous woman, Ms. West. Maybe, though. I'm still doubtful, really doubtful, but maybe. What does make sense for sure is going to Zurich, to the bank. We need to know more about why they all want the file. We need to know whether all that money really is hidden away at Staehelin & Co."

She smiled. "So… Head for Switzerland now, or another night here?"

His answer was just what she wanted. He started to pull off her t-shirt, pushing her down into the comforter as he found her mouth.

Chapter 48
Yan Wu

Ivan's Russian friends had found a match for one of the Italian addresses of the girl's past acquaintances. The girl's former nanny, more than a decade years ago, had been sent a package by DHL from Kigali, Rwanda. The FSS had cast a very wide net, eventually using their computers to check the address of every package sent from that part of Africa for a thirty-day period. It turned out that one of those packages was sent to the nanny, at an address near Pisa, and that address then turned up on the Russian computers' searches.

Ivan reacted immediately. An hour after the report arrived, they were on their way from Rome with a team of four men on loan from the Russian Embassy following them in a black van. They arrived at the nanny's house just after nightfall. Fortunately, it was a rural address, and very isolated. She and Ivan approached the house, pretending to be stranded motorists. The old woman let them in, offering drinks and food, as well as the phone number of the best mechanic in the next town.

The woman hadn't understood, at first, what Ivan was doing when he produced the pistol, from beneath his jacket. She offered money, whatever they wanted. Then Ivan asked about the girl and, after a flicker of surprise, the woman feigned ignorance. She first denied ever knowing or hearing of any Sara West or recognizing the photograph they showed her. Then she pretended to dimly recall her, from when she was a nanny, fifteen years ago. But she hadn't heard from the girl since then. Absolutely not.

Ivan hit the old woman, hard, across the face, sending her sprawling onto the floor, blood pouring from her nose. Then he dragged her into the kitchen and slammed her onto one of the chairs, and slapped her again, blood spraying out of her nose over the plate of biscuits that she had started to prepare for them. He tied her hands behind the back of the kitchen chair with a length of rope, then told her, in a low, menacing voice, that he would cut out her eyes if she did not tell the truth.

Despite the threats, the woman began to recover her composure. She repeated her denials, insisting that she hadn't seen the girl for years. He slapped her again, hard, spraying more blood across her clothes. This time, the woman only stared back coldly at him, then said something solemnly to them in Italian.

Yan had a bad feeling about the old woman, that she wasn't going to break, no matter what Ivan did to her. She saw that in the woman's eyes, and the way she held herself now. Ivan warned the woman again, then started to roll up the sleeves of his shirt. She left the two of them and began to inspect the other rooms.

She could hear the blows, and the woman's cries, as she looked around the house. She looked first through the trash bin, just next to the back door. She found the discarded wrapper to the DHL package right away, addressed to the woman from the UN airbase in Goma. She smiled to herself. The girl was clever, she thought again. She took the wrapper with her and stepped into the next room, which looked like a home office. Then she saw it. Lying in a neat stack on the desk was a thick file of German documents, copied incongruously onto a light pink paper, which was apparently the woman's stationery.

She checked that the door to the office was closed, then switched off the light so the embassy guards couldn't see what she did. She collected the stack of papers and carefully placed them at the bottom of her daypack, under a windbreaker, a pair of binoculars, and her Uzi. She zipped the pack shut, slung it over her shoulder and left the room, making sure not to disturb anything. When she left, it was as if she had never been there.

Ivan was still at work on the old woman in the kitchen. Her face was now a discolored mess. Her blouse was ripped open, down to her waist, and cigarette burns were dotted across her breasts. She was half-conscious, head tilted forward, chin resting on her chest. Ivan was washing his hands in the kitchen sink, his shirt splattered with the woman's blood. He was cursing to himself in Russian.

"She's a strong one," Yan said.

"Stupid bitch. She hasn't said a thing." He cursed again in Russian.

"She is old. Someone her age may not last much longer," she said. "She may not know much more anyway."

Then she produced the DHL wrapper. "Show her this. Tell her we know."

Ivan did as she suggested. The woman ignored him, mumbling what sounded like a prayer, in Italian, through swollen lips and broken teeth. He cursed again. Then he slipped the plastic wrapper over the woman's head, holding it tight around her throat until her legs began to kick wildly. She had seen him do this before. She had been sure that this was what he would do with the wrapper. It was why she had showed it to him. At the last possible moment, he released his grip, pulling the plastic bag off the old woman's head.

The woman gasped desperately for air, paused for a moment to catch her breath, then spit into his face, a thick gob of blood and saliva. He roared in anger and hit her again, brutally hard, sending the chair toppling over backwards against the counter. There was a dull, hollow crack as the woman's head hit the counter. Ivan swore, wiping the woman's spittle from his face, then set the chair upright again.

The old woman did that on purpose, she thought. The woman wanted to provoke him, to goad him into killing her and ending it. And the fool fell for it. She smiled to herself. The woman's secret was her secret now. They could help each other. Ivan stomped out of the room, cursing, in search of a towel.

After he left, she checked the woman's pulse. She was still alive, somehow. Quickly, first making sure that Ivan was still cleaning up in the other room and that she couldn't be seen from the outside, she took the DHL wrapper and placed it over the woman's head again, then held it tight. She stood on the woman's feet so she couldn't kick, then kept the bag in place until the woman's struggles slowed and finally stopped. And then she held the bag in place a little longer, just to make absolutely sure.

When she heard Ivan stomping back, still cursing to himself, she eased the bag off the woman's head and carefully placed it back on the counter, exactly where Ivan had left it. As he came into the kitchen, she was checking the woman's pulse, looking up at him with a mixture of concern and frustration.

"I think she's gone," she said.

"Stupid fucking whore," he shouted, then stopped and checked the woman's pulse himself.

After a moment, he cursed in Russian, and kicked the woman's body hard in the chest, toppling the chair again. The old woman's body was tiny now, like a small bird tied to the chair. She didn't stir.

He left the kitchen again and began to search the house, ripping it methodically apart, room by room. He dismantled every bit of furniture, inspected every drawer and file, kicked down walls and checked under floorboards. He was meticulous. But he found nothing, not a thing. Surprise, surprise, she thought to herself. At last, hours later, he gave up, slumping into what remained of an easy chair in the living room. She sat next to him, offering a comforting arm.

"I don't think there's anything here, honey," she said.

"I know. God damn it. The girl must have come to pick up the file. She must have beat us here. We were so fucking close."

"But we're on their trail, baby. We're closer. We'll get them soon."

He nodded.

"Let's get the men to wipe this place down, then torch it," she said quietly. "Better not leave a trail."

"Yes. That's right. Then back to Rome," he said in resignation.

She stroked his arm, smiling to herself. The day had been full of surprises. But good surprises. In fact, things couldn't have gone any better.

They left Alexei's team to clean up the house and rode together back to Rome. She calmed him, explaining patiently that the old woman couldn't have told them anything more, as they drove through the Italian countryside. Telling him that they were on the girl's trail, that they were ahead of the Americans. After an hour or so, his frustration subsided and he fell asleep, his head resting on her shoulder. She let him sleep against her, snoring wetly, while she thought.

She thought about the file, hidden now in her pack, and the chain of events that brought it to her. She thought about the things she needed to do next and the mistakes she needed to avoid. And she thought about the girl, wondering where she was now, and where she would go next. She was still thinking about the girl when they reached the outskirts of Rome and the city's darkened store fronts and churches began to roll past the limousine's windows.

Chapter 49
Jeb Fisher

They left the hotel quietly, Jeb taking the suitcase outside, while she paid for their stay, counting out the fresh 100 Euro bills. She followed him down the street for a few minutes, then into a side street. A late-model Fiat convertible was parked at the end of the block.

"Like I said, I was shopping."

She pretended to scowl. "It's on the list, though?" she asked.

"Of course, just like we said."

He had wanted new transport. The chances that the motorcycle's owners would discover its disappearance increased each day. He found the Fiat in a locked garage, next to a storefront with a sign announcing that the shop was closed for the next two weeks. If they were lucky, the car wouldn't be missed until the owners returned from their vacation. In any case, the convertible would take them safely as far as the Swiss border, which was all they needed from it.

They drove all morning, past Milan and further north towards the Alps. He headed for one of the Italian mountain resorts, where there would be a crossing point over the border into Switzerland. Along the way, they talked, fleshing out their life histories, past loves, and plans for the future. They mostly stayed away from mentioning the file, her backpack now packed securely in the new suitcase, instead pretending to live in a little bubble of make-believe normalcy, like lovers on vacation.

Then, for a couple of hours, he drove in silence, while she napped. He used the time to plan how they might survive a confrontation with the men that were hunting them, trying to work out how the Americans and the Russians would react to different scenarios. Almost any way he played it, though, the showdown that she wanted produced bleak results. One man against forty or so trained agents was just about impossible to overcome.

But he kept thinking, kept imagining different scenarios. As the Alps came into view in the distance, the outlines of a plan for dealing with Kerrington and the Russians began to emerge. It was a long shot, probably crazy, but it was better than the other alternatives he came up with.

She woke up in the early afternoon, then leaned over and kissed him, before saying that she was starved. They stopped for a late lunch at a country inn a kilometer or so off the road. There was no menu, and the waiter brought them steaming bowls of hearty white bean soup, accompanied by olive oil and parmesan cheese, followed by a plate of spicy veal sausages. They declined the offers of wine, plus additional courses, settling instead for expressos.

As they left, she slipped her arm around him. He thought how he didn't want this to end, holding her tight, feeling the warmth of her body, as they walked to the car.

He didn't think it would be difficult to cross the border. They drove to Lecco, a sunny town on the shore of Lake Como, on the border with Switzerland. It was a picture-perfect Alpine village, framed by the waters of the lake and snowy peaks, streets lined with quaint chalets, decorated with window boxes of bright red geraniums. The air was fresh and clean. The town was busy with tourists, drawn by the scenery, hiking, and food.

He left her with the car while he strolled around the picturesque squares, stopping for cappuccinos, all the while hunting for tourists who looked like them. After a couple of hours, a perfect match appeared. A few minutes later, he had taken the stranger's backpack while the owner inspected local handicrafts, going to a café restroom to remove the passports and cash. Half an hour later, he repeated the process with a striking Australian backpacker, who matched Sara's description as well as anyone might. He kept her backpack, as well as her passport, and returned quickly to the Fiat convertible. He smiled innocently at her as he climbed into the car and pulled away from the curb.

They drove back down the winding road through the valley, then parked the car in a long-stay parking lot near a train station not far from the Swiss border. The station was almost empty. An old woman sat behind a glass ticket-counter, but otherwise the station was deserted. He bought two tickets to Zurich, paying in cash, and they went out onto the platform.

He left her for a moment, while he went to use the toilet. He almost missed the stake-out. The man was seated on the railway platform, behind a large shrub, his face hidden by a newspaper, just another bored commuter waiting for a train. But the reflection in the window behind the man showed something else. The man was watching Sara intently. He consulted a photograph that he took from his jacket pocket, got up abruptly, and headed towards the entrance to the station.

Jeb hurried after the man, stalking him along the platform, ignoring her puzzled stare. He caught the man halfway to the door to the station, grabbing his hand as he started to make a call on his phone. The man whirled around, pulling a switchblade from his windbreaker. Jeb stepped past the knife thrust, then head-butted the man in the face while getting one hand on the man's throat, before slamming him against the wall. He took the man's knife hand and reversed the blade, then buried it with the same motion in the man's chest.

The platform was still empty. He gestured for her not to move, then searched the man quickly, finding nothing of interest, apart from a color photograph. It was a recent picture of Sara, pulled off her university's website. He dragged the man's body along the concrete floor, and deposited it in a cleaner's cubicle, jamming the door shut so that the body wouldn't be discovered until the next shift.

He hurried back to where she was waiting. She was shaken, watching him wordlessly. He showed her the photograph, explaining that the man must have been with Kerrington and Reid. He couldn't let the man report that he'd seen her. If he had, Reid would have men on their trail in a matter of hours. She'd nodded then, saying she understood.

Then their train arrived, pulling into the station precisely on time. A few minutes later they were riding north, sitting silently in a first-class compartment of the train. He was still on edge from the confrontation with Reid's man. And she was withdrawn, the way she had been after he killed the Libyan militiamen.

They crossed the border into Switzerland without incident less than twenty minutes later, a bored Swiss police officer glancing at their passports and backpacks before moving on to the next compartment. He breathed a sigh of relief that the scrutiny had been cursory and that there were no computerized checks for stolen passports.

They sat in silence in their compartment for the next couple hours, before she fell asleep again, turning away from him to the window, still exhausted from the last four weeks. He stayed up, watching the Swiss countryside while she slept. He thought again how different it was from the jungle and desert. Tidy and neat and ordered. But beneath the surface, just as dangerous as the jungle. Maybe more dangerous, as the stake-out at the train station showed.

He dismissed those thoughts and turned to more practical necessities — like where they would sleep in Zurich. He ruled out hotels and hostels. The Swiss were notoriously rigorous when it came to requiring production of passports at hotels and, before long, reports of the two passports that he had stolen would reach the police. In turn, that would inevitably alert Kerrington, and maybe the Russians, as well as the local authorities. And so, it was easy to figure out where not to stay. It was a lot harder to figure out where to stay. He was still working on that problem as their train reached the outskirts of Zurich, the neat villages and farmland giving way to suburbs and schoolyards.

Chapter 50
Franklin Kerrington III

He was staying at the Savoy Hotel, a stately Art Deco building overlooking the Thames River. He had reservations for dinner with the head of MI5, the British intelligence agency. They had known each other for years and had exchanged innumerable favors. They both looked forward to catching up on the state of the world.

After drinks at the bar of the Savoy, they enjoyed a meal of Highland beef and a bottle of claret at one of London's most distinguished clubs, just off Waterloo Place in St. James. They commiserated over the short-sightedness of their respective political clients and compared notes on the stock prices of several leading defense contractors. Their information about the companies was much more detailed than that of any securities analyst. They were both very wealthy men, but that was no reason for either one not to look after his investments.

His host's chauffeur dropped him back at the Savoy just before midnight. He went out on the balcony of his suite and stood there watching the late-night traffic creep along the Thames, enjoying an after-dinner cigar and listening to Reid's latest report. It was in line with his expectations.

Two passports had been reported stolen near the Italian border with Switzerland earlier that day, from an American man and Australian woman. The owners of the passports matched Fisher and West's descriptions. Reid also said that the two passports had been used later that day to cross the border into Switzerland. That was no surprise. It was what he had thought Fisher would do.

Reid also reported that the body of one of the local contractors they had hired had been found an hour ago at an Italian train station near the Swiss border. The man had been killed with his own knife. It looked like Fisher's handiwork, but

Gary Born

they couldn't be sure. There was apparently no video footage of either Fisher or West. They were still checking, but it looked as if the two had managed to avoid train stations with security cameras. This wasn't a surprise to him either. He didn't think Fisher would make mistakes.

Reid wondered aloud why Fisher and the girl had entered Switzerland, rather than remaining in Italy or trying to fly to the United States. Crossing into Switzerland involved more borders and greater risks, and then left them boxed up in a small country. Kerrington listened silently to Reid's question, deciding not to suggest an explanation. Instead, he directed Reid to shift all his men north, to Zurich, Geneva, and other Swiss cities, focusing on hotels, public places, and transportation links. He also made a note to himself to pull in CIA operatives from around Europe to add to the boots that Reid already had on the ground in Switzerland. He would have to manage their roles, and to come up with an explanation within the Agency for the operation, but the risks were worth taking.

After he finished speaking with Reid, he hung up and remained out on the balcony, despite the evening chill, lost in thought. He knew why Fisher and the girl were taking the risk of traveling to Switzerland. He hadn't told Reid, but it was obvious. They went to Switzerland for the money, the Nazi money that they thought would be in secret deposits in one of the Swiss banks. He smiled to himself. Maybe Fisher wasn't such a Boy Scout after all.

He wondered how much money might still be in the Swiss bank accounts. He didn't know. In fact, he couldn't even guess. But it could be huge. Who knew how much the Nazis might have hidden away. It could easily be billions of dollars. Or more.

The realization also made it easy to see where Fisher and the girl would end up. The place to find the girl and the file would be the bank, whatever bank held the Nazi deposits. That's where they would go. He made another note to order CIA surveillance of a half dozen of the leading Swiss private banks, the ones that had been doing business in the 1940s.

There was one more thing to do. He picked up the phone again and had his secretary arrange a flight in the morning on one of the Agency's private planes to

Zurich. Breakfast first at the Savoy with the CEO of a major British energy company, then an early flight to Zurich. He needed to act quickly now. Fisher and the girl had the files from the Nazi plane. Those files might enable the girl to extract more information from whatever Swiss bank they were headed to. He had to stop that from happening. And to stop other people from learning about the file. He had to get to Zurich, now, and retrieve the file himself, before the girl caused any more difficulties.

Chapter 51
Jeb Fisher

They left the train in Zurich's suburbs. They needed to be even more careful here. Kerrington and Reid, as well as the Russians, might have guessed that this was where they were heading, and then staked out the city's main train stations. So, when the train stopped at one of the last suburban stations outside the city, they disembarked and found a taxi. He gave the driver directions to the city center and, when they arrived, he left her in a quiet bookshop cum café, browsing through books on the Swiss banking industry, while he went to find somewhere they could spend the night.

He found the kind of club he was looking for after an hour or so. It was on a noisy street, with a mix of other bars and restaurants. It was named "Christopher Street," and the club's clientele was overwhelmingly male, sleekly groomed, and toned. He went to the toilets, emerging a few minutes later looking as if he were at home in the dimly lit surroundings. He had put his long-sleeve shirt into his pack, leaving only a tightly fitting white t-shirt. His hair was slicked back, and his jeans were pulled low on his hips.

The bar was long and black, lacquered and shiny. Plush easy chairs, upholstered with black velvet, were clustered around low tables. Black-and-white posters of Hollywood starlets covered most of the wall space, while jazz played on the sound system.

The barkeeper was burly and tattooed. The man eyed him appreciatively for a moment, then took his order. He nursed the beer for the next hour, hardly touching it, waiting for the club to fill up. When it did, he struck up conversations with half a dozen young men, drifting away after a few moments in each case, leaving disappointed suitors in his wake. Finally, after a couple of hours, he found Simon

— a slightly built young man in his early thirties, with dirty blonde hair and large brown eyes.

Simon said that he was still a student, in law school at the University of Zurich, living in an apartment that his father provided. He confessed that he actually didn't go to class very often. The professors were old and boring, and he could take as long as he wanted to graduate. His father would find him a comfortable job, in the legal department at one of the Swiss banks, once he was finished. Simon said that he wasn't lazy. Lots of his friends in Switzerland did the same thing. It was normal. He hardly ever came to places like this, he also said, but he had just broken up with his boyfriend, who moved back to London. He didn't have any roommates and his apartment was very quiet, too quiet even, he said with a smile.

Jeb confessed shyly that he had never been to a club like Christopher Street. He had never had the courage, even though he wanted to for a long time. He was here in Zurich on business, for meetings, and decided to finally try it. He left the comment hanging in the air between them, then looked, shyly again, into Simon's eyes. He didn't pull away either, when Simon stroked his arm, admiring his physique, asking how often he worked out. He blushed, blurting out that it embarrassed him, in public, but still didn't pull away.

He didn't resist when Simon suggested a few minutes later that they go back to his apartment for a drink. He also didn't protest when Simon touched his chest while he waited for their change at the bar, the bartender looking enviously at the two of them. Simon drove them home, only fifteen minutes away, in a dark blue Jaguar. The interior smelled of cologne, fragrant and cloying. Simon let his hand stray onto Jeb's knee as he worked the gearshift, smiling to himself at the good fortune of his evening.

Simon parked in the back of his apartment in a deserted alleyway. The apartment had its own entrance and, like Simon had said, was very quiet. The neighbor was an American banker — very hot, Simon said, but straight — who was almost never there. He wasn't there tonight either, Simon told him as he let them into his apartment.

Simon's taste in home furnishings was like his car. Dark grey Italian leather sofas on a light-colored pine floor, with color-coordinated curtains. Modern art hung on the walls. Simon took him by the hand and led him to the bedroom, his palm a little sweaty now with anticipation, then turned at the door, putting one hand on his hip and looking up at him.

"This is really your first time?" Simon's voice was thick with desire.

"It would be. But I have some bad news," Jeb replied apologetically.

Then he pinned the smaller man's arms behind him effortlessly, with one hand, his other hand covering Simon's mouth. He forced the younger man down onto the bed and explained what was going to happen.

"I won't hurt you. I promise. You just have to do exactly what I say. If you do, everything will be fine. But if you make a noise, shout or do anything like that, then I will hurt you. I don't want to, but I will. Do you understand?"

Simon nodded, wide-eyed in fear.

"I'm going to let you go for a moment. No sounds. Right?"

He looked at the smaller man, waiting for a reply. When Simon nodded again, he released his grip and told the man to sit on the bed. He found a long silk scarf in the closet, and used it to gag the young man, apologizing for the precaution as he worked.

Next, he found a length of soft hemp rope, coiled up in another closet next to a variety of sex toys. He used it to tie Simon securely to a large, heavy armchair, which he dragged into a windowless storeroom in the basement of the apartment. Then he searched Simon carefully, taking his phone and a Blackberry, as well as his keys. He reminded the young man again not to make any noise, or to try to escape, before locking him in the storeroom.

When he was done, he checked the apartment, making sure that Simon really lived alone. Then he left, locking the apartment door. He used Simon's car keys and drove the Jaguar to the center of Zurich and parked. He found her seated in the back of the bookstore, just beginning her second book on Swiss banking. She paid for her coffee and purchases, then walked with him down the street. She smiled when she saw the car.

"You've been keeping interesting company," she said, after he let her into the car and she took a breath of the scented air.

"You just wait," he responded with a grin.

As he drove back to Simon's apartment, she gave him a lecture on Swiss private banking. She started at the beginning, explaining how the Swiss banking industry developed from small, privately-owned banks in the eighteenth and nineteenth centuries into a major international business for Switzerland.

The foundation of the banking industry's growth had been simple — it was secret, numbered Swiss bank accounts. Banks allowed clients to put their money in secret accounts, not bearing their names, and instead identified only by numbers. Secret numbers, that only the clients knew. And the banks also refused to disclose information about these numbered accounts to anyone, including to government tax authorities, prosecutors, or jealous spouses. The Swiss Parliament had approved this system in 1934, when it adopted one of the world's strictest bank secrecy laws. After that, the Swiss banks could tell potential clients not just that they were allowed to keep their clients' accounts secret, but that they had to do so.

After WWII, the Swiss banking industry grew explosively. Depositors from around the world brought money that they wanted to keep secret to banks in Zurich, Geneva, and Zug. Corrupt politicians, tax cheats, drug lords, and arm dealers all came to Switzerland to hide their ill-gotten gains behind the veil of official bank secrecy. All the gleaming bank buildings, generous corporate philanthropy, and glitzy annual reports rested, at the end of the day, on the foundation of secret, numbered Swiss bank accounts and dirty money.

She continued. "And you know who else took advantage of this little system? Our Nazi friends. The ones whose files we have. As far as we know, all their piles of money are sitting happily in a few of those nice numbered Swiss bank accounts."

"Wow. That's crazy," he said.

When she was finished with the lecture, she went silent, then turned away and watched through the window of the Jaguar as he drove through the deserted streets of Zurich's suburbs, as if she was lost in thought again. He left her alone, thinking that she must be back in the jungle.

He didn't ask her how someone could access the Nazi bank accounts. He hadn't seen anything in the file that answered those questions, but he thought that there must be documents somewhere, documents that would give the Nazis access to their money. Somewhere, someone must have had the numbers of the accounts and instructions on accessing them. He wondered who. He wondered if it was her. And if he could really trust her after all. Maybe that explained her silence.

While he was pondering that, they reached Simon's apartment. He parked in the alleyway, right where Simon parked before. Then he took her inside and explained what he had done, who Simon was and what they would need to do to keep him from escaping or hurting himself. She wasn't happy, but eventually agreed that there wasn't another option.

He checked to make sure that Simon hadn't tried to escape. The young man was just where he had left him, staring over his gag out of sad brown eyes. Jeb apologized again, then locked the door to the storeroom and rejoined her in the kitchen.

She said that she was starved — they hadn't eaten all day and began to inspect Simon's refrigerator. The young man had excellent taste. She hesitated when he volunteered to make dinner, and then admitted that she was impressed when he produced a very authentic spaghetti carbonara with the ingredients that were on hand.

After dinner, they sat next to each other on the bed, surrounded by Simon's collection of stuffed animals, sipping their drinks. The food lifted her spirits. She thanked him for making dinner. And for saving her life again, at the train station. She also said that she was sorry for being withdrawn. Arriving in Zurich, where the Nazi bank accounts were, had put her on edge. She would be better soon.

They were silent for a few minutes, listening to music from Simon's sound system. Then, he told her that he had a plan for dealing with Kerrington's men and the Russians. A plan that might not be completely crazy after all. She kissed him on the cheek but told him to wait. They could plan in the morning. She just wanted him to hold her now. They switched off the bedside lights and curled up, her back against his chest, his arms wrapped around her. He thought he could feel her sobbing in the dark, but when he leaned around her, she was already asleep, eyelids fluttering as she dreamt.

Chapter 52
Maximilian Staehelin

He stood by the desk in his office on the top floor of the bank. He had just put down the telephone. He took off the hand-tailored jacket of his suit, folded it carefully, and laid it on one the chairs. He was perspiring slightly, damp patches just visible at the armpits of his shirt.

He had been dreading that phone call for much of his adult life. He tried to avoid the caller, first telling his secretary to get rid of her, but the woman persisted. He eventually took the call.

It was a young American woman. She gave him a single password, one from the protocol. One from *that* protocol, the very old one that he wished had never existed. But it did exist, as he knew very well. She referred to it, several times, and repeated the password. She insisted on meeting, to discuss what she called her accounts. She insisted that the meeting happen that afternoon, at the bank's headquarters on Bahnhofstrasse in Zurich. She said that she expected him to comply scrupulously with the protocol.

He had been non-committal. He said that the bank very much appreciated her call, but that he would need to consult with his colleagues. He also said that he wasn't sure what protocol she meant, but that he would check internally to see if he could identify what she was referring to. He asked if there was a number that he could reach her at? She refused, reminding him of the importance of banking secrecy in Switzerland. Then she insisted again that the bank follow the protocol, and that he stop playing games. She ended the call by announcing that she would arrive at the bank's headquarters at 2 p.m. that afternoon and that she expected him to be there to greet her.

He tried to calm his thoughts. He imagined ways that the call might be a hoax or an extortion attempt, which he could no doubt manage. But then he remembered the intelligence reports that he had received the week before, describing the Nazi plane wreckage and the unusual intelligence activities. And his thoughts returned to the conversations with his father, twenty-five years ago, about the Nazi deposits.

He remembered his father telling him for the first time that there were some secret, off-the-books accounts with the bank. His father didn't say at first, when he was still a young man, how many accounts there were, or how much they contained. Instead, his father said that the accounts had been opened in accordance with a secret agreement, which had been signed between his grandfather, for the bank, and a very special depositor, who insisted on absolute secrecy. It was a depositor who also insisted that its deposits never be recorded on the bank's books. His grandfather had done that — had opened the accounts the way the depositor demanded.

Strictly speaking, his father had said, this was not correct. Swiss banking law was very clear: all deposits, including numbered accounts, must be reflected in the bank's books. But, his father had explained, these accounts were special ones, for a very important client of the bank, that dated back to before WWII. Later, he said that the secret agreement was signed by a high-ranking Nazi general, almost at the end of the war, and that the accounts were arranged by Adolf Hitler himself. And, his father explained, the accounts were enormous, billions of 1945 US dollars, and that the bank had committed, for obvious reasons, to maintaining their absolute secrecy. The bank also accepted a protocol governing how the accounts would be handled and accessed, which was detailed in a secret agreement with the Nazis.

All of that alone would have been bad enough. It would have been the source of some serious legal and public relations problems for the bank, but it might have been manageable. But there was more, which was even worse. Much worse.

His father went on to explain how he later used some of the funds in the Nazi accounts to support the bank during difficult times. The money that he took had never been repaid into the German accounts. And, on other occasions, his father used the secret accounts to support the family's lifestyle. That money also had never been repaid. In total, his father had taken billions of dollars from the accounts over the years. At least. He wasn't sure exactly how much he had taken. He didn't want to check. And nobody had ever inquired about the accounts. Not once, in all the years since 1945.

Staehelin was shocked when he learned these secrets. The disclosures led to sleepless nights and angry shouting matches with his father. Eventually, however, he came to terms with this legacy. And when his father retired, and then passed away, Staehelin continued the tradition of secretly using the accounts for his and the bank's purposes when the need arose. He used the accounts liberally during the terrible days of the 2008 financial crisis. Without those funds, Staehelin & Co. would have failed, like so many of its competitors. Of course, like his father, Staehelin never informed anyone, not even the bank's directors and lawyers, about any of this. He had also never told his wife about the accounts.

All these awful memories replayed themselves that afternoon. Even worse images followed when he thought about the future. Staehelin shuddered at the thought that the deposits might be discovered. He, and his father before him, had broken dozens of laws in hiding the Nazi deposits, and then siphoning money out of the accounts.

At best, he and his father had falsified the bank's accounts and stolen money from the bank's depositors. Not small amounts of money, either. Over the years, they helped the bank and themselves to billions of dollars. If that were discovered, the bank and the Staehelins would be ruined. They would go from being pillars of the Swiss financial community, and respected philanthropists, to common criminals. They would go from being billionaires to being penniless.

Staehelin thought of his wife, a beautiful woman from one of England's best families. And their twin daughters, about to begin college that autumn at Stanford in the United States. He couldn't bear to imagine the humiliation they would endure. He imagined the lurid press articles about the Nazi bank and the greedy banking family, the lawsuits and regulatory investigations, his wife's reaction, his children's shame, the prison sentence. He could hardly bear to contemplate any of this.

The damp patches at his armpits had grown larger, and he felt little rivulets of perspiration trickle down his stomach. His hand trembled when he took a sip of tea, this time splashing the liquid onto his shirt sleeve, leaving a wet stain. He forced himself to sit down at his desk, to take deep breaths, and then to consider his options.

A quarter of an hour later, he picked up the telephone and called the head of the bank's security. Pierre Dupuy was a very ambitious young man from a good family, which had long-standing business with the bank. He had personally selected Mr. Dupuy, then promoted him rapidly to his current position. Mr. Dupuy could be relied upon to help deal with this problem. Staehelin was sure of that. He asked Dupuy to come to his office, then began thinking about how to handle the American woman.

Chapter 53
Sara West

She arrived at the bank just before 2 p.m. Jeb had come with her, stopping the taxi five blocks away from Staehelin & Co's office. They had worked through this part of their plan carefully, going over it step by step several times that morning. She would walk the rest of the way to the bank by herself and enter the building alone. He would stay outside, a few blocks away, waiting in case she needed help. They purchased cheap mobile phones, which she could use to call him, but only if she had to.

She would go into the bank and confront Staehelin, the bank manager she had spoken with on the telephone. She would demand information about the numbered accounts referred to in the file. Her demands would probably be met by more stonewalling and delay from the bank. But they would start the process of getting access to the accounts.

More importantly, her visit would almost certainly be picked up by Kerrington and the Russians. They would both find out, through their informants and electronic eavesdroppers, that she was in Zurich with the file, and that it led somehow to Staehelin & Co. Both the Americans and the Russians would then send their men to the bank and wait for her to return. They would wait until they thought that she had the file with her, and then their men would grab her. They would take the file, and then they would dispose of her, as well as him. That, at least, was what their plans would be. Those plans didn't reckon with Jeb. Or his plans.

She put those thoughts out of her mind and concentrated on this part of their plan, their first step, baiting the trap. She walked along the carefully manicured length of Bahnhofstrasse towards Staehelin & Co.'s headquarters. She looked around the street, watching for signs that she was being followed. But she saw nothing out of the ordinary. So far as she could tell, nobody paid the slightest attention to her.

She wore jeans and her battered mountain boots, which left her feeling very out of place. Bahnhofstrasse was Zurich's most glamorous shopping avenue, lined with elegant stores, their windows filled with watches, furs, jewelry, and designer clothes. The streets were orderly and clean, with neatly trimmed shade trees every ten or twenty meters. Elderly women drank coffee and ate pastries with generous helpings of whipped cream in open-air cafes, while tourists browsed through trendy boutiques and art galleries. Nobody raised their voice or crossed the road against the traffic lights.

Despite the civilized setting, she felt more exposed than she did in the Ugandan rainforest, the familiar knot of fear in her stomach returning. The same people were chasing her, with the same intentions. It was just that they were in their element, instead of hers.

The knot in her stomach tightened even further as she walked the final block to the bank's entrance. She was sure that she was unwelcome, or worse, at the bank. Jeb would be some protection — actually, lots of protection — but he was a few blocks away and might not get there in time. She was on her own once she went inside.

She entered the bank through metal doors that opened automatically when she approached. Two security guards with earpieces stood discreetly just inside the doors. The reception area was spacious, with easy chairs and low tables arranged on polished grey granite floors. Original artwork hung on the walls, highlighted by hidden lamps.

The receptionist was an elegantly coifed woman in her forties, seated behind a gleaming teak desk, wearing what looked like a designer label dress and expensive pearls. The woman smiled and welcomed her warmly, notwithstanding her jeans and boots, asking if she wanted tea or coffee while she waited until Dr. Staehelin was free. She declined the offer of coffee. And she felt anything but welcome.

Her own bank at home was in a non-descript shopping mall and looked like a used car salesman's office. She couldn't imagine how much it cost to decorate just the reception area of Staehelin's bank. And she wondered what Staehelin had instructed his guards to do about her. She slipped her hand into the pocket of her jeans, reassuring herself that the phone was still there.

Dr. Staehelin's secretary appeared at exactly 2:10 p.m. and greeted her coolly. The secretary was just as perfectly groomed as the bank's receptionist. She led the way through a pair of internal security doors, manned by more guards, and then into a private elevator up to the next floor, before they arrived at one of the bank's conference rooms.

The conference room must have been used for very special clients of the bank. It was even more imposing than the reception area. Rich wood paneling ran from floor to ceiling, with a collection of Old Masters displayed on the walls. An eighteenth-century chandelier hung from an intricately stuccoed ceiling. Thickly embroidered velvet drapes ensured absolute privacy. After the secretary had left, an elderly waiter in a dark suit appeared and asked whether she would care for anything to drink. She declined again, and then waited for Dr. Staehelin to arrive for their meeting.

After another ten minutes, Dr. Staehelin made his entrance, apologizing for keeping her waiting and repeating how much he had looked forward to meeting her, and how intrigued he was by her most interesting story. He repeated the waiter's offer of a beverage and, when she refused once more, still insisted with a smile that the waiter bring them two glasses of champagne. He inspected the bottle carefully when it arrived, before nodding his approval to the waiter and gesturing for him to pour. He settled into a chair next to her, pulled it further away from the table and turned slightly so they could face each other, then straightened his impeccably tailored suit jacket.

"So. Your telephone message was most interesting, as I have said, Ms. Warren. Can you provide us with a little more background? You know," he said with his most winning smile, "private banking is a people business. We like to know our customers."

Her stomach was still knotted with tension, but she smiled back, play-acting the way he was. "Yes, Dr. Staehelin, people are so important."

She ignored the glass of champagne that had been deposited in front of her. Instead, she put her badly worn windbreaker on the table and reached into one of the pockets.

She extracted a copy of the protocol from the jacket, then carefully unfolded it and placed it on the table. She made the copy earlier that day, in Simon's home office, while Jeb was showering. She put the paper just where Staehelin would be able to see it. The entire document was only three pages long. She put all three pages on the table, side by side. Staehelin shifted uneasily in his seat as she smoothed out the creases in the papers. He started to take a sip of the champagne, then thought better of it, instead just inspecting the rim of his glass.

"You know this document, Dr. Staehelin?" she asked.

It wasn't really a question. He pretended he thought it was a question.

"Hmm. I'll have to take a look. May I?"

She ignored his query, watching him pick up the papers. He took a pair of gold-rimmed spectacles out of an elegant case, put them on, and studied the pages. He pretended to read for several minutes, lips pursed, with a slight furrow on his brow. He looked as if he was wondering what to say next.

Finally, he exclaimed, "My goodness. This is quite old. What an interesting document. Very interesting indeed. I am most grateful for you bringing this to my attention. Fascinating..."

She watched him coolly.

He rambled on. "Yes. Just fascinating... Yes... It is... You wouldn't mind if I made a copy, for our historical archives, here at the bank? I hope not. We try and collect little curiosities, like this one."

He forced a smile, not quite as winning as before.

She smiled back, looking right at him. She felt better now.

"You can have all the copies you like, Dr. Staehelin. But you don't really need them, do you? You have one of the originals of this protocol, don't you?"

It still wasn't a question. She was sure that he did. He cleared his throat, then glanced at her, then back at the sheets of paper in his hand. They trembled slightly now.

"Perhaps, perhaps, I may have seen something like this sometime before. It's so long ago though. I cannot really say…"

He shifted uncomfortably again.

She leaned forward. "You see, the protocol is on the bank's letterhead, and it is signed for the bank by Herr Werner Staehelin and Dr. Wolfgang Staehelin. Look there. Werner Staehelin was your grandfather, am I right?"

"Yes. Of course. He was indeed," Staehelin said.

He avoided her eyes. He was still staring at the protocol.

She held up the next page. "You see the list of accounts. Bank accounts. Those are accounts here, at Staehelin & Co, correct?"

That wasn't a question either. She knew the accounts were with the bank. He took off his glasses and placed them back in their carrying case.

He was silent for a moment. He rubbed his forehead, then grimaced slightly. "They might be. There could be bank accounts… Maybe here… Yes, I suppose they might," he said.

"Do you see the code words there, next to each account?"

She pointed to the typewritten lines on the protocol.

"Those are the code words that someone would need to give you, to get access to that account, right? That's how the numbered accounts work, isn't it?"

"Well, that would usually be true. One cannot really generalize so well. It's very complex…," Staehelin replied, shifting uncomfortably again in his chair.

"Dr. Staehelin, I'm giving you the passcodes for these accounts. I want access to the accounts. Now. I want to see the account records. Now."

Her voice was firm and cool. It concealed the tightness in her stomach. She wasn't nearly as confident as she sounded. What would she do if Staehelin refused? What if he called his guards?

Instead, Staehelin cleared his throat, nervously, then said, "Ms. Warren. You have my full assurance, my word of honor, as a banker, that you shall be provided everything that you are entitled to. This is a matter of utmost importance to the bank, to me. We always keep our promises."

He went on. "But this whole matter requires careful study. We cannot open up the bank's files without a sound legal basis. Swiss banking rules are very precise, very strict," he said, slipping into lecture mode.

He looked again at the protocol. "This paper is a copy, I see now. It is not the original. Where did you come by this paper, may I ask?" His brow furrowed deeply now.

She smiled again. "I have the original. Seals and all. But you don't need to see it. All you need is for me to give you the account numbers and the access codes to the accounts, which I have just done. Now you need to give me the account records."

He cleared his throat. "That won't do. This may be a fraud, for all I know. You are a delightful young lady, but we must follow procedures. We must follow the regulations. I will have this document investigated immediately. It will be given our complete attention. But you must cooperate as well. Our lawyers will insist on reviewing the original of this paper. The one that you say you have."

He continued. "Perhaps you return next week. This time next week. With the original. And we can see what progress has been made."

He smiled hopefully.

She looked at him evenly, her heart racing. "I'll be back tomorrow. At 2:30 p.m. I expect to be able to review the account records then." She kept her voice even and cool.

He pushed his chair back from the table and started to shake his head.

She sensed his weakness, and continued, "If not, then I will turn this over to my lawyers."

She didn't have any lawyers. She had never had a lawyer in her life, but the warning sounded serious to her. "Or to the authorities and the press," she concluded, looking squarely at him.

He shifted uneasily again. "Ms. Warren, I have promised the bank's cooperation. Our full attention. But 2:30 tomorrow is impossible. Absolutely impossible. Let's say the day after tomorrow. You have my word that we shall do our utmost to assist."

"Fine."

She stood up, then folded the protocol and returned it to the pocket of her windbreaker. They stood there facing each other for a moment. He towered over her, his impeccably tailored suit contrasting with her jeans and hiking shoes. Then he buzzed for his secretary.

While they waited, he pretended to make small talk. "Can I arrange for our car to take you to your hotel?" he asked. "You are staying where? The Baur au Lac, I assume? It's such a lovely hotel. I adore the garden."

She hadn't heard of the Baur au Lac but guessed that the hotel didn't have many guests like her. She replied sweetly anyway. "No, thank you. I'll make my own way back. It's a lovely day for a walk."

She smiled at him again, and then said good-bye.

Staehelin's secretary led her back to the reception area, offering a perfunctory good-bye. She left by the front entrance and walked down the street towards the lake. Two heavily built men in dark suits, one on either side of the street, followed her, just the way Jeb said they would. She pretended not to notice and continued towards the lake. Her stomach tightened again. She fought the urge to hurry as she made her way past elegant shops and well-dressed people who looked like bankers and accountants. Instead, she followed the plan that she had worked out with Jeb earlier that day.

There was an old-fashioned street-trolley station, where several different trolley lines met, just at the end of Bahnhofstrasse, at the edge of the lake. She needed to walk through the station to get to the lake. She could see Jeb scanning a newspaper on a bench in the middle of the station, right where they had agreed he would be. He caught her eye momentarily, then nodded his head imperceptibly towards a trolley, waiting on his right.

The two men were walking faster, narrowing the distance between them and her. She forced herself not to look back. Jeb stood up just as the trolley was about to leave, and stepped on, holding the door open behind him. She had just crossed the street, and hurried a half-dozen steps, making it onto the last car as the trolley doors closed behind her. The trolley car was filled with commuters and shoppers. Most of them were focused on their phones or newspapers. They all ignored her.

The trolley pulled away from the station, at first moving slowly, then picking up speed. She finally allowed herself to look back towards the station. She could see the men who followed her from the Bank standing helplessly on the other side of the street, as the trolley headed along the shore of the lake. She turned around and made her way to the next car, where Jeb was waiting.

He looked up and winked as the trolley clattered along the lake. He was seated next to the window, watching the men who had tried to follow her, while he chatted with an elderly, white-haired Swiss woman, who reminded her of Maria. He had her backpack on his lap and she could see the outline of one of the knives from Simon's kitchen through the nylon material. It made her feel safer.

Chapter 54
Ivan Petronov

Their limousine drove past the Colosseum to the airport while Rome slept. The day before, one of Alexei's men had called with reports of CIA operatives from all over Europe arriving in Zurich.

He hesitated to fly off to Zurich on what might be a wild goose chase. But Yan had convinced him. Where else would the Nazi's banks be? Zurich was the center of the Swiss financial industry, in German-speaking Switzerland — it made perfect sense, she thought. If that was where the Nazis would put their money, it was where the girl would have to go. In the end, Yan was adamant that they go to Zurich, which was hardly ever how she reacted. They had left for Zurich on a private jet the next day, leaving Rome just before the sun rose.

They were staying at a villa just outside the city, looking over Lake Zurich. It belonged to one of his Russian friends, a former KGB officer who had settled down in Switzerland to help service the financial needs of Russia's latest generation of oligarchs. He was happy with the accommodations, particularly the private chef, who came with the property and specialized in Russian cuisine.

Lunch was served on the patio overlooking the lake. It began with caviar, herring, pickles, and sour cream, then continued with borscht and thick, juicy pork cutlets, and finally ended with blinis and fruit. Vodka and several bottles of Georgian wine completed the meal. When they were finished, he took a long afternoon nap — nearly four hours — awakening rested and eager to continue their hunt.

Alexei had assembled a new team to track down the girl, and deal with the Americans if that became necessary. A dozen men and women, all former FSS or Spetsnaz. A number of them had served in Donetsk or Syria and were seasoned veterans of close combat. He had insisted that Alexei provide a team that wouldn't be blindsided again by the Americans. Alexei demanded ridiculous amounts to cover expenses, but this time he delivered an impressive product. And he also came to Zurich personally to make sure that the team actually delivered.

Alexei's team was housed in a former KGB safe house, which had found its way into the hands of a Russian entrepreneur, who continued to work with the FSS. It was a run-down, three-story apartment building, located in one of the very few working-class neighborhoods in Zurich. It was a place where the comings and goings of hard-edged foreigners attracted little attention.

Alexei gave orders for the team leaders — two ex-FSS men in their early fifties — to meet with them at the safe house that evening. They were instructed to keep the rest of the team away from the house during the meeting. He didn't want anyone to see either him or Yan unless absolutely necessary.

They took a car from the villa to the safe house in the early evening. They parked the car a few blocks away, where Alexei and one of the FSS men waited. The four of them walked the remainder of the way, past non-descript apartment houses covered with graffiti. There was no elevator at the safe house and they climbed to the top of a dark stairwell that smelled of cat urine. They met in the kitchen of a third-floor apartment that had four locks on the door. The kitchen was almost as dirty as the staircase. A pile of unwashed dishes filled the sink, and the floor hadn't been mopped in weeks.

Despite their accommodations, the two new team leaders — Vladimir and Gregori — were experienced and diligent. They provided a detailed review on all the members of the team, with biographies and psychological profiles, as well as their equipment. Then they outlined their plans for tracking down the girl. Four teams of two agents each would rotate surveillance of banks, hotels, and public transportation hubs. The surveillance would be round the clock. Another team was dedicated to locating the American's headquarters in Zurich. Alexei and Vladimir would remain at the safe house, to command the entire operation, while Gregori would accompany the team staking out the financial district.

When the presentation was done, he asked questions about the team's equipment, security, and contingency plans. Gregori and Vladimir had answers for everything they were asked — nothing flashy, but solid, careful preparations. Both he and Alexei were satisfied with the arrangements. Yan was as well. The new men were not muscular cowboys, like the men on their prior team, but sober, serious professionals. He felt more confident about the mission than he had for weeks.

They left the safe house just before 9 p.m., walking down the unpainted stairwell with Alexei, and then back to the car. The driver was waiting and drove them back towards the villa. They talked along the way, walking through where they thought the girl would most likely be found.

They dropped Alexei near the Russian Embassy, then continued home. Yan was quiet on the ride back, and when they arrived at the villa, complained about an upset stomach and said she might want to see a doctor in the morning. She went to bed early, but not before telling him that she was happy with Alexei's team and sure that the mission was back on track.

He stayed up and had a late supper of the chef's Armenian specialties — roast lamb kebabs, eggplant with garlic, warm lavash flatbread, and pungent harissa. With a couple of bottles of Georgian wine.

While he ate, he imagined finally securing the Nazi accounts. And he thought about the days ahead. They were so close, he was sure of that — so close to the dream he had chased for more than a decade. All they needed to do was find the girl and her file. Once they did that, billions, maybe tens or hundreds of billions, of dollars would be his. The girl and her file were here in Zurich, somewhere only a kilometer or two away. They just had to be careful and they would find her. It was just a matter of time again. And then they would be wealthy, wealthy and powerful, beyond imagination. There would be no limit to what they would be able to do.

She was sound asleep when he came to bed. He watched her for a moment before he turned off the light. She lay there, head nestled in the curve of her arm, a soft smile on her lips. Her hair was thick, a luxuriant mane covering her shoulders. He felt his excitement start to rise, but then decided to let her sleep; tomorrow would be a long day. And he could have her tomorrow, or whenever he wanted. She was always there, waiting for him, anytime he chose.

Chapter 55
Yan Wu

She woke very early. The sun was just rising, finding its way through the morning fog over the lake. She made herself a cup of tea, not bothering to wake the cook, and drank it quickly in the kitchen. She left a note for Ivan, saying she was going to see a doctor about her stomach, and that she would be back as soon as she was finished. Then she took her handbag and slipped out into the morning chill.

She took a trolley into the city, and then a taxi to an address a few blocks from the main campus of the University of Zurich. It dropped her near the university's School of History just after 7 a.m. The building was silent, with students and staff yet to arrive. She went up the stairs of the minimalist, glass-and-steel building, until she reached the third floor. There were no guards or receptionists, just like the afternoon before, when she had scouted the building.

She walked down the deserted corridor, her shoes clicking against the stone floors, along the row of closed office doors and empty seminar rooms, until she reached Room 345, Professor Dr. Stefan Greimsucher's office. She knocked lightly. In a moment, a stout man in his early sixties opened the door with a toothy smile. He wore grey flannel trousers, an open-collared cream shirt, and a dark green cardigan, plus a heavy dose of cologne.

He surveyed her appraisingly as he ushered her into his office. It was a large room, for an academic office, with one window open to let in the morning air. The room was lined with bookcases, overflowing with books in a handful of languages. Stacks of papers were arranged on what little space remained on the bookshelves, and then piled in rows along one wall. Classical music played from an old-fashioned sound system that stood behind the professor's desk. A stand with a dozen pipes rested on the desk, and the air was heavy with the scent of pipe tobacco.

He waved her to the sofa, which stood against one wall, and asked if she would like coffee or a drink. She declined, with a demure, slightly embarrassed shake of her head, as if she were over-awed by the suggestion that he would serve her. She had dressed for the occasion in a short, dark blue pleated skirt, no stockings, and a white blouse, with three buttons left undone. Her hair was pulled back in a ponytail and she wore a pair of horn-rimmed glasses, like a particularly diligent university student. He waited until she was seated and then sat next to her on the sofa, clearing away a stack of books that separated them.

He smiled widely at her again. "So, Ms. Zhang. I am sorry to pull you out of bed so early. But my schedule today is dreadful. Just dreadful."

She looked up at him, as if struggling to find the right English words, then answered in accented English. "It is my honor, Professor Doctor. My honor to be able to spend even an hour with a scholar of your reputation. My professor in China, in Nanjing, Professor Tan, he has described your works to me so many times. It is like a dream for me to attend to you in person." She blushed slightly.

Professor Greimsucher smiled even more broadly. "Ah yes. Professor Tan. A very able student. I remember him well."

She looked down. "You know, we revere scholars in China, scholars like you, Professor."

He moved a little closer. "You need not revere me, Ms. Zhang. I am just an ordinary man. A normal man who has learned much about Swiss banking."

He struggled up from the sofa, his weight making it a momentary challenge, then crossed the office to his coffee maker and tinkered with its settings. When he was satisfied, he made two cups of espresso, then brought them back to the sofa, insisting that she try a European coffee. She blushed again, but accepted the cup, avoiding his glance while intently studying the saucer.

After a moment, he went on. "You said yesterday on the telephone that you had found some documents? Banking documents that somehow seemed unusual to you? Do I remember well?"

"Yes, yes. My German. It is so poor. I am very embarrassed. But may I show them to you?" she asked, in a hesitant voice.

"Of course. By all means."

She leaned forward from the sofa to reach into her handbag, her blouse falling away from her breasts for a moment. He watched hungrily. She arranged the stack of documents which she selected as the most important from the copy of the file on her lap, then handed him several of them. He reluctantly pulled his gaze away from her cleavage and scrutinized the documents. He skimmed quickly through the first few pages, his expression bored. Then he paused on a document. He read it slowly, a frown beginning to cloud his face. When he reached the end, he looked again at the first page and began to reread it.

"Let me see the others," he said, a little sharply, after a moment. The papers now had his attention.

She complied, handing him another stack of documents that she had selected from the file. He read them as well, pausing at a few passages. Then he looked at her, still half-frowning.

"Where did you get these papers?" he asked.

"In Nanjing. In the historical section of our library, the archives. I was the first person to check them out. I made copies of them to bring with me. I am sorry about the quality of the paper, but it is all that I could find. All that I could find in Nanjing."

He mulled that answer. She leaned forward again, to find the notebook in her handbag. His eyes followed her hungrily again, like a hawk watching a mouse.

"It is so important for me to understand these papers. They are an important part of my thesis. I would be so much in your debt if you could help me understand them. I cannot even understand the German text. It is so complicated," she said, looking slightly ashamed.

He moved closer to her on the sofa and laid the first document out, partly on her leg and partly on his. "Very well. We, bankers, enjoy being in the position of a creditor," he said, holding her eyes.

She blushed again slightly but returned his gaze.

He smiled at her and edged closer. Then he explained: "So. I am afraid that I must tell you that these documents have to be forgeries. Very sophisticated, very clever forgeries, but forgeries nonetheless. I would need to see the originals to be 100% certain, but already I am quite clear."

She looked crestfallen, although she had expected exactly this response from him. "Why? How is that? What do you mean?"

He explained, in professorial tones. He explained that one document purported to be a memorandum, addressed to Adolf Hitler, from a Nazi economics minister at the end of WWII. And that the memorandum described a supposed plan, a supposed top-secret plan, to assemble a fund for the Nazis to use in the post-war period. This plan was described as having been completed, at least partially, with the funds being deposited in a Swiss bank, hidden behind a web of front companies and nominees. The amounts described were enormous, with tens of billions of dollars in assets being collected from all over the Third Reich.

He paused at this point and rolled his eyes, tapping the side of his forehead with one stubby forefinger. "Nonsense, of course. There are no records of anything like this happening, or even being planned. None that I know of. No historian has ever suggested such a thing, either in Switzerland or anywhere else," he concluded, shaking his head with disapproval.

She felt a wave of relief wash over her, quickly replaced by excitement. It was true then. Ivan's hypothesis, built on a handful of reports he found in ancient KGB archives, which he then connected in a flash of insight years ago, was correct. She had seen the KGB files and had always believed his theory, but this was rock-solid confirmation. The memorandum described exactly the secret Nazi fund that Ivan had surmised. And it had come from the Nazi plane, just like the other fragments of intelligence that he had found said that it would.

"Can that be true?" she asked, her voice uncertain. In fact, she was completely certain. Her excitement rose.

"Of course not. This is just a very clever fake. To play a practical joke on some unsuspecting scholar like you," Professor Greimsucher explained.

"How much money does the memorandum say would be hidden?" she asked, hesitantly again.

He laughed again. "If we believed this nonsense, it would be tens of billions of dollars. Maybe more. In 1945 dollars... A complete fantasy, of course," he said, rolling his eyes again.

"Where do the documents say that the funds would be deposited?" she asked. "Perhaps there is some contradiction that we could use to expose the fraud?" She looked up at him.

He thought for a moment, then nodded. "Perhaps. Perhaps we might write an interesting expose. Perhaps speculate about who would concoct such a story."

"Which bank, Professor?" She leaned closer to him, her bare leg brushing his now. "Where would these Nazi accounts supposedly be located? If this weren't a fake."

"Yes. Staehelin Private Bank. Here in Zurich. See. One of the other documents you gave me. This one. It is supposedly an agreement, a protocol, between the bank, Staehelin & Co., and the Nazi minister, one Herr von Wolff. Preposterous. Completely absurd. Staehelin & Co. is the most respected of all our private banks here in Zurich. It has been for generations. The very best family. The bank even funds one of my colleague's positions here at the university. Perhaps this is some malicious competitive trick," he mused.

"And the protocol. What exactly does it say?" She leaned closer, her leg pressed against his now.

He leaned closer and then translated the protocol for her, reading out the account numbers and passcodes, and the agreed procedures for accessing the accounts. He shook his head with a smile as he read.

"Really. This is most ingenious. All of the details are so authentic. So precise. Exactly the way a genuine agreement of this sort would appear. But it's all nonsense of course."

She carefully wrote down everything he said in her notebook, especially the account details and passwords. When he was finished, she handed him another document that interested her and smiled.

"And this one? I am so indebted to you, Professor. I will be so grateful for your help."

He smiled again, then translated the second document as well, or at least most of it. "This is a transfer deed," he said. "Completed except for the name of the transferee."

"Where?"

"Just here. This blank space."

"What does it do? What would the purpose of the document be?" she asked.

"It would transfer all of the legal rights to an account to the named transferee."

"There are many documents that look like that one," she said, showing him several other pages from the collection of papers that she had selected the day before.

"Yes. Very clever. There is a separate transfer deed for each of the different bank accounts. Yes... And look.... Look here. They match the accounts on the protocol very precisely. Like I said, a very clever fraud."

He paged through the documents, shaking his head again and smiling. "Someone went to a great deal of trouble to make this look perfectly authentic. Most ingenious, I must say."

"If they were real, would these documents be valid?" she asked. "If there really were such accounts at the Staehelin Bank? Were the forgers so clever?"

"Yes, yes. They would be. At least the originals would be. Perfectly proper in Switzerland," he nodded vigorously. "This is exactly how such accounts were managed."

She smiled at him and said, "I don't know how I will ever be able to thank you, Professor."

His eyes glittered, watching her intently again. She looked back, holding his gaze now. Then she leaned forward and reached into her handbag once more. She brought out a slim black comb and unfolded it carefully, making sure she did not cut herself on the blade that was concealed in the handle. She leaned over towards him in one fluid movement as he sat frozen on the sofa, staring wide-eyed at her. She smiled again at the look on his face as she drew the blade smoothly and evenly across his throat.

The blood from his neck spurted out onto his shirt and sweater, drenching them in dark, red wet. He struggled frantically to hold the blood back, making wheezy, gurgling noises.

She stood up from the sofa and waited patiently a few moments for him to die, then checked his pulse. Satisfied that he was dead, she searched his pockets and found his office keys. She also took his pocket diary, which noted the appointment that morning with one Ms. Zhang, from Nanjing University. She tucked it into her bag, along with the comb and the papers she had brought.

She made sure she left nothing behind, turned out the lights and locked the office door behind her, making sure to wipe the door handle for fingerprints, then walked back down the silent hallway and left the building. The campus was still empty. She took a trolley to the center of the city, then slipped into a public toilet, emerging with a new hairstyle and a different skirt. She caught a cab back to the villa, arriving well before Ivan awoke. This time, she directed the cook to serve her tea and then sat on the veranda, watching the waves on the lake, lost in thought, waiting for their day to begin.

Chapter 57
Franklin Kerrington III

Zurich was his favorite city in Europe. The Baur au Lac Hotel always delighted him. It sat on the shore of Lake Zurich, near the city center. His suite overlooked the hotel garden, a lush green rectangle, lined by trees, leading down to the shore. The windows of the suite opened onto a sweeping view of the lake, stretching off in the distance.

He had breakfast in his hotel room, watching the clouds play across the lake. He was ostensibly in Zurich for high-level governmental consultations about money-laundering and intelligence-sharing. He had a series of meetings planned in the afternoon with his counterparts in the Swiss intelligence and bank regulatory agencies, then a press briefing, followed by dinner with the CEOs of two banks at a local restaurant. They were all old friends, and he looked forward to seeing them.

In the morning, though, he had the girl and Fisher to attend to. That, of course, was the real reason he was in Zurich. He took a taxi to a square in the suburbs of the city, then walked ten blocks to the neighborhood where Reid's men were staying. He went into a lakeside café and sat at a quiet table at the back, waiting until Reid arrived.

They hadn't sat face-to-face for several years. Reid had aged, with more grey in the hair at his temples and deeper wrinkles around his eyes. Kerrington remembered when he had first met Reid, more than twenty years ago, when the man was still young, just back from an abortive coup attempt in West Africa and eager for more action. Despite the grey hair though, Reid still exuded the same vigor he had decades before, ordering a large plate of local Swiss sausages, then attacking the food with enthusiasm, while delivering his briefing.

While Reid talked, Kerrington imagined the team's preparations. There would be a storeroom at the safe house stacked with weapons and ammunition — HK 416s, MK 7s, and other standard special forces weapons, as well as specialized gear, including night vision goggles, tear gas and masks, explosives, drones, and the other equipment of modern warfare. The members of the team would be cleaning their weapons, then storing them in their rooms. Reid's deputies would be holding briefings on the girl and Fisher, laying out the responsibilities of individual teams. Lookouts would maintain a watch over anyone approaching the safe house.

He felt a pang of regret that he was not there, on the front line, anymore. He had never consciously decided to retire from active operations, but at some point, twenty years ago or so, he stopped taking part in the action. Live operations weren't the sort of thing that the Deputy Director of the CIA could join.

This time might be different, though. This time, he might need to be there, on the front line, when they cornered the girl and Fisher. He wanted to be absolutely certain that he, and nobody else, not even Reid, retrieved the file from the girl. He also wanted to be sure that neither the girl nor Fisher discussed the file with anyone.

The prospect of being on the front line didn't bother him in the least; on the contrary, the thought of action produced a surge of excitement. He realized how much he missed the action, how much he missed the rushes of adrenaline and the gritty reality of combat. He decided to see it as a silver lining to the file's dark cloud.

Reid was optimistic. Sure, the girl had surprised them. She surprised them several times, as had Fisher — the stupid shit. Who would have thought that the guy was such a Boy Scout? That had to be the explanation for what he did — some confused idea of justice, or something. It was either that or the money. Maybe Fisher and the girl had agreed to sell the file and split the proceeds. Or maybe they were planning to try and access the Nazi accounts themselves.

But it didn't really matter, either way. Reid's team was even larger and better equipped this time. They had twenty operatives, a mix of men and women from a variety of nationalities. They were all highly experienced, almost all with service at the CIA, or, in a few cases, other friendly intelligence agencies. There was an arsenal of high-tech weaponry at their safe house. At Reid's request, he had dispatched a truck, with diplomatic status, from one of the CIA locations in Poland, laden with weapons, ammunition, and other supplies. The team would be ready for whatever Fisher, or the Russians, or anyone else, could throw at them. They had picked up no hint that the Russians were still in the game, after the fiasco in Goma, but Reid was taking no chances.

Their immediate objective was to locate Fisher and the girl. Reid had teams of agents scouring the city, checking all the most likely places. They were also secretly hooked into Swiss security networks and were monitoring feeds from video cameras around the city. Sooner or later, they would pick up the girl's trail. Then the team's orders were simple: Grab the girl and Fisher, get the file, and kill anyone who got in the way. Then deliver the file to Kerrington and exit the country. Reid had promised again that they could execute successfully. And, if the girl really was in Zurich, that they would find her before long.

"We're also working on where the girl is going. Why would she be in Zurich? The working hypothesis is a meeting with a buyer for the information from the plane. A buyer with Swiss connections — maybe Arab or another Russian," Reid explained.

Kerrington nodded but didn't reply. He hadn't told Reid what he knew the file contained. That was a handicap for Reid's hunt, a big one. But he couldn't let Reid, or anyone else, know what the file might reveal. Still, he could nudge Reid in the right direction. Just a bit more.

"There's one more thing. I've had some chatter from the NSA suggesting that Fisher and the girl may be headed to a bank. Maybe one of the older private banks," he said.

Reid nodded. "We'll have some of the guys focus on banks then. We can stake out the larger ones."

He nodded with approval this time. He toyed with giving Reid even more information about the file, then decided against it. He couldn't afford letting Reid have that sort of leverage. He couldn't trust anyone with the information the file might contain.

"One last thing," he said, signaling the waitress for the bill. "Once we locate the girl and the file, I'll be going in with you. Make sure there's equipment for me — a Glock, plus body armor. Better have a balaclava too. That's true for the whole team."

Reid looked up, surprised, then paused. "Sure thing," he replied after a moment, but didn't look happy.

Kerrington didn't mind the fact that Reid was uncomfortable. It would make him all the more diligent, knowing how important this was to his principal benefactor.

He paid the waitress in cash. Then they left separately. He walked along the lake for half an hour or so, watching sail boats skimming across the waves. The next few days held many risks. He was navigating in uncharted waters, filled with dangerous rocks. If he made a mistake, it could be the end of his career, his reputation, his family. He put those risks aside and focused on the hunt. It still excited him, after all these years — the thrill of action. It might be risky, but it was even more exhilarating.

By the time he reached the Baur au Lac Hotel, he was in high spirits. He crossed the hotel lobby to greet his Swiss intelligence counterparts — a tall, patrician figure in a finely tailored suit who looked every inch the scion of American industry and effective head of the CIA.

Chapter 57
Jeb Fisher

He left Simon's apartment early in the morning. It was Sunday and the roads were almost completely empty. He drove out of the city, up into the mountains overlooking the lake. An hour away from Zurich, he turned onto a gravel track. The road led through a thick pine forest to a quarry, carved out of the side of a hill. He had found the site on the internet two days before, and then studied it carefully on Google Earth.

When he reached the site, he parked the car on the side of the track. The quarry was deserted, as he expected. The front gate was padlocked shut and an electrified fence, with warning signs posted every fifty meters, surrounded the site. There were a handful of buildings inside the fence. He paused in the undergrowth to inspect them and the surroundings more carefully.

When he was satisfied there was nobody inside the quarry — no cars or motorbikes and no watchman or signs of life — he slipped out of the bushes. Then he used a long metal stake that he brought from the car to short-circuit the electric fence, and a pair of wire cutters to cut a hole in the wire mesh. He chose a place behind a stand of bushes, selecting a location where it wouldn't be noticed, and then slipped into the quarry. He walked quickly to a low, sandbagged structure, set away from the other buildings, and descended a stairway that led below ground level to a heavy metal door.

The door was a challenge. There was no window, and the hinges were on the inside of the door. The lock also proved impossible to pick, despite his best efforts. Finally, a crowbar inserted between the door and the doorframe levered a gap that let him force the door open.

The underground room was packed with explosives for use at the quarry. He worked quickly, filling two large duffel bags with containers of blasting powder. The powder came in brightly labeled, shoe-box-size containers, that fit neatly inside the two bags. He carried the bags back to the van, unpacked their contents and repeated the process twice more. On the last trip, he added a handful of detonators to his stash.

When he was finished, he had two hundred kilograms of high explosives stacked in the van. He covered the boxes with blankets from Simon's apartment. They would protect the explosives from both curious eyes and any unexpected accidents.

He made a final trip back through the fence to another building, which housed the site's offices. It took thirty minutes or so, but he eventually found a small safe in one of the rooms. He used a pneumatic drill, which he brought with him from the storehouse, on the safe's lock. After ten minutes, the lock gave way. He emptied the safe's contents of €20,000 in cash, which went into one of the duffel bags, along with the detonators.

The forest was still empty as he turned the van around and returned to the main road. He drove carefully back to the city and left the car parked next to Simon's apartment. He made sure that the explosives were still hidden from sight, then found a taxi and made his way back into town, to one of the city's seedier neighbourhoods.

It took a couple of hours, but he finally found a man willing to sell him an automatic weapon. It was a mint condition Uzi, plus twenty-five magazines of ammunition. The whole package cost €10,000, which he paid out of the money from the quarry. Next, he stopped at an electronics store and purchased a small hand-held camera. Something with a long battery life that could film for a couple of hours or so. He paid with cash again.

He returned to the apartment with his purchases, pausing to put the Uzi into one of the duffel bags, together with the detonators and a dozen boxes of blasting powder. Then he let himself into the apartment, bringing the duffel bag with him.

She was curled up on a sofa, reading another book on the technical aspects of Swiss banking law. He kissed her on the back of the neck, then settled in next to her on the couch. He looked over her shoulder, trying to follow the dense German prose and its description of assignment deeds under Swiss law. He wondered why she was so interested in the subject. She noticed that he was trying to follow and put the book down, then slipped her arm around him.

"Wow. I thought my day was tough," he whispered.

She laughed. "Yep. This is awful. I can't imagine who would ever want to be a lawyer." She went on, "How was your day? Did you get what you wanted?"

"Yep. All good. Make sure you don't play with matches near the van...," he said.

"OK. Sounds scary."

"Very. But not for us."

"So... I was shopping too. You hungry?" she asked.

When he said that he was, she led him by the hand to the kitchen. A chicken was roasting in the oven, the smell triggering a rush of saliva. He realized that he hadn't eaten all day. She watched him swallow and laughed.

"Mr. Fisher. You are so transparent."

He laughed and shrugged his shoulders, remembering at the same time his deception in Lucca and wondering if the same were true for her. Then she handed him a glass of wine and a piece of cheese. The wine was perfect — a rich red from somewhere in France with an unpronounceable name. The cheese was just as good, thick and creamy, on a piece of freshly baked bread.

They sat next to each other in an alcove in Simon's kitchen, watching the chicken roasting in the oven and sharing the glass of wine. He told her about the quarry and how he'd bought the Uzi. She told him more about the Swiss banking industry. It felt like they had just come home from work with stories about the office. He wished that were true, and that they weren't about to start a gun battle that would probably kill them both. He forced that thought out of his mind and leaned against her as she took another sip of the wine.

After dinner, he went back to work. He unpacked the detonators, checking each one carefully, and then attached them to the containers of blasting powder. When he was finished, he repacked the duffel bag and took it back outside to the van. It was dark and he worked undisturbed for another hour. When he was finished, he rearranged the blankets that covered the explosives, locked the van's doors, and surveyed the car with satisfaction. It was perfect. The van looked exactly the way it had before. But now it could devastate a medium-sized building — a building like the Staehelin & Co. headquarters, for example. All he needed to do was deliver the bomb to the right place.

Then he went inside. She was curled up in the bedroom, sound asleep in the midst of Simon's soft toys. He didn't disturb her, instead turning off the light and slipping into bed. He managed not to wake her, and then sat awake, watching her in the glow of the bedside clock, thinking over the past two weeks, trying to sort out his feelings. After an hour or so, he realised that he wasn't going to find the answer, at least not tonight, and slipped his arm around her, pulling her against him and cradling her head to his chest. He was asleep in minutes.

Chapter 58
Maximilian Staehelin

He stood in his office, wondering whether to take the phone call. His secretary said it was another young woman, someone different from the American woman who called previously, but who insisted on speaking about the same accounts. He didn't want to take this call any more than he wanted to take the previous one. But he had no choice this time either. He braced himself and waited for the woman to be connected.

The woman identified herself as Ms. Lee. She said she was a banker from Hong Kong, representing a very wealthy client. Someone of great mutual interest, who was eager, very eager, to work together, to cooperate, as friends. She could assure Dr. Staehelin, as a colleague, that her client was a man of the utmost good faith and seriousness.

He paused for a moment, then welcomed her warmly to Zurich, on behalf of the bank, and thanked her for the call. He promised his cooperation in assisting her and her client.

She went on. "My client has a specific interest in your bank, Dr. Staehelin. He is the owner of certain accounts at your bank, quite large deposits in numbered accounts. He has asked me to discuss a review and orderly allocation of these amounts." She spoke with what sounded like an English accent.

"We are fully at the service of any of our account holders," Staehelin said. He worried about where the conversation was headed.

"Excellent." Then she read off a series of account numbers, followed by a series of passcodes.

"That should be sufficient, I understand, for access to the accounts?" she said.

He swallowed, then steadied himself and thanked her for the information, assuring her that it was most useful.

But he went on. "Unfortunately, Ms. Lee, we have serious concerns about these account numbers and passcodes. We have reason to believe that they are fraudulent, perhaps connected to a criminal plot. A very serious criminal scheme. We are investigating the matter, but you should know that it is an extremely grave subject. We may need to advise the Swiss banking authorities about these requests."

She laughed lightly, not at all impressed by his bluff. "Dr. Staehelin. We both know that these are quite real, quite proper accounts. I have the documents, including agreements signed by your bank, to prove this. And I am sure that you have not contacted the banking authorities. So, we can stop playing that little game with each other. I am also very sure that a bank of your reputation and standing would not be mixed up in anything fraudulent or illegal." She was polite, but there was a cold edge of threat in her voice.

She continued. "You may be concerned about an American woman, who has been inquiring about the same accounts. I must warn you about this person. She is an imposter. And she is dangerous, I understand wanted by authorities in several countries. I believe my client has proof of this. She may be arrested. In my client's view, she should be arrested. That would help in solving the problem. It would help us both. Both of us, Dr. Staehelin. If one thinks carefully about it."

He reflected for a moment. "Why should I believe you, Ms. Lee, rather than the American woman? Perhaps you are the imposter. Perhaps both of you are."

She responded right away. Her voice was warm and resonant. "I can give you my word, my client is very respectable, very wealthy. He is also a very reasonable, fair businessman. Even generous. He is certainly not greedy. I would need approval for any final terms, but he has told me that he is willing to share the funds in these accounts. Share the funds on an equitable basis. Share the funds with the bank. With you, Dr. Staehelin."

He reflected again. His sense of dread eased ever so slightly. Maybe this woman wasn't a problem. Maybe she was a solution.

"That is of course constructive," he said. "If, and I only say if, your client indeed has all of the original documentation, recording his rights to these accounts, we would be open in principle to a fair and equitable resolution of this matter. That goes without saying."

She answered immediately. "Excellent. Let me make a suggestion," she said. "Perhaps you can arrange a meeting, where we can confront this American woman. And examine the documents she claims to have. I assure you, I can demonstrate that she is an imposter."

He thought again for a moment. This woman, this Ms. Lee, might be even more of a problem than the American woman. But he needed to decide. Better to confront them both, maybe play them off against each other. And make this woman bring the proof that she said she had. Flush her out and see if her threat was real.

He replied cheerfully, "Yes, we can do that, Ms. Lee. Come here, to the bank's office, at 2:15 p.m. Tomorrow. I will make sure that the American woman is present as well. Naturally, you should bring original copies of all the documentation. That is necessary for authentication in a case such as this. I am sure you understand."

"Perfect. I will do that. And I look forward to meeting you in person. Also, my client and I look forward to working with you. Together, I have no doubt we can achieve some very fine results. And avoid some very serious problems." The edge of menace was back in her voice.

"Please convey my best wishes to your client. Tell him that I am sure we can work together. That we can avoid any problems. For either of us, Ms. Lee. And thank you for calling. I shall see you here tomorrow."

He put down the phone and looked out the window of his office, watching the sailboats on the lake, running from the wind. He felt like one of them, blown by forces out of his control. He frowned, wanting this to end. But now, at least, he saw a possible way forward.

It was risky, but he thought again that this Ms. Lee might be a solution, not another problem. He could share what was left in the accounts with her and her client, if she really had one. And put an end to the whole long nightmare of Nazi accounts. Bury it forever, and return to the quiet, ordered respectability of his life. And he didn't really have a choice. He couldn't risk either woman going to the police or the press. That would be a disaster. He had to play along with them both to make sure that didn't happen.

After a few moments, he picked up the phone again and called Mr. Dupuy, to check on the security arrangements. On his instructions, the security detail at the bank had already been doubled. He ordered Dupuy to double it again, to sixteen men. He also insisted that the men be the best that Dupuy could find on short notice, with military training, and that they be armed. As heavily armed as they could be. And he directed that the security team be ready to respond, around the clock, at a moment's notice. Then he put down the phone and looked back out of the window, watching the sailboats, blown by the wind across the lake.

Chapter 59
Yan Wu

She woke very early again. She made herself tea and sat alone on the veranda of the villa, looking over the lake. It was cloudy, and the wind whipped up ragged froth on the tops of the waves rolling toward the shore. The wind stirred her hair from time to time. Despite the breeze, she didn't shiver, or use one of the woolen wraps strewn about the chairs on the veranda.

She sipped her tea, going over the things that she would need to do that day, checking and rechecking her plans. And gathering her resolve.

At exactly 9:00 a.m., she got up and walked into the kitchen. The stone floor was cool against her bare feet. The chef was up now and she sent him away, ordering a variety of provisions from the local market, which she said she wanted immediately.

Then she made coffee for Ivan. She prepared it just the way he liked, strong and thick, with frothy hot milk. After the chef departed for the market, she took a small vial from a padded compartment inside her handbag and added its contents to his coffee. She stirred the coffee carefully, making sure not to let the liquid touch her fingers. Then she unwrapped two croissants and carried them, along with the coffee, into their bedroom.

He was still asleep, sprawled across the bed, his body hairy and pale white in the morning light. She set the breakfast tray down on the bed stand, retrieved her handbag from the kitchen and closed the bedroom door behind her, silently locking it. She opened the curtains next, letting in the sunlight, then switched on the bedside lamp. After a moment, he stirred, shaking his head, as if to clear away the vodka from the night before. He looked blearily at her. She didn't usually wake him in the mornings.

"Relax, baby. Breakfast in bed. For a change," she said with a soft smile.

He made an effort to smile appreciatively. She knew perfectly well that he didn't care much for breakfast in bed, or for anything else prior to noon. She sat on the edge of the bed, next to the breakfast tray, then lifted the coffee cup and saucer, handing them fluidly to him. Her hand was steady, the way it always was. He took the saucer from her with both hands, holding it before him like a child, now half-seated, propped up against the headboard, still partly asleep.

"Today could be a big day. I dreamt we caught them," she said, tearing one of the croissants in half and handing it to him.

She realized just a second too late that she had made a mistake. The saucer and coffee cup, plus the croissant, were too much for his liquor-clouded mind to deal with just after waking up. As if in slow motion, she watched him reach, greedily, for the croissant, as the coffee cup slid off the edge of the saucer, toppling over his bare leg, the dark brown fluid splashing over his thigh and onto the bed sheets. He swore in Russian, mopping the coffee off his leg with the sheets.

"God damn it. That hurts. Fucking stings," he cursed.

She watched, half-frozen, as red welts began to spread angrily across the skin on his thigh, like flames across a sheet of paper.

"Shit. It stings, fucking stings," he swore.

He looked in bewilderment at his skin, which was starting to blister, staring at the bright red patches on the white of his thigh.

She held her breath and eased quietly off the bed, then picked up her handbag from the floor, and placed it on the edge of the bed.

"Let me get you some ointment," she said quietly.

He ignored her, still staring at his thigh, a puzzled look on his face. She reached silently into her purse and took out her comb, unfolded it, then slipped onto the bed behind him, her legs bare against the sheets. She paused for a moment to take in the scene — him, naked and helpless on the bed, still staring at his skin, burnt and blistering, with her, rising up above him, dressed in white, at the edge of the bed. And then, in slow motion once more, the sweep of her blade across his throat. Severing his jugular, his larynx, and most of the rest of his windpipe.

He half-turned, blood gushing out of his throat onto the sheets, staring at her with shock and confusion. She stepped slightly away from the bed, then leaned forward, so that he could see, and wiped the blade on his leg, leaving a glistening streak of blood against the white of his skin. She stood there, in her white dress, barefoot, hair soft around her shoulders, razor held delicately in one hand, and watched him die. She didn't look away. She didn't smile, didn't curse him, didn't do any of the other things that she had so often dreamt about doing. She just watched him struggle, clawing at his throat, then flailing helplessly. His eyes were wide with disbelief. And then she watched him finally die.

When he stopped breathing, she checked his pulse. Satisfied, she covered the body with the comforter, plus a spare blanket from the closet. She surveyed the scene. It looked just as if he had over-indulged, again, the night before. His head, burrowed into the pillow, greasy hair and pallid skin, were all that one could see. She closed the bedroom curtains again, switched off the light and closed the door, locking it behind her, and taking the key.

Then she went to the kitchen and made herself another cup of tea. She took it, and the remaining croissant, out to the veranda and had breakfast, waiting for the chef to return with his shopping. When he did, she thanked him and told him to take the next three days off, giving him a generous tip. She said she would do the cooking for both of them. The chef was delighted by the news. He was gone in twenty minutes.

After he left, she collected Ivan's laptop, mobile phone, and wallet, and packed them with her things, before wiping her fingerprints from every surface she might have touched in the past week. Then she locked the door to the villa and left, walking a dozen blocks before hailing a cab. She directed the driver to a small, anonymous hotel near the city center, where she checked in using a new credit card and passport. Nobody knew that she had them, not even Ivan. She had arranged her new identity two years before, in preparation for a moment like this.

After she was settled, she called Alexei, using Ivan's phone. She told him that Ivan had drunk too much again and that she wanted to check on the progress of the search. He was unsurprised at Petronov's plight and reported no sightings of the girl. She said that she would check in again later in the day. After she hung up, she changed her clothes, choosing a conservative, dark blue pantsuit for the meeting with Staehelin at the Bank. Then she left, walking through the neat, respectable streets of Zurich, until she reached Bahnhofstrasse. She was early, so she stopped in an open-air café, ordered hot chocolate, and reviewed the next steps in her plan while she nursed the drink.

Chapter 60
Sara West

They returned to the bank just before 2:30 p.m. She had been nervous all day, a ball of fear burrowed deep in her stomach. There were too many moving parts and uncertainties in their plan.

Jeb told her that last night, laying out all the things that could go wrong. She insisted on going forward anyway, despite his worries. But she knew he was right to be worried. The plan was crazy, and the odds of her getting out alive were tiny. The odds of either of them getting out alive were tiny. He had told her that again in the morning, holding her tight and asking her again to call it off or at least delay it.

But she refused. She insisted that she had to do it, that they had to do this. And he had agreed, finally, after trying everything he could to change her mind. When she refused, he had just held her, as they lay together in Simon's bed.

They left the apartment at 1:30 p.m. He drove the van, packed with the explosives that he had armed the day before. He was wearing a blonde wig, that she greeted with an expression of amused sympathy. He also wore the uniform of a local office supply company. In addition to the explosives in the back of the van, there were three other packages of blasting powder, stacked neatly on the front seat of the van. He had rigged each of the packages of explosives with a detonator, which he could activate with a call from three disposable mobile phones he had also purchased the day before.

He drove into the center of Zurich and parked the van in a side street, a couple blocks from the bank. Then they left the vehicle and walked to a restaurant across the street from the bank's main entrance. He went inside and took a seat by the window, where he could watch the street. Concealed under his jacket was the Uzi.

A dozen and a half magazines for the weapon were stacked in the duffel bag that he carried with him. She left him there, allowing herself one last look as he watched her go, through the restaurant's window.

Their plan was simple. He would wait at the restaurant and watch the bank while she went inside. He would watch for Reid and his men, and for the Russians. If they arrived, he would be ready to drive the van into the basement delivery area of the bank. He had scouted the bank the day before, and was sure that he could talk, or fight, his way past the security. Once inside, he would position the van, and its load of explosives, next to the bank's power supplies, then make his way upstairs. He would leave the remaining explosives where they would cause the most damage to Reid and the Russians.

They didn't really expect Reid or the Russians to try and grab her today. There was no sign that they had seen her two days ago, when she went to the Bank. And he'd seen none of Reid's men, or the Russians, when he scouted the bank yesterday. He didn't know how they missed her. But it didn't matter. The purpose of her visit today was to try and get their attention again, to bait the trap once more. But if he were wrong, and either Reid or the Russians were waiting at the bank, he would be ready to take them out. He hoped that wouldn't happen. The plan was for everyone — Reid's men and the Russians — to show up at the same time. But if it didn't work out that way, he would still be ready.

She waited until exactly 2:30 p.m., then walked to the bank. She made no effort to disguise her identity, and stopped several times along the way, to inspect store windows, lingering at pedestrian crosswalks, out in the open where she was easy to see. Then she went into the bank, pausing again at the top of the front steps for a moment.

The reception area was no more welcoming this time than before. And the knot in her stomach was even tighter. She was bait, not just walking into the lion's den, but walking into the lion's den as bait. Whether or not she made it through the day depended on Jeb. One man against a few dozen opponents. Assuming he was there to fight them. She wondered again if she could really trust him. What would a man do for five or ten billion dollars? She wished she were back in the jungle, where the world was simple and clear-cut.

Then Staehelin's secretary arrived and escorted her to the conference room, the same one where she met with Staehelin before. She waited once more in the midst of its opulence, this time standing, wondering what Jeb would do if things got nasty. She wanted to reach into her handbag, to find the phone that Jeb had given her and call him. But she thought that there would be surveillance cameras watching her every move. So she pretended to admire the view out over the lake.

The black-suited waiter returned and asked for her order. She dismissed him again. She thought they should know by now that she wouldn't want anything to drink. Staehelin arrived ten minutes later. He greeted her perfunctorily, with none of his previous pretended attentiveness. She didn't mind. She knew where the conversation would go. He came quickly to what he thought the point was.

"So, Ms. Warren. Or whoever you are. Let's see the originals of the documents you say you have. As we discussed."

She ignored his demand. It was what she had expected.

"Give me access to my accounts," she replied coolly. "The way we discussed last time. I gave you the account numbers and passcodes. If not, I will turn this matter over to my lawyers and the banking authorities. I told you that before."

He didn't blink an eye. "I doubt that. Whoever you are. Let me tell you now, very clearly, that I believe you are an imposter, a fraudster, a criminal."

This was also what she had expected. He was bluffing. She was ready for that. She was just about to tell him about the law firm that they had hired, the day before, and the reporters she had approached, with tantalizing little hints.

Then he stood up, before she could reply, and walked to a door at the side of the conference room, opening it so that someone else could enter the room from an adjoining office. The woman was petite, Asian, and stunningly beautiful, dressed in a dark blue pantsuit, with hair falling softly around her shoulders. Her features were delicate, almost child-like, with dark, solemn eyes, innocent and gentle. She looked perfectly at ease. This wasn't in the plan.

Staehelin pretended to introduce them. "Ms. Warren. Allow me to present Ms. Lee. Ms. Lee, this woman calls herself Ms. Warren. Let's come to the point. You will excuse me if we do that."

He went on. "You both have told me various things. Outlandish things, about supposed accounts from seventy years ago. I am inclined, quite frankly, to call the police. Neither one of you has produced a single original document to justify your requests. For all I know, you are both part of some elaborate hoax, working together to steal from innocent clients of the bank. I asked you for original documents before. Both of you. Where are they?"

She was struggling for an answer when the Asian woman responded sweetly.

"Dr. Staehelin. Rest assured. We are having the originals sent here. From Hong Kong. I apologize for the delay. I fully understand your concern. But it's 9,000 miles away. They will be here shortly, I am assured."

Staehelin turned pointedly from the Asian woman to her. This wasn't in the plan either. She stuck to her script.

"Dr. Staehelin. I have already given you the account numbers and passcodes. As you know, very well, that's all that the protocol requires. Now. Please stop your foot-dragging and give me access to the accounts, before I call my lawyers."

Staehelin smiled. "My dear Ms. Warren. And also Ms. Lee. I am afraid I haven't explained clearly enough. You both have arrived here, in my offices, coincidentally on almost the same day. You both claim the same accounts, using the same passwords, showing me copies of the exact same documents. Here is Ms. Lee's copy. Where is yours now, Ms. Warren? Or whoever you are."

He produced a copy of the protocol. A copy Ms. Lee gave him. It looked like her copy, the one that she showed him two days before, except this copy was on pinkish paper. Pinkish paper just like the pink-colored paper in Maria's copier. Just like the paper that she and Maria had laughed at, because it looked so amateurish, in her house, just outside of Lucca. Just like the paper that should be safely hidden in Maria's house.

She struggled to breathe, to try and listen to what Staehelin was saying to her. The tight ball of tension in her stomach suddenly dropped, like a rock falling off a cliff, carrying her down in a dizzying descent. All she could think was that the Asian woman, Ms. Lee, had copies of the file. On pink paper. There was only one copy of the file. That copy was with Maria. In Italy. On pinkish paper.

The Asian woman was smiling sweetly at Staehelin. Her hands were folded neatly, demurely, in her lap. She looked almost like a teenager, her hair was clipped back, showing off the soft, even tone of her skin, and the delicate shape of her ears and cheeks. Her eyes were fixed on Staehelin, large and liquid.

Somehow, this woman must have found Maria and then taken her copy of the file. Maria was a mother to her. Maria would never have given the file to that woman, or anyone else, willingly. Her stomach filled with dread, of what might have happened to Maria, and an aching guilt, that she was to blame for it. For putting Maria in the way of this woman and the killers who helped her. Just like she had put her father in their way.

She realized that Staehelin was speaking to her again. She struggled to focus on what he was saying, to sit upright, as if everything were fine. She realized that she was failing horribly. She didn't know what to do.

"Ms. Warren, or whatever your name is …You know, I can see now that you do know, this this is a very serious matter. Frankly, I should telephone the police right now. But I won't. I'm a generous man."

He continued, firm and assertive now, playing the role of the distinguished bank director.

"You may leave. Just go. But don't come back. Don't come back unless you can provide legitimate proof of your preposterous stories. I gave you one chance already to bring me the documents you say you have. Now, go. Leave before I call the police."

He walked to the door and opened it, dismissing her with haughty authority.

She noticed Staehelin and the Asian woman exchange glances, but she couldn't react. Numbly, she got up and walked, half in shock, across the plush carpet of the conference room, down the long hallway, into the elevator, and then across the vast stone floor of the reception area. She was dimly aware that the Asian woman and Staehelin followed her, the bank director helping her with the door.

The sun was still shining brightly outside, as she stood on the steps of the bank, searching for Jeb among the pedestrians who were walking up and down Bahnhofstrasse. She had never felt so lost in her life.

Chapter 61
Yan Wu

She stood behind the blonde girl, at the top of the stairs to the entrance of the bank, waiting for Staehelin to go back inside. The girl was looking up and down the street in front of the bank, searching for someone, probably her American friend.

As Staehelin said good-bye, she reached into her handbag and took out the comb, silently unfolding it, then wrapping her hand in her scarf. She stepped closer, right next to the girl, and put an arm around her shoulder, as if to comfort her. She held the girl tight, as she tried to pull away. The blade of the razor was poised just against the girl's throat, right at her jugular. She leaned next to the girl's ear, as if they were old friends or lovers, then whispered to her.

"Don't move. The thing against your throat is a blade, a razor blade. If you struggle, I'll kill you. I'll cut your throat. Do you understand?"

She hadn't planned this. She was taking a chance. A big chance. But this was an opportunity that was too good to pass up. The girl nodded, her eyes continuing to search the street.

"Walk down the steps with me. Right now, but slowly. Then over to that taxi. No games or I'll kill you."

There was an empty cab just in front of the bank. The girl hesitated, then complied. She guided her to the taxi, then opened the back door and half-pushed the girl inside the cab.

"Tell him to take us to the hotel where you're staying," she whispered.

The girl hesitated again. She let the blade rub against the girl's throat.

"I'll do it. Don't make me. And no games," she whispered.

The girl gave the driver a street address, eyes still searching the crowd outside the taxi. The driver grunted, then started the car and drove out along the lake. While he drove, she kept the razor firmly on the girl's neck. It took fifteen minutes before they stopped on a quiet suburban street.

She whispered into the girl's ear. "This isn't a hotel. I said no games. I'll cut your throat. You'd better believe me."

"I'm not staying at a hotel. This is where I'm staying," the girl responded.

"It better be. Give me the keys," she demanded.

The girl fished into the pocket of her jeans and produced a single house key.

"It's the side entrance," the girl said defiantly.

She paid the driver, tipping generously, so she didn't need to take her arm from around the girl's shoulder. Then she asked the driver to help them out. They'd had a bit too much to drink, she giggled. As he walked around the car, out of sight for an instant, she slammed her open hand against the side of the girl's head, stunning her, then opened the door and helped the driver ease the girl's limp body out of the car. They both chuckled, the man shaking his head at the girl's condition.

She debated whether or not to kill the driver and take his car, but then decided not to. On balance, it was too risky. And she didn't need the car. She let him drive away, leaving her holding the girl upright, standing in front of the address that the girl had given.

After the cab left, she guided the girl along the side of the house. The path was flagstones, uneven and mossy, shaded in rhododendron bushes. The girl could barely walk, stumbling on the footpath and dragging her feet like a sleepwalker. When they reached the door she shook the girl, who struggled to raise her head, then slumped back against her. The girl was out cold. She must have hit her harder than she intended.

She leaned forward, fitting the key into the keyhole, then unlocked the door and pushed it open. It was dark inside. She waited a moment for her eyes to adjust, then peered into the house again.

The girl chose the perfect moment, twisting out of her grasp just as she was leaning forward into the darkened hallway. Then, instead of trying to escape, the girl lunged forward, driving her against the door. She struggled to regain her footing, but the girl kicked her, viciously, in the stomach, knocking her onto her back in the front hall of the house.

The girl still didn't run, but sprang after her, face alive with hatred. She grabbed for her razor, found it and then slashed at the girl, simultaneously regaining her feet. The girl retreated through the doorway, but then, when she followed, slammed the door shut on her arm. She dropped the razor again, stifling a scream as the blade sliced her palm and the massive door clamped her forearm against the frame. She pried the door open, but the girl kicked her again, hard, in the stomach, knocking her down once more. She grabbed for her handbag and found the pistol, hidden at the side, and pulled it out. The girl retreated once more, graceful as a cat, and forced the door shut, just as the pistol barked and a bullet slammed into the heavy wooden frame.

She scrambled to her feet again and tried to open the front door. But it was locked now, from the outside. Without a key, she couldn't unlock the door. She cursed, then searched for a window that she could climb out of. Everything on the ground floor was barred. She had to hurry now. The girl would call her American friend, or maybe the police.

She searched the ground floor of the apartment for the papers the girl had to have, finding nothing of interest. She ran up the stairs to the next floor, anxiety rising. Maybe there was nothing here. Maybe the girl's American friend had the documents. Or maybe they were hidden somewhere else.

And then she found it. It was in the bedroom — a badly worn backpack, hidden under the bed. And inside the backpack was a thick sheaf of papers, with the originals of the documents that she had taken from the old woman in Lucca. They looked identical to the ones she had taken from the woman. Her heart leapt. She flipped through the papers, then placed the entire stack in her handbag and ran to the rear of the house.

It was a three-meter drop from the bathroom window to the ground, but the earth was soft. She landed easily, then climbed the fence into a neighbor's yard and sprinted to the street. She walked fast, away from the house, then turned right, sprinted for another hundred meters and turned again. A cab passed, its lights on, and she flagged it down. She directed the driver to a suburban train station, paid him and waited for fifteen minutes. Then she walked a few blocks and flagged another cab back to the hotel where she had checked in that morning. She walked silently past the reception, then climbed the stairs to the second floor.

She locked the door to her room and took out the file. The papers were old, many faded and brittle. But they were exactly what she wanted. They were the originals of the documents she had found near Lucca. She allowed herself another surge of elation. Six years. More for Ivan. And now she had it. Who knew how much money was in the accounts, but it would make her wealthy. Rich and powerful beyond her wildest dreams. Beyond anything that a peasant girl from China could ever imagine.

She went into the bathroom and drew herself a hot bath, scalding hot. Then she undressed and soaked, for more than an hour, letting the pain from the girl's blows drain out of her. She grudgingly respected the girl, escaping as she had, as well as delivering more than a little punishment. A worthy adversary. But not quite good enough. She settled back into the water and began to think how to finish her dealings with the good Dr. Staehelin.

Chapter 62
Jeb Fisher

He hadn't seen her come out of the bank. They expected that she would be in the bank at least an hour. He was watching anyway, in case she came out early. And then, for an instant, just the wrong instant, he was distracted.

He had been sitting unobtrusively in the restaurant across from the bank's entrance, when he spotted a familiar face. One of the men from Reid's team, walking arm-in-arm along the street with a young, dark-haired woman. They were trying to make it look as if they had eyes only for each other, but in fact, they were both focused on the entrance of the bank — watching it intently.

He let them continue up the street, then checked the crowds around the bank again. Before long, he spotted another familiar face, an ex-colleague at the Agency, seated in a car just down the street. He scanned the crowds once more, this time more slowly. There would be others, he was sure. After a moment, he shifted his eyes back to the entrance of the bank. It was only by chance then, that he glimpsed Sara as she disappeared, together with an Asian woman, into a taxi. He wasn't sure, but it looked as if the woman was holding something to Sara's throat.

He sprinted after the cab, ignoring the shouts from the waiter in the restaurant, demanding that he pay his bill. He hailed a taxi, then directed it to follow the cab with Sara and the Asian woman. But it was his afternoon for bad luck. His taxi was stopped at an interminably long traffic light and then caught in traffic. All his threats and promised tips did nothing to get the driver to try something creative.

He finally ordered the taxi to return to where he had parked the van, desperation rising. He could hardly believe it. In the space of ten minutes, he had lost her. Almost certainly because she had been abducted by the Asian woman. He tried the mobile phone that he had given her. Once, twice, a half dozen times. No answer. He climbed into the van and headed back to Simon's apartment, driving as fast as he dared. He realized how desperately he wanted to find her, how lost he felt at putting her in danger.

He screeched to a halt in front of Simon's house, just as his phone rang. It was Sara. She was there, in the bushes next to the house. The key to the house was in the front door. He took her inside, then checked to make sure that the house was empty. She was half in shock and shaking with anger. She ran up the stairs without a word, then returned, carrying the empty backpack. Her face was a mask, eyes cold with rage.

He made her collect her things, telling her that the house wasn't safe anymore. While she did that, he released Simon, and then drove the two of them away in the van. He didn't know where else to go, so he drove out of the city, stopping at a rest area looking over the lake. It was deserted.

Then he held her as she told the story of the meeting at the bank, the appearance of the Asian woman, the copies of the file that the woman produced, her abduction, the fight, and the missing file with the original papers. At first, she was half-panicked, words tumbling out. But part-way through the story she caught herself and described the rest of the events of the last few hours quietly, in a calm, almost detached voice. When she was finished, they were both silent for a while.

"We could walk away now," he said. "They have what they want. They don't need you anymore."

"I'm not walking away," she said flatly, her voice hard and cold.

He tried again. "We could go away. I can make it happen. I think. Just the two of us. Me and you together. A new life."

"I'm not giving up," she answered.

She paused and looked at him. "I love you. I might as well say it. You know it anyway. I love you. Unconditionally. But they killed my father. My friends. Now Maria. They are evil. I won't ever, ever walk away from this."

"Baby. I can't go through another afternoon like today. I love you too. Desperately. I couldn't bear it when I thought I'd lost you. Don't make me do that again." He pleaded with her, begged her.

She looked at him, like she hadn't really seen him close up before. But then shook her head again.

"No. I won't. I can't. I wouldn't be me."

"OK," he said, after a few more moments. "Then we need a plan. And we just lost our only real leverage. If we don't have the file, we've got nothing. Nada."

She looked at him again for a very long moment, grey eyes even, but as if they were watching something far away.

Then she spoke, softly, hesitantly. "I didn't tell you the truth, baby. I'm sorry."

He interrupted her. "I know, honey. But sweetie, I wasn't honest either. I know where you went in Lucca. I followed you that night. I watched you and your friend make the copies of the file. And I'm sorry too. I really am. I should have trusted you. We should have trusted each other."

He leaned across the front seat of the car, careful not to disturb the packages of explosives, and tried to hold her in his arms, pulling her against him and hugging her tight.

She pulled away though, and looked at him, at first stunned. Then she laughed, through her shock and tears. "Oh my God. You followed me? And that was the night we made love. The first time. Oh my God. I can't believe it."

She was silent for a few moments. Then she leaned over and held him tight, across the front seat of the van.

After another moment, she went on. "Actually, not telling you about the copy of the file wasn't what I meant," she said.

"I wasn't honest with you another time. About something bigger. I never showed you the whole file. I kept out the most important papers, the documents that you need to get access to the accounts with the Nazi's money. I never showed you those papers. I kept them hidden."

He looked at her wordlessly.

She continued. "So, that Asian women, whoever she is, she didn't get the whole file. She got most of it. But she didn't get the most important parts of the file. They're still hidden They weren't in what she took."

He didn't know whether to curse or laugh. He sat there staring at her, half in disbelief, half in relief.

"Well, I guess it's my turn to say 'Oh my God.' But you must be kidding, you couldn't really have done that," he finally said.

She shook her head. "No, baby. I'm not kidding. Here they are."

She opened the hidden compartment of her backpack, where the rain shield was stored, and took out the elegantly embossed leather folder with the Nazi swastika still visible on the front. Inside were a few dozen sheets of paper, old and brittle. A neat stack of official looking deeds and contracts, all with the letterhead of Staehelin & Co.

"These are what Staehelin wanted from us," she explained. "This is what he wanted from me and from the Asian woman. These are the originals of the documents that you really need in order to access the accounts. To get the money in the accounts. And we still have them."

He shook his head. "Oh my God," he repeated.

Then, "Why? Why did you hide them? Why did you hide them from me?" he asked.

She shrugged. "You must know why. I thought you were probably after the money. The money in the accounts. I didn't trust you. I'm not sure I could have trusted anyone then. After everything that happened. It's not easy even now."

"You told me now," he said.

"Yes. I did. Maybe I finally trust you now." She looked at him, evenly and unblinking.

He realized then, what she had just done, what she had just laid in his lap. He looked down at the thin set of papers, the keys to more money than he could imagine, more money and more power than anyone could imagine, lying there. He took her in his arms again, holding her tight.

Then he whispered, "I don't know how we got here, but I know that I love you. I always have. Since that first moment, in the hotel in Goma. And ever since."

She held him tighter then, clinging to him with both arms wrapped around his neck. After a moment, the shock and anger hit her again and she sobbed uncontrollably against his chest. He held her while she cried, like a child.

After a while, her sobs subsided. "I'm sorry," she said again. "I didn't want to. To lie to you. It never felt right."

"You know I was never in this for the money," he said, looking at her.

She looked down, then back up at him. "I know. I always wanted to believe that. I know now."

They were silent for a while, just holding hands in the front of the van.

Then he said, "We still need a plan though. Now what do we do?"

She replied without a moment's hesitation. "It's exactly the same as before."

She went on. "We just use these papers to get Kerrington and the Russians to the bank at the same time. Plus that Asian woman. And then payback. That's your part." Her voice was flat and cold again.

He shook his head, partly in disbelief, partly in admiration. Then he explained how the plan would work. Simple, but effective. And deadly. It was her turn to shake her head. And then they left, taking the van back into the center of the city, headed to the bank, her hand on his shoulder while he drove, both of them quiet, at peace, thinking about what had just happened. And about what lay ahead.

Chapter 63
Reginald Reid

It had been a bad day so far. It seemed to start well. They almost got the girl. Just after 3:00 p.m., one of his men spotted her leaving the Staehelin Bank, a private bank in the center of the city. The girl was with an Asian woman who they knew nothing about. The two women had descended the stairs at the bank's entrance, then gotten into a taxi. His men moved in immediately to follow the cab, but then somehow lost it in the traffic. It had been shit luck with traffic lights changing at all the wrong times.

And then it took more than two hours to track down where the taxi with the two women had gone. When they had finally done so, he accompanied a team of four men that rolled up at an address in one of Zurich's best suburbs. They forced the front door and then searched the apartment with a fine-tooth comb. But they were a couple hours late again and there was nothing there for them to find.

It was clear that Fisher and the girl had spent nearly a week at the apartment. The dazed law student, who they found hiding in the bedroom, confirmed that, ID-ing Fisher and the girl from their photographs and then describing his days of captivity. Apart from that, though, the apartment yielded hardly any clues.

Instead, they found only a mystery. Reid spotted the bullet, lodged in the wooden frame of the front door. It had been fired upwards, by someone who must have been lying on the floor of the entrance hall. There were signs of a scuffle in the hallway as well, with fresh marks on the walls and drops of blood on the floor.

He wondered who had fired the bullet, and why. They were sure that the girl and Asian woman had come to the apartment, alone, that afternoon. The taxi driver who they finally tracked down described the blonde girl's intoxication but hadn't seen any signs of hostility. Maybe the two women had tried to double-cross

Fisher, and he caught them. Or maybe the Asian woman took the girl hostage, and Fisher tried to free her.

The truth was that they didn't know what happened at the apartment. There were no bodies and no signs of either the girl or the file. And they had virtually no leads. The only thing they knew was that Fisher and the girl would need a new place to stay. Either with or without the Asian woman, whoever she was.

He reported the results of their search to Kerrington on his encrypted phone as they drove back to the safe house. Kerrington was furious that the girl had slipped through their fingers again. He didn't understand how she had gotten into the bank without Reid spotting her in the first place. Or how she then left the bank without a tail. And now how they had no idea where she had gone.

"What the fuck are you guys doing?" Kerrington demanded.

"I know. It's shit. I reamed the teams. But we are where we are. At least we're getting closer."

"Fuck that." Kerrington was angrier than ever before.

He went on. "Some fucking Chinese bitch found the girl? And you can't even follow her? Or watch the front door to a bank? What's wrong with you?" Kerrington demanded.

"I get it. It won't happen again. I guarantee it."

"There's a bright side," he continued. "We know now that it's the Staehelin Bank, right? We can focus my guys there. She'll come back. And when she does, we'll be there. We'll be there in force."

"You fucking better be. One more failure and you are done. Forever."

Kerrington hung up, leaving Reid staring out of the window of the van. He was tired of Kerrington's bullshit. Really tired of it. He wasn't a magician. And if Kerrington hadn't stuck him with Fisher, none of this would ever have happened.

He wondered what the girl really had, what Kerrington wanted so badly, what it had to do with the bank. It must be something really special. Kerrington didn't need money, that was for sure. He'd never gone after something this way just for money. What would explain this effort, and all these risks? It must be unbelievably important. Maybe that's what turned Fisher — the chance at something so big that even a Boy Scout might go rogue.

He wondered how much it would take for him to go rogue on Kerrington the way Fisher did. He'd never even toyed with that kind of idea before. This gig with Kerrington was too good and Kerrington was too dangerous. But with Kerrington's bullshit, maybe the world looked different.

Just then, his phone rang. It was Johnson, one of the men at the Staehelin Bank. They had spotted the girl again, entering the bank. Just a minute ago. The bad day just turned good again.

Chapter 64
Franklin Kerrington III

They were getting very close now. Just forty minutes ago, Reid called to report that his men had spotted the girl and Fisher leaving a cab a hundred meters or so from the bank, then walking quickly to its entrance. The girl was carrying a large handbag that looked as if it were full. Fisher had his hand in his jacket pocket and was scanning the street for tails. Fisher hadn't spotted any of Reid's men, and both he and the girl disappeared into the bank.

He ordered Reid to get his men, all of his men, ready to go into the bank on his order. He was sure that the girl had brought the file to the bank. That would explain the handbag, as well as Fisher's presence. He must be there to make sure that both she and the file stayed safe. And maybe to make sure that she didn't run off with either the file or the money.

Reid moved quickly. He deployed teams on each street corner around the bank, plus a dozen agents, with full complements of weapons, in vans across the street from the bank's entrance. In addition to a dozen and a half men carrying MK 7s and HK 416s, they had a heavy machine gun, rocket launchers, and tear gas grenades. They were ready to pull out all the stops when they went into the bank. Reid told him that it would make Goma look like a PTA meeting if the Russians showed up.

Reid also sent two agents into the bank, on the pretext of opening an account. They both had pistols, tucked into ankle holsters where they would not be seen. They were also equipped with audio surveillance gear, enabling Reid and his men to monitor movements inside the bank.

After receiving Reid's report, he left his suite in the Baur au Lac and met Reid a couple of blocks from the hotel. They went to a panel truck parked one street from the bank. It looked from the outside like a moving van, but actually housed a high-tech command center. Two technicians monitored the twenty-five or so field operatives that circled the bank. They also monitored all communications going into or out of the bank, with a little help from the NSA.

He seated himself in the truck, dressed in a charcoal grey suit, as if he were attending a board meeting at one of the companies he owned. He was impatient for more updates from the field. He didn't want to delay any longer in putting this whole problem to bed.

"No sign of either the girl or Fisher inside," Reid reported.

"They probably went upstairs. Maybe to Staehelin's office. He's the CEO. They'll be dealing with him, I'd think."

He paused, then asked Reid, "We've got the back entrance, parking garage, windows — all staked out?"

"Yep. Nothing, nobody will get in or out without us knowing it," Reid replied.

"OK. That's critical. No fuck-ups." He could have said "no more fuck-ups," but that went without saying.

Reid nodded. He was about to reply when one of the technicians waved him over, handing him a set of headphones. After a moment, Reid put the conversation onto a speakerphone. It was someone at the bank, male, with a Swiss accent, speaking on the telephone with a woman. Her accent was hard to place — vaguely English, with hints of an American or Singaporean accent. The Swiss man had telephoned the woman and was asking why he hadn't heard from her, whether her client was still interested in the arrangements they had discussed. His voice sounded nervous.

The woman hesitated a moment, apparently surprised, but then answered smoothly. "Naturally, Dr. Staehelin. I received the originals of the documents from my client this morning, just as we discussed. My client is a man of his word. I am looking at them as we speak. I thought that we agreed that I would call you when everything was in order. Has something changed?"

The man paused for an instant, then said: "Excellent. Very good news. Nothing has changed. But I would of course like to inspect the documents as soon as possible. After the incident with the American woman, I must be meticulously correct. But on the assumption that your clients' papers are authentic, then we would be delighted to proceed on the basis we discussed yesterday."

The woman cleared her throat. "We are happy to hear that. Very happy. There has been one new development though. My client considers that a one-third share isn't appropriate in the circumstances. He insists on an equal share, 50/50."

The man paused. She continued. "He was very insistent on this point."

The man replied after a moment. "I can certainly recommend an increase in the one-third share to our board. Let me suggest that you review the account records. I have had them retrieved and readied for your inspection. You will see, they are very extensive. And the amounts we are discussing are quite substantial. There is no need for anyone to be greedy."

"It's not a question of greed. It's a question of fairness," the woman replied. "You have my client's decision. I will be happy to inspect the records. As soon as possible, in fact. But there is very little flexibility on the share," she said.

"I understand. Perhaps you can come to the bank later today with the documentation. Say, in an hour and a half, at 7 p.m.?"

"Fine. When we have finished the review, my client will want to initiate transfers of the funds immediately. That will happen tonight, I assume," the woman said.

"Tonight is impossible. The clearing house agencies don't accept transfer requests after 4:00 p.m. But we could initiate transfers first thing in the morning. At 8:30 a.m."

The woman replied. "Very well. I will see you at 7 p.m."

After the phone line went dead, Kerrington stood up. "Well. That makes things even clearer. It looks like either Fisher and the girl, or this woman, have the file. The woman will be here at 7:00 p.m. Let's make sure that West and Fisher don't leave before then. As soon as the woman arrives, we go in. And we go in hard. Whoever has the file, we grab them. Work up a plan now and run it past me in half an hour," he ordered.

"OK, boss," Reid responded.

"And try to figure out who this woman is. Check the voice prints with the NSA. I'll make sure that they're expecting your call."

Kerrington waited while Reid conferred with the technicians, then stood up and told Reid he was going out for ten minutes. He walked to the back of the truck and let himself out, impatient for the action to begin. He couldn't bear being cooped up in the van for another instant.

But there was something else as well. There was something that being back in action, and that the phone call they had intercepted, crystallized for him. He needed to think about it. In peace and quiet. He headed away from the bank, along the well-kept streets, past elderly Swiss couples walking small dogs, parents with well-behaved school children, and dark-suited businessmen.

He continued towards the lake, lost in thought. It was an orderly, prosperous society, just as it should be. It was civilized. But that harmony and prosperity depended on something else, something much less orderly. It rested on the vigilance, and the strength, of men like him, who kept chaos at bay. Without men like him, none of this would exist. He marveled at how these placid, contented people had no idea what their quiet, comfortable lives really depended on.

He remembered a quotation, one from Nietzsche. Nietzsche said the world was divided into hunters and hunted, birds of prey and herds of sheep. That was true. These self-satisfied Swiss burghers were sheep. Staehelin was also a sheep. Even Reid and Fisher were sheep. Greedy sheep, but still sheep. It was only men like him, very few men, who were birds of prey. Men who saw the world for what it was, who truly understood it, and who had the courage and strength to master it. To take what they wanted and to mold it to their will. The way his father and grandfather had. Now, it was his turn. He fingered the wristwatch, the one his father had given him.

The phone call that they intercepted had gotten him thinking. This mission was not just about retrieving and destroying the file. The mission was not just about damage control or fixing a problem. There was an opportunity here as well. An enormous one. After he had dealt with West and Fisher, and with this new woman, whoever she was, then he would deal with Staehelin as well. If there were secret Nazi bank accounts at Staehelin's bank, then he would take them too. Once he had the file, he would take the accounts for himself. He would decide later whether to share with Staehelin, like the woman on the phone, or not.

He let himself imagine the amounts that were in the bank. He wondered how much was in the accounts. It could be staggering, even for him. More money than anyone could conceive. And more power. More power than even the Deputy Director of the CIA could wield. It would be a whole new chapter in the Kerrington dynasty. A bigger, more exciting chapter.

He reached the lake, invigorated, and watched the sailboats riding on the waves. He breathed in the mountain air. He loved the thought of being on the front lines again. Especially with this new prize. He was impatient for it to begin. He turned around and walked back towards the bank, past the tidy shops and crowds of well-dressed pedestrians. He looked for all the world like one of the Swiss businessmen, returning home to the suburbs after a day at the bank. A bird of prey waiting among the sheep. He smiled as he walked.

Chapter 65
Yan Wu

She sat on the bed after speaking with Staehelin on the telephone. She went over her plans again. She thought through what might go wrong, what the Americans, the bank director, and the girl and her friend might do. There were risks at every step. But this was still the best option. She would go to the bank and finalize arrangements with Staehelin to transfer the money that was in the accounts. And then she would leave. There wasn't any better way to do this.

She used Petronov's phone to call Alexei. He picked up immediately.

"Ivan?"

"It's me. I've got instructions from Ivan for you though. They're urgent."

"Where's Ivan? What's going on?"

"No worries. Everything is on track. Better than good. Ivan's on his other phone. He'll call you as soon as he can," she said.

She continued. "Listen. The girl is at the bank right now. Ivan spotted her himself five minutes ago. Going into the main entrance on Bahnhofstrasse. I don't know how you missed her. Ivan wants me to go into the bank myself, with your team as back-up. Ivan's worried about the Americans again. He wants you to make absolutely sure that the rear entrance to the bank is clear. Clear for me to go in around 7:00 p.m. and for me to get out a couple hours later."

"OK. We can do that. There'll be a team of five men outside the back entrance, at all times," he promised.

"Make that seven men. And send someone around the front of the bank. Check whether the Americans are there. And if so, how many. Then report back to me or Ivan. Use this phone. Don't let the Americans see you, and don't engage them. Unless they try and enter the bank. If they do that, while I am inside, then give us a heads up and go after them with everything you've got."

"Got that. We'll do it and report back," Alexei promised.

She left for the bank a half hour later. The razor was in her handbag, together with her Glock. She made sure that the Glock was fully loaded, with the safety off. She carried another pistol, a tiny Beretta, in the small of her back. She also took a shoe-box sized package of plastic explosives, like the ones she had used on the freighter off Kenya. Alexei had provided it to them three days ago, on her instructions, together with the remote-control detonator that she had specified. She double-checked to be sure that her passports and credit cards were in her wallet, so she wouldn't need to return to the hotel.

After she finished packing, she changed clothes, putting on her running shoes and a loose, baggy sweatshirt. With a pair of sunglasses, she would look like a rebellious teenager, reluctantly headed home after school. When she was ready, she took a taxi, taking her to the main Zurich train station, leaving her suitcase in one of the lockers off the main lobby. If things went as she planned, she would pick it up that evening on her way to the airport.

She walked from the train station to the bank. She pulled the hood of her sweatshirt up and put on the sunglasses. Along the way, she stopped at a kiosk to buy a Coke. She carried it with her, sipping through a brightly colored straw. She stopped at another store and replaced her purse with a backpack, arranging the contents so they would be easy to reach. Then she headed to the rear entrance of the bank.

Alexei's men were easy to spot. Much too easy. Two of them loitered in front of a women's fashion shop, pretending to speak on their phones. A couple parked nearby, in a white Peugeot, were studying a map intently.

She called Alexei again, telling him she was about to enter the bank. He assured her that his men were in place and ready. He also said that there was a heavy American presence. He wasn't sure how many, but at least a dozen agents, probably more. They were concentrated on the front entrance of the bank, but there must be others in the area whom they hadn't ID'd. She should be cautious. They looked professional. But they hadn't spotted Alexei's team.

"That's good. Don't forget, Alexei, we hired you because this team is supposed to be the best. Not like Goma. And we're paying you as if they are. If the Americans get rough, you better be there, with your whole team. And don't let them beat you again." Her voice was cold.

"Of course. Don't worry about that. We'll be there. But it may get nasty. Nasty and loud."

"Understood." She took the edge off her voice. "I'll be going into the bank in ten minutes. Make sure the Americans don't try and move in while I'm there. It may be a couple hours that I'm inside."

"Got it. We'll keep them, and anyone else, away from you," Alexei assured her.

"Great. That's critical. Ivan should be in touch shortly. But if he isn't, don't worry. He has a lot going on just now."

Then she hung up. Ten minutes later, she walked up to the bank's rear entrance, which employees and publicity-shy clients used. Staehelin had given the security guards her name, and instructions to admit her. A minute later, she was on her way up to the conference room, escorted by one of the guards.

She stopped in the restroom on her way, leaving the package of plastic explosives in the electricity closet, next to the bathroom. Then she armed the detonator, checking again that it was fully charged. She hoped that everything would go smoothly, and that she wouldn't have to use the explosives. But if she needed distraction and darkness, then she would have them.

When she was finished, she let the guard escort her to the conference room. Her stomach tightened in anticipation. As they walked, she wondered just how much money was in the accounts. She allowed herself to imagine what she would do with the money, and then dismissed those thoughts as the guard ushered her into the room.

Chapter 66
Maximilian Staehelin

The American holding the pistol was trim, a little sun-burnt on his forehead, with short brown hair. He wore jeans, a dark t-shirt, and a pair of well-worn running shoes. His movements were calm and deliberate, first, as he directed Staehelin to sit, and then as he checked the conference room and adjoining office for cameras or microphones. He moved around the room as if he had been there a hundred times before, and as if he, not Staehelin, owned the building.

The blonde girl, who had called herself "Ms. Warren" earlier that day, was dressed like the man, in faded jeans and a dark sweatshirt. She was inspecting the binder of account records that Staehelin had collected for Ms. Lee. The binders were arranged in neat rows on the mahogany table in the center of the room. It was a substantial collection, going back some seventy years, for multiple accounts. The girl seemed to read German perfectly and was methodically working her way through the early years of the accounts, laying some papers to one side, returning others to their original places.

The girl and her friend had arrived an hour ago, just as the bank was about to close. She phoned from the reception, saying that she had the originals of the documents that he wanted. She also said that she was tired of his games, and that they needed to meet now, or she would go to her lawyers, and maybe to the press. He didn't believe that she really had the documents, especially not after the way she had behaved that afternoon. Nonetheless, he didn't see any reason not to inspect whatever it was she had, and he agreed to meet the girl downstairs.

Before he went down to the reception, though, he telephoned Mr. Dupuy and instructed him to put security on alert and to take three of his men and wait inside the conference room on the second floor. He also told Dupuy that he was meeting with a very difficult client, who was suspected of stealing sensitive documents from the bank, so he should bring his most reliable men. Then he went down to the reception to meet the girl.

He was astonished, but the girl did have what looked like originals of his grand-father's protocol and the ownership documents for the secret accounts. She reached silently into her backpack and extracted a thin leather folder that contained a few dozen typewritten pages, many of them on the bank's 1940's stationery, embossed with a stylized Nazi eagle and swastika, bearing his grandfather's unmistakable signature, scrawled in faded blue ink. Somehow, this young woman, dressed like a student backpacker, had come into possession of papers that gave her the keys to billions of dollars — and the power to bring down his bank.

He forced himself to nod calmly as he inspected the girl's documents. He hadn't trusted himself to page through the papers himself: she might have seen his hands trembling. But she paged through the documents, one by one, showing him what they were. He had little doubt that they were authentic. When she was finished, he carefully straightened his suit jacket, then stood up.

"Well, these papers do look a little more serious. Of course, I am no expert, but they appear genuine," he said with a broad smile.

She looked up at him coolly, waiting for him to continue.

"Please, come upstairs, Ms. Warren. I will ask one of our in-house experts to review the documents. Just a formality. And in the meantime, you may inspect the account records."

He reached for the thin folder of papers that she held. She didn't give him the papers. Instead, she stood up, turning away from him, and slipped the folder back into her pack. She slung the pack over her shoulder in a single easy motion and looked at him again.

"Sure, let's go upstairs. The same conference room, I assume. And I'll have that glass of champagne now." She smiled.

He frowned at her refusal to hand over the files, then caught himself. He would have more than enough time to take the file from her once they were upstairs. Dupuy and his guards would be waiting in the conference room, ready to deal with her and take the file. The bank was almost closed now, and there would be no customers or staff to listen, if they needed to get rough with the girl. It might not be very civilized, but it would be effective. He smiled at her as they walked to the private elevator. He ushered her into the elevator and they rode up to the second floor in silence. His throat tightened in anticipation of what would come next.

The corridor was empty. Dupuy would be inside the office next to the conference room. He opened the door, directing her into the room, then rang for the waiter and her champagne. It arrived a moment later, and he toasted her grandly. He smiled at the girl's naivete, wondering how she would react when Dupuy and his men took the file away from her.

A minute later his smile vanished. The American man appeared suddenly from the office adjoining the conference room. Dupuy and three of the bank's security guards were on the floor of the office behind the man, bound and gagged. The American had an automatic weapon in one hand, holding it with casual ease, as he directed Staehelin to stay seated and be quiet.

The American searched him for weapons and then gave him very careful instructions. He spoke quietly, in polite tones. But he made things brutally clear: if Staehelin made any noise, or any effort to escape, he would be killed. The American was going to give Staehelin instructions about what would happen in the next few hours. He would follow these instructions, precisely and to the letter. If Staehelin wanted to see his wife and children again, then he would do exactly what the American told him to do. Nothing else. If he did that, they would let him go. If not, then he would be killed.

He nodded dumbly, struggling to swallow. He didn't understand how the American had gotten inside the bank, or what the two planned next. But he could tell that the man was dangerous, very dangerous. He would do what he was told and pray that the man kept his word.

The American instructed Staehelin to call Ms. Lee, telling him exactly what to say to her. They walked through the script three times, until the American was content. When he placed the call, the American and the girl listened intently. After he was finished with their script, they directed him to end the call.

Then they had ordered him to make arrangements for security to admit Ms. Lee to the bank, and to bring her up to the conference room as soon as she arrived. They shouldn't check her for weapons. The bank should also double the number of guards at the front of the bank and be on high alert, particularly at the front entrance. They should be ready for a possible armed robbery. Then the two Americans sat down to wait for Ms. Lee's arrival. While they waited, the girl inspected the account binders that were arranged on the table. The American man sat next to him, eyes never straying far.

An hour later, just after 7 p.m., the phone in the conference room had rung. It was the security guard, reporting that he had admitted Ms. Lee, and was bringing her upstairs. The American nodded and got up from his chair, checking that the safety on his weapon was off. The girl also got up and moved to the office adjoining the conference room, first returning the account folders on the table to exactly the places they had been when she arrived. The American followed her, leaving the door to the office open, so that he could watch Staehelin. He kept his gun out and ready. As he left the room, the American repeated his earlier warnings.

The woman who called herself Ms. Lee arrived a few minutes later. This time, she was dressed like the Americans, in jeans and a dark sweatshirt. The security guard ushered her into the room, then left, closing the door behind him, just as his instructions specified. As soon as the door closed, the American stepped out of the office into the conference room. He trained his gun on the Asian woman.

"Put the pack on the table. Gently. No quick moves." His voice was low and firm.

She complied. Then the blonde girl appeared from the office behind him, walked back into the conference room and picked up the Asian woman's backpack. She checked it quickly, removing the bulky file of papers, which looked like the originals of the documents that Ms. Lee had promised. The girl flipped through the documents, skimming a few of them, then nodding to the American.

Then the girl looked further in the pack, finding a pistol, which she extracted and slipped into the waistband of her jeans, and a phone, which she put on the table. After she finished searching the backpack, the American man handed her his own gun, which she trained on the Asian woman. The man then walked around the table and searched the woman, finding a small pistol in the back of her jeans, which he handed to the blonde girl. When he was finished, the American directed the Asian woman to sit at the table, hands in sight on the polished surface.

Then, the American man picked up the woman's phone. He demanded the PIN code and then spent a few minutes scrolling through the woman's contacts and calls. When he was satisfied, he questioned her about a few of her contacts, then directed her to telephone the man she called Alexei. He told her exactly what to say — that she didn't have much time, that the Americans were coming into the bank and that he needed to move in now, with all his men. She did exactly what she was instructed to, then handed him the phone. He pocketed it wordlessly, then joined the blonde girl at the head of the table.

He wondered what they would to do next. They made no preparations to leave. The American checked his weapon, then removed a dozen or so magazines from his backpack, arranging them on the table in front of him. He took a second weapon, a pistol, out of the pack, tucking it into his jeans. Then the man made himself comfortable in the chair and seemed to settle down to wait. The girl did the same. Neither one spoke.

After a few minutes, the blonde girl stood up and disappeared into the office adjoining the conference room, returning with a bottle of Coke from the hospitality bar. The two of them shared the drink, trading sips out of the bottle and glances as if they were teenagers waiting for a movie to start. They both seemed perfectly relaxed.

He wondered if they were crazy, maybe some sort of lunatics. Breaking into a bank, surrounded by heavy security, with documents worth a fortune, then sitting there as if they had no plans to leave. He could not imagine what they intended

They must be insane. At some point, his guards would detect them. And they would be surrounded by nearly twenty heavily armed men. Whatever their plan, they were the real prisoners, not him.

Twenty minutes later, sounds of gunfire and explosions began. The American and the girl exchanged smiles. It was as if they had expected this. The Asian woman shifted uncomfortably in her chair from time to time as the noise increased. Initially, there were a few isolated gunshots, like raindrops on a windshield. After a few moments, the individual cracks turned into a steady patter, occasionally drowned out by the clatter of machine guns or by small explosions. Cries of pain and the crackle of walkie-talkies added to the cacophony.

It sounded as if a small battle were being waged on the bank's premises. He couldn't imagine what was happening downstairs. He was only glad that he had quadrupled security over the last few days. That would surely be enough to stop anyone who attacked the bank. His men would surely come to the rescue.

The smell of smoke and cordite began to seep into the room. The American and the girl still made no effort to leave, instead only trading glances and calmly checking their weapons once more. They really must be crazy, he thought again. In contrast, Ms. Lee's composure began to waver, as she shifted uneasily in her seat, fiddling with the charm around her neck. After another five minutes or so, the American and the girl exchanged nods, before the man took out a phone and placed a call. A moment later, an enormous explosion shook the bank violently, followed by a lull in the gunfire and screams of anguish.

He was terrified now. There must be dozens of men fighting downstairs. His security wasn't trained for a full-scale battle. And now these explosions. The American must be trying to destroy the bank, maybe to kill them all. After the explosion, the American got up and walked around the table to the door to the room. The man was listening intently now, ears pricked, to the sounds coming from downstairs.

The American opened the door to the room and peered into the corridor, looking in both directions, then listening again to the gunfire and explosions. The girl kept her gun on Ms. Lee until he closed the door and returned to the table.

After another moment, the American removed a second phone from his jacket and made another call. Another explosion shook the bank, this one much closer to the conference room. The American and the girl exchanged smiles again and continued to wait. It was bizarre, he thought. It was as if they expected the battle, and wanted it to continue, just the way it was.

He struggled not to tremble. He was sure now that he would die here, either at the hands of these lunatics or when the battle below moved up to their floor. And he would die in disgrace. All of the papers that the two women had brought were here, together with the bank's records of the secret accounts. The whole world would know the awful Staehelin secret. He shuddered again.

But then, in his despair, another thought came to him. Perhaps, he thought, there might also be a silver lining. If the file and the records, all the records of the accounts, were destroyed, in a fire caused by a bizarre criminal attack, his problems would be solved. All the evidence of their secret would disappear forever. He would have nothing to hide anymore. And if Ms. Lee, Ms. Warren, and their friends all died in this attack, so much the better.

He needed only to keep his head down, and stay out of the way, letting all these crazy people dispose of one another. Then he could go back to his banking business as usual. The thought helped him regain his composure. He took a deep breath and smoothed his jacket, then started to think about how he would explain this incident to the press.

Chapter 67
Franklin Kerrington III

He was crouched near the entrance to the bank, surveying the battleground. They had taken casualties. Lots of them.

Reid ordered his teams into the bank shortly after 7 p.m., the way that they had planned, just after the Asian woman arrived. She had told Staehelin on the telephone that she had the file. A few minutes later, Reid's stake-out inside the bank reported that a Chinese woman had showed a stack of papers to one of the guards and then been ushered upstairs.

It was pretty clear. Either the Asian woman had the file or Fisher and the girl had it. Whichever it was, the file was at the bank and this was the time to go get it. On his instruction, Reid's men went in with almost everything they had, two dozen heavily armed agents barreling through the front entrance.

He had expected resistance, but they walked into something close to an ambush. The bank's security guards were on their home turf, deployed behind marble reception desks or metal sculptures. They were well-trained and well-equipped, and it seemed as if they were expecting an assault. Reid lost a third of his men just getting past the guards. Eventually, the superior numbers and grenades of Reid's team prevailed, but it was a bloody fight.

And then they ran into the Russians, who came charging into the bank through the back entrance. They were even better trained and equipped than the bank's guards, with their own heavy weapons and grenades. Running firefights raged through the reception area and staircases. Machine gun fire shattered the building's windows and extinguished the lights on the ground floor, leaving the men fighting in smoke-filled twilight. The stench of gun powder and smoke filled the air, along with the racket of small arms fire and cries of wounded men.

He worried that they would run out of time and the Swiss puliᴄᴇ would arrive before they found the girl and the file. Or that they wouldn't be able to get past the Russians. The Russians' men were tough, experienced in street fighting and well-armed. And they fought viciously, regardless of the casualties they took.

He crept forward to where the fighting was most intense, and watched a young American empty his weapon into the torso of a bald, heavily muscled Russian fighter, then toss a grenade up the stairway to the second floor. The explosion was followed by more screams.

Reid's man dashed up the stairway, in full combat gear, weapon at the ready as he took the stairs two at a time. He was met, in turn, by another deafening explosion, and his body tumbled back down the stairs, face and arms bleeding from a dozen wounds. Two more of Reid's men took his place, this time more cautiously, and after a few exchanges of fire, and another grenade, began to clear the second floor.

Reid came up to his side in a half-crouch. Soot covered half his face and the hair on the back of his head was singed. His shirt was scorched along one shoulder, and he bled from a shrapnel wound on his forearm. His report was cautious, but upbeat.

"We took heavy casualties, sir. Less than half a dozen men still up."

Reid went on. "But it was a lot worse for the others. At least thirty of them dead, maybe thirty-five. There are no hostiles still up on the ground floor and we're clearing the second floor now. I'm pretty sure that's where the girl and the file are. One of the bank's guards told us. After a little persuasion." He smiled crookedly. "We should be there in another few minutes."

"Good job. I don't have to tell you that we really need to hurry."

"Right. It's only been ten minutes. We've got another five minutes before the police get here I reckon."

"The exit route is clear?"

"Yep. Helicopter on the roof. Or ambulance out back." Reid smiled at him.

"When we go in for the file, just me and you. Nobody else," Kerrington said.

"You armed?" Reid asked.

"You bet." Kerrington brandished his Glock and smiled. "I still love this shit." He adjusted his balaclava.

Reid was hesitant. "OK, but be careful. Fisher's the one to worry about. Maybe we bring someone else with us? Just one guy. Johnson — he's solid."

"Fine. You're right," Kerrington conceded. They couldn't take chances with Fisher. He could worry about Johnson's reliability later. First things first.

He paused then, for a moment, signaling Reid to listen. They were crouched behind what remained of a large marble sculpture, which stood near the staircase in the front of the bank's reception. The entire ground floor was dark, and thick with smoke. He had heard the sound of footsteps moving stealthily on the granite floor, from the other side of the sculpture.

He signaled Reid to keep his head down. Seconds later, two Russian fighters crept out from behind the reception desk, headed towards the stairs. One of the Russians was older, with short-cropped hair. The older man's colleague whispered in Russian, which he could just make out. "Alexei. Up the stairs, then at the end of the hallway."

The man called Alexei nodded and inched forward, both men scanning the debris surrounding the staircase. Kerrington gestured silently at the Russians with his weapon, motioning for Reid to take the younger man and taking Alexei for himself. Reid nodded and brought his HK 416 to bear on the younger fighter, then raised his other hand.

On Reid's silent count of three, they both opened fire on the Russian soldiers. His shot caught the older Russian in the back of the head, blowing off the side of his face and killing the man instantly. Reid's shot must have missed or been deflected by the younger Russian's body armor. The man wheeled, swinging his machine pistol around towards the two of them.

Kerrington smiled. He was still good at this. He shifted the Glock to the younger Russian. Reid struggled with his HK 416, trying unsuccessfully to track the Russian, who leveled his own weapon at them. The man was about to fire when Kerrington calmly squeezed off another head shot from the Glock. He caught the man in the forehead, dropping him in his tracks.

"Fuck," Reid said. "I screwed that one up. Thanks for saving my ass."

Kerrington didn't reply. Reid was right about his mistake. It was stupid. But he didn't mind just now. He was still savoring the thrill of back-to-back kills, after so many years away. Nietzsche's metaphor about birds of prey and sheep came back to him, unbidden, and he smiled. He wondered again how much money might be in the accounts at the bank. How much money he would be able to take for himself.

Reid crouched down again behind the sculpture and whispered into his walkie-talkie. A minute later, he received an all-clear signal for them to head up to the second floor. His men had mopped up what was left of the Russians and the bank's security guards. They were all dead – forty-five men or so, scattered around the bank's first two floors. The gunfire had stopped, replaced by an eerie silence, punctuated by occasional moans and the crunch of glass beneath the remaining agents' boots.

The air was even thicker now with smoke. Sirens and car alarms wailed in the distance. They climbed the stairway, picking their way through the aftermath of the fighting — bodies, discarded magazines, empty cartridges, and chunks of masonry. The second floor didn't look quite as much like a battle zone, but it was still littered with debris and scarred by blast marks and bullet holes on the walls.

Reid motioned towards a door at the end of the corridor, then crept over to the four surviving members of his team. He sent one man downstairs, and two upstairs, to secure their exit routes. Reid beckoned for the fourth man, who must be Johnson, to accompany him, then came back to where he was crouched. Together, they edged forward, through the half-light and wreckage, to the doors of the bank's main conference room.

Reid nodded for Johnson to lead. The agent pulled down the door handle and pushed the door inwards, then peered into the conference room. A single shot caught him in the face, sending him sprawling back into the corridor. He stared blankly up at them, out of his one remaining eye, his body motionless. Reid dropped back into a crouch, hugging the wall of the corridor, signaling him to stay back. They waited in the darkness for several long moments. The hallway was silent.

The voice came from behind them.

"Get up and walk into the room. Leave your weapons on the floor. Now."

It was Fisher. When they didn't move, Fisher continued. "I said now. Don't make me tell you again."

This time, they obeyed. They put their guns on the floor and walked into the conference room. It was like entering another world. The room was peaceful, its wood-paneled walls, paintings, and curtains untouched by the battles that had raged in the rest of the bank. The chandeliers in the room glowed warmly, as night started to fall outside. The plush carpet was clean, free of debris or bodies, and the surface of the conference room table gleamed, as if it had just been polished.

An Asian woman sat quietly on one side of the conference table, hands folded on the tabletop, in front of a collection of old-fashioned binders. The blonde girl, West, stood across from her, holding an Uzi submachine gun. A middle-aged man in a business suit, his hair in disarray, sat alone at the far end of the table. The man looked very frightened.

Fisher followed them into the room and closed the door behind him, shutting out the occasional moans and crackling of fires that burned downstairs. He kept his Uzi at the ready, his eyes scanning the room. He motioned for them to sit at the table, facing the window.

Fisher spoke, his voice low and confident. "Let's start with exit plans. Reid, how are you getting out of here?"

Reid hesitated. Fisher shot him in the foot. A single shot, perfectly placed. It served its purpose.

Reid talked. "Fuck. Why'd you do that? Fuck, fuck, fuck."

Reid's shoe was leaking blood. The pain must be excruciating. Kerrington was impressed. Fisher was as good as his record said. Such a shame that the man went rogue. Someone like Fisher would have been a tremendous asset.

"Don't make me ask again." Fisher's voice was menacing.

Reid spoke through clenched teeth. "Fuck. In the back. An ambulance."

"How many men?" Fisher demanded.

"Just the driver."

"What else? You never have just one exit," Fisher said.

Reid hesitated and Fisher shifted his weapon slightly. Reid talked again.

"Fuck. You fucking shit. On the roof. A copter. Just the pilot, plus one guard."

Fisher turned away from Reid, satisfied with his answer. "Good. Now. Gentlemen. Ladies. We're going to play a game. True confessions."

The blonde girl stood up from her chair, leaving him, Reid, the Asian woman and the bank director seated uncomfortably around the table. Then the girl took a small handheld camera out of her pack and tinkered with its settings. When she was finished, she trained the camera on the bank director.

"Dr. Staehelin. You're first. Tell us who you are, then describe these accounts. The ones that these binders here on the table are for. Look into the camera. Speak clearly too. The whole world is going to watch."

Fuck. He didn't like where this was going. Fisher really was a Boy Scout. And the girl must be too.

The banker blanched, then shifted uneasily. The man looked as if he were going to cry. Fisher swiveled his weapon, training it on the banker.

"I'll do you too," Fisher threatened in a low voice.

The banker squirmed, then started to sob. Fisher moved closer and repeated his threat, this time in German.

The next few seconds were a blur. The Asian woman continued to fiddle nervously with the charm on her necklace, and as Fisher focused on the banker, she gripped it firmly in one hand. An explosion detonated in the bowels of the building. The lights flickered and then went out, plunging the room into darkness.

He heard the woman push her chair away from the table, then grab for something on the tabletop. He heard Reid as well, fumbling for his pistol, concealed in an ankle holster. Fisher and the girl made no sounds.

Two shots rang out, bright flashes coming from their side of the room. He heard a thud and a groan, followed by glass shattering. Then more shots in the dark, this time in their direction. Another groan, followed by the sound of a body hitting the floor.

He kept low, creeping for the door in the pitch dark. His foot hit something soft, something soft and wet. It whispered something in German. It must be the banker. He wondered who had shot the man, then moved on, inching towards the door into the corridor. Another shot shattered the silence, coming from where the Asian woman had been sitting, followed by the dull thud of an impact across the room.

Then the lights in the room suddenly came back on, no doubt powered by the bank's emergency generator. For a split second, the room was frozen, as if caught on film. The Asian woman was on one knee at the far end of the room, a pistol in her hand, the weapon trained across the table. Reid was at the other end of the room, his pistol out as well. Fisher was crouching next to the table, sheltering behind one of its thick wooden supports, in front of the window.

All three began firing at once. Fisher shot Reid twice, squarely in the head. The Chinese woman shot Fisher, catching him in the left arm, before he ducked under the table. Fisher fired twice more, under the table, in the Asian woman's direction. She remained silent.

He lay on the floor next to the banker's body, keeping his head down while trying to watch Fisher and the Asian woman. He heard soft, rustling sounds from Fisher and the woman, as they both maneuvered slowly around the table. He eased his own pistol out of his ankle holster, then continued his slow crawl towards the door.

An arm appeared at the far end of the table, as someone began to creep out from behind one of the table's supports. The arm was wet with fresh blood. It must be Fisher, bleeding from where the Asian woman shot him. He eased his pistol forward, waiting for Fisher's head to appear from behind the support.

If he got Fisher, it would be just him and the Chinese woman. Those were pretty nice odds. Plus, a couple of Reid's agents were upstairs. Those were great odds. Everything was going to end nicely, even better than he had planned. He waited patiently.

Fisher's head appeared, slowly, as he soundlessly inched his way around the table, hunting the Chinese woman. He tightened his finger on the trigger of his pistol, waiting for Fisher to come directly into his line of fire. The image of a falcon, a bird of prey hunting among the sheep, came to him again. He smiled, gently tightening his finger on the trigger.

A single shot rang out. It struck him in the back, right above the heart. The impact slapped him against the floor, knocking his head against the wall. As his vision started to go dark, he looked behind him and saw the blonde girl, crouched at the other end of the table, her gun still leveled at him. The last thing he could see, before the world went black, were her eyes, cool and grey, watching him lying there on the floor, next to the banker's body, blood pouring out of the wound in his chest. After that, there was nothing.

Chapter 68
Sara West

The Chinese woman was gone. They searched the conference room, then the adjoining office and the hallway, but there was no sign of her. Only the bodies of Staehelin, Kerrington, and Reid, sprawled on the carpet around the table. Sirens were wailing nearby now.

"We've got to go," he said.

"OK," she answered.

She picked up the backpack with the file from the table, then collected the account records that she had marked earlier. They were all that she would need.

"Shall we fly or drive?" she asked.

"Let's drive. I think it's a surer thing," he said.

"OK, baby. You're in charge." She smiled at him.

They hurried into the hallway, then down the stairs. He led the way, keeping an eye out for survivors from the firefight. The ground floor of the bank was a scene of total devastation. Emergency lighting cast a harsh glare over a tangle of bodies, wrecked furniture, and large pieces of walls and ceiling. The floor was littered with spent cartridges and discarded weapons and splattered with blood. A half dozen fires burned, their smoke mixing with the stench of gunpowder. Outside, the sirens were very close now. She hoped he had a plan to avoid the police.

He led them to the rear of the building, then down a flight of stairs and outside. As Reid said, a large white ambulance waited nearby. He went ahead, leaving her by the staircase, hidden in the shadows. He slipped up to the driver's side of the ambulance, tapped on the window, then waited for it to open. When it did, he delivered a vicious blow with the butt of his gun and then dragged the unlucky sentry out of the vehicle, leaving him on the pavement.

He climbed into the driver's seat, opened the passenger door and waited for her to get in, then pulled the vehicle out onto the street. He switched on the siren after half a block and sped away, past the oncoming motorcade of police and military vehicles. It looked like he had a plan after all. She should have known. She smiled to herself.

He drove fast, for ten minutes, headed out of town, then switched off the siren and continued to drive, following the shoreline of the lake.

"Thank you, honey," he said when they were clear of the oncoming traffic.

She smiled. "Any time. You'd have got him anyway."

She was sure that he would have.

He shook his head. "I don't think so. I thought he was on the other side of the room. I think I would have been dead."

"So you owe me one. I think that makes the score ten to one or something," she said.

They were silent for a moment. She thought about what they had just done. They had survived. They were still alive. Somehow, despite the odds, they had survived. And they had retrieved the file. And avenged her dad, at least as much as she could. It was hard to believe, almost too good to be true.

"So, we got them, pretty much all of them," she said after a moment. "Kerrington, Reid, Staehelin, all the Russians. They're all gone. All of them," she continued. "All the ones who killed my dad."

"We didn't get the taped confession," he said. "But that won't matter. We've got the file and the account records. We did it."

He was right. They really had done it. Actually, he had done it. She hadn't done much more than watch.

"You know, you are pretty impressive, Mr. Fisher. What were the odds? The ones you said were impossible? fifty to one or something?"

She smiled at him. He watched her for a moment, then looked back at the road. He was quiet while he drove, as if he were concentrating on something. After a few minutes, she reached over to him across the driver's seat.

"Thank you for doing that. I know you didn't want to."

She leaned against him, as he drove, and kissed his arm, then pulled away abruptly. Something was wrong.

"What's this?" she exclaimed, touching his shoulder, her hand coming away wet and red.

"Just a scratch, honey. No worries," he said.

"That's no scratch. Stop now. Let me see. Stop the car," she demanded.

He pulled the ambulance over, then let her turn the interior lights on and they inspected his wound. His arm was bleeding heavily, but it was just a graze. That wound would be fine. But that wasn't the real problem. He had also taken a pistol shot in his chest. It missed his heart and lungs, but it was bad. The wound in his chest was oozing blood. Lots of blood.

"Turn around. Now. You need to get to a hospital. And fast." Her voice was tight. She was worried and afraid. His wound looked serious.

He turned the ambulance back onto the road, but he didn't head back to Zurich, the way she insisted. Instead, he kept driving away from the city.

"We can't, baby," he said. "If I show up at a hospital with a gunshot wound, we're caught. Maybe dead, if there are still bad guys on their feet. But certainly prison time. For both of us. That's not in the plan."

"You're shot. And bad. You have to get help. You're hurt bad, honey," she said.

He was just as adamant. She looked at him in the light from the dashboard, watching him drive, blood dripping down his shirt, face taut in the half-light. He didn't look back, and instead stared into the darkness ahead of them as he drove them further away from the city.

Chapter 69
Jeb Fisher

He drove along the lakeside road, putting as much distance as he could between them and the bank. After another twenty minutes, he saw what he had been looking for. It was an empty house by the side of the road. He knew that they needed to stop. His chest wound was bad, a lot worse than he had realized. He needed to stop the flow of blood. And get some painkillers.

He stopped the ambulance by the house. A sign announced that it was for sale. The house was right on the road, but he drove around to the back and parked the ambulance where it wouldn't be seen by passing cars. There were no neighbors. He got out of the vehicle, then inspected the house for alarms before breaking in the rear door. They went inside. He checked the house for occupants, then turned on the lights. It would do, at least for the night.

He went back outside to the ambulance, climbed into the back, then found bandages, antiseptics, and painkillers. He paused as he left the vehicle, surprised by the lack of Swiss cleanliness. A bloody handprint was smeared on the inside of one door, the leftovers of the ambulance's last mission. He closed the door and returned to the house.

It took them an hour of washing and bandaging. The wound was bad, but he had been lucky. The bullet missed everything vital, then exited out of the back of his shoulder. They washed his torso thoroughly, with water and antiseptic solution, then applied antibiotics and bandaged him to stop the bleeding. She gave him water and painkillers, then made him stretch out on a couch in a room next to the kitchen.

He was just drifting off to sleep when the Chinese woman appeared. She was standing in the doorway, holding an Uzi. One leg of her jeans was dark brown, from a wound in her calf. She limped as she moved into the room.

"Get over there, by him," the woman directed Sara. She waved the Uzi for emphasis.

Sara got up from the chair where she had been sitting and came over to stand by him. His shoulder was aching again. Like his head.

"Where's the pack? With the files," the woman demanded.

Sara hesitated. "In the front room. On the sofa," she finally said.

The woman backed up slowly to the door of the room and glanced briefly inside the adjoining room. Then she cursed and stepped quickly back into their room. Sara had disappeared. He wondered what she was doing. The woman checked the room behind her, then craned her head to peer into the kitchen. Satisfied, she disappeared through the doorway, then apparently thought better of it and returned.

"Listen now," the woman shouted. "Get back here now, with the backpack, or your boyfriend is dead."

He prayed that Sara would stay silent. That she would take the file now and run. That she wouldn't be so stupid as to walk back into the Chinese woman's grasp.

His heart fell. Sara stepped silently through the kitchen doorway, the pack dangling from one hand.

"Leave him alone. Here it is." She proffered the pack.

The woman couldn't suppress a chuckle. "You are so predictable," she said, smiling, half to herself.

She kept the Uzi trained on Sara and took the pack from her.

A shrill alarm coming from the kitchen shattered the quiet of the night. The Chinese woman glanced at the door to the kitchen, confused for an instant. Sara was on her in a heartbeat, a serrated kitchen knife suddenly gleaming in her hand.

She slashed at the woman's throat, catching her instead on the upper arm. The woman yelped in pain, then rolled away gracefully, trying to bring her Uzi to bear. Sara followed, stalking the woman, wielding the knife now with both hands. The woman slid to the left, avoiding the blow, and triggering a short burst from the Uzi. The bullets thudded harmlessly into one of the walls of the living room.

The woman stepped back and then brought the Uzi around, training it on Sara. Jeb lunged, as hard as his shoulder would allow, tackling the woman around the waist, pulling her down onto the floor with him. She fired another short burst from the Uzi, this one into the ceiling, releasing a shower of fine white powder that filled the air. He used his weight to roll her over, forcing her underneath him, directing the Uzi away from Sara and between the two of them, its muzzle pointing harmlessly into the air. She fought back viciously, but he leaned against her, overpowering her with his bulk.

Sara grabbed the barrel of the Uzi, then wrenched it free, jerking it out of the woman's grasp. When it was free, she turned the gun around and pointed it at the woman's head. The woman smiled. Then she raised her other arm, from underneath him and pointed the tiny, wicked-looking Beretta at Sara. Sara pulled the trigger on the Uzi. Nothing happened. The woman kept smiling.

He shifted his weight, before she could shoot, throwing his body over the woman's arm, trapping it underneath his chest. Then he heard the pop, like a firecracker, and felt the searing pain in his abdomen. He cried out in agony, white fire coursing through his gut. Then another pop, and more pain in his stomach. The Chinese woman pushed him off her, then pointed the tiny Beretta at Sara again.

He could barely see, and his whole chest was on fire. But he could still deliver a brutal kick to the woman's wounded leg, his shoe slamming into her calf. She winced and Sara was on her again, this time using the stock of the Uzi to batte the woman's arms and head. The Beretta went flying across the room and Sara the woman again, hard, across the face. The woman slumped, but when stepped back to deliver a final blow, the woman squirmed away, springing feet like a dancer, then disappearing into the next room.

Sara retrieved the Beretta, then followed the woman. Three minutes later she was back. He could tell from her face that she hadn't found the woman. She knelt by his side, first anxiously inspecting his new wounds, then crying silently. Her tears fell like raindrops onto his face.

His chest hurt less now. Maybe the painkillers had kicked in, he thought. He looked down at his stomach and could see only blood, a pool of deep crimson blood leaking out of his body, soaking his clothes, spilling onto the floor. It wasn't the painkillers. It was the new wound in his stomach. He wasn't going to make it. Not this time. He knew that now.

He looked up at her. She was radiant, blonde curls tangled and afire, eyes liquid, cheeks flushed. Like when she had made love to him that first night.

"Oh, Jeb. Jeb," she sobbed. "You're hurt so bad."

That brought him back, for a moment. Focused him again.

"In my wallet. Find the card. It has an address in Germany. Go there. You'll find money, passports, whatever you need." He paused, struggling for breath.

"I love you. I always did." He tried to swallow. "Bury me up in the mountains. Away from all this. Where they can't find me. And think of me, baby."

"Jeb. Don't. You can't, honey. I love you. You can't go now. You can't leave me." Tears were streaming down her cheeks now.

"I love you too, honey. But I can't. I just can't."

His last words were a whisper, like a child drifting off to sleep. And then he was gone.

Chapter 70
Yan Wu

She was fully recuperated. The wounds to her arm and leg had healed, with only minor scars. Her nose had taken cosmetic surgery but was more delicate now than before. She was even more beautiful.

She sat on the patio of her penthouse suite on the top floor of Shanghai's most exclusive sky-rise. Her suite stretched over two floors, filled with an impeccable collection of Chinese antiques. Classical music, Beethoven, played in the background. She looked out across the Bund into the harbor.

She had been lucky. The American man had nearly seen her, in the darkness behind the deserted house, when she had limped silently away from the ambulance where she had hidden. And the blonde girl almost found her, out in the Swiss mountains. The girl nearly stepped on her, the first time, before she returned to the house and the man. And then the girl almost caught her again, chasing her through the mountain forest in the night with unnerving determination. Stalking her relentlessly across the mountainside. In the end, sheer luck saved her, in the form of a motorist stopping to pick up the lone woman waving for help in the early morning twilight on a country road. But for that stroke of fortune, she had little doubt that the girl would have had her in another few minutes.

But she had escaped. She made her way back to Zurich. Then she collected the suitcase with Petronov's belongings from the train station. And, over the next several months, she painstakingly unraveled his financial empire, then liquidated it at an auspicious moment.

He had been very wealthy. And now she was very wealthy. Plus, there was the life insurance that she had secretly taken out, against his death. Her lawyers needed to fight for a while, but the insurance company finally paid out. Another lar sum. She hadn't gotten the file, but she had gotten his fortune and more. And now her freedom. At last. The little peasant girl was finally free.

She heard the sound, a rustling noise, behind her to the left. She rolled off her chair, tumbling like a gymnast, her hand simultaneously finding the Beretta that she always kept by her side. She ended up crouched behind the massive terracotta pot of one of the palm trees on the patio. Her weapon, the safety off, was trained on the head of the intruder, her hand steady as a rock.

It was only June. Her maid. June had strict instructions not to surprise her, never to appear unannounced. She shook her head, critically, ignoring June's nervous giggles and efforts to explain. She padded silently back to the deck chair on the patio where she had been sitting and picked her sun hat up off the floor.

"I said never to do that. Never. One day, I'm going to shoot you," she said in Mandarin.

June blanched and disappeared without a word.

She settled back into the chair and wondered about the girl. She wondered what she had been doing for the past seven months. What the girl would do next. She had covered her trail well, very well, in case the girl still wanted revenge. And there were layers of security in the building, more than Petronov had ever used, to keep her safe. Plus her pistol. She really didn't need to worry.

She turned her attention back to her book. It was poetry, classical Chinese poetry. Her latest hobby. She forced herself to focus on the characters, their layered meanings, the elegance of the meter. She had been trying to concentrate on the poems for the last hour. After another twenty minutes, she gave up, put the book to one side and stared out across the water. She wondered whether the girl would ever let her go.

Chapter 71
Sara West

She looked across the lake as the sun began to set. Her eyes were grey, like the waves washing against the shore.

She had come back to Zurich to finalize arrangements with the bank. This time she stayed in a hotel, using her real name. It wasn't the Baur au Lac, but it had a beautiful view of the lake.

She buried her father first. She buried him in a family cemetery on a ridge outside the small town in New York where she had grown up. The funeral was attended by colleagues and former students, from around the world. The preacher's sermon moved her father's friends to tears. He had been praised as a teacher, a researcher, a mentor, a father, and a man. She was the only one who hadn't cried, her reservoir of tears exhausted from the last month. Instead, she laid him to rest at the funeral with a flower and a kiss. And later that night, when the crowds had gone home, with a prayer at his grave, alone on the hilly ridge, out in the countryside, where she knew he would feel at home.

She said goodbye to Maria next. She found the simple gravestone in a tiny cemetery looking over Lucca, from another rocky hillside. She still hadn't cried, even though she spent the entire day by the tombstone, remembering the woman who had become her mother. She laid her to rest with another flower, when the parish priest told her that the cemetery was closing and that it was time to go.

She buried Staehelin & Co. and Kerrington after that. She found lawyers, first ones in her life, to review the documents in the file from her backpack, then to pursue the bank and Kerrington's estate in courts around the world. newspaper reports had done most of the work for her, followed by the gov investigations and prosecutions. Neither Staehelin nor Kerrington's survived the first day's press and the lawsuits and prosecutors had taken what was left of their fortunes.

She didn't ask for much in the settlements that followed, instead demanding only that the money from the bank's liquidation be used for charities in Uganda and scholarships in the names of Jeb's parents. She also insisted that the money be used to repay a long list of people in Italy and elsewhere, whose names were recorded in Jeb's neat handwriting on a few sheets of stationery from their hotel in Lucca. Then she made sure that the contents of the file were preserved in an archive open to the public. Multiple books about the file were already underway.

She buried Jeb last of all. She buried him out in the mountains, the way he had asked, away from people and towns. She hadn't gotten permission from anyone, but she found a way to get him to another hilly ridge, this one high up in the Swiss mountains. There hadn't been a sermon, or any crowds. It was only her. This time the tears did come, as she let herself cry for both of them. Crying for him, and for them, and for what might have been, before she rolled the boulder closed in front of the cairn that she built for him up on the ridge. And then she said goodbye.

She looked out of the window of the hotel, across the waters of the lake. She felt the soft kick in her stomach, then eased herself up from the chair. She wondered where the Chinese woman was, what she was thinking. Then she wrapped the shawl around her stomach, against the evening chill, and looked back over the lake. She wondered whether the boy would look like Jeb.

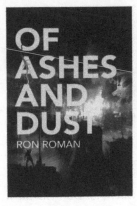